The Grindhouse Chronicles Collection

Book 1: Smoothen Silky: Demon Fighting
Pimp

Book 2: Midget with a Chainsaw

Book 3: Curse of the Blue Diablo

Book 4: Pestilence A-Go-Go

Book 5: Smoothen Silky Vs The WereCougar

SMOOTHEN SILKY: DEMON FIGHTING PIMP
© 2018

CHAPTER ONE

The atmosphere inside the Guilty Growler was as enticing as a hobo orgy. As soon as Rose set foot inside, she was assaulted with crunchy power chords and the underlying musk of daily drunks that hadn't showered in weeks. Boisterous bellowing permeated the crowd from a group of half drunk frat boys in pink polo shirts clustered around the end of the bar.

The walls were grungy with nicotine and spat beer, dented from years of punk rockers smashing around with abandon. The soles of Rose's thigh high boots stuck to the floor as she circled the throng of sweaty rockers. She managed to move with grace despite this, and swung up onto a bar stool, careful to keep her flowing black dress from brushing against any spilled muck.

She lived a glamorous life.

When she crossed her legs and leaned forward to rest a delicate looking arm on the bar, her green eyes swept the room in a quick arc. One of the pink shirts leaned in, yelling to his friends about something over the music, and when he motioned to her, she sighed. Predictable little university kids with their fake swagger and unending bullshit.

The band screamed one last garbled line into their far too cranked microphones, and the frontman leapt into the crowd. The cacophony of notes ringing out died down, and the stage lights lowered, house lights brightening and breaking the anonymous spell of the dance floor.

Drunken dancers that had been slamming into each other hollered and stumbled over each other, eyes adjusting to the ambient light. Some stared awkwardly at their previous dance partners, unsure of whether or not they were still interested in spending more time together. Rose didn't envy them.

"We don't get too many women like you in here," the bartender said as he stepped in front of her, taking advantage of the fresh quiet to address this new customer. He took in her plump lips and flawless skin leading down a slender neck to a prominent collarbone and the swell of luscious cleavage beneath.

The bartender was middle aged and may have been handsome once, but at this point he looked like he'd around the block too many times. He was rough around the edges, and not in the way that Rose usually found intriguing or endearing.

He seemed like he was the perfect embodiment of the Guilty Growler. What

kind of name was that for a bar, anyway?
It made her envision a very sad looking
pussy.

"What can I say?" She shrugged,
sweeping her waterfall of crimson curls
over her shoulder. "I like the
atmosphere."

"Hey, baby, how you doin'?" It was
the Pink Shirt that had been motioning to
her moments ago, and she rolled her eyes.

"Well, at least I _did_ like the
atmosphere," she said to the bartender,
and his lips curled into a wry smile. The
exchange went right over Frat Boy's head.
She wasn't surprised. It was amazing that
these dolts made it into post secondary
with their empty heads. They sure didn't
have any street smarts in her experience.

"Hey buddy, get my new girl here
whatever she wants." He didn't take his
eyes off of Rose's blush pink lipstick as
he spoke, pulling a twenty dollar bill out
of an obscenely fat wallet.

"I'll take a double scotch on the
rocks," she said, eyeing Frat Boy's wallet
as he made a show of how difficult it was
to fold it back up. "And the change," she
added, and the bartender stifled a
chuckle. He liked her sass, and the way
she was playing this kid. These fraternity
idiots were just as out of place as this
chick. He didn't normally attract their

type of crowd, and wondered if they'd headed out here on a dare. Kids these days still dared each other to do shit, right?

"Coming right up, ma'am," the bartender said, and turned to pluck the bottle of Scotch from the wall behind him.

"So, what's up, baby?" Frat Boy tried to turn up the charm, leaning in a bit with a leer that made Rose's skin crawl. "I'm Moses. You come here often?" His blue eyes were slightly hooded, and he eyed her like he was sizing her up for purchase. In a way, he was. That's what guys in bars did.

She wondered briefly if this guy had ever successfully picked up a woman in his miserable little life. The bartender slid a surprisingly clean glass full of amber liquid across the bar with a smattering of bills behind it.

"First off, my name is Rose, <u>not</u> baby," she said, voice level, and lifted her drink in her perfectly manicured hand. "Second off," she began, and then shot back the drink in an expert display of opening her throat. She slammed the empty glass back down on the counter and smacked her painted lips together in disappointment. "If he keeps pouring drinks like that then no, I won't be coming here often."

The bartender huffed as she folded up the extra bills and slid them into the top of her dress. She spun the stool so she was facing away from the bar, watching the band packing up their instruments. They'd been good, at least for a punk band whose job was to just make as much noise as possible. If she were here for pleasure, she'd have been shaking the drummer's sweaty hand right about then. He'd been throttling those drums like his life depended on it, and moving one's entire body in such a fast rhythm was beyond her.

Moses snapped his fingers to catch the attention of the bartender.

"Yo dude, get your ass over here," he said pompously, and the older man leaned towards him with his lips pursed. "You're going to pour her the strongest drink you got, cause I plan on getting me some of that tonight. You got it?" The pink clad boy motioned to Rose, and the bartender raised his eyebrows, abashed. "I said, you got it?" Moses clenched his fist for effect, and the bartender rolled his eyes.

"Yes sir, I'll take care of it," he replied, trying to keep his professionalism in check. He didn't want any trouble with these university kids, but this woman had insulted him and his drinks. If she wanted to stoop to screwing a pack of frat boys then that was her prerogative. He swallowed his sense of moral conduct and started pouring some very old--and not terribly legal--German moonshine into a glass.

There was a <u>plonk</u> on the wooden bar and Rose glanced back at the new drink the bartender had procured for her. It looked like cloudy water and she raised a perfectly sculpted eyebrow, catching a whiff of fermented fruit and maybe honey. That definitely was not a regular drink for a fine upscale establishment.

"Five dollars, please, ma'am," the bartender informed her, and her mouth curled down into a pensive frown. She hadn't ordered the damn thing, and she sure as shit wasn't going to pay for this swill, whatever it was.

She turned a manipulatively softening gaze on Moses, green orbs big and round and oh so inviting. He opened his mouth but no sound came out, and he reached blindly to grasp the bills that had been sitting by her previous drink. When he remembered that she'd shoved them in her bra, he almost scowled, but then caught her fuck-me eyes again.

"Fine," he groaned, and produced his ridiculous wallet once more.

"Thank you," she batted her eyelashes at him as he paid for the drink.

"Moses, my name's Moses," he blurted,
wanting to hear his name come out from
between those squishy cocksucking lips.

"I don't care, sweetie." A ghost of a
smile crossed her face and she turned back
to the crowd, fresh drink in hand, to
watch the patrons fully disperse. She
wasn't surprised that none of them were
sticking around for last call based on the
quality of the drinks in this dive.

Even the rest of Moses' frat friends
strolled out the door, not even looking
back to see what their buddy was doing.
They probably assumed that he was going to
pick Rose up, and didn't want to get in
the way. Maybe the plan was for him to be
by himself, oh so harmless and inviting,
to get her to head on over to the frat
house where--surprise!--there are four
more dudes to fuck.

<u>Not tonight, bucko</u>, Rose thought
bitterly.

Moses took a deep breath and leaned
in again, going in for another try. "Well,
I'll give you a reason to care," he
purred, lowering his voice into what he
thought was a sexy husk. "Why don't we go
back to my place and I'll part your red
sea?"

The red haired woman in the black
strapless dress froze, and then very
slowly turned her head to look at him. He

was smirking at her with false bravado, clearly nervous about how she was going to respond.

She tried to keep a straight face, she really did.

But she couldn't stop the laughter bubbling up from inside her. It came in massive waves, and she had to support herself on the bar to keep from spilling her drink as she nearly doubled over. She gasped for breath, great heaving guffaws sucking the life out of her lungs, and the more she tried to stop, the worse it got. She squeaked out unintelligible words as she cackled, trying to say something, anything to make it stop. Her gut ached.

Moses frowned, almost pouted. The bartender's head dropped into his hands, and he stifled his own laughter, making a mental note to add this kid to his list of losers that couldn't pick up women. He'd be a proverbial cash cow, buying drinks for chicks that would never go home with him.

"Seriously," Rose finally managed to wheeze the word. "Does that line ever work?" She slammed a fist down on the bar to accentuate another fit of giggles. "Part my red sea?" She set her drink down to avoid dumping it all over herself, though she was sure some had already sloshed onto the floor in her mirth. "I'm…

I don't even know what to do with that.
I'm speechless."

Moses shoved off of the bar stool
with a snarl, and stormed out of the
building, slamming the front door behind
him. Rose leaned her head on her elbow,
laughs subsiding to little hiccups as she
turned her amused eyes on the bartender.

"As you can see, we get some really
sad individuals in this place," he spread
his hands for effect.

"Yeah, I can see that." She shook her
head and downed the drink, nearly spitting
it back up as she giggled again. "Is it
too late to get one more?"

"I'm afraid so," he said, and glanced
at the clock. It was past last call. She
shrugged in understanding, looking
apologetic for asking, but he put up a
hand. "However," he stated, scooping up
the scotch bottle once more. "After seeing
what you had to go through, I think I can
make an exception." He smiled as he poured
the drink, genuinely feeling that this
woman deserved the extra drink.

However insulting she'd been at the
beginning, she'd dealt with that
university kid with sass and style. The
bartender couldn't help but respect her
for having such a thick skin.

The door burst open just as he was
sliding the glass across the bar, and Rose

swiveled to see Moses return. He was
flanked by the four nearly identical
clones of him, pink shirts and all. Their
eyes were maniacal with rowdy glee, and
she pursed her lips, a small sigh escaping
her lips.

They did <u>not</u> look like they wanted to
play nice.

"Okay fellas, you all had your shot with the ladies, but we're closed," the bartender said in a jovial but firm tone. He didn't like the look of these assholes, especially busting back in here after the show between Rose and Moses. He didn't think that him returning with his pack of puppies was a good sign, and hoped he could defuse this situation. "Go on home and sleep it off."

The five-pack ignored the nervous looking man and stalked towards Rose like predators circling prey.

"Don't worry, I deal with this all the time," she threw a wink back at the bartender to calm him down, but also as a display of relaxed dominance to the frat boys. She wanted them to know that they weren't rattling her cage one bit with their attempt at intimidation.

"Is this the bitch?" One of the pink shirts spat, and she leaned back on her elbows, crossing her mile long legs casually.

"Yeah, that's her," Moses confirmed. "Let's teach her a lesson. Nobody laughs at Moses."

"That's enough, boys," the bartender cut in, despite Rose's insistence that she could handle herself. "Leave now, or I'll call the cops." He wasn't about to let five guys at this one woman, no matter how chill she was about the whole situation.

"You shut the fuck up," Moses growled, a deep guttural noise that made the bartender's blood run icy cold. The frat boy's wide eyes had an eerie glint to them, and man behind the counter could swear that his skin was pulsing. "This is between me and the bitch," Moses continued, his voice having dropped two octaves.

Rose hopped down off of the bar stool as if heading off to catch a ride home, and the pink clad guy's hand shot out lightning fast to grasp her bicep.

"You just fucked up bad, frat dick." She narrowed her eyes and slipped her hand instantly down into her boot, producing a retractable police baton.

Steel slinked out and expertly hit flesh with a loud smack. Moses let go of her arm to grasp his cheek in shock. That reaction earned him two more hits, leaving a matching welt on the other side of his face and a far more painful strike to his twig and berries.

Rose reeled forward with her pointed toed boot and slammed it into his stomach, knocking the wind right out of him. She wound her fingers into his hair and jerked

him to the floor, stomping on his ribs
with a grunt.

His four buddies were positively
vibrating with excitement, their eyes
emanating that same shiny glow of their
comrade. One of them lunged forward, and
Rose dodged out of reach, vaulting up onto
the bar.

The bartender dropped to the floor
like a stone, seeking refuge under the
counter. Rose ran down the length of the
bar, sliding off of the end to dart into
the next room. She needed to funnel them
somehow, take them one at a time.

Unfortunately, they knew better than
to pop into the room in a perfect line,
and bustled in all together. Moses parted
them like the red sea, and the image made
Rose snicker at his awful pick up line
once again.

"You little bitch," he snarled, his
lips curling back to reveal double rows of
razor sharp teeth. "I'm gonna take your
soul for that."

The frat boys all started to glow
together, their skin darkening and
hardening into scaly flesh. Their teeth
grew longer, their eyes redder, their
noses upturned into little buttons on
their faces. They looked more like
hairless scaly pugs, and Rose couldn't
help but grin at the image.

She widened her stance, preparing to defend herself as best she could against the onslaught of frat pug demons.

"Prepare to die." Moses' voice was unrecognizable. Rose opened her mouth to make a snarky comment regarding his cliched speech, but a sharp whistle cut through the empty bar beyond the door.

The lights from the dance floor were bright enough that the fluffy humanoid silhouette remained in shadow as his heels clicked along the floor.

"Now I <u>know</u> ya'll ain't thinkin' of hurtin' that pretty little thang." His soft drawl was sly and intimidating all at once as he reached the doorframe. When the light from the small room illuminated a man in a long impeccably white suede coat, it was as if all the air went out of the room.

He grinned and reached beneath the long garment, producing a shiny 9-iron. He set it in front of him with a flourish, head down on the floor, as if it were a cane.

"Who the fuck are you?" Moses blurted, incredulous. This guy looked like he'd just walked out of a costume store, and to waltz on up in here and interrupt their important business?

"Silky," the pimp said, voice matching his name, "Smoothen Silky."

"Well, <u>Silky</u>," Moses addressed him with a sneer, "you picked the wrong whore to stick up for. Looks like we're gonna have to take your soul too." He shoved one of his buddies in the shoulder, and the pink clad demon lunged forward, a flurry of clawed fists.

Silky planted his feet and easily dodged each punch, the demon getting more and more frustrated and sloppy as his lashes continued to miss. Finally the pimp flicked the golf club upwards, catching the frat boy in the chin. The demon staggered back, and there was a little <u>shink</u> as a blade slipped out of the end of the club.

Silky jabbed forward, and embedded the blade right into the frat demon's crotch, eliciting a piercing shriek that had the rest of his buddies covering their scaly ears.

Rose leaned against the back wall, crossing her arms to watch the action. Another frat boy leapt forward, and Silky flipped the 9-iron with expert grace, swinging it in a quick arc that decapitated his attacker like butter.

Moses screamed in rage, shoving his other two packmates forward as Silky did a backflip out onto the dance floor. His fur coat billowed in a fluttering arc and when he landed in a power stance, somehow not

dislodging the majestic hat from atop his
head.

He held the club out to the side and
jutted his free hand forward, flipping it
palm up and motioned for the demons to
come hither.

The first one to get close led with
his fist, and Silky grasped him at the
tricep, slicing up with the bladed club.
The demon squealed like a pig as the pimp
tore his arm clean off, tossing it into
the air like a graduation cap.

He used the momentum to spin and
fling the club at his furthest attacker as
the armless body crumpled to the floor in
shock. Spinning with the ferocity of a
lawnmower blade, the weapon slicked clean
through the demon's throat, embedding
itself in the far wall. Blood waterfalled
downwards, staining the pink polo with
crimson, and the glow of his eyes
flickered out as he expired.

The head toppled over onto the floor
and rolled perfectly into the doorframe,
the dead shocked expression causing panic
to bubble up in Moses like a fountain.

"What are you gonna do now, pimp?" He
yelled at the man who had just single
handedly killed his crew. "You're
unarmed!"

Silky simply grinned, gold grill
glinting in the tungsten lights,

illuminating the word SILKY embedded in his mouth. The severed arm dropped into his waiting hand with a squelch.

"You was sayin'?" He taunted, swinging his new weapon back and forth like a baseball bat. Blood spattered everywhere, bits of torn flesh bobbing back and forth with the motion.

Moses flexed his claws and stalked forward with purpose, heart pounding and eyes on fire.

Silky peered at the hand beneath the wrist he'd been using as a handle, and inspected the tight fist of the punch that had never landed. He glanced at Moses, who was shaking as he slowly moved across the dance floor.

"Naw, you's looks like a bitch," he teased, and peeled open the fingers of the dead hand. "So you's gonna get slapped like a bitch."

Moses lunged forward, claws extended, but Silky easily unleashed a hellish volley of slaps from a comfortable distance. Like a farmhand whipping a rented mule, he rained down a savage beating until the demon was cowering on the floor.

"Please, no more!" Moses cried, and Silky actually paused, staring down at him with disgust.

"For shit's sake, ya can't even take your whoopin' like a man?" He asked, ignoring Rose's <u>humph</u> of disapproval from the doorway. The frat demon didn't move from the floor, still covering himself as best he could with his arms, and the pimp sighed in exasperation.

He tossed the arm behind him like a crumpled up piece of trash and turned away from the shivering demon. He opened his hands to Rose in a shrug, giving her a friendly smile, and she rolled her eyes. She reached up and wrenched the 9-iron free from the wall, tossing it to him like a good little caddy.

Moses let out a battle cry, and Silky turned on his heel, bringing the club up instinctively. Steel hit steel as the demon tried to come down with a pipe, but the pimp easily sput his body down the frat pug's arms to flank him.

Moses tried to turn, but he wasn't fast enough for Silky, who landed a crushing blow right on top of his head. The mouthiest and final frat boy fell to the dance floor with a wet slap.

Silky stood tall, his club upright in front of him, in a regal pose. He didn't move at all, and Rose raised her eyebrows at him expectantly.

"Give it a rest already," she urged, motioning to him.

"Wait for it," he replied, and she crossed her arms, wondering what in the blazes he was talking about.

"Wait for wh-"

"Shhhhh, wait for it," he repeated, and she looked around the room, exasperated and confused.

The front door burst open and a short guy bustled in, dragging a comically large fan behind him.

"Sorry boss," he said in a thick Spanish accent, kicking aside demon bits to position the fan just right. He brushed a stray hunk of skin from the nearby outlet to insert the plug, and the fan whirred to life.

The breeze caught Silky's jacket and blew it gently. "Oh yeah, that's what Silky's talkin' about." He leaned his head back, closing his eyes momentarily, decadent skin taut over high cheekbones. His heart shaped chin sported an impeccably trimmed goatee, soft full lips curling into a catlike grin.

"Who the fuck is this?" Rose blurted, motioning to the random Spanish guy she'd never seen before. Silky ignored her, spreading his legs into a power stance, shiny white penny loafers almost blinding and impossibly clean despite the carnage around them. His strong massive hands clasped each other on the handle of the 9-

iron, fingers adorned with shiny baubles that glinted in the soft lights.

He was a statue of epic pimp and circumstance in a sea of devastation, with a firm brow that took no shit and gave no fucks.

"Okay Enrique, that's enough," Silky finally broke his pose to wave at the fan bearer. "Muy bueno, Silky's dismissing ya." He reached into his coat and held out a twenty to the short man.

"Thank you Mr. Silky, thank you!" Enrique praised thickly, and then unplugged the fan, dragging it back out the door. Rose stared down at the smear of demon blood left behind and then raised her eyes back to the smug pimp before her.

"You hired a little Mexican dude to make you look cool?" She raised a hand to her forehead, but in the grand scheme of things, she didn't know why she was surprised.

"Hey now, Silky don't need nobody to make him look cool," he chastised with a click of his tongue. "Silky's just tryin' ta help a brotha out. He's too young to be pimpin, y'know?"

"So you pay him to follow you around with a fan." Rose stated, voice almost tired. She knew asking him anything more would just raise more questions, and she didn't have the energy for that.

"It's a hero pose, baby, every great hero's gotta have one." Silky grinned at her, and she shook her head.

"Un-fucking-believable," she muttered.

CHAPTER THREE

Rose strode over to where Moses was softly groaning on the floor. His head was mostly caved in, but demons had stamina, and he was still coherent enough to talk to her.

She toed him onto his back, flopping him easily, and then pressed her boot into his crotch and leaned. A choked sob clawed its way out of his throat and she glared down at him.

"What are you doing this far out of town?" She demanded. "I didn't think you demon frat boys left the college area. Not enough stupid drunk sorority girls around this week?"

"Actually, there aren't," Moses groaned.

Rose snarled and backhanded him, sick of these chauvinist frat dicks thinking they were gods gift to women.

"Damn baby, nice technique," Silky complimented her.

"Thanks." She continued to beat Moses' face in, letting out her frustrations with him and his pack of douchebags harassing her.

While she was at that, Silky headed around to the rest of the bodies, using his ceremonial blade to dispatch the demons for good. Soon the dance floor was sticky with melted demonic goo.

Rose plonked down onto Moses' chest hard, straddling his shoulders so she could press his cheek down into the pungent muck that was all that was left of his friends.

"You see that?" She cooed. "That's going to be you in just a minute." He simply whimpered at her words, trying to close his eyes against the carnage. "Now, you're going to tell me what you're doing this far away from home," she demanded.

"There weren't enough stupid drunk sorority girls around this week!" Moses cried, an edge of hysterical sarcasm to his gravelly voice.

She hauled off and punched him with three quick jabs to the throat.

"Stop that!" He gasped for air, croaking the words through a crushed larynx.

"Tell me what I want to know," she said, voice cold as ice, "and I'll make it go quickly."

"How many times do I have to tell you?!" He cried hoarsely. "The sorority girls are all at Palm Meadows Resort! It's spring break, you dumb bitch!"

Rose scowled at him and reached into her boot for her own ceremonial knife. She paused, then decided to punch him a few more times. She stood before plunging the knife into his chest to avoid getting melty demon goo all over her dress.

What a messy fucking night.

"God_damn_ demon frat boy fucks." Rose muttered as she wiped off her ceremonial knife to return it to her boot. "Christ, I need a fucking shower."

"Settle down there, sista girl," Silky said with a wink, and waved for her to follow him over to the bar. "We's got some work to do first. Where your shit at?"

She reached into her left boot on the outer thigh, opposite the knife holster, and produced her phone.

"Whoo-eee, what else you got in them boots?" Silky waggled his eyebrows as they took a seat at the bar. She busied herself with unlocking her phone, not wanting to admit that she had rigged up the thigh highs because she couldn't find her matching purse for this outfit.

The smooth pimp set his trusty golf club down on the bar, and leaned forward, peering down to see the cowering middle aged bartender still in the fetal position on the floor.

"Yo, cracka, can we get some muthafuckin' service up in here?" Silky asked, and the bartender had to take a second to marvel at how jovial and

compliant the man's tone was even when
barking orders.

"What… what were those guys?" He
stammered, peeling his fingers out of
their white knuckled fists. He hadn't seen
much, but what he _had_ seen had been
complete insanity. And what he had heard…

"Those honkies were part of a demon
cult bent on destroying the world, ya
dig?" Silky waved his hand with a
flourish, motioning to the entire world
revolving around him.

"The frat boys?" The bartender asked
incredulously, slowly moving up into a
sitting position. His eyes were massive
and confused as he gazed up at the couple
above him. He should have known as soon as
a woman that hot wandered in that it was
going to mean epic trouble.

"You's goddamn right the frat dicks!
Shit," Silky leaned on one arm, lowering
that shoulder to shoot the man on the
floor a conspiratorial look. "Frat boys
are bad enough, but these needledicks will
do more than fuck your daughter in the
ass. They's gonna take her soul, too."

"But…" The bartender let out a ragged
breath, mind swirling with the
information. "I don't have a daughter," He
stammered.

"It's a metaphor, you ignorant
cracka!" Silky rolled his eyes. "Now you

gonna give us some fuckin' service or does Silky gotta come back there and do this shit?"

The bartender snapped out of his haze of fear, remembering that he was first and foremost the owner of this fine establishment. And serving these people that kept him from becoming demon chow might be in his best interests. It would also be a good distraction from the cold panic threatening to blow his sanity open over having almost just died at the hands of demonic university students.

He straightened up, smoothed his hair back, and pulled on his customer service face like a mask. He got to his feet and desperately tried to ignore the carnage of demon goo spattered all over his bar. He wondered how much a cleaning service would charge to deal with this, because he wasn't sure that his mop bucket would be able to handle this.

Not now, not now. Customer service.

"Apologies," he said with a slight bow of his head, setting his hands flat on the counter to address his customers directly. "What… what can I get for you, sir?"

"Gin and juice muthafucka, what else you think Silky's gonna drink?" The pimp flashed him a wide smile, and then wagged a warning finger at him. "And don't you go skimpin' on the gin, either!"

"Coming right up," the bartender nodded, and glanced at Rose, who was pumping away on her phone's touchscreen. "Scotch for the lady?" She nodded her head absently in approval, and he turned to make their drinks, forcing his hands to stay steady.

The drink he'd made prior to the pink demons busting back inside had been knocked to the other end of the bar, half of it sloshed all over the wood.

"What you got, girl?" Silky peered over Rose's shoulder to see there was a video call waiting to go through.

"Just getting set up with the Agency." She propped the phone up on its case so they were facing it, and nodded her thanks to the bartender as he slid a glass to her. "Should be up in just a moment."

Silky took a sip of his drink, and as soon as the ambrosia hit his tongue, elation washed over him. He pointed at the bartender with an appreciative smile.

"God<u>damn</u>, that's my boy! Whoo-ha!"

"Good evening Silky," a professional voice emanated from the phone and the pimp turned his grin on the screen

"Boss-man," Silky raised his glass in a toast to the white collared man in the frame.

"How did the sting operation go?" The Boss asked, straight down to business. His salt and pepper hair was slicked back as always, beard perfectly manscaped on his hard edged face.

"The operation was a success, Sir, we got their destination," Rose replied, straightening up as she spoke to her higher up. "Palm Meadows Resort, it looks like its down by the coast."

"Palm Meadows?" The Boss furrowed his brow, and glanced away from the camera, likely looking up the place as Rose had before calling. "Hmm… this isn't good."

"What's goin' on, Boss-man?" Silky prompted, taking another swig of his delectable drink.

"Are either of you familiar with The Princess?" The Boss asked, finally turning his gaze back to them.

"Ain't that the tall skinny bitch demon?" The pimp countered, lips twisting up in thought.

"She's not just a tall skinny bitch, Silky," the Boss replied, and the bartender blinked at the phone. He couldn't help but to eavesdrop, and hearing the words 'skinny bitch' coming out of this professional looking guy's mouth was surreal. But what came next made him almost drop the glass he was polishing. "She also has an enchanted rack."

"Enchanted rack?" Rose blurted in exasperation. "You've got to be fucking kidding me."

"I couldn't be more serious, Rose," the Boss said in a no-nonsense tone. "In most cases, diamonds are a girl's best friend, but in her case, it's those magnificent tits."

Rose shot back the rest of her scotch and shoved the empty glass back at the bartender. He scrabbled for it, not wanting to look like he was listening intently to their conversation. But why would they be having it so openly in front of him if it wasn't okay for him to hear it?

He had a sudden vision of being on the smooshing end of Silky's golf club, and swallowed hard. No, if he'd heard or seen too much they'd have killed him already, right? They wouldn't be keeping him around just to make drinks. These people seemed reasonable. They only killed demons, right?

The bartender fought to keep from shaking scotch all over the counter as he gave himself his mental pep talk.

"Several years ago," the Boss began, his voice a lilting cadence comparable to a news reporter, "she sold her soul in order to win a beauty pageant. And if the swimsuit contest had been last, she would have won. She had the judges eating out of the palm of her hand with those hypnotic hooters." There was a slight shift to his shoulders, and Rose imagined that out of frame he was holding an imaginary pair of tits on his chest for effect. Such professionalism. "Unfortunately for her, the evening gown she had chosen for the last phase of the contest covered up just a little too much cleavage. They lost their power, and she ended up tripping on the dress in her frustration and falling off of the stage.

"Before she could try to hypnotize the judges and the crowd again, she'd already lost the contest. After that, she set off across the east coast, leaving a trail of very happy looking corpses." The Boss finished, and looked down out of frame again. A text rolled down from the top of Rose's screen and she brought it up, revealing the Boss' picture message of a few crime scene photos.

They all revealed very dead men, pelvises crushed to smithereens as if they'd been literally fucked to death. Each had a glassy eyed lifeless stare, but their mouths were curled up into the creepiest of happy smiles. Rigor mortis had locked their arms in their final resting position; straight out to the front with the hands in a clear groping position.

"Poor crackas," Silky said with a sigh, shaking his head as Rose flipped back to the video feed. "So what does this mean to Silky?"

"According to our intel, she was last spotted heading towards the Palm Meadows Resort," the Boss said. "I need both of you to get down there as quickly as possible and find out what's going on."

"Silky's callin' the hos right now," the pimp pulled his phone out of his inner jacket pocket and waved it as he spoke. "We's be down there by mornin'."

"Rose, I'm sending you the info on a safe house that you'll be staying at." The Boss met her eyes as she lifted her fresh glass of scotch to her lips. "It's in a semi-nice neighborhood… so do try to take care of it."

"Silky don't make no promises," Silky piped up as he dialed a phone number, leaning back against the bar casually. He

was the pinnacle of relaxation, and Rose
entertained the idea for a split second of
kicking the bar stool out from under him.

"I understand," the Boss nodded,
killing the moment for her. Silky did as
Silky did, and she didn't <u>have</u> to work
with him if she didn't want to. Regardless
of his over the top ways, she did enjoy
his company.

He definitely kept things
interesting.

"Oh, and one more thing," the Boss
added, "I'm sending out a new recruit. His
name is Kerr. Silky, I need you to break
him in."

"Oh," Rose replied with a chuckle,
"don't worry, he'll break him in alright."

"I'm sure he will," the Boss said
with a firm nod. "Report back to me when
you have more intel."

"Will do, Boss-man." Silky waved and
then started yammering into his phone at
one of his hos. Rose gave the Boss a
salute and ended the call, slipping her
phone back against her thigh.

She stood up, shooting the last of
her drink, and pulled out the bills she'd
scooped from Moses earlier in the night.
She tossed them on the counter as Silky
finished his call, following her lead and
getting up from the bar stool.

"Thanks, barkeep," Silky said with
his signature grin, and offered Rose his
fuzzy arm to escort her to the door. Using
his golf club as a cane, he swaggered them
to the front door as the bartender looked
on in bewilderment.

When they reached the door, Silky
opened it and gave Rose an exaggerated
bow. She chuckled and gave a fake curtsy,
rolling her eyes out of habit but secretly
finding the gentlemanly gesture endearing.

"Who are you?" The bartender called
just before they stepped out into the
night.

Silky reached into his coat,
revealing a pair of massive sunglasses
with sparkly bling all along the rims.

"Smoothen Silky," he purred, sliding
the glasses onto his face with
unimaginable grace. "Demon fighting pimp."

CHAPTER FIVE

"What the shit is this?" Silky spat as he turned his metallic purple El Dorado into what could only be described as Suburbia Hell. "Silky ain't stayin' at a place like this."

The sun was shining happily as if they hadn't been covering a bar in demon goo the night before. Every house looked cheerful, bright, and exactly the same. Rack 'em, stack 'em, and pack 'em.

"Come on, it's not that bad." Rose replied, motioning for him to pull over in front of a modest house. "At least there's no white picket fence."

"You ain't helpin' any," he muttered as he accelerated up the driveway, pulling up the parking brake with more force than necessary. "Sides, Silky thought we's supposed to be at the coast? Silky don't see no fuckin' beach."

"Of course, the Agency is skimping on resources." She shrugged as she exited the car, her long legs bare in the tropical heat. She'd opted for a simple sundress and flip flops that day, not wanting to draw any attention with full on Agency garb.

Though Silky drew attention wherever he went, especially with that car. But there was no toning down Silky, and she

did feel nice and cozy in the lavender
shag interior. It was definitely built for
comfort.

"We're about a mile inland," she told
him, retrieving her backpack from the
floor and slinging it over her shoulder.
"You're not really dressed for the beach,
anyway."

"Silky's dressed for every occasion,
baby," he flipped open his powder blue
coat and put a hand on his hip as he
exited the car, taking a beat to pose with
his trusty club.

When he decided that the proper
amount of time had lapsed for Rose to
admire his majestic getup, he relaxed and
took in the front of the house again.

"Goddamn cheapass honkies," he
sneered, and she turned away from him,
stomping up the front walk.

"Oh, quit your bitching," she
retorted, "you never know, it could be
nice inside."

She opened the door and appraised the
shiny hardwood floor. She strutted into
the living room and ran a hand along the
cream colored couch, admiring the simple
decor and minimalist furniture. It was
contemporary, like something out of an
Ikea catalogue, but not unpleasant.

"Awwwww, _hell_ no," Silky drawled as
soon as he stepped over the threshold,

waving a hand in the air like a lunatic. "Silky ain't livin' with this shit."

"What?" Rose crossed her arms as he turned right back around and went back through the door. "Wait! Where are you going?" She ran to the doorframe and peered out at him, noting that he wasn't getting back in the driver's seat to leave.

He strutted up to the trunk, and opened it, inclining a little bow of his head.

"You hos ready to do some work for ole Silky?" He asked, stepping back, and Rose's eyes near popped out of her head as he helped a blonde woman step out of the back of the El Dorado.

"What do you need, baby?" The woman asked, straightening her black miniskirt and adjusting the red and white polka dot halter top that just barely reached the underside of her breasts.

"Silky wants you hos to clean this place up." He motioned to the house, and then extended his hand to help a second woman step out. She had chocolate brown hair in high pigtails, and wore a bright pink babydoll dress over bubblegum heels.

"What is this, Felix's magic ho bag?" Rose muttered as she saw a third woman spring onto the sidewalk. This one had hair as black as ebony, and was clad in denim Daisy Duke's with a blue and white plaid bikini top that just barely covered nipple.

Rose felt like she was looking at Charlie's Sluts, and she crossed her arms at the fact that the pimp kept one of each hair color in his trunk at all times. Of course there was no redhead, and she narrowed her eyes at the thought that <u>she</u> was the redhead. A perfect set.

"Pimpify it, babes!" Silky spread his arms, leaning back and wildly waving the golf club at the house. As the women hopped to, he slapped one with the short shorts on her toned ass and she squeaked out a giggle. "Oh yeah, that's right," he appraised the reverberation of her globes under his hand.

Rose jumped out of the way of the three hos bustling through the door, a flurry of tanned skin and impossibly high heels.

"What the fuck is this?" She demanded, stomping back down the walkway towards her partner. "You had hos in the fucking trunk this whole time?"

"Aw, settle down, baby," he held up a hand to stop her. "Silky's gotta have his hos on the road with him. Gotta keep the income flowin'. And these ain't just run 'o the mill hos. Trixie, Mixie and Dixie are Silky's prize bitches."

"Unbelievable." Rose pinched the bridge of her nose.

"Hey, don't get too mad at ole Silky, now," he reached into the blankets the women had been laying on and rummaged around. "I gave them some toys for the trip, they was entertained." He produced a neon pink vibrator and Rose scoffed, slapping it out of his hand.

"Really?!" She slammed the trunk shut, nearly severing his hand, and he shot her a thousand watt grin.

"Them hos is makin' themselves useful," he said as the sunlight glinted off his golden grill, and started back up towards the house. "Right now they's fixin' up the place for ole Silky here."

When they entered the living room again, Rose stopped dead. There were leopard print covers on the couches, lava lamps lighting the dim space with the curtains drawn, and a massive painting of a pimp in black velvet hanging over the fireplace.

"Where… how…?" Rose stammered, and then shook her head. They must have had this stuff stashed in the house somewhere. Or they'd gone back out to the trunk? The more she thought about it, the more her head started to hurt.

"Now <u>this</u> is what Silky's talkin' about." He gave a little wiggle of his hips in excitement.

"These hos work fast, I'll give them that," Rose said, putting a hand to her forehead.

"Silky's got 'em trained right," he said, licking his lips at the three women on the couch. They were celebrating their quick and efficient job with some very close cuddling. "The slower they work the less money Silky gets."

"I'm going to get things set up in the office," Rose turned away from the tangle of limbs and lips in the pimpin' living room. "I'll call for you when I'm up and running."

The blonde ho extended her arm and curled her finger up in a come-hither motion.

"You do that," Silky says, a spring in his step as he jaunts into the living room. "Silky can find something to occupy himself in the meantime."

CHAPTER SIX

The humidity was soul crushing that
day, especially for someone not used to
it. The confident young man that strutted
up the sidewalk in east coast suburbia
felt like he was breathing soup. He hoped
the house had air conditioning.

He stopped short at the pimpmobile in
the driveway, and had to double check his
phone to make sure he had the right house.
The car was the most conspicuous thing
he'd ever seen. He stepped up onto the
porch and set his suitcase to the side,
straightening his shirt.

He rapped on the door firmly,
straightening his spine. This was the
first day of field work, and he wanted to
make a good impression. Nobody answered,
and he knocked again, leaning to the side
to peer in the window.

There was a creak as the door opened.

"Hey, I'm Kerr, I was sent…" he
began, and then his jaw to hit the floor
when he turned to face a scantily clad
blonde bombshell. "Here… by the… wow."

"Yeah, I get that a lot." The woman
giggled, shifting her weight so that her
perfectly curvy hip jutted out enough for
her to rest a soft hand on it.

"I can imagine," Kerr said, composing
himself. He tried desperately not to look

her up and down, but her tits were magnetic, and practically bursting out of her tiny red halter. "A woman as beautiful as you, I'm sure that you have guys lined up around the block to be with you." The words tumbled out of his mouth as he quickly raised his eyes to her face.

He had to be professional. This couldn't be an agent, for sure, with her plump painted lips and colorful eyeshadow. He swallowed hard, forcing down the awkwardness at being so attracted to her.

"I did that once, but it hurt a lot," she said, putting a finger to her chin in thought. "I think you can still order that movie though, if you can find the right website."

Kerr blinked at her, an image flitting through his head of this sultry siren being plowed by a bunch of guys at once, and then physically shook himself back to reality.

Professional.

"Oh," he stammered. "You don't say."

"Yeah, that was my biggest seller," she said, poofy curls bobbing on top of her head as she nodded enthusiastically. "Or, wait, was is the one I did with Big Jim and Truck Turner?"

"Okay, moving on," Kerr said, trying to steer the conversation in a less porn related direction. "The Agency sent me.

I'm supposed to meet with a Smoothen Silky?"

The woman looked him up and down, appraising him a little more in depth after hearing where he was from. He was dressed business casual, beige slacks and a white button down shirt.

Suddenly a soft looking pastel blue sleeve snaked around her and pushed her behind the door. Kerr blinked a few times at the tall guy that looked like he'd just walked out of a pimp convention. But there couldn't possibly be anyone else more deserving of a name like 'Smoothen Silky'.

"You must be-" he started, but the pimp stood in the doorway defiantly and cut him off.

"Twenty dollas!" Silky yelled, squaring his shoulders.

"Excuse me?" Kerr stood up to his full height as well, though he was more than a little intimidated. He was just over six feet tall, and not used to having to look up at anyone. But this guy was a beast. He had to be at least half a foot taller than the new field agent.

"Silky said twenty fuckin' dollas!" The pimp tore his ridiculously huge sunglasses from his face, the glittering of gems on the sides nearly blinding.

"Uh, you need to borrow twenty dollars?" The recruit scratched the back of his head nervously.

His face suddenly stung like a bitch, and it took him a few seconds to realize that the pimp had backhanded him clean across the face.

"Muthafuckin' dumbass honky." Silky leaned down so that his nose was a hair's breadth away from the guy on the doorstep. "You owe Silky twenty dollas."

"Owe him… err… you… twenty dollars?" Kerr stammered, a flush creeping up his face from the slap. It was more humiliation than pain, and he wasn't sure if he was as excited for this job as he'd initially been. "For what?"

"You's been takin' up his ho's time," Silky said, his voice menacing, but somehow still smooth as chocolate.

"What? Her?" The recruit motioned to the woman who was now peeking out from the living room along with two other sets of eyes. "She just answered the door."

"And you took up her fuckin' time," Silky replied, at this point exasperated that this moron wasn't getting it. "Her time is worth twenty dollas."

"But…"

"Silky knows ya don't want to be takin' food outta Silky's mouth, now do ya?" His voice lowered an octave, and Kerr swallowed hard.

"No," he replied thickly. "No, Sir."

"Now look," the pimp suddenly leaned back against the doorframe casually, checking his perfect nails as if he hadn't just been threatening as all hell. "Silky ain't one to judge what another man is into. Some wanna tap that ass, some wanna yodel in the fuckin' valley, and some just wanna chit-chat. Silky's down with it, he's cool as a fuckin' cucumber." He slid his hand through the air to indicate how level he really was about the whole thing, and Kerr found himself nodding, even though he was still a bit lost. "Now, do you know what those three got in common?" Silky raised an eyebrow, pulling his sunglasses a little ways down his nose.

"Um," the recruit swallowed again. "No, Sir."

The pimp grinned. "They all paid Silky twenty dollas."

At the sight of the golden teeth spelling <u>SILKY</u>, Kerr blinked a few times and realized that he wasn't going to win this one.

"Um. Okay." He sighed and reached into his pocket, pulling out his wallet. He held out a twenty dollar bill, and Silky snatched it out of his hand, running it under his nose like a cigar.

"Silky appreciates your fuckin' business." He bowed his head slightly, and then slammed the door.

"What the fuck just happened?" Kerr muttered to himself, momentarily stunned by the interaction. If this was par for the course field work, his job was about to get a hell of a lot more interesting.

He knocked on the door again, squaring his shoulders to try to show he wasn't intimidated. Silky threw open the door.

"Whaddya want, cracka?" He barked. "Ya got another twenty?"

"No, Mr. Silky, Sir," Kerr innately winced at how awkward he sounded, but shoved away his embarrassment. "I was sent by the Agency. I'm Kerr, your new recruit." He raised his chin, and Silky pulled his sunglasses clean off of his face.

"They sent Silky _your_ dumb blondie-blue-eyed country bumpkin ass?" His tone dripped with incredulity, eyes condescending. "Goddamn Silky's gettin' too old for this shit." He sighed at the determined gaze on Kerr's face. "All right, grab your shit and come on."

The recruit let out a breath of relief, and grasped his suitcase quickly, rolling it behind him as he followed the baby blue clad pimp inside

Kerr's eyes darted all over the living room, noting the decor that was vastly different from every other room of the house. He set his suitcase next to the couch, trying to ignore the two women snuggling up to the woman who'd answered the door. They seemed very friendly.

"What the fuck you think you's doin, cracka?" Silky snapped.

"Um," Kerr said, and took a deep breath. He really needed to work on not sounding like an idiot every time his superior asked him a question. "Just putting my stuff down?"

"Ah, Silky gets it," the pimp replaced his sunglasses onto the bridge of his nose despite the dimness of the room, and cocked his head. "You think you's just gonna come on up in a brotha's house and throw your shit down? That it, honky?"

"No, Sir, I'm sorry I just-"

"Just what?" Silky barked. "Just what, cracka?"

"I'm sorry." Kerr shrugged, and grasped his suitcase so that it was clean off the floor, not even on its wheels anymore.

"You's sorry?" Silky cupped a hand around his ear and waited. "That all you got to say for yoself?" He snatched up a

golf club that had been leaning up against
the wall, and Kerr took an involuntary
step back. "Honky, you best keep yo shit
up off the floor before Silky shoves these
loafers so far up yo ass you's gonna be
spittin' pennies."

"Spitting pennies?" Kerr blurted in
his nervousness, and Silky scoffed,
lashing out to slap him in the back of the
head.

"They's penny loafers, muthafucka!"
He lifted his foot and rested it on the
edge of Kerr's suitcase to show him the
shiny white shoes. "Silky gonna have to
teach your inbred ass everything?
Goddamn."

He sighed and lowered his foot, the
heel hitting the carpet with a soft thud.
He waved for the recruit to follow him,
wandering through the doorway at the back
of the living room towards the basement.

"What's down there?" Kerr asked as
Silky opened the door, motioning towards
the stairs that headed down into darkness.

"That's where you stayin'," the pimp
replied.

"Down there?" A burst of anger flared
up in Kerr's chest as the stress and
humiliation bubble burst.

"Down there." Silky smiled.

"But that's the basement," the
recruit snapped.

"Whoo-eee, you's an observant muthafucka, ain't ya?" Silky leaned on the door and crossed his feet at the ankles.

"Years of Agency training, what can I say?" Kerr retorted before he even thought about it, a smart ass tone shining through in his exasperation.

"Get yo cracka ass down there before Silky whoops it," Silky threatened in a menacing tone.

The recruit clenched his jaw and stepped down onto the wooden staircase, the door slamming into his back before he was fully inside. He stumbled down a few steps, pain exploding in his forehead as he bonked his head against the low ceiling.

He mumbled a few curses under his breath, and ducked down into the area that looked like it was more for storage than a real basement. There were boxes piled from floor to ceiling, and a tattered reclining lawn chair that looked like it had seen better days.

Kerr dropped his suitcase on the concrete floor and collapsed into the chair. He leaned back and settled in, staring at the wooden beams overhead.

There was a creak and groan, and the chair collapsed, pain reverberating up his spine like lightning as his tailbone hit the cement floor.

He rolled onto his side, throwing an
arm over his eyes as he hissed in pain.
This was going to be a long
assignment.

CHAPTER EIGHT

Kerr finished placing his things on the makeshift shelf he'd created out of the boxes, and then sat back on the decently comfortable bed he'd managed to make up. A few of the bigger boxes had been full of comforters, so he'd crafted a pallet out of cardboard and layered blankets on top.

He stretched out on his homemade cot and pulled out his phone, scrolling aimlessly through his Twitter feed before his stomach growled loudly. It was getting to be around dinnertime.

Why was he hanging out in the basement anyway? Silky had sent him down here, but was he really just going to stay down here until he was called, like a dog?

Kerr stood up and stretched his arms up over his head, relishing in the sweet crackle of his back and shoulders as he did so. Enough was enough. Smoothen Silky was his superior, but Kerr had done his time at the Agency. He would prove himself or die trying.

He opened the basement door with authority, and then strolled through the kitchen into the living room with as much confidence as he could muster. He'd never had a problem with the other recruits; he needed to stay in that mindset here.

"There you is, let's get this shit started," Silky waved him over from his perch on the couch, surrounded by his women. The two on either side snuggled up to him like a Silky sandwich, and the third straddled his back, hands working at his bare shoulders. The pristine powder blue coat hung artfully on a coat rack behind them, an imposing presence all on its own.

Kerr stopped short, bravado forgotten when he realized he'd been fucking around in the basement when he was supposed to be in a strategy meeting. "Sorry, I wasn't aware that-"

"That's yo problem, Wonder Bread, you wouldn't be aware of shit on a sandwich," Silky tilted his head down, eyeing the recruit from over the top of his sunglasses.

Kerr squared his shoulders again, determined to keep his cool. Mere minutes after vowing to do better he was already being insulted, but instead of arguing he needed to just face this head on. Grunts always got the abuse, right? He had to just take it in stride and eventually he'd get to be the one knocking around new recruits.

He turned to the opposite couch to sit, and his breath caught in his throat at the woman sitting there with her laptop. She hadn't been around with the other three earlier, fawning all over Silky. In fact, she didn't look like she belonged in the pimp room at all.

Thick red curls draped over creamy shoulders, a pale yellow sundress hugging a shapely body. Mile long legs stretched out, ending at bare feet that braced themselves on the coffee table.

Kerr blinked a few times and gulped as he sank down into the couch, and she immediately turned her bright green eyes on him. It was as if he'd been stabbed in the gut by her glare, and her deliciously full lips pursed as she exaggerated looking down at his thigh pressed up against hers.

He coughed nervously, not having meant to plop down right against her, and backed up so that he was at the opposite end of the couch. He caught a faint whiff of lavender as he slid away from her, and resisted the urge to lean forward and bury his nose in her hair.

So professional, he mentally chastised himself, and forced his gaze to Silky, who had gotten up to pace.

"Alright, so we's got a job to do down here," the pimp began as he strutted back and forth along the crimson shag carpet. "And you know what? We's gonna get it done hella quick so Silky can go soak

up some of them rays and pick up a ho or
two. Or three."

The women on the couch giggled,
stroking each other with seemingly
practiced sensuality. Kerr forced his
eyeballs to stay glued to his superior,
ignoring the ridiculous amount of sex
appeal oozing all over the room.

"So, what's the plan?" He asked,
proud of how firm his voice sounded.

"The plan is for you to shut the fuck
up and let Silky talk, suga cube," came
the sharp retort, and Kerr sat back
against the plush couch cushion. He
resisted the urge to mime zipping his
mouth shut, and continued to stare at the
pacing pimp.

"Rose, what you got for ole Silky?"
He pointed at the luscious redhead with
the laptop.

"Well, I've pulled up rental records
for the houses in this area," she said,
and Kerr wanted to slam his head against
the wall at the husky tone of her voice.
How did anyone work in these conditions?
It wasn't fucking fair. "There are half a
dozen fraternities that have rented
houses, and that's just the ones that we
know of."

"Right, right." Silky wound his
fingers in a circle to encourage her to go
on.

"We'll have a couple of the ladies out on the town trying to get an invite to one of the parties," Rose added, motioning to the three scantily clad ladies on the couch.

"Who's our objective?" Kerr spoke up, injecting himself into the strategy meeting with an air of authority.

"Look at that, the slack jawed yokel finally axed a relevant question." Sarcasm poured from Silky's voice like a waterfall, but Kerr decided to take it as a compliment, however backhanded it was.

"Our target is this woman," Rose turned her laptop to reveal a photo of a bleach blonde beach babe in a tiny bikini and a pageant sash. "She's a nasty demon and we're trying to figure out why she's here for spring break."

"Why frat parties?" Kerr asked with a shrug. "I mean, a woman that hot should be pretty easy to spot. Why not just drive around and look for her?"

"It's more complicated than just following your dick." Rose closed the laptop and leaned forward to set it on the coffee table. "The fraternities that we tracked down all have demon possession affiliation. For the most part, they use the fraternity as a front to harvest souls."

Kerr was impressed with the woman's articulate nature, and felt a little badly for sexualizing her so hard when he first saw her. She seemed to be the most professional person in the room.

"With that tall skinny bitch in the mix, we's pretty sure somethin' big and fuckin' bad's goin' down here." Silky emphasized his words with swoops of a 9-iron. Kerr eyed it but was too afraid to ask.

"So, when do we leave?" He inquired instead, itching to get out there and show off his skills.

"Whoo-ah there cracka, you's thinkin' you ready for the field?" Silky stopped and put his hand up, palm out.

"Damn straight." Kerr quenched his nervousness and stood up. It was now or never. He had come here to show the Agency what he was made of, and if he had to stand up to a pimp and his hos to do it, then that's what he was going to do. "I graduated top of my class at the Agency, blowing away the competition. Besides, they sent me to you, didn't they?" He motioned to Silky with a conspiratorial grin. "Surely they're going to send the best recruit to the best field agent, aren't they?"

"Oh, you's a savvy muthafucka, ain't ya?" Silky threw his head back and barked a laugh at the flattery. "Okay, okay, Silky's gonna give you a shot. You just go on back down to yo hole and ole Silky will let you know when it's time to get outta here."

Kerr mentally high fived himself, totally surprised that the pimp seemed impressed by him. "Really?" He caught his childish hopeful tone and coughed to try to cover it up. "Yeah, alright."

"Go on now, buddy, Silky's gonna talk to Rose here and get yo plans all set up nice," his superior said, shooing him off like a cat.

"Alright, Mister Silky," Kerr couldn't quash his excitement this time. A real field mission. This was it. He was doing it. "I won't let you down." He added, and scurried off back into the kitchen, grabbing a box of crackers on the way by the counter.

"Silky's sure you won't!" The pimp called after him, and when the basement door closed, he turned to share a conspiratorial smile with Rose. "That cracka don't know what he's in for."

Silky descended the wooden steps into the basement, nose twitching at the smell of dank cardboard. At the bottom, his mauve hat grazing the low ceiling, he turned to see Kerr dancing off to the side.

No, not dancing, shadowboxing, it looked like. Some kind of kung fu shit, that was for sure.

"Whatchoo doin' down here?" Silky asked, and Kerr didn't respond. He was about to make a comment about how it was rude for a ho not to answer a question when she was asked, but then he realized that the kid was wearing earbuds.

He extended his trusty golf club and poked the recruit in the back, eliciting a yelp as Kerr leapt into the air, bonking the top of his head into a wooden beam.

"Ah, shit!" Kerr yanked the earbuds out, thrash metal blasting out of the little nubs. "Sorry sir, what's up? Did you say something?"

"Silky asked what the fuck you doin'?" His superior asked, motioning to the earbuds and his shirtless and sweat sheened torso.

"Oh, just doing some training before my first mission," Kerr explained, excited to get to share some personal details with him. "See, it's a way for me to relax, and the music-"

"Silky didn't ask for yo goddamn life story, honky." The pimp held up a hand to stop him from rambling on.

"Sorry," Kerr replied immediately, keeping his posture formal. He was vaguely aware that he probably smelled pretty bad, and needed to get upstairs to shower before any of the ladies got too close to him.

He was amazed at how put together and shiny the pimp was, having changed into a dusty deep purple suit and jacket. The feather proudly spewing from the top of his massive hat brushed against the wooden beams of the ceiling, and the recruit couldn't help but feel a bit mesmerized by it.

"And quit apologizing so damn much," Silky continued, tapping the golf club on the kids head with a hollow <u>pock</u>. "Man, you's worse than a ho. Where's that cracka I saw upstairs, huh? Silky needs a honky that believes in himself."

"Alright." Kerr blinked at him, amazed that he'd just gotten a pep talk from the guy that had spent most of the day insulting him. "No more apologies. What's the mission?"

"That's more like it, muthafucka," Silky clapped the kid on the back. "One of

Silky's hos got picked up by a couple of those frat boy fucks, and they invited her to a party. She's s'posed to be bringin' a friend so's they can do a little striptease thing."

"And where do I fit in?" Kerr asked, turning off the music still blasting from the tiny speakers.

"Silky don't like to send his hos out without protection, ya dig? Usually they be gettin' a taser and a set of ball clamps. But seein' as how you wanna shot and all, Silky's gonna send you instead."

"I get to be a bouncer?" The kid beamed, puffing out his chest. "Fuck yeah, I can be a bouncer. I look great in a muscle shirt. The ladies will go crazy for these guns." He flexed his biceps with a sly grin.

"Whoa, whoa, whoa, settle down there baby boy," Silky stifled a laugh at the recruit's train of thought. "You ain't gonna be dressin' like that."

"Why not?" Kerr lowered his arms in disappointment.

"Cause if you do that they's gonna know that you a bouncer." The pimp raised his eyebrows, not sure how this green as hell agent wasn't understanding.

"Well yeah, and I'll intimidate them." Kerr flexed his biceps again.

At that, Silky threw his head back, gold glinting as he bellowed a laugh. "Boy, you couldn't intimidate a one legged crack whore with that apple pie fuckin' face o yours," he said with an amused grin that refused to go away.

"So what am I going to do?" Kerr scowled. "Be one of the strippers?"

"Cracka, this is an undercover mission," Silky threw up a hand in exasperation. "We's tryin' to get infomation, not collect money from these fools. You's gonna have to blend in." He reached into his coat and pulled out a very specific article of clothing.

"Oh, hell no," the recruit protested, shaking his head. "You can't expect me to… no."

"You's wanted field work, ole Silky's got you field work."

"But I didn't know it involved… this."

"That's what you be fuckin' gettin' for not askin'," Silky replied jovially, and tossed the garment at Kerr's head. "Get a fuckin' shower and put that shit on, cuz you's leavin' in five minutes."

"I can't believe I'm dressed like this," Kerr muttered, and both Rose and Silky's blonde ho stifled giggles.

"Don't be so hard on yourself," the redhead said while fighting a grin. "It looks fine. Right, Trixie?"

"Yeah," Trixie agreed, "it really brings out your eyes."

Kerr scowled, and picked at the hem of the pink polo shirt he'd been forced into wearing. "This fucking sucks."

The roar of the waves seemed to accentuate his mood, swooshing up into the sand with more force than seemed necessary.

Rose clenched her jaw, pursing her lips to keep from bursting into laughter. "Pink looks good on you," she tried to assure him, and Trixie let slip a snicker.

"I swear to god, if I could go back in time I'd find the person that decided pink shirts were a good idea and beat the ever living fuck out of them," Kerr promised, and cracked his knuckles for effect. "I'm a man, dammit. The only legitimate reason for owning a pink shirt is if a red towel got thrown into the wash."

"Are you done?" Rose raised an eyebrow at his outburst. It really wasn't

that big of a deal, but she wasn't about
to tell him that. He was acting like a
hormonal teenager. Who said guys couldn't
wear pink?

"No, I'm not done!" He cried. "My
manhood feels dirty from this! Hell, I
feel like my manhood's shrunk from this!
In fact, I'm going to do something about
it." He motioned to Trixie with a
determined stare. "May I?"

She shrugged sheepishly, putting her
hands on her hips. "Uh, ok?" Her tits
looked like they were ready to burst from
her low cut shirt, and she assumed he was
going to reach out and grab them.

Kerr simply took a long, deep look at
her cleavage. He drew in a breath, held
it, and then released. "Okay," he said,
voice almost zen. "I feel better now."

Rose rolled her eyes at him, and he
fought the urge to give her the finger as
his phone trilled in his pocket.

"This is Kerr," he greeted without
looking at the caller ID, and stood tall,
flexing his biceps in Rose's direction.
She wondered if he was going to start
beating his chest.

"Twenty dollas!" It was Silky, and he
yelled so loud that Kerr had to pull the
phone away from his ear. Rose leaned and
whispered something in Trixie's ear and
they shared a giggle.

"Huh?" Kerr scowled. "For what?"

"You takin' an extended look at those fine-ass titties," Silky drawled.

"How the fuck did you see that?" Kerr slapped a hand to his forehead, eyes darting around. "I thought you were back at the office?"

"Silky's a hi-tech pimp," he explained. "We's on a mission, remember? We's gotta know what's goin' on at this party, ya dig?"

"But how did you-"

"See you titty gazing?" There was a laugh through the phone. "Silky has his hos wired for video. Best way to get a good look at a honky's face is to put a camera at melon level. Cuz when they look that good you <u>know</u> a brotha's gonna check that shit out."

Kerr glanced at the tiny brooch on Trixie's shirt that he hadn't noticed before, and then leaned over the cleft between Rose's tits. "You got a camera in there, too?" He asked, and she growled.

Before he could react, she smacked him four times in the back of the head, and he sidestepped out of her reach.

"I am <u>not</u> one of Silky's hos, thank you very much," she snapped. "I work for the Agency."

"Fair enough," Kerr put his hands up in surrender, and then remembered the phone call, returning the receiver to his face. He kept a close eye on Rose, just in case she felt like smacking the shit out of him again.

"Alright, time to get yo game faces on," Silky advised. "You's almost at the party."

"Yo, Silky?" Kerr asked innocently.

"What up, cracka?"

"You still charging me that twenty bucks?"

"Goddamn right, Silky's got muthafuckin' bills to pay."

Kerr turned and buried his face in Trixie's ample breasts, and her squeak of shock quickly turned to titters of amusement. He let out a happy moan at the soft pillows against his nose and cheeks, and then straightened up, regarding her with a warm smile.

"Hell yeah, milady." He inclined his head in thanks. "Just wanted to make sure I got my money's worth."

"Remind Silky to whoop your ass later," the pimp said sharply through the cell.

"I'll add it to the list," Kerr replied with a jovial tone, happy to be keeping it light. Regardless of hot chicks beating him up with a pink polo shirt, he was getting paid to motorboat titties. Agency life was good.

Inside the palatial frat house, Rose squeezed Kerr's shoulder gently as a little show of support for his first mission. He shot her a quick smile of appreciation, and turned to offer one to Trixie.

There were sudden hands all over his arms, and his first reaction was to kung fu the shit out of whoever was grabbing him. But he stopped himself just in time, remembering that he was an undercover frat idiot.

"Whooooooo!" One of the frat boys grasping him cheered. "Newcomer!" The other three shoved him towards the kitchen island that was covered in various bottles of beer and liquor.

"Funnel!" A second guy pumped his fist into the air, and Kerr raised an eyebrow as people poured into the kitchen from other rooms, chanting.

"Funnel! Funnel! Funnel!"

Trixie put a hand to her mouth and giggled, and Rose leaned in close to her ear.

"Just work the room," she said over the hooting and hollering from the kitchen. "I'm going to find out what's going on after the party. I need you to try and get as many faces on camera as you

can, then Silky can run them through the
demon database."

Trixie nodded, but then wrinkled her
nose in thought. "What's a database?" She
cocked her head in thought.

"Don't worry about it, hon." Rose
gave her shoulder a little pat. "Just go
do what you do best and we'll handle the
rest." She smiled warmly, and Trixie
nodded. She flounced off into the kitchen,
blonde curls bouncing behind her.

The redhead turned to the living
room, moving casually away from the
kitchen, admiring a few of the abstract
paintings along the way. It had a large
sunken sitting area, with built in sofas
covered in pillows and cushions. There
were a few couples getting hot and heavy
on various surfaces, but Rose quickly
spied a nervous looking guy sitting by
himself.

His posture was stiff, and he seemed
like he was trying too hard to look
relaxed and casual. Rose strolled up to
him, put a hand delicately on her hip,
and leaned a bit at the waist, motioning
to the cushion beside him.

"Is this seat taken?" She asked,
voice sultry sweet. He blinked at her
through his thick rimmed glasses, and then
turned his head left and right, as if
checking to see whether she was actually

speaking to him. "Um. No, ma'am," he had a slight southern twang that she couldn't help but find endearing.

She clasped her hands in front of her, waiting expectantly.

"Oh, sorry," he stammered, shuffling a little to the left. "Would you like to sit down?"

"I thought you'd never ask," she replied with a smile, and slid onto the cushion next to him. She turned to face him, crossing her long legs campfire style and leaning forward a bit to give him a cozy view over her cleavage.

"So." A flush crept up his cheeks as his gaze flickered down and then back up again. "Are you having fun?" He looked like he wasn't sure how to sit, with her in such a friendly relaxed pose.

"It's all right I suppose," she shrugged, and offered him a small smile as he drummed his fingers on his knees, struggling to find something to say.

"It looks like your boyfriend is having a good time," he blurted, motioning towards the kitchen where the guys were flipping Kerr over for a keg stand.

"Boyfriend? Him?" She barked a laugh. "Oh, no, no." She glanced back over at the green rookie, dressed in pink desperately chugging beer upside down at a frat party. He was unknowingly doing his job well, at least. He kept the house boys occupied so that she and Trixie could work the room.

"Well, he's missing out," her companion said shakily. "He'd be lucky to have you." The compliment, however sweet and probably genuine for such a nerdy guy, didn't really faze her. Rose wasn't the romantic type, and had a twisted feeling that his kind words were just a way to get her to take her pants off. She always had that twisted feeling, having been burned so many times in her life.

"Aw, thank you, sweetie," she said with a warm smile, and leaned a bit closer to him. She reached out and put a hand on his arm, and he looked down at it, gulping hard. "So, tell me…"

"Roy," he blurted. "I'm Roy."

"Roy." Rose let the name fall from her lips as if she'd been rolling it around in her mouth first. He gulped again. "So tell me, Roy, what is a nice guy like you doing hanging out at a party like this?" It was cliche, but she knew she didn't have to pull out the big guns on this guy. He was already putty and all she'd done was say his name out loud.

"I didn't want to be left alone in my dorm…" He shrugged. "So the guys said if I bought the beer I could come along."

Rose opened her mouth to reply, but two frat boys strolled up looking like they were about to alpha-hole all over the place.

"Hey, Reggie," one of them said.

"It's Roy," Rose piped up, and Polo Shirt #1 shot her a sleazy grin.

"Whatever," he drawled, and then turned back to Roy. "We need more beer. Go get some." He reached out and ruffled the nerd's hair.

"Okay," their target replied meekly, and Rose pursed her lips.

"And <u>you</u>," the sleazeball dragged his gaze up over Rose's form, leaning down to get a better look at her. She resisted the urge to punch him in the throat. Causing a scene wouldn't help her blend in any. "You should come hang in the kitchen," he continued, and she rolled her eyes.

"Not interested," she waved him away. "Leave my friend and I alone."

"<u>Friend</u>, huh?" The second guy laughed, and smacked his buddy on the arm for emphasis. "Fuckin' loser got friendzoned!" They high fived and turned to leave, cackling all the way.

"Go get more beer!" The first one called back over his shoulder, and Roy stood up from the couch.

"Sorry to cut our visit short, but I'd better do what they want," he said apologetically, genuinely put out that he couldn't sit next to this bombshell anymore. "They have all my school stuff, and said if I don't keep them supplied with beer they'll toss it all in the bonfire."

"And you're going to take that from them?" Rose raised an eyebrow.

"Yeah." He shrugged. "But… but it was really nice to meet you. The party's moving to the beach later tonight if you want to come by."

"I think I might, Roy." She smiled up at him, and his cheeks grew pink again.

"I'll see you tonight…" he trailed off, realizing that he didn't know her name, and extended his hand to her.

"Rose," she introduced herself, shaking his hand, and his blush deepened at the contact. He was so pathetically adorable that she almost wanted to knock him out and put him out of his misery.

"Rose," he stammered. "Bye Rose, see you tonight." He turned abruptly on his heel and scurried towards the door. Rose smoothed her jeans, straightened her tank top, and got to her feet. There wasn't anyone in her immediate vicinity to chat with, so she figured she'd take a post within saving distance of Kerr and hopefully Trixie would be done working the room soon.

She positioned herself casually against the wall close enough to jump in

for Kerr, but far enough away that those
sleazebag fucks from earlier wouldn't
think she wanted to hang out with them.
She took a sip from her red Solo cup of
water, and glanced at the front door as it
swung open with a whoosh.

It was almost as if all of the air
went out of the room. An incredibly tall
thin woman with long thick blonde hair
swept inside, face perfectly painted to
emphasize her doe eyes and high
cheekbones.

Rose fought to keep her composure at
the sight. It was the Princess.

Roy stepped aside to allow her to
pass before he could leave, and offered a
smile. His gaze lowered to the epic tits
near spilling out of her corset top, and
it was game over.

His jaw dropped open, drool visibly
running out of the corner of his mouth,
and his eyes went wide as saucers. She ran
a long hot pink fingernail up the curve of
his throat, and grasped his chin in her
hands.

He reluctantly allowed her to raise
his face back to hers, and she leaned in
so that her lips were so close he could
almost feel them against his. She
whispered something, and he couldn't
understand what she was saying, but his
body felt compelled to just

He walked out the door, lopsided grin on his face, massive tent in his pants, and she slammed the door behind him with a flourish.

Rose cocked her head, observing the way the demon moved with catlike grace. She wore ridiculously tall stiletto sandals, and walked on them like a ballerina, gliding around the room like a specter. Rose couldn't deny that the woman was beautiful, but knowing that there was a demon in the space where a soul should be made her beauty intensely creepy.

Trixie was sandwiched between two guys in polo shirts, innocently motioning to her own well endowed, if not enchanted tits.

"Yeah, my one girlfriend says that they're too big," she was saying, "but my other girlfriend thinks they're not big enough. What do you guys think?" Both sets of eyes were glued to her bouncing tits as she pushed them up and down for effect. Rose vaguely wondered how that looked on Silky's end through the camera.

The Princess strolled on past them, and like the pied piper, the two guys fell into step behind her. They tried to peek around her shoulders as she walked, catching glimpses of her cleavage. Rose shook her head, and quickly strode over to Trixie once the demon was out of hearing range.

"We've got to go, now," the redhead took Trixie's hand, noting that the woman looked mildly put out at the guys' ability to walk away so easily.

"Okay," she turned her eyes on the kitchen. "What about Kerr?" She pointed to the lump on the kitchen island, and Rose sighed. He was passed right out, and somebody had dunked his hand in the sink. The giant wet spot on his slacks showed the results of that lovely little prank. At least in this state he wouldn't be a target for the Princess.

The demon beauty queen was quickly growing her horde of followers, and disappeared in a mass of bodies as she stepped down into the middle of the living room.

Rose tugged Trixie towards the kitchen. "Let's get him and go."

They grabbed Kerr's legs and swung them down over the side of the island counter. He groaned and sputtered, and Rose barely sidestepped his stream of vomit. It hit the tile with a squelch and he heaved again, the smell of stale beer and stomach acid wafting up to the women's noses.

Trixie didn't even bat an eye at the smell or display, slinging his arm over her shoulder. Rose opened her mouth to breathe, gingerly hopping over the river of beer puke to grab Kerr's other arm.

"Ugh," she gagged slightly, but swallowed it down as they exited the kitchen, Kerr giving a half moan and half cry as he drunkenly flopped between them.

"Ah, this is nothing," Trixie said offhandedly. "You should see some of the nasty shit that comes out of dudes."

"I don't know if you mean that literally, and I don't really want to know," Rose replied, wrinkling her nose.

"Y'know, y'know somethin'?" Kerr slurred as they stumbled down the front walk, head lolling onto Trixie's shoulder. "I love you's guys…" He slipped down her collarbone, landing face first into her cleavage. "Special, 'specially you," he mumbled into her flesh, "with, with the boobs."

"Oh, who's a cute drunk little bear?" Trixie cooed, petting his head like a kitten.

"Yeah, thazz nice," he praised her.

"We really need to get him back," Rose watched with disdain, and the blonde agreed.

CHAPTER TWELVE

"What in the hell's goin' on up in here?" Silky bellowed as the women dropped Kerr into a heap in the foyer.

"We had to get out of there pretty quick once the Princess showed up," Rose explained, as the recruit on the floor started to roll back and forth like a turtle stuck on its shell.

"You, you's gotta fun-nay jacket." He broke into a fit of high pitched giggles as he pointed at Silky.

"That skinny bitch showed up?" The pimp cocked his head at Kerr, watching him finally manage to roll over and start attempting to crawl around on the hardwood.

"Yeah, and she got every guy there," Rose replied, stepping to the side to avoid Kerr's elbow as he slithered to the living room carpet. "Except him."

"Why didn't she get him?" Silky demanded. "Cracka like smokin' dick or somethin'?"

"He might," the redhead shrugged as Trixie slipped past her to take a spot on the couch with her sisters. "Or it could be because he was passed out drunk."

Kerr turned on elbows and knees like a stoned hermit crab, and buried his face in the bottom of Silky's jacket.

"God<u>damn</u>, cracka!" His superior cried, and kicked him square in the chest. He flopped backwards into the living room, and rolled his head to look up at the three women on the couch.

"Eyyyyy," he chortled, "iz the Three Cocksketeers!"

"Why you's gettin' drunk on your first field mission?" Silky shook his head in disappointment. "Somebody wanna get ole Silky a cup of coffee? We's gotta get this honky sobered up."

"He didn't have a choice," Rose protested as Dixie scurried off to the kitchen to grab some coffee. "He distracted the frat boys so we could operate."

"Oh, now you's defending his ass?" Silky cocked a perfectly sculpted brow.

Rose pursed her lips. "Well."

"Tell ole Silky somethin'," he said conversationally, though there was a hint of sarcasm in his tone. "While wonder bread was gettin' lit the fuck up, what exactly did you find out, huh?"

Dixie returned from the kitchen with a steaming cup of coffee, likely bitter as an old nurse from sitting on the hot plate all day.

"Thanks, honeybunch," Silky said sweetly, accepting the mug. The dark haired ho beamed at the endearment and

practically skipped back past Kerr, who
made a mad grab for her leg as she moved.

"Dixxxxiiiee!" He missed her leg, and
faceplanted into the shag carpet.

"Well," Rose cleared her throat,
turning back to Silky, "they're having a
party on the beach later."

"DIXIEEEE." Kerr squeaked out another
of those high pitched giggles and pointed
at her, arm wavering. "I… I can make your
south rise <u>again</u>." He hissed the last few
words, raising his fist and clenching it
for emphasis.

"Huh?" Dixie and Trixie shrugged at
each other. Then Trixie turned to Mixie
and they exchanged blank stares. Then
Mixie leaned forward to look at Dixie and
they shared yet another shrug.

"It's okay hos, Silky don't know what
in the fuck he's sayin' neither," their
pimp piped up, and Kerr turned, eyes
lighting up at the coffee mug. "Here,
kitty kitty, come to ole Silky for some
fuckin' milk," he cooed, backing up along
the hardwood to coax the wobbly recruit
out of the living room.

As soon as Kerr crossed the threshold
off of Silky's shag carpet, his superior
jabbed the mug forward, flinging the
entire cup of hot coffee directly into his
face.

The recruit stayed still for a split second, drunk brain not registering what had just transpired.

But then his nerves caught up with his head and they were on <u>fire</u>. He started to scream as his entire face started to burn up, feeling like it was melting down onto the floor.

Rose winced as Kerr went down on his forehead, the rest of this body writhing about.

"You was sayin'?" Silky prompted her, and she blinked, turning her gaze back to him.

"We should be able to apprehend one of the frat demons at this party to find out what the Princess is doing to them." She squared her shoulders, back to business. "They were all over her, and we had to extract Kerr, but on the beach in the dark we should be able to get one of the demons alone. The Princess might not even be there."

"All right, Silky'll buy that," he gave in, and leaned down to inspect Kerr's cherry red face. "You sober now, bitch? Or does Silky need to get you another cup o' joe?"

"I'm good," the recruit moaned, rolling away from him. "I'm good…"

"That's what Silky likes to hear, he does!" The pimp clapped his hands and

tossed the mug behind him. It hit the
floor and smashed into pieces. Rose
winced. Why did the Boss trust them to
stay anywhere nice? "Get your shit
together, and be ready to leave in two
hours!" Silky bellowed, and Kerr staggered
to his feet, still moaning.

"Ugh, you still reek like booze and
barf," Rose wrinkled her nose at him as he
swayed in front of her.

"Whoo-eee, you ain't wrong, sista!"
Silky held his nose dramatically, and
wandered off into the living room. "You
can be payin' one o Silky's hos to bathe
you, honky, or maybe if you axe Rose real
nice she'll do it up for free!"

Kerr raised his eyes to hers and she
waved her hands in front of her
frantically.

"Oh <u>hell</u> no," she said. "You can
bathe yourself, thank you very much." He
swayed as trudged to the stairs, taking a
deep breath before lifting a lead foot to
land on the first step. Rose bit her lip
as he managed to get up two steps before
slipping and falling on his face.

"I'm good, I'm good," he whimpered,
and struggled to get back to his feet. She
pinched the bridge of her nose.

"Ugh, I'm going to regret this," she
muttered, and hooked one of his arms over
her shoulders to help him up the stairs.

"You are <u>so</u> not going to regret this," Kerr promised, trying to slip his arm further around her.

"I'm not bathing you, I'm just helping you up to the bathroom, you horny drunk idiot," Rose snapped. "And if you are anything less than gentlemanly I will kick your ass back down the stairs, understand?"

He lazily curled his fingers into an a-okay sign, and then went full dead weight on her. She grunted and heaved, realizing that she was willingly carrying a half sober recruit up a flight of stairs in suburbia so he could shower before escorting her and a prostitute to a frat party.

She couldn't say that Agency life wasn't interesting.

CHAPTER THIRTEEN

Kerr peeked out through the hay-like grass, peering down at the beach through his binoculars. They were night-vision, and he almost wished he'd worn sunglasses to stare through the damn things as the remains of his headache pulsed in the back of his head.

But he was better off than he could have been. The vomiting at least had blown most of the alcohol out of his body before it had started to digest. He'd been lucky that Rose and Trixie had been able to get him out of there, and away from the Princess' evil wiles.

"There doesn't look like there are too many of them," he said quietly. "That's good, right?" The beach behind the fraternity mansion had a bonfire that glowed a headache inducing white in the glow of the night-vision. But around it were a few staggering figures and some couples hanging off of each other in various positions up and down the sand bar.

He flipped to regular vision to try to save his eyeballs--and his piercing forehead--the strain and watch for Trixie's signature blonde pouf.

"Could be," Silky shrugged, reclining in the pop up chair he'd brought. "Depends."

Kerr shuffled back through their camouflage, raising an eyebrow at his relaxed superior. "Depends on what?"

"Just depends, cracka," Silky threw a hand up dismissively. "Just depends."

The recruit sighed, not particularly enjoying being told facts without being taught how those conclusions were come to. He was supposed to be learning, right? He dug in his pocket for the little bottle of Advil that Trixie had procured for him, and popped two, swallowing them dry.

He felt a surge of bravery as he parted the grass again, taking a deep breath to ask the question he'd been burning with all day. "So what's your story?" He asked, as casually as he could muster.

"What you talkin' about, honky?" Silky barked, bending a leg at the knee to rest his mint green clad arm over it. He was the pinnacle of relaxation, massive sunglasses under an equally large hat, light green velvet to match his jacket.

The recruit had no idea how he could even see in those massive glasses in the dark, but questioning Silky's fashion choices seemed like a step too far.

"You." Kerr sat back again, eyeing his eccentric superior. "I mean, how the hell does a pimp end up working for a demon hunting agency?"

"It's a long story, cracka," Silky drawled. "We ain't got time for that shit."

"Don't have time?" The recruit scoffed. "We're hiding in birdshit infested grass waiting for a bunch of frat boys to drink themselves to death. I think we've got time."

"Aight," the pimp sighed, leaning his head right back in his chair. "You wanna know what Silky's all about, wonder bread? Here you go. Silky's a muthafuckin' angel."

Kerr blinked at him. "What?"

"Is you deaf or somethin', boy? Silky said he's an angel."

"A pimp angel." The recruit rolled his eyes, and turned back to the grass, poking the binoculars back through. "Look, if you didn't want to tell me your story, you could have just said that."

"Silky's tellin' the truth, muthafucka." The pimp's voice raised an octave at his subordinate's attitude. "Silky's been a top dog pimp for years, but he's always encouraged his hos to use the money they be makin' to better 'emselves. Go to school, get 'em an education and shit. Hos can't fuck forever, ya dig."

"A pimp with a heart of gold," Kerr joked.

"Goddamn right, honky," Silky snapped. "Now you gonna let Silky finish, or you gonna keep fuckin' interruptin'?"

"By all means, continue," the recruit chuckled, and backed up through the grass. He turned and sat on his haunches as the pimp slid off of his beach chair.

Silky grinned his golden toothy grin as he reached out and poked his pointer finger right into the middle of Kerr's forehead. The younger man went crosseyed with curiosity as he tried to focus on the finger, and then the wind went out of him as his center of gravity pitched forward.

Kerr blinked and realized they were standing in a massive hall, set up like a posh banquet but full of the sexiest and sluttiest women he'd ever seen. The color scheme was all deep crimson and gold, and tits, just tits everywhere.

"What the-" he stammered, but was speechless as he realized there were two Silkys standing in front of him. One in the same peppermint getup as before, and another in a far more outlandish leopard print suit and coat, complete with a golden cane and a hat that had to be at least three feet in diameter.

"As Silky was sayin'," spearmint Silky said, and his doppleganger didn't even notice his presence. Kerr's lower lip moved up and down but no sound came out. What was happening? "About three years ago, Silky was hostin' his annual Fuckin' For A Future reunion dinner for all his former hos that made somethin' of themselves."

That explained the sexy women everywhere. Some were sitting at tables, some were dancing on them. Some had a man or woman on their arm, others were grouped together, catching up. There were random men spattered about the group, clearly Johns that had been invited for the current hos to proposition. Ever the businessman, Silky was.

Past Silky strutted up onto the stage, spotlight flashing off of his epic grill. He had a woman on either side of him, each in a long pastel elegant gown that would have looked like something out of a prom had there not been mounds of soft flesh bursting out of the extremely low necklines.

Cheers erupted throughout the hall, and Kerr stared around wide eyed at the uproar. Everyone was hooting, hollering, up on their feet to applaud. This pimp had clearly made a difference to a lot of people.

The on-stage Silky spread his arms, motioning for everyone to settle down. It took a good two minutes until everyone finally stopped whistling and took their seats again, giving him their undivided attention.

"Ladies and gentle-hos," he began, and a chuckle rippled through the crowd. "It's damn good to have all's y'all together again this year. My sweet ass Lola graduated from Nursin' School with fuckin' honors last month!" He clapped his hands and there was more thunderous applause. The woman to the left of him blushed hard and waved shyly to the audience, clearly not used to such praise.

She turned and kissed Silky on the cheek, and he patted her backside lovingly. He turned back to the crowd, but as he opened his mouth to say more, there were two sharp cracks, and then all hell broke loose.

Kerr had been so fixated on the show that he hadn't noticed the man with the gun stand up from his table, and pop off two rounds directly into Silky's chest. The hos on either side of him shrieked as he fell to his knees, looking down at the blood pouring from his heart in shock.

In slow motion, people lunged forward on top of the gun man, but it was too late. The leopard clad pimp fell back onto

the stage, the tears of his hos dripping
down onto his lifeless face as they tried
to rouse him back from the dead.

The scene slowed down even further
until it was completely frozen, and Kerr's
eyes darted around, his heart pounding. He
nearly jumped out of his skin when minty
Silky put a hand on his shoulder.

"That cracka ass came in undercover,
sent by a rival pimp to infiltrate Silky's
banquet." He motioned to the guy that was
flattened beneath a tableau of angry hos
and their dates. "He wasn't happy at the
amount of his hos Silky had gotten out of
the game and thinkin' about them futures."

"Damn," Kerr breathed, looking up at
the anguished faces of the women frozen
over Silky's body. "You try to do the
right thing."

"Damn is right, cracka," the
nostalgic pimp sighed. "Well, ole Silky
was faced with a dilemma." A bright light
washed over the stage and a silver form
materialized before their eyes, floating
down to wash over the dead man.

It slid over him, and the pimp let
out a shocked gasp, crab walking backwards
from the women over him that were frozen
in time. He clutched at his chest that he
remembered being full of bullets, and
gazed open mouthed at the vaguely humanoid
wisp floating above him.

"Smoothen Silky," an ethereal female voice floated down around the room, "you have changed many lives for the better in your short life."

"What in the fuckin' shit is this?!" Silky exclaimed, and leapt to his feet, personality winning out over shock as he pointed at the wisp. "Silky just fuckin' died, how the fuck is he still standin'?"

The voice chuckled. "We want to offer you the chance to ascend to the heavens, Smoothen Silky," it purred, and he pursed his lips.

"Silky's not too surprised he wasn't endin' up there in the first place," he admitted. "But Silky ain't no chump, what's the catch, cloud lady?"

"Help us with the war on demons, child, and you will live forever in the land of the angels," the voice proclaimed, and he barked a laugh.

"The war on fuckin' demons?" He picked up his cane and struck a regal pose at center stage. "Silky was born for that shit."

The scene melted away and Kerr had that anti-gravity feeling before falling back into the grass. He blinked. The grass. They were back at the beach.

"Understand, honky?" Silky leaned back in his chair once again.

"Not really," Kerr shook his head. "I mean you changing lives or not, why would they recruit a pimp?"

"You a thick muthafucka sometimes," the pimp sighed. "If you's a demon and you make yo way up to this world from the depths of hell, what's the first fuckin' thing you gonna go lookin' for?"

The recruit screwed up his lips in thought. "Food?"

"Hells, no!" Silky threw his hands up. "You's gonna go lookin' for a piece of ass! That's why Silky was recruited. Cuz even up in heaven they know that Silky's got the best pieces of ass in this world and the next."

Kerr rubbed his forehead in disbelief. "That's… quite a story, man. Not sure if I really believe it all, but it is a hell of a story."

"Bitch, Silky showed you his fuckin' memories, what more does ya need?" He humphed at Kerr's shrug, and then lowered his sunglasses. "Believe this, cracka," he said, and his eyes glowed into shining orbs of bright blue light.

The recruit cried out, backing up a bit in the grass. "Alright, I'm with you," he assured him, "just, ugh, stop doing that, it's creepy."

"Aight, muthafucka, then get your snow white ass back to work here," Silky's eyes immediately lost the shine and fell back to their normal chocolate brown.

Kerr gladly turned to look back through the grass, deciding not to ask any more questions for the moment. He'd bitten off more than he could chew with that one. Though a lot of things made more sense now, even with the fantastical story he'd just been told. He was hunting frat demons, so why was it so outlandish to think that there were pimp angels too?

"I've got eyes on Trixie, she's leading a frisky polo shirt down the beach," Kerr reported, innately shuddering at his own stint wearing one of those atrocities.

"That's Silky's fuckin' cue." The pimp stood up, flicking the chair expertly into a neat little package that he stowed away in his amazingly spacious jacket. He drew his golf club and motioned for his recruit to follow. "Rose'll be finishing up the interrogation room, let's skedaddle."

CHAPTER FOURTEEN

Trixie giggled as Roy tickled her ass while they crossed the threshold into the back of the beach house. Rose had procured this place for the night to interrogate their mark. Trixie whipped around and sashayed backwards through the sitting room, licking her lips as she went.

"Slow down there, big boy," she winked at him. "Let's get inside my bedroom, first."

"Oh I plan on getting inside, alright." Roy grabbed her wrists and pulled her flush against him. "Inside them pants. Whoo-haa." He kissed down her throat, suckling at her collarbone, and she pushed at his chest.

"Wow, you are a frisky one," Trixie said, laughing nervously as he held her in place.

"Shut up, baby, you're ruining the mood," he said, voice hard, and wound a fist into her hair roughly. Warning bells went off in Trixie's head, and she didn't think that she was going to be able to get this guy back to the interrogation room before he overpowered her.

She wriggled out of his grip, nearly managing to scurry away before he grabbed her bicep in a strong hand.

"Where you going, baby?" Roy leered as he dragged her back against him. "I got what you need." He lowered his mouth to her cheek and slid his hand down her hip, toying with the waistband of her shorts.

"Okay, that's enough." She shoved against him as hard as she could, and he snarled, backhanding her with enough force that she fell to the carpet.

"You're going to wish you gave in, bitch!" Roy hooked his hands in the collar of his shirt and jerked down, ripping it clean open. Trixie shrieked, holding her cheek, and scrambled backwards as fast as she could despite her lightheadedness.

"Muthafucka!" Silky's voice boomed, and Roy turned just in time to meet a jewelry adorned hand that sliced his face clean open. "Silky's gonna teach you to hit his fuckin' ho."

Rose burst into the room as Roy hit the ground, gun at the ready. She knelt to check over Trixie as Kerr stepped in behind Silky, leaning down to jerk Roy up by his hair.

"Piece of shit," he muttered at the shirtless frat boy, and Rose's breath caught in her throat as she recognized him. She noticed Roy's glasses laying on the carpet, having fallen in the scuffle, and put them on his face, blinking in shock.

"Get his ass hooked up," Silky
ordered, and she nodded firmly, hauling
him out of the room by his arm.

"Trixie!" Mixie squealed from the
hallway, clearly having come from the
kitchen if her flour dusted apron was any
indication. "Are you okay?" She scurried
over to her fallen sister ho, who smiled
up at her.

"I am now." Trixie ran a hand through
Mixie's honey brown locks, and shakily got
to her feet. They clutched each other and
then Mixie slid a hand around the back of
the blonde's neck, pulling her in for a
sweet kiss.

Kerr slid a twenty dollar bill out of
his pocket, holding it out to Silky as he
gazed at the two beautiful women
comforting each other. The pimp grinned
and took the bill, patting his recruit on
the shoulder before leading him to the
interrogation room.

When they entered, Rose had Roy tied
securely to a chair, and was standing in
front of him, one hand thoughtfully on her
chin as she scrutinized his face.

"Fuckin' buzzkill bitches!" He spat,
writhing against his bonds. "Cocktease
cunts! Get me a fuckin' beer, I'll drink
alllll the fuckin' beer and show you who's
the fuckin' man! My dick is so big I can
fuck your ass from all the way over here,

bitch, just bend over and fuckin' take it!" He continued to shriek obscenities at her, and she turned to her coworkers, bewildered.

"I can't believe that he's acting like this," Rose said, crossing her arms.

"He's a drunk frat dick, what did you expect?" Kerr shrugged.

"You don't understand, he wasn't one of them," Rose insisted, "he was a geek that got blackmailed into buying beer."

"People get crazy when they're drunk," Kerr replied, scratching the back of his head nervously. He didn't want to bring up his stint earlier that evening, as he was still a little embarrassed by his behavior.

"Dammit, it's more serious than that," she snapped.

"We's gonna know soon enough," Silky cut in. "Where's Silky's smart ho at?"

"Her name is Kiki," Rose muttered under her breath.

As if on cue, the door opened and a dark haired woman in a white cropped blouse and red kilt strode in. Kerr's jaw dropped to the floor at her almond shaped eyes accentuated by delicate glasses on her flawless face. Her shapely calves were adorned with white knee socks, and the playful black mary janes on her feet had an impossible heel that still didn't even

get her more than a head shorter than
Silky.

"Sorry, Silky," she was out of breath
as she lifted an aluminum case onto a
table in the corner. "It took a little
longer than I thought to run the tox
screen."

Kiki opened the case, producing a
laptop, and slid a USB stick out of her
lacy red bra.

"That's okay, baby," he purred as he
leaned over the computer with her. "Didja
get what Silky needs?"

"Yes, I did," she replied excitedly
as her fingers flew over the keys. "I ran
a full blood tox screen and a DNA scan on
him." Her slight lean revealed the lower
curve of her ass out of the bottom of her
ridiculously short skirt, and Kerr
fingered another twenty dollar bill in his
pocket in case the pimp turned around.

Rose rolled her eyes and moved up
next to the sexy schoolgirl, peering down
at the computer screen. Roy's bellowing of
profanities lowered to lewd talk about
schoolgirls and their teachers, and Kerr
clocked him on the back of the head.

"Let me just bring up my data so we
can analyze it," Kiki was saying as Silky
sat down, appraising her long creamy legs.

"Mm, mm, _mm_, ole Silky would analyze
that _all_ night long." He winked, and she

giggled as she worked. Kerr marveled at Silky's charisma, and not for the first time. But you don't get to be the most famous pimp in heaven if you're not charming.

Kiki's face hardened. "Oh no, this isn't good at all."

"Talk to Silky, baby, what we got here?" He leaned forward, but the graphs on the screen didn't mean anything to him.

"Slut, get over here and sit on my fuckin' face, I bet you taste so fuckin' sweet," Roy babbled, and Kiki furrowed her brow, turning around to face their bound prisoner.

"This guy is sober," She said, and the other three stared at him, wide eyed.

"I'm going to go out on a limb and say that isn't good," Kerr piped up.

"Come on baby, spread your fuckin' legs, Imma tear you in fuckin' half," Roy continued.

"How can someone be that annoying and be sober?" Rose crossed her arms, eyeing him warily. She had known something was up as soon as she'd seen that it was Roy who had tried to assault Trixie. Even if he'd been lying earlier that day, pretending to be a victimized nerd to get some ass, this was too insane for him to have been fully acting.

"Silky knows a brotha's goin' to go balls out fo a nice set o' titties, but god<u>damn</u>, this skinny bitch done drove this cracka crazy."

"The Princess did this?" Rose motioned to him. "She can do <u>this</u>?"

Kiki turned back to the computer, and shook her head in worry. "Silky," she tugged on his sleeve.

"What is it, baby girl?" He leaned over her.

"There's something much worse," she said, and both Rose and Kerr immediately turned to look. "This is what a normal DNA chain is supposed to look like." Kiki pointed to a diagram she'd brought up on the screen. "And this is his DNA chain. See the extra lines here, and here?"

"What you tryin' to say, sweet cheeks?" Silky asked.

"I have a theory, but it'll be confirmed in a moment when the program is done running it's calculations," she replied, biting her lip.

"DNA chains? How can she do all of this?" Kerr blurted.

Silky smiled proudly. "Kiki here was the charter member in Silky's Fuckin' for a Future program. Graduated with a masters-"

"Doctorate," Kiki interjected.

"Silky apologizes," he replied, putting a hand over his chest to emphasize his guilt. "She graduated with a doctorate in some fucking techy mumbo jumbo that yo dumb ass wouldn't understand, dig?"

"You have no idea what it is, do you?' Kerr raised an eyebrow.

"Not a fuckin' clue." Silky nodded.

"Okay," Kiki said, and everyone leaned back in again. "This first line is some sort of spiritual trigger. It's something that can alter DNA on a spiritual level, often driving the victim insane."

"Okay?" Kerr shrugged. "So what's the problem?"

"When the spiritual trigger is activated, the victim's soul is ripped out and they spend all eternity in a painful void," Kiki explained.

"Still don't see a problem," he shook his head. "Who cares if a bunch of dickhole fratboys lose their souls?"

"Muthafucka, think of Silky's profits!" The pimp smacked Kerr on the back of the head. "If all these dumbass white boys get their souls ripped out, then who's goin' to partake in Silky's fine ass assortment o' hos?"

"And it's not just that," Kiki added, "often when such a trigger is activated it is for something much more sinister."

"Such as?" Rose prompted, lips in a thin line.

"The most common use is to summon a legendary demon." She adjusted her glasses on her face, turning back to Roy.

"Legendary demon?" Kerr asked. "What do we do if that happens?" He cracked his knuckles.

"Be somewhere else." Kiki shoved his fists down with a sigh. "Those demons are powerful enough that they've been sealed away by the Agency's predecessors. They have been increasing in power, and since they've been locked away in their own personal hell, they typically come out very, very pissed off."

"Wait, you work for the Agency too?" Kerr stared at her, taken aback.

"Of course I do." She shrugged. "Why?"

"Just…" He motioned to her outfit, and then ran the hand through his hair to try to recover his possible rudeness.

"Just because I'm a professional doesn't mean I can't dress up in a sexy outfit." Kiki winked at Silky, and he tipped his hat to her.

"Truer words ain't never been spoke, baby doll," he purred, and she giggled.

"So," Kerr prompted and coughed, trying to direct the conversation away from his hormonally charged question. "Legendary demons have escaped before?"

"We try to make sure it doesn't get to that point," Rose replied, taking her bottom lip between her teeth as she continued to watch Roy thrash about and yell.

"But it <u>has</u> happened before?"

"The last time it took 17 agents to bring it down." She looked him dead in the eye. "Only two walked away."

"Okay." Kerr gulped. "Let's make sure it doesn't get to that point."

"Oh, fuck," Kiki blurted, snapping everyone to attention. "We're in trouble."

"Talk to Silky, baby," Silky leaned forward.

Her almond eyes were wide as she turned to him. "The second chain is a tracer strain."

Kiki slammed the laptop shut, shoving it quickly back in the aluminum case.

"Get the other hos and get outta here," Silky pointed a finger at her, and then turned quickly to Rose. "You be takin' care of our boy there and then get out the back. Wonder bread, you be comin' with Silky to the basement."

"The basement? What?" Kerr threw his hands up. "What's a tracer strain?"

"Goddammit you honky numbskull, how in the fuck did you pass yo entrance exam?!" Silky grabbed the back of the recruit's collar and hauled him through the house. "Tracer strain means they know where we's at, they's trackin' us."

"Oh," Kerr mentally smacked himself. "Fuck."

"That's right, fuck." The pimp nodded as they reached the basement door. There was a sound of glass shattering as he opened the door and waved the recruit inside. "Good luck, cracka."

"Wait, what about you?" Kerr asked in a panic.

"Hos before bros, muthafucka," Silky gave a little salute, and held out his 9-iron like a baseball bat. "Once they's safe Silky'll be back to get you."

"But-"

"Get yo honky ass down them fuckin'
stairs!" His eyes blazed.

"Alright." Kerr scowled and
reluctantly descended the steps.

Rose sighed as she unsheathed her
ceremonial knife, looking down at Roy with
sadness in her gaze. He really had been a
nice nerd.

"I'm sorry, Roy," she said sincerely.
"You didn't deserve this."

"Go fuck yourself, bitch-" he
started, spittle flying from his maniacal
mouth, but she cut him off by burying the
blade into his skull.

He disintegrated into demon gunk
right before her eyes, and she pursed her
lips at the fact that it was
indistinguishable from any other demon
gunk. The poor guy had deserved better.

She reached up to touch her cheek in
shock, finding a tear there. She brushed
it away with a ragged gasp and shoved any
more thoughts of Roy out of her head. It
was time to get the fuck out of dodge.

Rose slid the knife back into her
combat boot and moved silently down the
hallway. She slipped into the kitchen, and
immediately vaulted over the island as
pink shirts barreled in from every angle.
She scrambled up onto the far counter,

hoping to get to the window over the sink,
but a firm hand clamped around her ankle.

She snatched a baking sheet from the
sink, whipping it in a tight arc to smash
into the frat dick's face. He dodged but
let go of her ankle to tuck and roll away,
leaving a second guy to pop up on her
other side. She swung her legs out of his
reach and leapt for the island again in a
twisted game of 'the floor is made of
lava'.

Pots and pans cackled against each
other as she bumped the hanging shelf with
her shoulder. She dropped the baking sheet
with a metallic <u>clang</u> onto the tile floor
and took a cast iron skillet in hand,
bringing it down hard on the head of the
attacker trying to pop up from below.

She swept her leg around with a
<u>whoosh</u>, aiming for another face to her
right, and when she missed, he jumped up
beside her. He grabbed the hanging shelf
of kitchen utensils and jerked it down,
stainless steel and iron crushing her
beneath the wooden frame.

She cried out and wriggled as hard as
she could, managing to slip out from
beneath the trap and hit the tile floor
with a hard <u>smack</u>. A heavy lump landed on
her back, knocking the wind out of her,
and she lost her grip on the heavy pan.
She reached out blindly as a fist wound

its way into her hair and yanked on a
drawer, wrenching it free and flinging it
back over her head.

It connected with something, and
wooden spoons rained down on top of her,
bouncing and clattering all around. Her
attacker grunted and she managed to squirm
away from him, his hands groping for her
legs as she did so.

She got to her feet and opened the
freezer door just in time to clothesline a
guy making a run at her, and he fell onto
drawer-head on the floor. She turned tail
and bolted for the door, but another frat
boy slammed into her midsection and
tackled her to the tile.

She screamed in frustration as
another one joined his friend, and between
the two of them they were able to pin her
before she could get at her knife in her
boot. She spat and kicked and shrieked,
but they overpowered her, flipping her
face down onto the floor.

"I will fucking _end_ you
motherfuckers!" Rose cried as they secured
her wrists behind her back with zip ties,
and then her ankles. One of them dislodged
the ceremonial knife and buried it into
the wall as they hauled the snarling
wildcat of a woman out the back door.

"Go on, babes, Silky'll see you
soon," the pimp in the mint green suit
handed Kiki the keys to the truck.

"You be safe, love," she ran a hand
down his face and kissed his lips softly,
languidly. He wanted to drop his cane and
bury himself into her right there in the
sand, but Smoothen Silky had a recruit to
take care of.

"Don't you be worryin' about ole
Silky," he said with a squeeze of her
tight ass, and bit his lip. "He's gonna be
just fine. You hos take care of each
other, now, get d'fuck outta here." He
watched them barrel into the truck, Mixie
at the wheel, and speed away towards the
parking lot.

He turned and jogged back to the
house, staying low in the shadows in case
of any uninvited frat dicks. He peered in
through the front window, and there was
nobody there. An angry screech filled the
air and his blood ran cold. That was
Rose's voice.

Silky barreled through the door,
hurtling through the house just in time
see through the back sliding door. There
were two pink shirts carrying Rose's
thrashing form off of the porch into the
sand. He lunged forward but two pink blurs
swept into the way, knocking him back.

"Silky's had e-fucking-<u>nough</u> of you needledicked pussies!" He lifted his 9-iron and his left leg, hopping in a graceful roundhouse kick that his opponents didn't expect. Upon landing, he jabbed out with his fist, connecting with a demon jaw, the force of his punch crushing cartilage and bone.

Two more polo shirts burst into the room and made to tackle him from behind, but he ducked and rolled under them. One ended up hitting his buddy like a bowling ball, but the other wised up and tucked his shoulder into a somersault to land on his feet.

Silky took advantage of the confusion to hurl his body into a front flip, bringing his heel down onto an upturned face. The <u>crunch</u> of his skull was telling and the pimp smirked as he lashed out with the golf club and caught another frat dick in the chin.

That one crumpled to the carpet, and Silky drew his knife, executing a perfect cartwheel and using the momentum to plunge it into the asshole's throat. He gasped in a series of squelching swallows and one of the other frat guys immediately hurled himself out the sliding door, running scared from the experienced killer.

The one with the flattened face moaned as he attempted to sit up.

"Where's you think you goin', pinkie pie?" Silky sneered, and drove his knife into the guy's ass cheek, causing a surprised scream to tear its way out of his mouth before he passed out from the sheer pain that had been rained down on him.

Three down, one to go, and that one was dancing back and forth in front of the sliding door. Silky raised an eyebrow as the frat asshole performed a pretty impressive dropkick and a few well executed punches to the air in front of him.

"Oh, you's gonna show Silky a thing or two, huh?" The pimp raised his eyebrows in skepticism. "Aight, bitch, come _on_."

Kerr started to case the entire basement, trying to ignore the thumping and clanging from upstairs. He feared Silky's wrath for not following orders more than the demons attacking the beach house, so he did as he was told. Rose and Silky could handle themselves.

His job was to take care of the basement.

He slowly moved in the darkness, straining his eyes. Every box and blanket down there looked like a humanoid shape, but nothing was moving. His senses were on such high alert that when the shriek of an angry woman pierced the air it seemed to slam into his eardrums like a skewer.

He'd found the window that he'd heard break from the top of the stairs, and though it was right at the top of the wall at ground level, he was tall enough to peer outside. The scream had clearly come from the beach.

His heart skipped a beat when he saw two frat dicks making off with his struggling and bound coworker.

"ROSE!" He yelled, and tried to aim his gun through the broken glass. They were too far away for a handgun. Fuck.

He took a second to decide whether to try to wriggle through the window and risk slicing himself into ribbons, or take the extra time to run back upstairs and out the back door. Every second counted.

He turned to make a mad dash for the stairs, and slammed right into a pink clad chest.

Kerr looked up into the glowing eyes of the biggest frat boy he'd ever seen, and curled his hand into a fist. But the guy was more beast than man at this point, and he grabbed the recruit's shirt, tossing him into the concrete wall like a rag doll. The wind tore out of him like a storm, and he coughed as he staggered to his feet, scrabbling for his gun.

The frat dick was standing stock still, eyes glazed as if thinking really hard about something. Before Kerr could find his gun, the guy turned abruptly like a robot, heading for the stairs.

The recruit's eyes widened when he realized that this brainwashed frat asshole probably was very much like a robot, and barked a laugh to get his attention.

"Where do you think you're going, dickhead?" Kerr wheezed, injecting as much bravado into his voice as possible. "You had enough of Kerr? Or are you just afraid that you're going to get your ass kicked?" He shoved his hand into his back pocket, retrieving a small device he'd been saving for a special occasion.

Polo shirt hesitated, his lips twitching into a sneer, but then back to a thin line as he turned to the stairs again.

"Oh, I get it." Kerr laughed, and injected his voice with as much smooth and silky attitude as he could muster. "You ain't nothin' but a pussy."

The guy whipped around, anger in his hellish eyes, and stalked back to where his heckler was bouncing back and forth from foot to foot.

"That's what I thought you piece of-" Kerr was cut off by the superhuman frat boy snatching his throat in giant hands and lifting him off of the ground. "Shit," he choked, but managed to slip the device under the pink polo collar as he slapped the asshole with his other hand.

The guy threw his forehead into Kerr's nose with a sickening crunch, and then dropped him in a heap on the basement floor. The recruit gasped for air as the frat dick marched away from him and up the stairs.

This fucking job.

Silky wrapped his bejeweled hand around the doorknob of the dining room, leaning down to give his prisoner a menacing grin.

"Where they takin' her?" He asked with sugary sweetness, and when he didn't get an answer, he slammed the door on the fucker's ugly face.

The frat boy groaned in pain, and it was music to the pimp's ears.

"Silky axed you a question, frat fuck," he said, "where they fuckin' takin' her?"

"You can't stop us…" the pink clad guy hissed, gargling blood in his throat.

"Oh yeah?" Silky slammed the door two more times, and then rapped the head of his 9-iron against his enemy's nose. "How's that feel, muthafucka? Now Silky ain't gonna ask again. Where they takin' her?"

"Fuck you, pimp." The words were even more garbled. "You lose."

Silky let out a cry of frustration and slammed the door completely, severing the asshole's head from his body. For good measure, he plunged his ceremonial knife into the center of that god awful pink polo shirt, reveling in the nasty goo that spread out over the carpet.

He skirted it as he sheathed his knife, heading through the kitchen around to the basement door. As he opened it, a bloody hand reached up from the stairs and Kerr groaned.

"Goddamn, cracka, somebody done fucked yo ass up." Silky reached down to grab the recruit's hand, pulling him through the door with concern in his eyes.

"Well." Kerr grinned through the blood pouring from his nose as he managed to stand up straight. "I guess it's better to have my ass fucked <u>up</u> instead of just plain fucked."

"Boy, this ain't no time for words of wisdom bullshit," Silky snapped, wringing his hands around the golf club's handle. "We's in some serious trouble."

"Tell me about it," Kerr replied, motioning to his likely broken nose.

"Cracka, I ain't playin'." The pimp narrowed his eyes. "They's got Rose."

"I know."

"They's got Rose and they's plannin' somethin' big." Silky started to pace, slamming the club against the tile with every step like a heavy walking stick.

"I know."

"Silky don't think you know, cracka." He turned and pointed the head of the club in Kerr's direction, eyes wilder than the recruit had ever seen them. "Rose ain't one of Silky's hos. We's got no way to track her."

"I know."

"Goddamn, Silky's gettin' tired of your shit, boy." Even through his words of panic, he still sounded cool as a cucumber, and the recruit marveled at how together his superior was in a time of crisis.

"Silky."

"Silky ain't finished. Your dumb ass got any idea what's gonna happen if we can't find 'em?"

"Silky…"

"_Bad_ muthafuckin' shit, that's what. We's gonna get our asses reamed, and that's even assumin' we's be survivin' this shit," Silky rambled.

"Goddammit would you shut the fuck
up, you ignorant pimp?!" Kerr cried,
throwing his hands up in the air.

His superior blinked at him, drawing
his shoulders back, cocking his head ever
so slightly. His deep set eyes narrowed
the tiniest bit and he clicked his tongue.
"Is you outta your goddamn mind, honky?"

"Even though I'm pretty sure I left
part of my mind on the wall downstairs…"
Kerr put his hands up in front of him,
taking a deep breath. "I was able to put a
tracker on the guy that was beating me to
a pulp. Which means we can track them with
this."

He wiggled his phone in the air, and
his breathing returned to normal as
Silky's mouth spread into a wide grin on
his face. He looked like a kid on
Christmas morning, eyes alight with glee
at the news.

"If we survive this shit, you's gonna
get a free ho on Silky," he promised,
slinging the golf club up to rest over his
shoulder.

"Really?" Kerr returned the smile,
bloody face and all. "Do I get to pick?"

"Don't be pushin' it, boy."

"Silky's choice." The recruit nodded.
"That's cool."

Silky clapped Kerr on the back and
barked a laugh. "My cracka's growin up so

fast!" He pretended to wipe a tear from his face.

"Alright, let's go save Rose." Kerr held up the phone, running the companion app to the tracking device.

Silky raised the golf club in the air like a sword. "Lead on, my honky!"

CHAPTER SIXTEEN

Rose twisted as best she could, but it was no use. These demons apparently had supernatural knot tying powers as well as their glowing eyes and ability to drink infinite amounts of beer.

"Save your strength my dear, you're going to need it." A regal voice declared, and a familiar beauty queen stepped up into Rose's view, complete with a crown.

Rose raised an eyebrow, not having expected this bitch to show up at the frat boy's altar party.

"The Princess," she pursed her lips, and started wriggling anew. This could not be good. The six frat boys kneeling around her half naked and bound form had been disconcerting enough. But this was probably going to end far worse than if they'd been in charge.

"You know who I am?" The blonde raised a delicate hand to Rose's face, drawing a pink fingernail down the curve of her cheekbone. "I'm impressed. I wasn't aware that the Agency knew of my existence."

"Well, what do you expect?" The redhead asked with her signature eye roll. "How many innocent people have you killed?

Ten, twenty? The Agency was going to get wind of you eventually." She hoped she could keep the bitch talking long enough for that very Agency to come to her rescue.

"My dear, the men that have fallen before me are but the tip of the iceberg," the Princess smiled daintily, drawing her fingernail down Rose's collarbone, reaching the swell of her lace clad breast. "After tonight, there won't be a man--or woman--that will be able to resist us." To accentuate her point, she took the bound woman's nipple through the thin silk of her bra and twisted it cruelly.

"Us?" Rose seethed with the sharp pain of it, but was determined to keep the conversation going. "What are you planning? Why am I here?"

"Patience my dear, patience." The woman looked like a valley girl but talked like a debutante, and it was really starting to annoy the agent who was being subjected to this tripe. "You mustn't tire yourself out yet."

"Yeah, because I'm going to need that energy to shove that tiara straight up your ass," Rose snapped, and the blonde stared down her perfect button nose at her foul mouthed prisoner.

"Not exactly what I had in mind," she said, and moved away from the altar, gliding with practiced grace behind one of the kneeling frat demons. "You see my dear, my powers are profound by mortal standards. Do you realize what an act of god it is to make half a dozen frat boys sit silently on the beach when there is a house party just one block over? Do you?" She slid her hand up over the guy's head, scratching behind his ear like a dog, and his eyes closed in elation.

The gentle <u>swish, swish</u> of the waves in the background were a strange soothing contrast to the twisted display.

"While you are doing all women a service with that, why do I get the feeling there's more to it than that?" Rose inquired wryly, realizing that she'd twisted her wrists raw at this point. She wasn't getting out of the ropes, her only hope of survival now was to stall as best she could.

"You're quite right," the Princess agreed, and slid a knife from the folds of her skirt, holding it to the frat boy's throat. "You see, I crave more power. I want more than just the admiration of annoying little schoolboys who have no idea how to worship a woman properly." With that, she fisted his hair and drew the blade across his neck from ear to ear without even a blink.

"Jesus Christ," Rose blurted as the pink clad body hit the sand. "You killed him."

"Yes." The Princess ran a finger up the blade, fraternity blood pooling along her skin. She reached out and drew a line down Rose's arm with it, causing the redhead to shrink away in disgust. "However, unlike so many of us, his death shall not be in vain. His death will help bring about a new order on this planet. His death, will help fulfill my destiny."

She stabbed the second frat boy in the heart, and he fell to the ground with a grateful smile on his face. She wiped the blood and and drew it down her prisoner's other arm, tattooing her with death.

"So what," Rose demanded, "are you going to kill me too, skinny bitch?"

"Oh no, my dear," the Princess tittered. "Your death, like these before you, will have meaning. But it will not be at my hands." She stabbed the third guy in the back this time, and then wiped the blade itself across Rose's forehead, leaving swipes of crimson on her creamy skin. "It will be at the hands of the King of the Beach."

"Who?"

"He is the one who will fulfill my destiny," the blonde purred, gutting the fourth frat boy with an expert stroke. His blood went along Rose's left leg, and then the fifth, down her right.

The Princess of death stood behind the sixth and final pink clad asshole, rubbing his chin in an almost sensual way.

"When this boy's blood hit the sand, the King of the Beach shall be reborn," she said, voice carrying on the sea's gentle breeze. "He will rise from the sea and take your life force for himself."

"Great," Rose sighed, "I'm a sacrificial offering?" The Princess' eyes lit up with a wistful nostalgia, and she stared down at the redhead with an almost tender longing.

"He's going to fuck the life out of you," she said. "You have been marked with the blood of the innocent. After he has your life force and consumes the innocent blood from you, he will be more powerful than anything that has walked the earth. After that, there is nothing your friends at the Agency can do."

"Don't be so sure, bitch." Rose smirked, eliciting a confused gaze from the demon Princess, and she turned to look at what the redhead had spotted.

"Alright, sugartits, Silky's here to put an end to all this bullshit." The pastel suede pimp stood with his legs apart in the sand, trusty 9-iron out in

front of him in his signature pose. Kerr
had his handgun aimed at the demon's face,
bits of paper towel shoved in his
nostrils.

"What are you?" The Princess' nose
wrinkled in disgust.

"Smoothen Silky and his honky
sidekick." Silky smirked. "And we's here
to whoop yo skinny little ass."

"I know someone who might take
offense to that," the Princess replied,
and pinched the frat boy's shoulder,
simultaneously snapping her fingers on her
other hand.

He stood up like a shot, turning to
the newcomers as he cracked his massive
knuckles. Kerr narrowed his eyes at the
nemesis he'd faced in the basement.

"God_damn_ that's one big ass fuckin'
frat boy," Silky let out an impressed
whoosh of breath.

"He's mine," the recruit grunted,
sounding slightly less intimidating with
his nose plugged.

"You outta yo mind, boy?" Silky
asked.

"Just be ready with that 9-iron,"
Kerr growled and stepped forward. "Alright
motherfucker, it's time for round two. I
hope you brought your A game, because
you're going to need it to walk away from

this one." He cracked his neck in a
display of dominance.

The frat boy was stone faced, under
the Princess' spell, and thundered towards
Kerr like a predator. When he was a few
steps away, the recruit popped a round in
each of his kneecaps, and screamed for the
golf club.

Silky tossed it, and Kerr snatched it
out of the air just time to smash the fray
boy down to the sand, crushing his head in
one swift blow.

"No!" Rose cried, letting out a sigh
of frustration. They'd played right into
the Princess' hands.

"That is cold fuckin' blooded,
cracka," Silky commended, and they both
froze as the Princess began to laugh.

"That can't be good," Kerr commented,
fist clenching around his gun. A flash of
light drew their attention, and they
looked up to see a glowing pod shoot down
from the clouds like a meteor and plunge
into the ocean below.

"You completed the spiritual
trigger," the blonde demon spread her arms
like wings, letting the breeze wash over
her. "The King has been reborn."

"Let's go get this bitch." Silky took
the 9-iron out of Kerr's hand, and the
recruit's arm fell limp. "Cracka?" He
smacked Kerr's shoulder, and realized his

line of sight was directly at the ample
cleavage of the demon before them.
"Goddammit." He backhanded his newest
coworker, knocking him to the ground,
useless.

"There's no man on earth that can
resist my tits!" The Princess cackled
madly. "I'll just have to use them on you,
instead!"

The pimp swung his trusty club around
like a bo staff, flinging frat boy blood
all over the place. The Princess furrowed
her brow at the fact that he was unfazed
by her tits, ignoring the crimson
splattering all over her.

"I don't understand!" She cried, and
tore the front of her shirt open, letting
her milk bags fly free. "Why won't you
submit to my tits?!"

"Cuz as voluptuous as them titties
are…" Silky grinned toothily and then gave
her a solid backhand, the smack
reverberating in the night air. "That shit
don't work on angels."

The Princess started to crawl away,
hand to her cheek in shock. Silky turned
to Rose, bound to an altar in nothing but
her skivvies, and rushed over. He'd never
seen his partner so helpless, and it lit a
vengeful fire in him that he normally
reserved for protecting his hos.

"We have to get out of here," she insisted as he used his ceremonial knife to cut the ropes. "I think she summoned a legendary demon."

"Silky hears you, babydoll," he assured her as he helped her to her feet. "As soon as Silky takes care of that bitch we's be on our way." He tightened his grip on the knife, but Rose slid a hand around his tricep.

"Don't worry about it," she said, "that cunt is about to get what she deserves."

"Okay, Silky trusts ya." He nodded to Kerr. "Let's get our honky and get the fuck outta here." They hurried through the sand to the recruit's crumpled form, and Rose reached down, snatching up his gun.

Silky smacked the kid a few times, getting quite a few good licks in before the lump started to stir.

"What… what happened?" Kerr moaned, and Silky hauled him to his feet by the back of his collar.

"You got caught staring at them enchanted titties, so Silky had to knock you the fuck out," the pimp told him.

"Fair enough." Kerr rubbed the back of his neck, and upon realizing Rose was standing next to him in lacy black lingerie, tried very hard to ignore it.

"Get yo ass movin, honky," Silky urged, giving him a shove. "We's gotta move." Rose cocked the gun for effect, and the three took off down the beach.

The Princess was still in shock. That ridiculously dressed man had raised his hand to her. Hit her like a common whore. She cradled her cheek, on her knees in the sand, tears streaming down her face.

An angel. Her miracle tits didn't work on angels. What was the point of all of this, then? She was supposed to get whatever she wanted. And right then, she wanted to finish the ritual.

She stood on shaky legs and turned to the altar, finding it empty. She stumbled over, tears still flowing, pulling more and more mascara with it. She grasped the ropes with white knuckles, and let out a frustrated cry, cursing the heavens for their plan-ruining angels.

She turned her head as something moved in her periphery, and her eyelids seemed to blink lazily of their own accord at the sight of a very wet and very naked toned god of a man slowly gliding through the sand.

She licked her lips slowly, and cursed how crazed she must look with her makeup all over the place. But realization started to set in, as she noticed that he

<u>was</u> literally gliding through the air. It wasn't just a graceful illusion.

When his eyes fell on her, zoning in on the blood spatters from Silky's golf club, her veins turned to ice.

"Oh, no," she whispered. "No, no, NO!" Her voice rose and she turned to run, but the man moved like the wind, practically appearing in front of her.

"Oh yeah, baby," the King of the Beach sneered down at her with lusty, murderous eyes, "you're mine."

"What the fuck are we supposed to do now?" Kerr blurted, sick of silence. Silky had been pacing the shag carpet in the safe house living room for a solid ten minutes without a word.

The only noise was the clickety-clack of Rose's laptop and the occasional clang of a pot or pan from the kitchen. He wasn't sure which two out of three hos was in there, but the tantalizing smell of baked goodies was distracting.

"Hello?" Kerr waved his hands over his head. "What the fuck do we do now? Just sit here and hope everything magically works out?"

"Calm down, cracka," Silky replied, flicking his hand dismissively. "We's don't even know what we's up against yet. Rose, baby, you's got the Agency yet?"

"Just holding for the Boss," the redhead replied, and set her laptop down on the coffee table, turning it to face the room.

"Aight, aight," Silky rubbed his hands together and sat down on the couch, leaning into frame. Kerr shuffled forward to do the same, and Rose backed up to allow Mixie access to the table. She was wearing an apron, and as she bent over to set down a tray of coffee and cookies,

Kerr realized she was wearing <u>only</u> an apron.

Silky cleared his throat and the recruit crumpled up a twenty dollar bill and tossed it without his eyes leaving the hos shapely ass as she walked away.

"You's gonna be puttin my hos through college, mozzarella." The pimp flattened the bill and slipped it into his jacket with a grin.

"Silky, what the hell is going on down there?" The screen flickered and a very concerned looking man appeared. "Our satellite surveillance is going crazy! In the last half hour the demon activity near the beach is up two thousand percent! What the fuck happened?"

"Well boss, it's like this." The pimp sighed. "That skinny bitch summoned a legendary fuckin' demon."

"Oh sweet mother of god." The Boss' eyes widened to what seemed like double their normal size. "Which one?"

"She called it the King of the Beach," Rose piped up.

"Excuse me," the Boss replied, blinking at the camera and leaning in as if trying to hear better, "what did you say, Rose?"

She leaned into frame to look at him. "The King of the Beach."

"Silky, I can't stress this enough," the Boss said hurriedly. "You must destroy it before it gets out of town."

"Silky plans on it Boss-man, but why's the urgency?" Silky raised an eyebrow. "What happens if this cat gets out o' the bag?"

"I was part of the team that had to bring this demon down back in the sixties." The Boss ran a hand up the back of his head shakily, and Rose marveled at the motion. She'd never seen her usually stoic and professional superior act so nervous. "This fucker is bad news, let me tell you."

"What was he trying to do? Kill everyone?" Rose inquired. "Wipe a town off the map?"

"Worse." The Boss pursed his lips. "His sole purpose was to turn the world into a giant spring break."

"That doesn't sound so bad." Kerr shrugged.

"Think about it this way." His superior's eyes hardened. "Would you want to live in a world where every guy acts like an annoying drunken frat boy?"

"No, that doesn't sound appealing," Kerr said immediately, mouth turning downward into a disgusted frown. "But what about the women?"

"The women all act like drunken whores."

"Okay, that <u>does</u> sound appealing." Kerr grinned.

"Well," the Boss replied, brow furrowing in annoyance, "much like in your everyday life, these women aren't going to pay any attention to you. The only thing on their mind is the King of the Beach. And that's the problem with this particular demon. If he gets his way, everyone in the world will be on permanent spring break. And since all of the men want to be like him and the women won't put out for anyone but him…"

"Nobody's fucking," Kerr finished, eyes round as saucers. "It'd be the end of the human race."

"Don't be worryin' Boss-man, Silky ain't gonna let that happen." The pimp saluted the laptop.

"I should hope not," the Boss said gravely. "I'm sending in the only reinforcements I have in the area."

"Who we gettin'?" Silky asked.

"TnT."

"Shit balls covered in gravy, Boss, that's all we need," the pimp said, slapping his knee.

"Good to hear that, Silky." the Boss nodded. "Rose, I'm sending the satellite images to you, as well as the coordinates

of where we think the King of the Beach
is."

"Got it, Boss," the redhead
confirmed.

"One more thing." He put up a hand.
"I don't know if TnT will be able to reach
you before you begin your assault. To be
on the safe side, I am sending him
directly to the site."

"Got it."

"Silky, if you fail this mission, we
may never be able to get this close to the
King again." The Boss clenched his jaw.
"The whole world is riding on your
shoulders."

"Silky's got you covered, Boss," the
pimp assured him. "Don't you be worryin'
yo pretty little head about it."

"That's good to hear." The Boss gave
a firm nod of his head. "Good luck." The
screen went black, and Silky scooped up a
fresh chocolate chip cookie from the plate
Mixie had brought.

"Aight, let's get this shit started,"
he said, and shoved the whole cookie in
his mouth.

Silky stood and headed over to the
bay window at the front of the house,
where a long leather case was propped up
in the corner. He pulled it from it's
leaning position, and caressed the worn
fabric like it was the skin of his lover.

"What are you doing?" Kerr asked, his curiosity getting the best of him as he approached, a cookie in each hand.

"We be in some dangerous times, honky," Silky said gravely, "so we be needin' all the help we can get."

"So, what, is there a bazooka in there?" The recruit shrugged.

"Bazooka's ain't got shit on this," the pimp patted the top of the bag lovingly. "Sucka, you know what this is?"

"Uh, no," Kerr mumbled through a mouthful of sugary dough, "I thought that's why we were having this conversation." His vision momentarily exploded as his superior backhanded him, sending crumbs flying everywhere.

"Don't you be gettin' smart around the Club, snowball," Silky snapped, and slowly lifted the tip of the case. He reached in and wrapped his hand around the battle worn handle of a rusty golf club. He pulled it out, inch by inch, reveling in the feel of comfort and power thrumming through his nerves as he clutched it.

"What in gods name is <u>this</u>?" Kerr threw his hands up.

"This here is Silky's Great-great-great grandfather's 9-iron." The pimp smiled fondly at the club, holding it horizontally in gentle hands. "Silky is a

fifth generation pimp. And this Club is
his connection to the past."

"But what good is this to us?" Kerr
asked. "It doesn't look like it could chip
you out of a sand trap, how is it going to
help us fight a demon?"

"Boy, let Silky fuckin' tell you
somethin'," his superior snapped. "When
you's at the demon killin' level that
Silky's at, you's be gettin' a legendary
weapon. This here be Silky's."

"Legendary weapon?" Kerr blinked.
"What the-"

"See, when ole Silky here was
transformed into an angelic demon bustin'
machine, they's offered Silky a legendary
weapon to fuck them demons up with," he
explained. "Silky coulda had anything.
Swords, guns, a holy fuckin' flame
thrower, whatever ole Silky wanted."

"And you chose this rusted piece of-"

"You best be watchin' that fuckin'
mouth, boy," Silky warned. "This here 9-
iron'll beat the shit outta you and rip yo
soul right outta that little white ass.
It's been blessed by the highers ups at
the Agency. Hell, even the muthafuckin'
Pope put his blessin' on this here Club."

"Alright, that's good enough for me."
Kerr put his hands up in surrender. "If
you think that thing is going to be able

to take this demon out, then by all means, use it."

"Aight." Silky nodded. "You's got yo shit together, cracka?"

"You know it," the recruit produced his trusty handgun and cocked it.

Silky grinned his golden grin. "Let's do this."

CHAPTER EIGHTEEN

Fueled by sugar and caffeine, the trio used the Agency's intel to track the King of the Beach to a small warehouse out in the middle of nowhere. After ditching the car a little ways away, they crept through the trees to peer down at their target.

The forest was eerily quiet, not a bird nor cricket to be heard. A dim ethereal glow fell over the roof of the warehouse from the moon above. Rose inhaled deeply, enjoying the scent of wood and grass. She much preferred this atmosphere to the beach. Being covered in sand wasn't her forte. She absently rubbed at her chafed wrists. Neither was being almost sacrificed to a legendary demon.

"Okay, how are we doing this?" Kerr hissed eagerly, ready to spring into action.

"Damn, you's an impatient little muthafucka, ain't ya?" Silky raised an eyebrow as the recruit bounced on the balls of his feet.

"I'm just ready to get this over with," Kerr replied with a sly smile. "I got a nice shiny ho waiting for me to save the world."

The pimp barked a laugh. "Aight, Silky likes your enthusiasm. You's head

down there and show this pimp what you be
made of, honky."

Kerr gulped, bouncing stopping
immediately. "By myself?"

"You scared, boy?"

"Well, no…"

"What you be waitin' for then?" Silky
urged, motioning to the building below.
"Hop to it, cracka, Silky ain't got all
fuckin' night."

Kerr took a deep breath and drew his
gun, cocking it with a flourish.

"Whoa, cracka, the fuck d'you think
you's doin'?" Silky exclaimed.

"Um," the recruit raised his
eyebrows. "Showing you what I'm made of?"

"You can't be goin' around usin' that
hand cannon, dumbass," the pimp hissed.

"Why not?" Kerr argued defensively.
He didn't have a fancy legendary weapon,
he deserved something.

"Cuz we's covert, muthafucka." Silky
sighed in frustration. "You go shootin
that thing off and we be up to our asses
in frat dicks. You want that?"

"Well… no." Kerr lowered his gaze.

"Goddamn right you don't, white bread
fuckin' meat head." The pimp rolled his
eyes. "Now go on and show ole Silky all
them fancy moves you be learnin' at the
academy."

The recruit holstered his gun, cracked his neck, and then cracked his knuckles. "Aight," he rolled his shoulders in tandem with Rose rolling her eyes.

"This should be good," she muttered as Kerr slipped off into the trees. He reappeared a few moments later, behind the two frat boys guarding the door.

He brought the side of his hand down to chop one throat, while simultaneously lashing out with his leg to kick the second one in the ribs. As they both collapsed, he brought his feet together around the first one's ears and twisted, snapping his neck in a clean break. He flipped forward, leg sailing up above him to land on the second one's neck, effectively crushing his windpipe.

Kerr stood, and cracked his knuckles again, admiring his handiwork as the second frat boy gasped the last few breaths of his life.

Rose and Silky strutted up casually, as if out for an evening stroll, and Kerr puffed out his chest. Silky slapped him in the back of the head.

"Cracka, this ain't any time to be posing," the pimp said, "we's got work to do." Rose snorted as she opened the door, motioning for the guys to enter with a pretty flick of her wrist. Kerr pouted at her as he slunk inside, shoulders slumped, and she rolled her eyes for the second time that night.

The halls were dead quiet as they moved through the bare concrete building. The vague smell of oil lingered in the air, and Kerr wondered what the warehouse had been used for.

"We's got the right place, or what?" Silky hissed, and Rose lowered her gun to show him her phone's screen. A blue glowing dot showed their location inside of a bright red hot zone on a map.

"This is the right place," she assured him. "There's something here, we just have to find it." They slowly moved in triangular formation into a large open space, likely the warehouse proper. There were cardboard boxes all over the place, adorned with large H's in an old font and logo that Kerr didn't recognize. This place must have been out of business for a long time.

As he was studying one of the boxes, it wiggled a touch, and he jumped back, raising his weapon.

"What the fuck was that?" He whispered, more to himself than anything, but all three were at attention as more rustling happened behind them.

"I've got a bad feeling about this," Rose said quietly, swinging her gun around, and Silky threw his hands up.

"Goddamn woman, why's you gotta go sayin' shit like that?" He turned to her, exasperated. "Don't you be watchin' no horror movies? Every time somebody says that shit they end up fucked. And not in the <u>good</u> way."

The boxes in front of Kerr shuffled as three frat boys bumped their way around them, lopsided grins on their faces.

"See?" Silky raised his club.

"It's just a couple of them," Kerr insisted, "we aren't fucked."

As if on cue, a multitude of frat dicks in pukey pink polo shirts slide out from boxes on all sides, circling the trio in a foreboding arc.

Silky glared at Kerr, mouth twisted into a condescending knot.

"Okay, now we're fucked," the recruit acquiesced, cursing his quick mouth.

The frat dicks start to close their circle, getting closer to the trio of demon fighters that stood back to back in a protective triangle.

"I hope you's be ready for this, cracka." Silky raised his trusty rusty club like a samurai sword. "This ain't gonna be pretty."

Kerr cocked his gun for effect, locking his elbow. "I'm ready, let's do this."

Rose slipped her phone into the side pocket of her tight cargo pants, and released her favorite retractable police baton with her free hand. "Let's get it on." She sneered, and with catlike speed, raised her gun and popped a bullet right between the eyes of the nearest frat boy.

His body hitting the ground like a wet rag was the catalyst that drove everyone to action, and the battlefield was a blur of pink as the group descended on their foes.

Kerr shot twice, then flipped his gun to smash another in the face, at too close a range to be firing. His free hand curled into a fist and he punched a nearby nutsack, bringing his knee up to crunch a nose.

Rose fired a belly shot, and then used the back of her doubled over victim to launch herself up onto a stack of boxes. Luckily the cardboard was filled with something firm, so she had easy footing on the stack, and started popping off headshots to cover Kerr and Silky.

The pimp himself whirled around with his club in a graceful swoop, white jacket fluttering behind him like angel wings. He raised his foot to kick a frat dick square in the chest, but a body flew into him from behind. He barely stumbled before flipping the guy over his head and righting himself, but his glasses fell off in the process.

As they shattered against the concrete, it was as if time slowed down for the wide eyed demon slayer.

"My glasses," he said, his voice a low husk. "You muthafuckas broke Silky's glasses." He raised his gaze from the bits of his broken soul on the floor and his chocolate eyes blazed with a rage like no other. "Aww hells no! You muthafuckas is gonna fuckin' DIE!"

It was as if he'd been possessed by a lion, and he swung the club so hard he took one of their heads clean off. With a kick and a thunk he completely crushed a skull, and when a pair of thick arms circled him, he slammed his head back, shattering cartilage.

Kerr drop kicked a pink shirt, and on the way down, managed to sink a bullet into his opponent's throat. The concrete floor was a crimson slip and slide at this point, with the amount of blood flying. He used this environment to his advantage, shoes slick as he spun, flinging frat boys into each other in a twisted game of bowling.

Rose ran out of bullets, and hopped from box to box, liberating another police baton from her other leg. She tapped the two together as if she were about to play

a wicked drum solo, and dropped down onto
one frat boy's shoulders. He grinned at
the woman's crotch right up against his
face, and died grinning as she snapped his
neck with her strong thighs.

Silky got into a tug of war with his
golf club, and screamed, letting go so
that the frat dick would slip and fall
into a pool of his dead buddies. The pimp
immediately hauled another towards him,
twisting and tearing an arm clean off with
a squelch.

Hand firmly planted around the wrist,
he used the decapitated shoulder to beat
his foe, who was too grossed out by the
removed arm to fight back with the club.
Silky liberated his legendary weapon from
his enemy's grip, and swung it in a
perfect golfer's arc, taking the frat
boy's jaw with it.

The bottom hinge of his mouth sailed
through the air, skin and blood flapping
behind it, and hit the concrete a good
distance away, directly in front of a set
of shiny black shoes.

CHAPTER NINETEEN

It was eerily quiet, the only sounds that of the trio's heavy breathing, and that made the sharp clap even more jarring. The three warriors reunited in the center of the bloodbath, battle worn and disheveled and covered in sweat and gore. They faced the source of the noise, and saw a tall and square jawed man with broad shoulders, clapping his hands in stark applause.

"Very impressive," he said, and his voice dripped with so much manliness that Rose felt her core clench. "I did not think my army of frat boys would be beaten so easily." He leaned down and gently lifted the jawbone from the floor, holding it up to his eyes for inspection.

"Yeah, well you best be gettin' used to disappointment, muthafucka, cuz you's next," Silky promised, widening his stance. He lowered his chin to shoot their foe a menacing glare, flanked by his teammates in an intimidating triangle.

"You have no idea what you are up against," the King of the Beach tossed the jawbone aside like a piece of trash, and flicked his hand clean of bodily fluids. "I have spent the last thirty years trapped in my own personal void. The only thing that I have done in that time is grow stronger. Far stronger than anything this world has ever seen."

"I can take him," Kerr murmured under his breath, so only Silky could hear him.

"What you talkin' about, cracka?" The pimp asked quietly, barely moving his lips so that the King wouldn't know they were whispering as he continued his speech.

"I still have one shot left," the recruit replied.

"Why the fuck you tellin' me about it?" Silky hissed. "Shoot the fucka and let's go home."

"Prepare to meet your end," the King bellowed, and spread his arms dramatically.

"You first," Kerr snapped, and raised his gun, firing a quick shot right for the demon's forehead.

The King grinned in the face of certain death, and raised his hand. The bullet slowed to a stop right in front of his face, and he plucked it out of the air as if it were no more dangerous than a butterfly.

"Cracka, Silky hopes you brought yo A game, cuz Silky thinks you's just made him mad," the Pimp warned, as the King turned the bullet over in his hand.

He smirked at it, then tossed it up in the air, bringing his hand down on top of it like a volleyball spike. The bullet

flew as if shot from a barrel, and his
Rose in the shoulder.

She flew backwards from the impact,
hurled into a pile of boxes behind a
crumpled heap of pink clad bodies.

"Rose!" Kerr dove over the corpses to
her side, dropping his gun to check her
over.

"I'll live," she grunted, and pressed
her hand hard against the wound. "Go get
that son of a bitch." She raised her green
eyes to his sternly, and he nodded,
recognizing it as an order from his
superior.

"If that is the best you can do, then
you are not worth my time," the King
declared, his hands glowing and then
bursting into flame.

Kerr rejoined Silky, eyes wide at the
fiery display of demon magic. He did <u>not</u>
like the look of that.

"You can deal with my army." The King
slammed his fist down onto the concrete
floor of the warehouse, palm open, and a
shockwave of red heat fluttered across the
space. The pimp and his recruit recoiled
as the wall of warmth flew through them,
but recovered in confusion, having
expected to be attacked by fire.

"Uh, guys," Rose piped up from behind
them, and the two slowly turned to see the
corpses on the floor starting to move.

Slick bodies, writhing against each other to rise again, bits of flesh peeled back from exposed bone. Grins wide with shattered teeth and lolling tongues. Concave heads, exposed brains, eyeballs drooping from their sockets and swinging about by sinewy nerves.

Kerr gulped. "Now what?"

A loud rrrrrip and a whirr broke through the air, followed by the steady thrummmm of a chainsaw. All of the living pairs of eyes turned towards an opening between two piles of boxes, leading from a hallway that had been previously uninhabited.

"What the fuck is that?" Kerr's heart pounded in his ears. Flaming demons, zombie frat boys, an agent down, and now somebody was coming at them with a chainsaw? How could this get any worse?

CHAPTER TWENTY

"That's TnT, baby," Silky's golden grin made Kerr's heart unclench the tiniest bit when he realized the chainsaw was on their side. "He's about to fuck some shit <u>up</u>."

A large shadow cast along the floor, a hulking frame holding what looked to be the biggest chainsaw Kerr had ever seen. He cracked his knuckles, ready for the tides to turn for them. Even the zombies seemed to be holding their breath.

The shadow grew smaller and smaller as it approached, and Kerr grew more and more confused.

When a legitimate midget walked into the warehouse, holding a regular sized chainsaw that looked oversized in his tiny hands, all blood drained from the recruit's face.

<u>This</u> was TnT? He was bald, he was buff, and had he not been just four feet tall he might have been intimidating.

The zombie frat boys snickered, and the midget narrowed his eyes at them. His steel gaze was so rough around the edges that Kerr blinked, and he could tell this guy had been through some shit. The gaze and the ease at which he held that chainsaw, as if he'd cut up a million motherfuckers in his life, told Kerr that

maybe what'd he'd seen at first glance
wasn't accurate.

"Oh, you think I'm funny, do you?" He
barked with the air of a man ten times his
size as he strolled towards the group of
pink shirts, now torn and stained with
crimson.

In a swift motion he sliced right
through the midsection of the zombie
closest to him, spraying blood and
intestine everywhere.

"Who's next?" The tiny agent yelled,
spittle flying from his mouth, and the
zombies immediately stopped looking
amused. The horde descended on him like a
tidal wave, and Kerr took a step forward,
but Silky blocked his path with the golf
club as severed limbs started flying up
out of the pack.

"Goddamn, that is one pissed off
midget," Kerr raised an eyebrow, and Silky
slapped him hard on the back of the head.

"They prefer 'little people', you
culturally insensitive honky ass cracka,"
he scolded, and the recruit blinked at
him, exasperated. "Now come on," the pimp
ordered, "let's get that muthafucka."

They turned to face the King, Kerr
throwing one more quick glance back at
Rose, who seemed to be enjoying the
decapitation circus happening in front of
her.

A flaming volleyball hit Kerr straight in the chest, and he looked down at it in shock before his back hit the cement floor, tearing the wind from his lungs.

Silky lunged forward, club raised, as the King spiked another fiery ball at him with expert form. King of the Beach, indeed.

"You best be keepin' yo goddamn balls away from Silky, muthafucka," the pimp declared as he dodged the projectile. The King simply smiled, and bumped two underhand serves in succession, sending multiple attacks.

Silky ducked and rolled and dove out of the way as he advanced, slowly gaining ground until he was within clubbing distance of the King. He swung in a fierce uppercut, and the slithery demon managed to dodge gracefully, moving like an animal.

Fire vs steel, spike vs Club, they danced, and finally the King managed to grab hold of the 9-iron in his large fist. His skin started to sizzle and spit at the contact, but he merely grinned, free hand exploding into little mushroom clouds of orange and yellow.

His flaming fist hit Silky like a battering ram, flinging the pimp clean across the warehouse into a wall of

cardboard, effectively burying him in
kindling. His grin curled up into a
sinister smile as he charged up another
volleyball, ready to rain napalm down on
his enemy.

"Hey King Pussy, you want some of
me?" Kerr snapped, and the King flung the
ball at him instead, knocking him back to
the ground.

"Too easy." The King sneered.

TnT cut through the last few frat
boys, rendering even their zombie forms
useless, and headed over to Rose. He
grasped the front of his tight T-shirt and
jerked it down, ripping the thin fabric
clean off of his chest.

"Been awhile, Rosie," he smiled, and
she returned the expression, gratefully
accepting the fabric. She wrapped her
shoulder as tight as she could and tied it
off, satisfied with her makeshift bandage.

She inclined her head towards the
King, who was gearing up to attack Silky
again. TnT shot her a wicked grin and
crept up to Kerr, who was slowly sitting
up. She got to her feet, shuffling low to
the ground and taking cover behind some
boxes. She held one of her sticks in her
good hand, ready to leap in if she was
needed.

The King turned back to Silky with a
malicious smile. The pimp stood up and

brushed himself off, wrinkling his nose a
bit at the singed suede.

"You be owin' Silky a new jacket,
cracka," he said, wrapping his hands
around the golf club tightly. "Silky's
gonna enjoy whoopin' yo ass."

"There is nothing you can do to me!"
The King declared with a laugh, spreading
his arms in incredulity. "I have waited
three decades to unleash my fury onto this
world, and I am surely not going to be
brought down by the likes of you!"

"We's gonna be seein' 'bout that,"
Silky said with a sly grin, dodging two
more volleyballs.

"You cannot dodge my balls forever."
The King raised his chin in defiance.

"Ain't gonna have to," the pimp
dusted off his shoulder like he'd already
won, and the King snarled, firing off
another. Silky lifted his club with
lightning speed, winding up and smacking
it like a baseball.

This caught the King off guard, and
he took the ball in the chest, stunning
him to his knees.

During this, Kerr had TnT by the
feet, and was swinging him around in a
tight circle, chainsaw growling away. TnT
opened his mouth, a loud battle cry
bellowing across the massive expanse. Kerr
let go of the little soldier's feet, and

the midget with the chainsaw flew across
the room like an arrow.

The King of the Beach turned just in
time to take the chainsaw right to the
face, blood splattering out in a wide arc
as the top of his head slid clean off.

TnT landed gracefully on his feet as
the legendary demon's body fell,
disengaging the saw. An eerie silence fell
over the warehouse.

"Muthafucka," Silky said, and kicked
the corpse a few times in the ribs. He
turned to Kerr, and slapped a firm hand on
his shoulder. "Good job, my cracka."

"Death by midget tossing," the
recruit confirmed with a nod, offering the
pimp a hopeful smile.

"That one definitely gets some style
points," Silky replied with a grin. "To
show my gratitude, Silky's gonna let you
pick out yo own ho."

"How about you just stop calling me
'cracker?'" He raised an eyebrow, and his
boss chuckled at his pronunciation.

"Whatever you's likin', honky."
Silky's grin widened.

"No, no, just call me Kerr," the
recruit insisted, waving his hands in
front of him. "Just once! I won't tell
anyone, I promise! I just want to know you
have at least a little respect for me,
after all this."

"You did a fine job, Kerr," Silky said seriously, brow furrowed, and his recruit smiled brightly. "Wipe that shit off yo face and let's get the fuck outta here." He shoved Kerr's shoulder, who immediately went stonefaced.

But as soon as the pimp turned to check on Rose, the recruit let the smile erupt across his features once again. He puffed out his chest and followed his boss--who appreciated him!--over to where TnT was helping Rose to her feet.

"Damn, baby, you fine," the midget smirked. "Am I tall enough to ride, or what?"

She rolled her eyes and brushed his hand off of her arm, pulling out her cell phone and leading the way out of the warehouse at a brisk pace.

"What'd I say?" TnT opened his free hand in question and Kerr chuckled.

"Don't bother barking up that tree, man, she's ice cold," he offered, and the midget looked up at him with an incredulous expression.

"Maybe for an apple pie motherfucker like _you_," he shot back, and Kerr crossed his arms with a scowl as Silky trilled a laugh.

They started to pick their way through the heaps of dead frat boy zombies, Silky's pastel loafers somehow

still clean. Kerr wondered if that was
another Angel power, the ability to stay
perfectly polished even during a chainsaw
battle.

"I wonder what our next job will be?"
He thought out loud.

"Silky don't care." The pimp
shrugged. "As long as ole Silky gets to
hurt some fuckas, that's all that
matters."

EPILOGUE

Deep in the belly of the warehouse, the body of the King of the Beach floated in a crimson ocean with only half a head. He was cold and useless now, except for the one pinky finger of his right hand that twitched slightly.

The head of a rusty 9-iron smashed down on that hand, obliterating it to smithereens.

"Aw <u>hell</u> no," Silky grunted as he continued to bring his legendary weapon down into the body of the demon. "We ain't havin' that shit."

When there was nothing left but a pulpy mess inside the pool of blood, Silky set down the club like a cane and spread his feet into a power stance. He raised his chin, sunglasses reflecting in the fluorescent light as he grinned, revealing his glittering golden teeth.

His jacket blew gently in the breeze, and he inclined his head to the Mexican man standing there with the comically large fan.

"Muy Bueno, Enrique."

Midget with a Chainsaw
© 2018

CHAPTER ONE

When Kyran walked into the Randy
Badger dressed in a fancy overcoat with
his slicked back hair, he knew that dingy
bar was the place he'd been looking for. A
lilting county twang floated from the juke
box, mixing with the haze of cigarette
smoke floating in the stale air. The
patrons were sparse, a few playing cards
in the corner, others staring at him from
a booth off to the side, but none at the
bar.

The juiced up bouncer by the door
looked disappointed at the tall rich man
with the jet black hair, looking like he
was ready for some rowdy customers to
knock about. Kyran gave him the smallest
of smirks; if the roided up idiot only
knew what the well dressed man was capable
of.

The bartender pretended to look
nonchalant with a few swipes of his cloth
on the counter; but his wide curious eyes
gave him away. He wasn't used to seeing
guys like this wandering around in this
dead town.

"What'll it be, mister?" He asked,
leaning on one hand and cocking his head.
He looked like he'd been around the block
a few times, but that was par for the
course in a town like this.

"I will take a double of your finest twenty five year old scotch. Neat." Kyran raised his chin as he reached the bar, eyebrows raising at the sly grin emerging on the bartender's face.

"Buddy, I don't know where you think you are, but we ain't in the big city," he drawled, spreading his arms. "We're in the middle of fracking country. Now look, if you want some kickass whiskey, I can get you something that'll fuck you up so bad you'll wake up in the morning two towns over, missing your pants."

Kyran slid onto one of the barstools with unusual grace for his tall frame. "I accept," he said simply, and the bartender shot him a bewildered gaze. It was a weird way to answer his diatribe, but he reached under the bar for the unmarked bottle there.

Was serving homemade whiskey illegal in a licensed establishment? Yes. Did it matter in this town, where it was the sheriff's own brother that made the swill in his basement? Nope. However, the flask that the newcomer had produced that was dribbling a thick red liquid into his glass… *that* was definitely not allowed.

"Whoa, whoa, buddy, you can't be doing that," the bartender leaned forward, as if he were letting Kyran in on a secret. "We might be in the middle of nowhere, but we still have rules, yeah?"

The man's eyes sparkled with amusement as he produced his leather wallet with a flourish, and slipped a fifty dollar bill onto the counter. He laid a finger on it and slid it towards the working man, a ghost of a smile on his face.

"And rule number one is that for fifty bucks, you can do whatever you damn well please," the bartender grinned toothily at him.

"Well, within some reason," a sultry female voice cut in, and Kyran turned to see a red haired bombshell glide up to the bar. She hopped up onto the stool next to him, and looked up at him with bright green eyes. He raked his eyes over the tight jeans and casual baby blue blouse that was just sheer enough to show the line of a tank top underneath. She smelled like jasmine and fresh cut grass with an underlying musk that was all woman, and it took all of his willpower not to consume her right there.

"You mean that fifty dollars is not enough for me to have my way with you?" His voice was a low husk, and her full pouty lips twisted into an amused smirk.

"All you're going to be able to do with that is buy me a drink and take pleasure in watching me walk back to my table," she replied, and he immediately snapped his fingers at the bartender. The man behind the counter obliged easily, having pegged this rich guy as a proverbial cash cow. The more fifties this guy dropped the better, and if it was at the expense of the hot redhead who'd been steaming up the windows in the corner, then so be it.

"Well, thank you darlin'." The woman inclined her head as she watched her drink being made. "So, what's your story? You look a little overdressed for this blue collar crowd."

"I am Kyran, and I have traveled a great distance to look for a very special person," he replied, words dripping from his lips like silk as he extended his hand to her.

"Traveling the world and looking for love?" She raised an eyebrow as she shook his offered hand. "Aw, are you one of those hopeless romantic types?"

"Something like that," Kyran replied wryly, disappointed when the warm flesh of her palm left his. Her hand was soft in that way that only a woman's could be. It looked delicate but he could feel power there, a strength thrumming just beneath the surface that intrigued him immensely.

"Well, I wish you the best of luck, although I gotta say, you aren't going to find too many hopeless romantics in this town," she said as she grabbed her drink from the counter. She stood up from the barstool and chuckled. "Just plain hopeless? Oh yeah, this town is packed with those. Well, it used to be before the wells got shut down and most everybody left. Pretty sure a quarter of the town is in this room at the moment." She motioned to the smattering of patrons behind her with a shrug. It was a sad state of affairs, this town.

Kyran swirled his cocktail beneath his nose, inhaling the tantalizing scent and then taking a sip, keeping his eyes locked on the woman's slender throat. "I do appreciate your candor…" he trailed off, realizing that he'd never gotten her name even though he'd offered his.

"Rose," she supplied, and he smiled. His favorite flower. He enjoyed peeling back the layers, each satin petal revealing another smoother one beneath.

"Rose, yes," he continued, "like I said, I do greatly appreciate your candor. It is refreshing in this day and age." It was refreshing in any day and age, really, but he wasn't about to get into that with her. He had always been impressed with a woman that would tell it like it is. Especially one with such luscious hips.

"I guess it is, isn't it?" She sighed and shrugged again, raising her glass to him. "Well, you have a good evening, Kyran. And enjoy my walk back." She winked at him and turned, and he lowered his gaze to her perfectly heart shaped ass as she did.

"Rose." The name left his lips before he could control it, and she turned her big doe eyes back on him. They were curious, and hid a sharpness beneath that he knew he shouldn't take for granted. There was no naiveté in that stare, though a man less calculating might think so. Kyran, however, was very calculating.

"Yeah, hon?" She drawled the question, leaning a little to the side, her free hand tracing the waistband of her jeans before resting there.

"Seeing as how you are confident I am not going to find who I am looking for in this town, I was wondering if you would care to join me for a while," he said with an impish smile. "I've spent the last week visiting nearby towns and coming up empty. It has been a long and lonely road, and I could use some company." His words didn't come out sounding as pathetic as he'd thought they would, and he saw no pity in

her gaze. Her full lips curled up into a
sly little smile.

"You want company, huh?" Rose asked,
eyes twinkling with mischief. "Hm. A few
questions before I agree."

He nodded, interested to hear what
this vixen's stipulations were. He didn't
think they would be too outrageous. And he
couldn't help but be more and more
impressed by her forwardness. This woman
definitely had an eye out for her own
safety and comfort.

"You gonna buy the drinks?" She held
up a finger to signify her first question.

"Just as a gentleman should," he
replied.

"And you aren't gonna try to show me
your dick later?" She raised an eyebrow to
go with her second finger.

"Those types of appearances are by
request only," he responded easily, and
she nodded.

"You don't bite, do you?" She asked,
and he grinned wickedly. "I'm just messing
with you." She laughed, and slid back up
onto the barstool. "Barkeep, another round
for my buddy and me!" She crossed her legs
and leaned on the counter, twirling a lock
of her hair around her finger playfully.

"Let us make life easy," Kyran said
and slid a hundred dollar bill across the
counter. "Just leave us the bottle if you

wouldn't mind." There was nothing money couldn't procure in this world.

"Oh, thanks, mister," the bartender replied, and left the bottle in between their two glasses. In addition to making their lives easier, it made his *job* much easier; and more lucrative, to be sure.

"So tell me, Kyran, where're you from?" Rose asked as she poured their drinks with practiced ease. He wondered if she'd been a bartender in her life, or perhaps she was just an alcoholic. Though he didn't think so. If she were, she'd likely have been sloppy at this point in the night. No, this woman carried herself with poise despite her blunt nature.

"I will be honest, I have spent so much time traveling and visited so many places that my beginnings are but a faded memory." He swirled the amber liquid in his glass wistfully.

"Oh, come on now, don't bullshit me," she scoffed. "You have to know where you're from. I mean unless you hit your head and got a case of amnesia."

"Best I can do is tell you that it is someplace in eastern Europe," he replied, and downed the drink in one fell swoop. "With so many wars over the years I am not even sure the village still exists. If it does, it would be a far cry from what it was when I entered this life."

"Now now, you can't be *that* old," Rose furrowed her brow with a shy smile. "You don't look a day over forty." That shyness didn't reach her eyes, however, and he didn't miss the slight inflection on the number 'forty'. He didn't want to get too excited; he was quite sure she was playing with him, but he wasn't one hundred percent sure. And there was no reason to get invested in a woman that wasn't one hundred percent.

"That's very kind of you to say, Rose," Kyran replied, chuckling as he produced his flask to mix another drink. "But I assure you, I'm older than I appear."

"Well don't you worry hon." She winked and ignored the strange goo that he was adding to his whiskey. "I like older men."

"Perhaps, then, my long search could be at an end." He lowered his eyes to her plump lips and she threw her head back in a laugh.

"Yeah, gonna need a few more drinks before then," she promised him, and he simply refilled her glass in response.

"My pleasure," he told her with a grin.

By the time the bottle was empty, the bar was as well. The bouncer stood at the door, arms crossed, watching the clock tick down in hopes that he'd get to throw these two out. At least he'd throw the fancy dressed guy out. The redhead, he'd make sure to get a good feel for her first.

Unfortunately for him, Kyran led Rose out the door with one minute to spare and another hundred dollar bill on the counter. She stumbled a little over the threshold, and he grasped her elbow tightly to keep her from totally bowling over.

She grasped his bicep with a giggle, and threw her free arm around his neck. Once she was back firmly on her feet, he took her small waist in his hands and gently pushed her away from him.

"That was quite an enjoyable evening, Rose," he offered politely. This was the sloppiness that he'd been worried about. But the woman beneath the booze was everything he wanted, everything he needed, he could smell it on her. He salivated at the very thought, and let her stumble ahead of him.

"Aw come on, hon, the night is still young!" she proclaimed, spreading her arms and spinning around.

"I'm afraid our relationship must change at this time," Kyran said, face betraying no expression. He dropped his car keys on the asphalt and Rose swaggered a few steps towards his car.

"You sure you're okay to drive? My place isn't too far, we could just walk," she said as she reached out the lean on the car, sliding something long and sharp from inside her loose fitting blouse. The glazed look in her eyes slipped away as she straightened her shoulders and whipped around. "Or you can just lay down right here!" She'd wanted to catch him in the back as he picked up his keys, but he was gone.

Her heart pounded in her ears as she gripped the stake tightly, standing up perfectly straight now, body at attention. She'd wanted to get him farther away from the bar to ensure the least amount of civilian interference, but when he'd dropped his keys she'd seen her chance. Now she realized she'd been overconfident, and this asshole was a lot older and smarter than she'd originally thought.

She strained her ears for any kind of noise, though she knew that these assholes were as stealthy as they come. She moved like a cat between the cars, senses on high alert. She knew she hadn't lost him, and that he was likely stalking her now, knowing that she knew what he was. This definitely hadn't gone according to plan.

Silence.

She looked left, and then right, and
then up, just in time to see a gleefully
grinning Kyran drop down onto her.

"So, what do you know about our trainer?" Briggs asked nervously, standing up as straight as he could. He wanted to make a good impression. He hadn't thought he would end up in training so fast, but he didn't want to look a gift horse in the mouth. He wanted to show the higher ups that they'd made the right choice.

"Heard he's a real hardass, but he's trained some of the Agency's best people," Franks replied with a shrug as he hopped from foot to foot. He was just happy to get into some hands on learning. He was so sick of sitting at a desk all day. He didn't belong in the classroom. He belonged out in the field, kicking the crap out of demons. He cracked his knuckles.

They were in one of the Agency warehouses, deep in the belly of weapon research and development. There were workers and scientists standing at tables here and there, clicking and clacking as they put together and took apart various weapons and prototypes.

"At least we'll be in good hands, right?" Briggs asked, glancing to the other side at Dale, who was leaning casually against the wall, tapping away at his phone. He just wanted to get this over with so they could go to lunch. There was a really cute chick that washed dishes in the mess hall that he was sure he could get to go out with him if he just asked her out enough times.

Robinson rolled his eyes, the tallest of the four. He opened his mouth to berate Briggs for being a pussy, but a loud yelling bark cut him off.

"Alright, line up!" The voice cried, and the four recruits immediately snapped to attention. Straight backs, face forward, hands at their sides. Regardless of personal preference and experience, they were trained military.

"Eyes on me, motherfuckers," the voice belonged to a four foot tall midget, and the recruits glanced nervously at each other in disbelief. He had broad shoulders and a smooth bald head, and strutted in like he was the biggest man in the building. "You probably think you're hot shit, that you are standing here because you're the best of the best."

He stopped in front of Dale, turned on his heel, and started to pace in front of them. "News flash, needledicks, you are *not* the best of the best. You're merely the best we could fucking find. Take a look beside you." He raised a hand and undulated it back and forth in a *tick-tock* motion. "The men on either side of you aren't going to be able to help you out. From this fucking moment forward, you are on your own!"

He stopped short, pointing a finger right up into Briggs' nervous face. "If you succeed, it's because you're strong enough. If you fail, it's because you're a *pussy*, and you should feel ashamed that you wasted my time! And when that happens, I fully expect a fucking apology letter in my mailbox, unless you want me to visit you at home!"

Briggs stifled a whimper, blinking rapidly at the tiny man's fist so close to his eyeballs. Franks rolled his eyes and the midget reeled on him, having spotted it in his periphery.

"Did you just roll your fucking eyes at me, maggot?" He cocked his head, eyes menacing, and Franks at least had the intelligence to look nervous.

"I'm... I'm sorry, sir," he stammered, and his superior waved for him to bend down to his level. Franks hesitated a moment, not realizing what he was supposed to do, until the midget snapped his fingers and pointed at the ground. He flushed with embarrassment, and slowly sank to his knees on the hard concrete floor.

"Something you need to understand,
boy," his superior said, voice low and
menacing, but still loud enough for the
others to hear. "You ain't half the man I
am. And given that I am already half a
man, what the fuck does that say about
you?" He turned and waved flippantly at
the recruit to stand up, and Franks slowly
got back to his feet, face cherry red.

Dale snickered.

"Did I say something to fucking amuse
you?" The midget stepped in front of him
and the recruit realized in that moment
that this little guy definitely had the
presence of a bigger man. He exuded power,
and if Dale wasn't careful he wasn't sure
he'd make it to lunch in one piece.

"No, sir, I apologize for my
outburst, sir!" He declared loudly.

"Holy fucking balls, man, that is one
thick accent," his superior raised an
eyebrow. "What hillbilly republic are you
from?"

"Uh, Alabama, sir," Dale cleared his
throat.

"Alabama, huh?" The midget chuckled.
"As fate would have it, I know some
fucking trivia about Alabama. Would you
like to hear it?"

Dale cleared his throat again, and
then nodded, thinking maybe he didn't
really have a choice in the matter anyway.

"Do you know what they call a fifteen year old Alabama girl who can run faster than her brothers?" His superior sneered up at him, and Dale shook his head. "Virgin," came the finishing blow.

Dale's face flushed as red as Franks', and he croaked a few times before any words came out. "But I… I never fucked my sister."

"Well then, maybe we should have recruited her because you must be a slow ass motherfucker," the midget replied, and Dale's mouth opened and closed, but no sound came out. "Oh for fuck's sake, don't tell me you're the Forrest Gump kinda slow too! God*damn*, at least that goofy motherfucker could run like the wind."

Robinson was growing tired of this tirade quickly, and cleared his throat loudly.

"Alright, Too Tall, you got something to say?" His superior strolled up.

"Just wondering how someone of your stature thinks it's wise to run his mouth like that," Robinson said, ever the picture of a stoic soldier. "Sir."

The shorter man couldn't help but me impressed by the balls on this recruit, lanky though he was. "Man, you *are* a bold one, Too Tall," he said, "I wonder, would you be willing to help me demonstrate the first lesson?"

Robinson grinned, puffing his chest out a bit. "Yes sir, I'd be happy to."

The midget lashed out and grabbed the large recruit's ankle, jerking it up while kicking his own boot towards Robinson's rear ankle. The swift movement sent him into a full split onto the concrete, and the tall man groaned in pain, flopping to the side in shock. He clutched at his crotch and rolled over to the side, and the other three recruits recoiled, fighting the urge to hold their own genitals in sympathy.

"Lesson number one," the midget declared, holding up a thick finger. "Don't fuck with a strong person who has a low center of gravity. Now, let's move on to lesson-"

"Excuse me, Agent TnT?" A young dark skinned asked, hands clasped studiously behind his back.

The recruits' eyes all widened, even Robinson who was still on the floor. They'd heard of TnT. Everyone had. But from the retellings and rumors, they'd all imagined a giant guy. Not this.

"You better have a good goddamn reason to interrupt my lesson," TnT turned away from the crumpled recruit to look the newcomer in the face. He wore a pristine white lab coat, black slacks, and a pair of thin rimmed glasses. There was a no. 2

pencil smartly angled behind his right ear, and he looked like he'd just walked out of a stock photo shoot for male nurses.

"I'm terribly sorry sir, but there is a call from the Boss, and he says it's urgent," the young man bowed slightly, and the midget nodded, appreciating the manners on this kid.

"Very well, then," he said, "who are you and what's your name?"

"Baptiste, sir, I'm your new attache," came the reply. "Whatever you may need, equipment, research, I'm your man." He straightened up and offered a small smile that reached his eyes.

"Well, Baptiste," TnT grinned. "Let me ask you then, do you know any yo momma jokes?"

"Excuse me, sir?" The attache furrowed his brow. He couldn't be serious?

"It's a simple question," the midget replied. "You said you're here for whatever I may need. Do you know any yo momma jokes?"

The young man shrugged. "Yes sir, plenty."

"Fantastic." TnT stepped beside him and motioned to Robinson. "You see that man there, the one clutching his recently destroyed manhood?"

"Yes, sir," Baptiste frowned, his own balls tightening at the sight.

"Good," the midget clapped him on the back. "You are to stand here and ridicule this man until I return." The young man looked down at him incredulously, then at the moaning recruit, and back again. "Well, what are you waiting for?" TnT asked impatiently.

"Yo momma is like a bag of chips," Baptiste said with a shrug as he stepped over to the recruit. "She's Free-To-Lay."

TnT barked a laugh. "You're going to go far in the Agency, kid."

TnT hopped into his office chair, swiveling it back and forth a few times before pulling against the desk to face his computer monitor.

"What can I do for you, Boss?" The midget asked, saluting the older man on the screen. He had slicked back salt and pepper hair, and a perfectly shaped beard with not a lock out of place.

"Sorry to pull you away from training the new recruits," he said, soft crinkling eyes conveying his apology. "How are they doing?"

"It's been a painful process for one of them." TnT shrugged with a smirk. "But I'll mold them into something useful."

"That's good to hear, but I'm afraid we're going to have to put that on hold for the moment." The Boss pursed his lips and folded his hands in front of him. "We have a situation." Those were words that no Agent ever wanted to hear. They bore a weight with them that dragged even the most experienced man's stomach to the floor.

"What's happening?" The midget's lips curled into a pensive twist. Something big must have been going on if they were interrupting training. The Agency needed new recruits badly. That's why they'd given TnT so many at once, and greener than he would have liked before getting to this point.

"Agent Rose has been investigating mass disappearances in some small fracking towns," the Boss said, and his face shrunk into a smaller frame as he showed a map on the screen. "There is a trio of small towns that were built around a giant dirt racing track. Over the past few weeks, several dozen people have gone missing in that area. Locals thought it was because the work dried up and people just moved on, but long time residents have also disappeared."

"So what's Rose found?" TnT asked. "What are we up against?"

"We don't know," the Boss replied. "The last communication we got from her was twenty-four hours ago. She missed her last two check-ins."

"She's *missing*?" The midget was incredulous. Something definitely was going bad in those fracking towns if it got the best of Rose. She was one of the Agency's elite. He clenched and unclenched a fist. This wasn't good.

"Yeah." The Boss nodded. "And you are the closest field agent we have. It's about a two hour chopper ride to the dirt track, which will be the drop off point. They do demolition derby events and stunt shows there, so there will be plenty of cars. Baptiste will assemble a kit for you with enough cash to acquire a ride. There are a couple of good ole boys who run the place, and from what Rose told me, they love greenbacks and are always in the market to sell."

"Which of the three towns should I head to first?"

"Head north, to Struckerville," the Boss instructed, "based on Rose's last report there is a dive bar in the middle of town. That should be your best bet."

"Alright sir, I'm on it." TnT nodded. "I'll bring her back."

"Whatever you need, let me know," the Boss promised.

The midget saluted. "Sir."

CHAPTER FOUR

Helicopter blades cut through the still desert air, reverberating sharply across the empty track. The *shoosh, shooshshooosh* was an unusual sight in such a small town, but the noise wasn't a problem for the residents of the Blackwell's Demolition Track.

The chopper landed next to a giant ramp with a row of beat up muscle cars lined up behind it, swirling dust in tiny tornadoes. TnT hopped down from the side, saluting the pilot and receiving one in return. He slung his duffel bag over his shoulder as the aircraft lifted off again, whipping wind loudly with its ascent.

As the chopper disappeared into the distance, TnT strode off towards the row of cars to have a look. He was a bit of a muscle car enthusiast, and was pretty excited to secure a ride here. They looked well loved, to say the least, but there was pretty much every make and model imaginable, and the Agent eyed his selection with glee and care. How to decide?

"It's a midget, it's a midget!" A high pitched male voice screeched, and TnT dropped his bag, adopting a defensive stance immediately. A large man lumbered towards him, massive arms swinging back and forth like a gorilla. "Look, George, it's a midget!"

"Whoa, calm down there, big fella," TnT held his hands up, palms out, eyebrows raised. What the hell was this guy's damage?

"Can I toss him? Please, George?" The big man stopped and hopped back and forth from foot to foot, looking like an excited kid in a candy store. He had sandy brown hair and blue eyes, the kind of all-American look that was classic on a Calvin Klein model but not so on this oaf. His glassy eyed gaze gave the impression of low intelligence, and the way the eyeballs seemed to bug out made him almost look alien.

"The fuck?" TnT blurted. A shorter skinnier man jogged up to them, putting a calming hand on the gorilla's shoulder. He had similar features, though a leaner stature, and a whole lot less crazy in his tired eyes.

"Sorry Nick, he's not like your friends at the county fair," George said gently. "I don't think he'd like that too much." Nick's lower lip quivered, and his gaze shot to the ground, shoulders slumping. "Aw, come on, Nick, it'll be okay. Why don't you go inside and play your game?"

The gorilla immediately stood up and smiled brightly. "Okay! Bye, mister midget!" He waved a gargantuan hand and turned, scampering back the way he'd come.

"What the fuck just happened?" TnT eyed George warily.

"Sorry bud, please forgive my brother," the thin man scratched the back of his head nervously. "I'm afraid our act has taken its toll on him."

"Your act?" The midget crossed his arms.

"Yeah, we're the Badass Blackwells," George motioned to the boards on the far side of the track. The font looked almost like graffiti paint, and the logo was a silhouette of two guys standing in front of a muscle car. It was—TnT had to admit to himself—pretty badass.

From the looks of it, the silhouettes were Nick and George, given the respective ape and beanpole shapes of the bodies.

"I do all the driving," George continued, "and my brother is the car surfer."

"Look man," TnT sighed, pinching the bridge of his nose, "I know I got shit to do, but I gotta fuckin' ask. What in god's name is a car surfer?"

"Well, Nick's big move is to stand on the roof of the car as I drive around the track, like he's surfing," his new acquaintance explained. "Once people got bored of that, he wanted to add in a wrinkle." He pointed to the giant ramp looming over them like a monument of insanity.

"I'm guessing that didn't go well?" TnT inquired hesitantly.

"Man, it went fan-fucking-tastic!" George blurted, eyes lit up like a Christmas tree. "The crowd went wild! We got four million hits on YouTube! Some of the big morning shows put it on the tee-vee!"

The midget sighed. "I meant for Nick."

"Oh, Nick?" The thin man scratched his head again, having the decency to look a little ashamed. "Yeah, he got fucked up pretty good. When the car landed, the front end dug into the ground, and then launched him up like a catapult. He must have done five, six flips in the air before landing on his head. Doctors spent six hours removing the pieces of helmet from his scalp. Those helmet people gave him a sponsorship deal out of it though, so he's happy."

"Christ, I miss civilization already," TnT muttered, pinching the bridge of his nose again.

"I didn't catch that," George prompted, leaning forward and cupping his ear.

"Nothing." The midget waved him off and then shouldered his duffel bag again, eager to get moving. "You got a car for me?"

"Yeah, right this way," came the reply, and George led his tiny acquaintance to the row of cars, all dented and dinged up. There were different colors of paint scratched across the surfaces from multiple collisions. "They ain't much to look at, but they're fast as hell, pack a lot of power, and will get you where you need to go."

"Did Baptiste relay my special requirements?" TnT asked, and ran his hand along the driver's window of a dark purple GTO.

"Yeah, he did," George replied with a nod. "You can go ahead and pick any car you want. We have them all rigged up with hand controls for the kiddie demolition derby next weekend."

"Man, y'all need some cable TV in the worst possible way." The midget ran a hand down his face in exasperation.

"Nah, we're outdoorsy types in these parts." George grinned, revealing crooked yellowed teeth with more than a few spaces peppered throughout his mouth.

TnT strolled down the row of cars, and stopped in front of a jet black '72 Boss 302 Mustang. He ran a finger up the hood with a ghost of a smile on his face, enjoying the mean beastly look of the machine. It looked like it was ready to spring into action, roar to life, strike fear into the cold dead hearts of his enemies.

"Mind if I take this one?" He asked, delight dancing in his eyes.

"You have some great taste in cars," George commented. "The keys are in it, ready to go. Where you headed?"

"Struckerville," TnT replied.

"Good deal." The lanky man pointed across the track to the open gate. "Just head out that exit, hang a right, then straight on for a few miles. You can't miss it."

"Thanks." The midget reached into the duffel bag and produced a thick wad of cash, tossing it over. "Here you go."

"Pleasure doing business with you." George used the stack of money to salute his tiny new friend, flashing his graveyard of a mouth once again.

TnT opened the door and tossed in his bag, jumping into the driver's seat with stellar grace. He fired up the car and grinned at the throaty roar of the engine. He ran his hands lovingly across the steering wheel, and grasped the paddles on either side for the gas and brake. They were crudely set up, but not the worst he'd ever used, and he punched the gas hard, spinning the wheels in a fabulous display of torque.

The engine sucked in air like a hoover of death, thrumming beneath him, a thundering bass roiling deep in his gut. TnT smirked at the vibration in the seat; he couldn't wait to get the lovely Agent Rose into this car.

CHAPTER FIVE

The bar in the middle of town had a few dejected workers hanging out at a few of the tables despite it being the afternoon. TnT strolled in as if he owned the place, eyes swinging around to assess his surroundings with expert speed.

The 'roided up bouncer seemed like he would be the sole problem.

"What do you want, little man?" He puffed out his chest, standing as tall as he could over TnT's four foot frame.

"I'm looking for a woman," the midget replied calmly, not intimidated in the least.

"Aw, did you lose your mommy?" The bouncer sneered, and more than a few of the card players at the far table guffawed at the joke.

"You know, I always hate coming to these backwoods inbred cousin fucking shitburgs of civilization because everybody is just so goddamn stupid," TnT spoke up, his stance still as relaxed as ever. "I mean come on, a little man and a mommy joke? That's all you got? Take some pride in your insults, dig deep, think of something creative. Or hell, at the very least, take a break from cranking your steroid shrunk micro-cock to MILF porn and google some good insults."

The silence was deafening. Even the bartender froze, cloth in hand against the age worn wood of the counter, toothpick hanging from his lip and threatening to fall to the dusty floor.

"But you know, I will give this to y'all," TnT continued, "this dumb shit bouncer is a brave motherfucker." The onlookers were confused by this. After that whole tirade, he was complimenting his opponent?

"Huh? Why's he brave?" A thickly accented voice called from the back, and the midget grinned.

"It takes a brave man to talk shit to someone at dick level," he said simply, and then head-butted the bouncer straight in the balls. The surprised beast fell to his knees with a grunt, and TnT immediately jammed his thick fingers into his nostrils, dragging him across the floor to the table of horrified onlookers.

"Now who has seen this woman?" He slammed a photo down on the wood, causing their beer glasses to clink dangerously. "Anybody?" The picture had come from Baptiste, a printout of one of a candid shot somebody had snapped of Rose. She was in a pale yellow sundress and white flip flops, superstar sunglasses perched on her head, holding back her long red tresses from blowing in her face.

The men glanced at each other in a panic, none of them knowing what to say or how to deal with the situation. TnT snatched up the photo and held it up to the bouncer's face, hauling him closer by his now very sore nose.

"Alright pencil dick, do you know this woman?" He demanded.

"I… I duddo her dabe…" He stammered, voice impeded by the little torpedoes blocking his airways. TnT removed them and shoved the bouncer down with his surprisingly strong foot, holding him to the wood floor. "She's been coming in here the last week and drinking alone. A couple of nights ago she met some well dressed dude."

"Who the fuck is he and where do I find him?" TnT asked, leaning forward on his foot, slowly crushing his opponent's throat as he did so.

"He never told me his name!" The guy croaked. "I've seen him around town. He's been renovating some office over on 3rd. I always see him when I'm driving home from my shift!"

"Driving home?" TnT narrowed his eyes. "Who the hell does office renovations at night? Wouldn't people be complaining?"

"Man I swear, I don't know," the bouncer pleaded, dark eyes wide and glassy. "This town is dying, so people are probably just happy there's money being put in. Or hell, man, maybe the neighbors are already gone."

The midget stepped back, leaving the bouncer to clutch at his throat and nuts in the fetal position. TnT *humphed* and snatched up one of the glasses of beer, opening his throat to down the entire thing in one fell swoop. He slammed it down on the table, pocketed the photo, and then stepped over the moaning man on the floor.

As he swept out of the bar, the one of the men at the table stared at his empty beer glass in disdain. But he glanced down at the floor; he knew better than to protest this little firecracker lest he end up like the broken bouncer at his feet.

That evening, TnT hopped out of the car outside of the offending office building. It was a ghost town over there, and he thought maybe the bouncer had been right that the neighbors had already left. Well dressed guys doing renovations in a ghost town office building only at night did not bode well for anyone. And there was no way that things were as they seemed in this situation. Especially with enemies

that had managed to pull one over on one
of the Agency's top elite.

He popped the trunk and dug through
his duffel bag. He selected a wild west
holster with two slots, and filled them
with his two ten inch mini chainsaws. He
rummaged until he found his multi-purpose
medium sized chainsaw and strapped it to
his back. With a series of *zzzzzt's* and
clicks, he was suited up and ready for his
mission.

He glanced around, and regardless of
whether or not the owner of this building
was really here for renovations, it was
clear that there had been actual
construction going on at some point. There
was caution tape, broken walls, debris and
workbenches all along the inside of the
fence, and that was just the outside of
the building. He didn't think this
equipment was all for show.

He stayed low and skirted the
building, finding a few guys casually
guarding the front entrance. TnT shook his
head at their uselessness, and slipped
through an opening in the gate to reach
the side door he'd spotted earlier. Upon
examining one of the work benches and
noting a thin layer of dust on one of the
wrenches, his theory about the tools not
being props confirmed.

The inside was a disaster. There was plastic sheeting hanging everywhere, and more benches full of tools along the walls. In the center of the wide open space he'd walked in on there was a giant hole in the cement, with prison bars across the whole top. That definitely wasn't standard office fare. He knelt at the edge, squinting down into the gaping hole, and wondered what the hell anyone needed to keep in there.

He swept the hole with a flashlight; no sign of Rose.

There was a shuffle and a sigh and he pressed himself against the wall, peering slowly through a doorway. Moonlight streamed through the window to dimly light the area, and he caught sight of a woman sitting on the floor in shackles. She was clad in jeans and a dank looking blouse, with a matted but very familiar shade of red hair.

TnT scoured the area with his eyes, making sure they didn't have company, and then rushed into the room. He skidded in front of her, and she simply blinked, the only indication that she was at all surprised by his arrival.

"Holy shit girl, I always had my suspicions about how kinky you were, but I never thought you were the chained to an

office wall type," he joked as he reached
up to examine her wrists.

"Get away from me!" Rose snapped, and
he froze.

"Whoa, what's wrong?" TnT asked, brow
furrowed. "Is it rigged to blow or
something?" He realized upon thoroughly
examining her expression that her eyes
were wide and full of trepidation. He'd
never seen this hot shot Agent ever look
even remotely close to afraid, and his
stomach knotted up.

She tilted her head to the side,
revealing two perfectly round puncture
wounds in the hollow of her throat. The
knots in the midget's stomach turned to
dread and he sank down into a squat. There
was only one creature that could create a
mark that pristine without killing their
host.

"He turned me into a vamp," Rose said
thickly, and he stared at her for a
moment, dealing with the shock of it.

"But… wait," TnT shook his head,
thinking harder about the situation. "If
you are a vampire, then why aren't you
trying to rip my throat out? Did they just
bite you now?"

"No, a couple of nights ago," she
replied, eyes hardening in anger. He could
easily identify the flames of rage
building in her expression.

"Well it's obvious it didn't take, then." He reached into the side pocket of his pants and produced some lock picking tools. "So we're going to get you out of here and figure this shit out later. Sun's about to go down and I get the sense we don't want to be here when it does."

She nodded reluctantly, and resisted the urge to just close her green orbs while he worked. Instead she kept them peeled, knowing that it was up to her to be her rescuer's eyes while he was occupied freeing her bonds.

He got her left wrist free and with surprising gentleness, and lowered it into her lap before getting to work on the other.

"Vamp!" Rose hissed as a shadow passed over the doorway, and a low growl reached TnT's ears. He dove out of the way just in time, and sprung up to his feet, drawing both his mini-chainsaws. He sent one skittering across the concrete to Rose, who immediately fired it up to work at the chain still binding her.

TnT grinned maniacally at the vampire, wielding his hunting knife sized chainsaw as he hooked his fingers in a *come hither* motion. The vampire, unused to people standing up to him, let out a roar and lunged towards the midget, making attempts to grab at him. TnT ducked and

slashed at every turn, the little chainsaw
making tiny cuts all over the demon's
body.

The vampire finally tried to come
down on his tiny opponent overhand, but
screamed in disdain as the little chainsaw
ripped down his arm lengthwise, leaving
him with two tattered dangling limbs in
his shoulder socket.

TnT lashed out and grabbed the
vampire's ankle, upending him, and then
wound a fist in his hair. The chainsaw
made quick work of the demon's neck, and
TnT tossed the vampire's head to the side.
It hit the concrete with a *squelch*, and
the midget turned quickly back to the
woman he'd been sent to rescue.

"You ain't gonna murder me, are you?"
He asked quickly as he helped Rose to her
feet.

"Only if you try and cop a feel, you
perverted little freak," she shot back.

"There's the woman I know and love."
TnT grinned.

"Come on, we have to get out of here
before Kyran shows up," she urged, green
eyes still darting all over the place. She
took a defensive stance and clenched a
fist, clearly on edge by the mere mention
of that name.

"Who the fuck is Kyran?" the midget
asked.

"That would be me," a velvety male voice said, and an impeccably dressed man with jet black hair rounded the corner. "Where you do you think you're going, my dear?"

"Yeah sorry bro, she's spoken for." TnT squared his shoulders and raised the mini-chainsaw in his hand.

Kyran chuckled pretentiously. "I'm impressed you have such a large voice for a man of such small-" He looked down at the expertly thrown little chainsaw that was now sticking out of his chest. He casually pulled it out and slid it back across the floor to the midget and the redhead. "You appear to have dropped this." He smirked, lips curling in a surprisingly elegant fashion. But one didn't live so long and so successfully without poise.

"That could be a problem." TnT looked down at the seemingly harmless weapon so carelessly discarded by the tough as nails vampire. "Thankfully though, I have a solution." He whipped the chainsaw from his back with a flourish, starting it up with a magnificent *thrummmm*. He let out a primal scream and lunged forward, slashing and stabbing at the vampire with excellent speed and accuracy; had it been a normal opponent.

Kyran was too fast. He dodged every slice with apparent ease, not even a single hair slipping out of it's shiny style.

Rose threw her mini chainsaw like a ninja star, and Kyran plucked it out of the air with yet another smirk. That moment of distraction, however, was all that TnT needed, and he managed to get his saw almost all of the way through Kyran's bicep before he stumbled out of the way.

The vampire looked down at his arm, hanging by just a few tendons, as unconcerned as if brushing away a fly. He turned to the workbench behind him and flopped his arm down onto it, pulling a staple gun from a smattering of tools.

The Agents stared as the vampire stapled his arm back on without even the smallest grunt or grimace of pain.

"We have to go," TnT said, "right fucking now."

"Agreed," Rose replied, and they bolted out the door.

Kyran finished his stapling job and lifted his hand in front of his face, wiggling his fingers as if they'd never been severed. He strode to the exit, just in time to catch a glimpse of the Mustang peeling out down the road.

"What kind of blood sucker was that?" TnT asked as he drove, speeding down the sparse streets of Struckerville. "Usually when they get cut, they scream like… well like they got cut with a fucking chainsaw."

"I don't know," Rose replied, shaking her head. "He's different from any vamp I've ever faced. When he jumped me the other night he was way faster than he should have been."

"Was he the one that bit you?" The midget raised an eyebrow from the driver's seat.

"Yeah, he was," the redhead sighed.

"We gotta talk to the Boss," TnT said firmly. "Something is up and it's not good."

CHAPTER SIX

"Rose, it's good to see you in one piece," the Boss said jovially, and the redhead saluted him with only a hint of sass. She'd managed to get a shower in while TnT set up his computer equipment in the seedy motel room the Agency had procured for them.

She towel dried her hair and adjusted her seat on the bed next to the midget, the two of them sitting within view of the laptop's camera. They'd set the computer on the end of the bed, lacking any surface in the room big enough for it.

"Not exactly in one piece, boss," she tilted her head so that he could see the bite wound.

"Did that just happen?" He gasped, and she shook her head, tossing the damp towel onto the floor.

"Been almost forty-eight hours now," she replied.

His brow furrowed in concern, and he hit the call button on his desk phone off screen. "Carol, can you please get Baptiste on the line?"

"What are you thinking, Boss?" TnT asked, concentrating on the laptop screen instead of the peaks of Rose's nipples sticking through the thin fabric of the grey tank top he'd loaned her.

203

"I worked a case damn near 30 years ago where a woman was bitten, but didn't immediately change," the Boss replied. "It was *not* pretty. What can you tell me about the man who bit you?"

"His name is Kyran," Rose said, though she wasn't sure how much her information would help. "He's a suave, well spoken individual."

"And the motherfucker doesn't feel pain," TnT added. "Damn near lopped his arm clean off, and he staplegunned it back together. Didn't even make a fucking peep." He mimed stapling his own arm for effect as a smaller window appeared in the corner of the laptop screen, revealing Baptiste's face.

"Good to see you, TnT." He nodded. "Miss Rose."

"Alright Baptiste, work your magic," the Boss instructed. "We have a name, Kyran, a woman who has gone forty eight hours after a bite without turning, and a vampire that doesn't feel pain. Compare that to the Garvin case I worked back in '86."

"I'm on it, Boss," Baptiste promised, and his gaze shifted from the camera to his own computer screen.

"TnT talk to me, what do you need?" The Boss asked while his researcher worked.

"Man, we gotta take this asshole down," the midget replied. "Can you get Silky out here?"

The well groomed man on the screen shook his head sadly. "He and Kerr are taking down a demon hive."

"What about Nantz?" TnT asked.

"Undercover recruitment operation," came the instant reply.

"Christ, is there anybody?" The midget scrubbed his hands down his face.

"You and Rose are it." The Boss shrugged. "Only warm bodies that could be of use in the field are the recruits you started training yesterday."

"Man, those kids would be cannon fodder." TnT sighed. "The only way I'd want them out there is if we were in a worst case scenario situation."

"You'd better get them geared up then, because it looks like you're facing off against an Ancient," Baptiste spoke up, and both Agents drew in deep breaths.

"I'm not well versed in Ancients, but I'm guessing if you earn a title like that, it's not so good for us," Rose put in.

"No, Miss Rose, it is not," Baptiste replied. "In a nutshell, they are stronger and faster than your average run of the mill vamp. They are also a lot harder to kill."

TnT pursed his lips, leaning forward. "How much harder?"

"Your usual tactics like beheading or a wooden stake won't do the trick," came the reply. "Don't get me wrong, it will certainly slow him down, but you'll need to get a little more creative."

"Creative, like throw him into a wood chipper?" TnT asked, and Rose raised an eyebrow at her companion. He shrugged as if to say *what*?

"I'm afraid that would just piss him off even more." Baptiste shook his head. "No, you'll have to inject him with a special UV serum that I will include in your care package. Basically, it's highly concentrated liquid sunlight. It won't kill him, but it will be enough to permanently paralyze him. Once you do that, we can put him in storage."

"What about me?" Rose cut in. "How do I not become a blood sucker?" She needed to know what the hell they were going to do about this. She refused to become the very thing she'd devoted her life to hunting. A chill ran up her spine at the thought.

"Your situation is a bit more complicated, Miss Rose," Baptiste said reluctantly. "Usually when you kill a head vampire, it releases his underlings from the curse."

"But we can't kill this motherfucker," TnT argued.

"This is true, but that's not necessarily a bad thing for you, Rose," the researcher said.

"Goddammit, how can this not be a bad thing?" She was starting to get frustrated with all of this back and forth. There had to be some kind of clear path here. A mission to complete. A plan.

"Well, according to my research, an Ancient will arise from their centuries long slumber to find an incredibly strong willed and powerful female to turn into a breeder," Baptiste said, and then set his mouth in a thin firm line.

"Oh yeah, that sounds so much better," Rose said, voice dripping with sarcasm. "What, this asshole wants to put a little fanged beast inside of me?"

"In a manner of speaking, yes." He nodded with a grim expression. "That's why the transformation has taken so long. His bite is strengthening your body so that you can survive the pregnancy. Over the course of seventy two hours or so, your body will become stronger and… um. I'm not sure how to put this exactly… more fertile?"

"Oh, fuck me," Rose cursed.

"In your current state, I wouldn't recommend that," Baptiste replied.

"So that do we do?" TnT cut in. "Just sit here and watch Rose become a vamp?"

"There is only one other Ancient birth on record, the Garvin case that the Boss worked on." The researcher leaned towards his computer, tapping his chin as he read. "The pregnancy lasted a week or so, but the woman didn't survive. Best we could tell is that she never turned full vamp because the Ancient in that case was trying to create a hybrid."

"A hybrid?" The redhead asked.

"Daywalker," Baptiste corrected.

"A daywalker?" TnT let out a deep whoosh of breath. "Boss, you faced off against one of those fuckers?"

"Back in '86, my partner and I took on this Ancient that was successful in knocking up his target," the Boss confirmed. "We finally tracked them down just after the kid was born, damn near ripped that poor girl in half. Probably had something to do with the vamp coming out like a six year old."

"They grow that fast?" Rose's face went white as a sheet as she imagined the implications of something like that happening inside of her perfect body.

"Oh yeah, rapid development to adulthood," the Boss continued. "We were busy with the Ancient while the kid made a run for it. As good as we were, we still

got our asses handed to us. The Ancient
kept us busy long enough for his offspring
to escape, then he just vanished."

"What happened to the kid?" TnT
asked.

"We tracked him for weeks across the
midwest." The Boss sighed. "He left a
trail of destruction unlike anything we've
ever seen. Probably helped that he didn't
need to sleep and could move freely at any
time. We caught up to him at this little
farm in Illinois, where he had turned a
family into blood suckers. It was just
like the Waltons, only more vicious."

"Were you able to kill him?" Rose
asked.

"We think so," came the hesitant
reply.

"You *think* so?" The redhead's voice
rose a notch in incredulity.

"Yeah, we stabbed and shot him with
everything we had, but he was still coming
at us," the Boss explained. "WE got him
out to the barn, stuck him with pitchforks
to keep him somewhat contained. Finally we
were able to get him into a wood chipper."

"Ha!" TnT fist pumped the air. "See?
My wood chipper idea wasn't so bad, was
it?"

"Sorry to rain on your parade, but
his guts started re-materializing as we
celebrated." The Boss shook his head.

"Craziest damn thing I ever saw, and coming from me that's saying something. So we improvised. We scooped up his remains and fed them to some hogs the farmers had. To be extra safe we threw the hogs into the wood chipper one at a time, collected their remains separately, and sent each of them to a different corner of the globe. So in theory, he could pull himself back together, but it isn't gonna be easy."

"That sounds like a nightmare and a half," Rose said, voice tired.

"Yes, it does," Baptiste agreed.

"But wait, if that's their goal then why aren't they out there picking up every woman they find?" TnT asked.

"Well, the woman has to be incredibly strong." The Boss gave Rose a pointed look, and she couldn't help but straighten up a bit. "And the mating ritual can only be done once every few centuries due to an Ancient having to build up the strength and whatnot."

"Christ, no wonder he's fucking pissed." TnT let out a deep whoosh of breath. "Only being able to get off every few centuries? Yikes."

"So, where does that leave me?" Rose piped up, eager to get back on track.

"My recommendation is that when we drop off the recruits, you hop on the chopper and come back to base," Baptiste replied. "We'll get you as far away from Kyran as possible, and with any luck in a couple of weeks the effects of his bite will wear off."

"Won't that leave TnT short handed?" She asked worriedly. Regardless of the fact that he kept stealing glances at her nipples--dammit, it was cold in there!--she still didn't want to leave the little asshole to face off against an unkillable vampire with nothing but four snot nosed recruits to back him up.

"Girl, get out of here, I don't want to be the reason you get knocked up," he scoffed. "Well, I mean I do, just not in this way." He winked at her, and she rolled her eyes.

"You are one perverted little troll, you know that?" She shook her head.

"That's why you love me." TnT grinned widely.

"Don't worry Rose, I've created something special to help TnT out," Baptiste cut into their banter. "I've made a slight modification to his preferred weapon, and created something I've dubbed Big Jim. Also modified some boots to help you get to decapitation height."

"I said it before Baptiste," TnT said as he held up a hand. "You are going to go far in this Agency."

"Okay, TnT, Rose," the Boss declared regally with a clap of his hands. "I'm going to get the recruits geared up. Chopper will be landing at the track in three hours."

"We'll be there, Boss." The midget saluted his superior. The video call ended and he closed the laptop with a sigh.

"Well, that was informative," Rose said, and stretched her arms above her head. "Why don't you get some sleep? We've got three hours to kill."

"I can think of a way to kill three hours, baby," TnT waggled his eyebrows at her and she rolled her eyes again.

"Don't you mean three minutes?" She asked, crossing her legs.

"Ouch, girl," he put a hand to his chest in mock offense, and she couldn't help but smile.

They'd stealthed in, leaving TnT's new muscle car far enough out that nobody would notice their approach. He knew that Nick and George weren't a threat, but didn't want to take any chances on letting anyone know they were there. This dirt track was pretty central, and if Kyran had tracked TnT's arrival... well, there was a chance that they could be compromised.

Rose scanned the dirt track, eyebrow raising at the giant ramp in the center. She couldn't help but be amused by the type of entertainment these back woods hicks enjoyed. She sat back down behind the wall where they'd chosen as a vantage point.

"How long until the chopper gets here?" She murmured.

"Assuming Baptiste's estimate is correct, just a couple of minutes," TnT replied, glancing up at the night sky.

"You think these recruits are going to be strong enough to help you take Kyran down?" She pursed her lips.

"Yeah, they'll be alright." He shrugged, and couldn't help the little swell of pride that the red haired bombshell was still worried about him. "Worst case scenario, they'll be decoys

while I get in there and do the dirty
work."

"That doesn't bode too well for them,
does it?" She chuckled, thinking of Kerr's
first field mission where she essentially
used him in the same way. Though the
danger was definitely not as great as it
would be for these new grunts.

"Well, it's either that or we let an
Ancient vamp roam free." TnT shrugged. "He
may miss his window to be your baby daddy,
but he could still build a fang army if he
gets pissed."

"I know." Rose sighed. "I just hate
it when we have to sacrifice the newbies."
As if on cue, the sound of helicopter
blades permeates the night air and they
both look to the sky.

"Sounds like they're inbound," TnT
commented, and as soon as the words left
his mouth, the revving of an engine joined
the cacophony.

"What the hell is that?" Rose
demanded.

"I don't know…" the midget replied,
though he had a sinking feeling he might.

"Sounds like a car," she hissed, and
he poked his head up out of their hiding
spot.

"Oh, shit." He pointed across the
track where a bright green mustang revved
away. Nick pulled a chain out from

underneath the front of the car and
attached it to the front bumper.

"What in god's name is that idiot
doing?" Rose asked, having poked her head
up to see what was happening.

"They're the Badass Blackwells," TnT
said with a shake of his head. "And if
they are going to do what I think they're
going to do, then there's a good chance
Kyran or one of his lackeys paid them a
visit."

"Wait, what the hell are they going
to do?"

"You see that ramp?"

"Are you fucking kidding me?" Rose
pinched the bridge of her nose between her
thumb and forefinger. Her companion shook
his head just as Nick climbed up onto the
trunk of the car. George popped the muscle
car into gear and the engine screamed,
tires spinning before finally grabbing the
dirt and launching towards the ramp.

The gorilla brother stood on the
trunk like a surfer, somehow looking
almost graceful despite his big boned
stature. The gleeful grin on his face made
it clear that he really loved doing
stunts, and even more telling was the fact
that he wasn't wearing a helmet.

TnT sighed. They'd been compromised,
and it was too late to do anything about
it.

The car flew over the ramp at high speed, and when the chain pulled taught the front end snapped downwards, catapulting Nick off of the trunk. He spread his arms in an almost beautiful swan dive, and then smashed through the windshield of the chopper. As the Agents watched on in horror and awe, the helicopter spun out of control and crashed, skidding along the dirt. It stopped inches away from the crashed car, the tail blade still whirring.

"Holy fuck, that was awesome." TnT breathed, and Rose turned to him, eyebrows risen into her hairline. "Well, I mean it's tragic and all, but come on. A fucking cartapult? Holy fuckballs, man." Her incredulity melted into a glare and the midget put up his hands in surrender. "Okay, fine, come on. Let's hope that the care package survived."

They hopped the track wall and jogged across the dirt. They slowed and readied their weapons as George kicked open the door of the Mustang, flopping out into the dirt with a whoop.

"God*damn* did you see that?!" He cried, throwing his fists into the air. "You didn't happen to get that on video, did you? Man that would have gotten us a billion YouTube hits! We'd be rich!"

"Hey asshole, you just murdered five people," Rose snapped, extending her baton with a *snick*.

"Yeah, but did you see how we did it?!" George grinned, and slowly got to his feet. The redhead glared at him, looking like the devil herself with fire in her eyes.

"Look, George, mister midget came back to play!" Nick cried happily as he climbed out of the wreckage. There was a substantial piece of glass jutting out of his forehead, but he didn't seem to notice as he dropped to the dirt, landing on his massive feet.

"That's right Nicky, why don't you go see if he wants to be tossed?" The lanky Blackwell asked, spreading his arms.

"Ok, George!" His brother agreed, and made a beeline for TnT.

"Guess I'll take the big one," the midget said, and ripped the cord of his signature weapon. It thrummed to life with steady ease, and TnT swung in a graceful arc as Nick burst into striking distance. The blade connected with the redneck's elbow, and he cried out in pain as it went deep, hitting bone. He grasped the midget with his free hand and spun around twice, whipping his smaller body against the wreckage of the chopper.

"Midget go wheeeee!" Nick screamed
maniacally, laughing despite the chainsaw
embedded in his arm.

George reached Rose and smirked at
the harmless looking baton in her hand.
She smirked right back at his
condescending look and swiped up with
lightning speed to hit him in the face
with it. As his hand flew to his nose, she
ducked and smacked the back of his knees,
and then leapt back up to catch him in the
chin.

"Bitch!" The lanky brother cried.

TnT scrambled to his feet, looking
desperately for a weapon, and settled on
the chain that had snapped itself from the
car during their stunt. It was about
fifteen feet long, and he detached the
hook that was still on the bumper and
started to twirl it around like a lasso.

George landed a vicious backhand to
Rose's face, and she reeled up with her
leg to kick him square in the chest.

"Ha ha, Mister Midget wants to play
cowboy!" Nick clapped his hands with glee.
"Okay, I play along!" He started a series
of little sliding kicks, looking like a
bull about to charge a matador. George
launched himself at Rose once again, a
flurry of fists, and she dodged his clumsy
attempts, landing blow after blow with her

baton. Clumsy or no, he was definitely
resilient.

Nick took off full speed directly for
TnT, who loosed the chain at his enemy,
the hook looping around a meaty leg. The
midget ducked under the gorilla's arms,
and jerked hard on the chain, causing the
big brother to go down on one knee. TnT
leapt up onto his shoulders from behind,
wrapping the chain around his neck and
pulled it tight.

George lunged for Rose again, arms
pinwheeling wildly, and she ducked,
shoving her head between his thighs. She
grabbed the back of his knees and stood
up, slamming him down on a spiked rotor
poking out from the wreckage.

He grunted in pain, sinking down the
rotor sticking out of his chest, staring
down at it with dejected disappointment.
He looked to Nick, and his eyes grew wide
and fearful as TnT tossed the free end of
the chain into the still spinning rudder.

Before Nick can even attempt to
compute what is going on, the rudder jerks
the chain, pulling him towards it. His
head flips up into the air without its
body, spraying his brother with a healthy
amount of blood in his last stunt. The
rest of his body gets tangled up in chain
and rudder blade, and guts squeeze out all
over the wreckage with a dull squelch.

"You okay, babe?" TnT asked, striding
to his chainsaw that had lodged itself in
the dirt.

"Just fine," Rose replied wryly,
"this asshole, on the other hand." She
motioned to George, who was still undead,
a scowl on his face as he assessed his
impalement.

"You going to finish him off, or
what?" TnT inquired.

"Figured we'd ask him a few
questions, first." She shrugged, and he
gave her a thumbs up. There was sudden
movement in the wreckage and they both
froze as a figure emerged from one of the
broken windows.

"Ah, this needledick," TnT rolled his
eyes at the sight of Robinson.

"Recruit?" Rose asked.

"Yeah, I may or may not have torn his
ballsack in half," the midget replied
sheepishly.

"Well well well, here we are again."
Robinson sneered and stretched, cracking
his joints. It appeared he'd become a
vampire, and his eyes lit up with glee at
the sight of his old superior. "Gonna be
fun teaching you a lesson, little man. I'm
gonna show you why you shouldn't fuck with
someone like me."

The two agents locked eyes from their respective stances fifteen feet away from one another.

"Cirque Du Soleil!" TnT yelled, and ran full speed towards her.

"Hah, run away, little man! I'll still catch you!" Robinson bellowed as Rose cupped her hands, allowing the midget to springboard off of them and into the air. She launched him as well as she could into the air and he stretched out his chainsaw arm, leading his aerodynamic flight.

Robinson stared at the display with paralyzed amusement, and realized too late what was happening as the blade implanted itself directly into his skull.

TnT landed on the handle, and tore up the cord with a throaty roar, the blade whirring to life. The midget rode his chainsaw all the way through his recruit, cutting him clean in half.

He admired his handiwork and turned off the motor, slinging the bloody weapon over his shoulder to saunter back over to his partner.

"We're getting better at that." He grinned.

"I agree," Rose replied, "but if we're going to keep doing it we really need a catchier name. If we use that too many times we might get a cease and desist letter."

"I'll see what I can come up with." TnT winked.

"In the meantime, I think we should ask our friend here where Kyran is hiding out." She turned towards George and crossed her arms.

"How the fuck should I know?" He threw his arms up in the air. "I don't even know who that is."

"Tall, well dressed guy," the midget said, "way out of place in this town."

"Oh, okay." Their prisoner nodded. "He came in about an hour before you got here."

"No shit." Rose rolled her eyes. "Now where is he?"

"I don't know, I haven't left the track in weeks." George shrugged, and then winced as it pulled at his giant chest wound.

"See, what's where you're mistaken," the redhead raised her foot, planting it on the vampire's stomach, casually leaning on it. He groaned as he sunk further down the rotor, tearing his chest open even further. "When a new vamp is turned, they have a kind of sixth sense about where the nest is. Like a vamp GPS."

"Oh yeah." His eyes lit up as he thought about it. "I guess I can see it in my head now. But I ain't gonna tell you shit until you get me out of here. I'm not gonna talk while being impaled."

The agents shared an amused look, and shrugged in unison.

TnT smirked. "Okay."

"Fuck you, you fucking psychopath!" George shrieked, at a high pitch the midget had never heard come from a man's vocal chords. "You turned me into a goddamn muppet!" Rose giggled, enjoying waving him around the deserted office building.

After TnT had liberated him of his arms and his entire lower half, they'd popped him in the trunk and brought him to the last place they'd seen Kyran. Upon arriving inside the office building where Rose had been imprisoned previously, the redhead had shoved a two by four up into his torso.

She wiggled him a bit to make him appear to be dancing.

"Yeah, well." TnT grinned wickedly. "Unless you want me to shove my hand up there and start moving your fucking mouth myself, I suggest you start telling us where we need to go!"

"Go to hell, half pint!" George was practically frothing at the mouth with anger. Had he still been alive, blood would have likely rushed to his face.

"You're one to talk." The midget sneered.

"This is getting us nowhere," Rose sighed, though she was definitely enjoying her little puppet show.

"Agreed." TnT nodded. "We need to up the ante. It's going to be light soon and I don't want to be stuck listening to this fuck the whole day."

"What do you have in mind?" She asked.

"Not sure yet," he admitted. "Maybe we could drive around town, see if he gives off an involuntary response?"

"That's better than staying here." She shrugged. "I can't imagine what they were planning to use this thing for." She kicked the steel bars that had been grafted over the hole in the cement floor.

"Birthing chamber, maybe?" TnT suggested.

"The fuck?" Rose's jaw dropped in horror.

"Think about it… human woman, lots of blood," the midget explained his thought process. "That's going to be difficult for a vamp to ignore. Down in a hole with the prison gate, makes it a lot tougher to get through."

"Ugh. I just." She stammered. "Nope. That's a whole lot of nope."

"What's wrong bitch?" George seethed. "You can rip someone in half, but you ain't lookin' forward to it being done to

you?" She growled and swung the vampuppet
like a baseball bat, smashing his face
right into a concrete door frame. His eyes
glazed over, stunned.

"We really need to get this moving
along," Rose said firmly. "Let's try your
driving idea." TnT nodded and they headed
outside. They were just about at his car
when he stopped abruptly, grinning ear to
ear.

"Crazy idea," he said, "you wanna get
your nails done?"

"I could go for a little pampering."
She grinned. She hefted George over her
shoulder and they strolled across the
street to a little strip mall. The end
unit was a day spa, and his eyes widened
at the implication of what they were
planning on doing to him.

"Sure you don't want to tell us what
we need to know?" TnT asked as he opened
the door for them.

"Fuck you!" George cried shrilly, and
Rose barked a laugh at the waver in his
voice. She led the way all the way to the
tanning beds, and flopped him down onto
one with a flourish. She slammed the lid
down and turned it on to the lowest
setting.

Agonized screams.

"How long do you think he can last in
there?" TnT asked casually.

"Oh the lowest setting, a few days."
Rose shrugged. "Had this real stubborn
bastard a couple years back, wouldn't give
up his nest. Found out these assholes are
pretty resilient when the wattage is low."

They looked down at the purple glow
and gave their vamp barbecue another
moment to enjoy his cookout before Rose
opened the lid.

"Okay George, that was a little
fuckin' taste there," TnT said, leaning
over to look the vampire in his seething
face. "So you gonna help us out, or is
Rose gonna have time to get her nails
done?"

"I hope Kyran tears you right open,
you little fucker!" The vamp screamed.

"You know, TnT, I think that foot
massager has your name written all over
it," Rose said, motioning to the row of
chairs along the far wall.

"I think you're right, Rose," the
midget replied. "Okay Georgie, we'll see
you in thirty, bud!" With that, Rose shut
the lid, and cranked the timer to thirty
minutes.

"No, NO!" The vampire shrieked, and
the two agents wandered off to pamper
themselves. Soon enough, they were
stretched out next to each other, TnT deep
in a foot massager and Rose painting her
nails a lovely shade of dusty blue. She

held out her left hand to dry and glanced over to see her partner was reading a woman's magazine.

"Anything good in there?" She asked.

"Reading an article called *Six Ways to Improve your Confidence*," he replied.

"More confidence is the last thing you need." She laughed.

"True, but I'm not sure these suggestions would help me out much anyway," he admitted. "The first suggestion is to buy a pushup bra."

"Well." She wrinkled her nose. "There's a horrific mental image that will haunt me until my grave." As if on cue, the bell for the tanning bed went off with a delicate *ding*.

"On a lighter note, our singed vampire torso has finished his first treatment." TnT grinned.

"Yeah, pretty sure that's going to be a more pleasing image than you in a pushup bra." She rolled her eyes and got to her feet. They strolled up to the tanning bed, the sound of sizzling and popping permeating the now dank smelling air. As Rose opened the bed, a puff of smoke billowed out, and she waved it away from her face, stifling a cough.

George let out a deep sigh of relief as they UV light went off, and TnT leaned over him and cocked his head.

"So now that you've had a chance to reflect on things, would you like to share what you know?" He asked in a conversational tone. "Or do Rose and I have time to do one of those water massages?"

"You know, for a pissant little town, this day spa is top of the line," she added.

"I know, right?" The midget agreed. "You know, I kind of hope he doesn't talk for awhile. I'd love to have a go in the sauna."

"Should we put him back in?" Rose inquired.

"I think an hour should give us enough time, don't you?" TnT held up his wrist for effect, though he wasn't wearing a watch.

"I saw in the pamphlet that they have a mud bath," she told him, and he shook his head.

"Better make it two hours, then," he amended.

"Okay George, see you in two hours!" Rose said jovially, and the vamp moaned in defeat.

"No, no, wait!" He protested weakly, his lips cracking from the blistering burns on his face. "Please, wait. I'll tell you what you want to know."

"That's the right answer, George," TnT said. "So, where can we find Kyran?"

"I don't know if he's there right now, but the safe house is 4221 Main Street," he blurted. "It's a big old house with giant white columns."

"There, was that so difficult?" Rose smiled.

"So…" he stammered. "What are you going to do with me?"

"Well, we need to check out your story, so I don't think we can kill you just yet." TnT scratched his head, as if in deep thought.

"Can you…" George whimpered. "Can you at least leave the light off?"

"Hmm, we can't very well leave you here," Rose said. "What if someone comes in to open up shop? Don't want to give you an opportunity to turn someone, now would we?"

"What are you going to do?" The vampire asked, but he was relieved that they wouldn't be leaving him in this infernal machine.

Within minutes, the agents had him bound and gagged, and in the trunk of TnT's muscle car. He screamed muffled obscenities through the fabric, but Rose slammed the trunk on him, uncaring.

"So, what do you think?" She asked, eager to get this over with but unsure

that they should be running to the new
address blindly.

"I think we need to call it in," TnT
echoed her thoughts. "Let's go get some
coffee and get the Boss on the line."

CHAPTER NINE

"Really? A cartapult?" The Boss laughed in amusement. "Man, that's ingenious!" Baptiste looked a bit uncomfortable in his window on the other side of the laptop screen.

"Boss!" Rose reprimanded sternly, and TnT chuckled, leaning back in the booth seat of the diner they'd found.

"Yeah yeah, sad too," he waved her off, though a smile still remained on his laugh lined face. "But damn, TnT, get that shit on video next time."

"Can we get back to the issue at hand?" Rose set her coffee mug down on the table a little harder than was necessary. "You know, the Ancient vampire that wants to impregnate me? We got a lead, so now I need some gear so I can be of some use."

"Miss Rose, I must stress again that you need to evacuate that town ASAP," Baptiste spoke up, worry etched into his forehead. "We can't risk Kyran being successful in creating a daywalker."

"And we also can't risk a pissed off Ancient vampire turning a major city into an undead army," she countered firmly. "He needs to be stopped, here and now. So unless you have more recruits we can feed into the meat grinder, I'm staying."

232

"It's a moot point anyway, because we don't have a chopper to get them to you," the Boss mused, shrugging his shoulders. "The one the hillbilly daredevils took out was the only one on base."

"So getting me some equipment is out of the question, then?" Rose asked wryly, and he nodded.

"Afraid so," he said.

"Not a big deal," TnT cut in with a smirk. "We're in rural America, so I'd bet my balls that there's a gun shop and a hardware store in this town. Hell, it's probably the same store."

"You are correct, Mister TnT," Baptiste agreed, looking off screen presumably to another computer. "Zeke's Bolts and Buckshot is half a mile from the diner. They should have everything you might need to make Miss Rose a formidable foe."

"Excuse me?" Rose bristled.

"My apologies, Miss Rose," he backtracked, eyes wide. "You are quite formidable, armed or not."

"That's better," she preened under his praise and TnT rolled his eyes. She stole a piece of his bacon and chomped on it, and he growled at her, picking up his fork like a dagger.

"Based on my research, Kyran needs to be neutralized tonight," Baptiste continued. "If he can't, ahem, plant his seed, his window will close. At which point we have to be concerned that he will take out his frustrations on a *big* population."

"But I thought these Ancients would only be around to mate before going back to sleep for a few centuries?" Rose raised an eyebrow in confusion.

"That's only if they're successful in mating," came the reply. "If they aren't, they need another way to burn through the energy they have accumulated. That usually involves wiping out a town or two. Which was bad hundreds of years ago, but if they were to reach a major populated area it could set of a vampire pandemic."

"How bad are we talking?" She asked.

"Hundreds of thousands of vampires within a matter of weeks." Baptiste calculated.

"Holy hell," she breathed, and TnT swallowed a mouthful of his eggs.

"Don't worry Baptiste, we'll save the day like we always do." He winked at the computer screen.

"I have no doubt," the young attache replied with a smile. "Have you opened your care package yet?"

"Not yet, we got a bit distracted last night." TnT grinned as Rose held up her pristine blue nails. The Boss chuckled and Baptiste just looked confused, imagining the midget sitting on Rose's lap, giving her a manicure.

"Well, when you do, call me if you have questions," he said simply, and TnT saluted him.

"Ten-four, good buddy," the midget replied through a mouthful of more eggs. He slammed the laptop closed and downed the rest of his coffee. "Well there Rose, you got your nails done and had a big breakfast, what do you say we go out and do a little shopping?"

"I painted my own nails, this diner is like the homeless man's Waffle House, and we're going to buy weapons so I can gut vampires like they are freshly caught trout," she listed off.

"So, you're a happy girl, then?" TnT asked.

She nodded, a sly smile playing her lips. "Goddamn right. Let's go."

"I'll start looking at hardware for some creative solutions," TnT instructed. "You go see if they have any silver." He wandered off into the hardware section of Zeke's Bolts and Buckshot, Struckerville's only hardware and gun shop.

"Yep," Rose agreed, and strolled up to the counter, languid grace catching the eye of the older heavy set gentleman behind the counter. He was wearing beat up jeans and a plaid button up shirt, and she stifled a disgusted noise at the trail of tobacco stains on his otherwise white beard. As if hearing her thoughts, he turned and spit a stream of brown goo behind the counter as she reached it.

"Well hello there, little lady," he drawled and leaned on his hands. "My name is Zeke, and I'll be happy to help ya. What are ya lookin' for today?" At least he was polite.

"Well I-" she began.

"Now now, let me guess," Zeke cut in, and put up his hands to stop her speaking. "You want a sporty little number for your purse. Oh, let me see here." He rummaged around behind the counter and pulled out a tiny pistol. "Here we go. Got this nice little nine millimeter. Sleek, compact, and it even comes in pink!"

Rose blinked at him, mind drawing a blank against the massive level of offense washing over her. She finally took a deep breath and composed herself. "I'm afraid I'm going to need something that packs a little more punch, but we'll get to that once we find the ammo."

"The ammo?" Zeke was more than a little surprised at her directness. This did not look like the kind of lady that would know anything about ammunition.

"Yes sir, I'm looking for silver bullets," she said, and it was the older man's turn to stare blankly at her.

"Silver bullets?" He raised an eyebrow. "You do know you ain't the Lone Ranger, don't ya? And he sure as heck ain't Tonto."

"It's complicated." She leaned on the counter, ignoring the stench of chewing tobacco to give her lithe body a tantalizing arc for him to admire. "Can you help me out?"

"No, I'm sorry little lady." He shook his head, genuinely regretful. "I ain't got anything exotic like silver bullets. Most people 'round these parts are simple folks that either want home protection of something for game huntin'. The only out of the ordinary ammo I have are the Holy Smokes."

"Holy Smokes?" Rose furrowed her brow. "What in the world are those?"

"Well, we got a lot of god fearing folks in these parts, so they want to do right by the lord," Zeke explained. "Genesis 9:3 says *Every moving thing that lives shall be food for you. And as I gave you the green plants, I give you everything.* That's god almighty giving us his blessin' to hunt the earth for our nourishment needs. So I came up with the Holy Smokes, the only biblically ordained shotgun shells for sale in these United States of America."

Rose blinked at him for a moment once again, and then a smile slowly grew on her face. "Hey, TnT, you… you are going to want to hear this."

"Hope it's good!" He barked from the shelves behind her, and strolled up as casual as if he were at a family picnic. "Because all I've found that would be useful is a machete!"

"Oh, it is." She motioned for him to join her at the counter. "Zeke, I'd like you to meet my friend, TnT. TnT, this is Zeke."

"Zeke, whatcha got for me?" The midget asked.

"Sir, I have Holy Smokes, the only blessed shotgun shells available for sale on the open market." The older man drawled, not fazed in the slightest by his customer's size.

TnT turned to Rose with intrigue in his eyes. "Did he just say… *blessed* shotgun shells?"

"Yes he did," she replied, smile wider now.

"Okay, wait a second," the midget put his hands up. "Who blesses them?"

"Well sir, in addition to being the town's handyman and gun dealer, I'm also the preacher that caters to this particular flock," Zeke replied, hooking his thumbs into his suspenders.

"So, you do it." TnT narrowed his eyes. "Come on, are you an actual priest or did you just get ordained through the back of a magazine?"

"Graduated from seminary school back in the 80s, came here to set up a church, and just never left." Zeke shrugged. "I'm as legit as the Pope, just without them fancy hats."

"What do you think?" Rose raised an eyebrow.

"I think at the very least it'll hurt like hell, so anything else would be a bonus." The midget grinned.

"I tend to agree." She nodded.

"So, what are ya'll huntin'?" Zeke leaned on the counter with a smile.

"Demons straight from the pit of hell that have arrived here to suck the very lifeblood from every last person in this town," TnT replied conversationally, as if chatting about nothing stranger than the weather that day.

"Okay, well just remember," the clerk said with a sly grin, "when you do shoot a liberal, bury 'em deep 'cause we don't want no feds coming 'round here and pokin' about." He winked, and Rose rolled her eyes. The midget tossed his agency card on the counter, a fancy number that didn't break the code of secrecy but allowed them to stock up wherever they needed to.

"Just give us all the Holy Smokes you got and a semi-automatic shotgun with the highest capacity you've got," he instructed, and Zeke saluted him, wandering off into the back room to gather their goods.

Rose crossed her arms. "Fucking small towns, man."

CHAPTER ELEVEN

"How many shots do you have?" TnT
asked as he opened the trunk, and Rose
clipped an ammunition belt around her
waist, slipping Holy Smokes in the shell
holes.

"Sixteen," she replied as she worked.
"No matter how many of those fangsters are
in there, I'm saving a few shots for
Kyran. He's far quicker than anything
we've faced, and hopefully these will slow
him down enough so that we have a chance."
The midget reached in and opened up the
case that they'd rescued from the
helicopter; Baptiste's care package.

"Sweet mother of god," TnT breathed,
and reached in to lift up the holy grail
within. It was a chainsaw nearly as large
as him, with a golden handle and a very
exciting extra feature. He laughed,
guttural and low in his throat, increasing
in volume to the point that Rose stopped
what she was doing to see if he was okay.

His eyes were crazed, wide with
maniacal power, and she raised an eyebrow.

"You may want to stand back," he
instructed, and she slipped behind the
car, hands still full of shotgun shells,
but intrigued to see what he was about to
do.

TnT reared back and threw the chainsaw forward, the blade detaching from a gauntlet like a flying guillotine. He wound up his arm, swinging it like a lasso of death, and loosed it at a nearby tree, the blades studded along the chain slicing through a branch like butter.

The midget cackled loudly and hit the trigger on the gauntlet, retracting the chain so that the saw whipped right back into his waiting hand. He turned to Rose, whose jaw was practically on the cement road.

"I…" she croaked, and then cleared her throat. "I haven't met Baptiste yet, but I get the sense I'd like him."

"Oh yeah," TnT purred, and stroked the golden handle with something akin to love. "This is pretty magical right here. I think Big Jim just became my favorite." He let out a deep sigh of happiness and then peeked back into the trunk. "Oh yeah, where are those boots?"

Rose finished loading up her ammo, and reached in to grab a pair of black work boots that were outfitted with metal braces. She set them on the ground and TnT kicked off his shoes, stepping into his new duds. They tightened around his legs automatically, and there was a low *whirr* as they powered up.

"What are these supposed to do?" The
redhead looked them up and down.

"He said they'd get me to
decapitation level." TnT shrugged. "So I
guess I'll jump?" He bent his knees and
leapt off of the ground, and let out a
roar of glee as he launched right over her
head. She laughed as he hit the ground
behind her, and his grin was wider than
ever.

"Oh yeah, these will work just fine,"
he said. She turned back to the trunk, and
produced two UV syringes, slipping one
carefully into the center back of her belt
so that she could grab it quickly with
either hand.

"Looks like we each get a shot at
him," Rose said as she handed one to him.
"So what's the plan when we go in there?"
The safe house didn't look out of place in
this run down neighborhood, being just
another abandoned house in the
neighborhood.

"Two story large house." TnT
shrugged. "Those fuckers could be anywhere
and we don't have any idea how many of
them there are. You take the left, I'll
take the right? Then we'll meet up before
tackling the second floor?"

"Works for me," Rose replied, and
cocked her shotgun with a sharp finality.

"Alright sister, let's do it!" The midget smiled so big he showed teeth, and pointed at the house with Big Jim.

The windows were boarded up, possibly to protect from vandalism pre-vamp infestation, but most likely done by the vampires themselves. There was very little sunlight, which was jarring coming in from the beautiful sunny day, but the power was on at least so they could see without having to sacrifice a hand for flashlights.

Rose took the left, shotgun in front of her, combat boots moving soundlessly across the wooden floor. She stepped through a dilapidated doorway into a bare living room, peeling yellow paint with a broken table to the far left. The two vampires sucking face against the far wall turned towards her, malice in their eyes.

The lady vamp cocked her head. "What are you gonna do with that, little girl?" She purred. "Guns don't do anything against us."

"Let's test that theory." The redhead grinned and shot her vampire make out partner in the chest.

He screamed and immediately spewed a spray of blood all over the cream colored walls, falling to the hardwood floor in a heap. Within half a minute, his body melted from the inside out, and the lady vamp's mouth dropped open in horror.

"Looks like your friend disagrees." Rose sneered, and pointed the shotgun at her new target, very pleased with her Holy Smokes.

TnT strutted to the right of the front door, into a massive dining room. The table and chairs looked like they would have been expensive once upon a time, topped by an impressive chandelier that was somehow still shiny in all the desecration. There was a gaping hole in the ceiling, indicating something had smashed through, possibly recently if the fresh dust on the hardwood was any indication. Maybe the vamps had gotten rowdy with one another.

TnT walked further into the room, chainsaw idling. He knew with the vampire superior hearing that trying to be stealthy was useless anyway, he might as well have his piece raring and ready to go.

Three male vamps decked out in cliche leather outfits dove in from the gaping double doors on the far end, and the midget turned at the soft *thunk* of two females hitting the floor behind him, apparently from the hole in the ceiling.

"You guys look like an emo fucking biker gang," TnT commented dryly, and one of the leather clad female vamps preened, as if he'd complimented her.

"What are you gonna do about it, little man?" One of the male vamps spat, spreading his arms, eyes blazing.

"I'm *so* glad you asked." TnT smiled, the laugh that had bubbled up inside of him out in the street coming forth like napalm. The vamp's expression flickered for a moment to worry at the maniacal look on this midget's face.

He threw his arm backwards in a sharp arc, the chainsaw flying away from him. One of the biker chick vamps managed to duck in time, but the chain hit her girlfriend's neck, the blades pinning her hand there as she tried to protect her face. The first vamp leapt back to her feet, a triumphant grin on her face for ducking the projectile, but the centrifugal force of the spin caused the saw to fly clean around the second vamp's neck and hit her right in the face.

The now chained vamp let out an angry shriek as her companion's head fell to the floor, and TnT took advantage of her distraction to leap gracefully up onto the oak table. He flung the gauntlet as hard as he could, the force of the captive vamp flying towards her three compadres causing the chain blades to sever her head, blood

squirting all over them as her body
smacked the floor.

Rose fired at her own chick vamp, but
the angry screaming demon managed to dodge
the bullet and get up close and personal
with her. The redhead flipped the shotgun
in her hand and smashed the butt of it
against the vamp's face, shattering her
jawbone. Her opponent shrieked and moved
in with a quick uppercut, but Rose caught
her arm with the gun and quickly flipped
it back, blowing the vamp's leg off at the
knee.

As the bitch went down, Rose drew her
machete and with a quick *shink* sliced the
vamp's head off, a slick line of blood
joining the wall.

TnT spread his feet in a power stance
on the table as one of the biker vamps
jumped up to greet him, the other two
circling the oak surface like sharks. The
midget leapt forward, the boots propelling
him into a perfect corkscrew, driving the
chainsaw right through the vampire's
chest. He followed it right through to the
other side in a firework display of blood,
hitting the floor in a roll. He kicked off
immediately, flying through the air to
slice the vampire shell's head off.

Rose trailed crimson footprints
behind her into the back room, what looked
like a trashed den with a giant hole in

the ceiling. She slowly and carefully approached the closet at the far end, figuring that if any of the vampires were still sleeping then this would be a likely spot. She ripped the door open and leapt back, readying her shotgun, but there was nothing in there.

There was a *thump* behind her as a vamp flew down through the ceiling, and the redhead ducked just in time to avoid the embrace of death. She threw her weight into the vamp's thighs, flipping him over her to tumble into the closet. Just as he sat up Rose shoved the barrel of the shotgun in his face, pulling the trigger to paint the closet a lovely shade of deep red.

TnT ran and launched into a front flip, loosing the chainsaw from the gauntlet to come down on top of one of the last two vampire's heads. The blade cut clean down through the head, stopping mid chest. The two sides of his head flapped back and forth as the midget retracted the saw, using his considerable muscle to fling the corpse at the remaining vampire.

They collided as TnT dove from the table, spinning in a tight whirlwind to behead the remaining stumbling vamp.

"You okay?" Rose asked as she entered the room from the far door, having done a complete sweep of her side of the house.

TnT responded with a maniacal laugh, turning towards her with glee in his eyes, covered in blood from head to toe. "This shit is fucking amazing!" He bellowed, and she chuckled, shaking her head.

"Any sign of Kyran?" She asked.

"Not yet," he replied, shaking his head.

A vampire suddenly dropped through the ceiling hole, and TnT glanced up to see another one squatting upstairs to watch the carnage. The midget grinned and shot the chainsaw up into him, retracting the chain and jumping at the same time in order to launch himself up to the second floor. He hit the vamp in the chest with his feet, toppling them both over to TnT could wrench the saw up through it's head.

Rose took advantage of the distraction to blow the landed vampire's head off, and looked up through the hole.

"Find some stairs," TnT instructed as he kicked the newest corpse down through the hole. "I'll start clearing them out up here!"

"On it," Rose replied, and leapt down from the table to head towards the front of the house. The midget turned on his heel and headed into the first bedroom, a massive one with what looked like an ensuite. It was likely a master bedroom at one point, judging by the size and the broken down four poster bed in the corner.

Two jean jacketed vampires strolled out from the ensuite bathroom, wielding machetes and hungry grins.

"Looks like you boys have leveled up a bit," TnT taunted. "Still not gonna be enough." He flung Big Jim without any warning, but the first denim clad vamp was quick and deflected it with his machete.

The blade embedded itself in the wall, and he sliced down hard, managing to sever the chain from the saw. The midget's blood boiled as the weapon went slack from the gauntlet.

"You. Mother. Fuckers." He retracted the chain halfway and wrapped the rest around the gauntlet, making a deadly bladed fist. The vampires lunged for him, and he rolled to the side, managing to mangle one of their thighs in the process. He narrowly avoided machete swings, and leapt up with the aid of his boots to punch one of them in the face.

The blinded vampire swung wildly, and caught his partner in the head. TnT took advantage of the Stooges falling all over each other to leap and kick them both in their backs with his fancy boots. They flew into the wall as if they'd been launched from a catapult, and the raging midget snatched up his weapon from the wall and through both of their heads in one fell swoop. He revved the blade, redecorating the master bedroom in red and grey.

Rose reached the staircase and took them two at a time. As she reached the halfway point, an arm burst through the drywall and grabbed her throat in an iron grip. She shot it through the elbow, hearing a muffled cry through the wall. She smashed at the stump with the severed arm like whack-a-mole, aimed the shotgun through the hole and fired. At the sound of retching and squelching from the Holy Smoke, she continued barreling up the stairs.

TnT kicked open the doors to the back room, a wide open space that was empty save for the single chair against the far wall housing an extra dapper looking Kyran. The midget narrowed his eyes at the nearly seven foot tall behemoth of a vampire looming beside him.

"Kyran!" TnT snarled, and the vampire preened under the sound of his name.

"I must say, I am impressed," Kyran said with a sinister grin. "In all of my years, I've only seen a handful of people that are capable of the pure delicious carnage you have displayed here today. I can't think of another soul this century that has taken out as many of my creations as you have." He put a delicate finger to his chin in mock thoughtfulness.

"Given that you're old as fuck, I'll take that as a compliment," TnT replied.

"You should," the vampire said jovially. "I'm *so* impressed, in fact, that I'm not going to kill you. Normally when people get bold and confront me, I peel the skin from their bodies while they're alive… all the while asking them if they thought taking me out was worth it." He spoke fondly of these memories, eyes glazed in happiness. "It's a torturous exercise that can go on for days if I pace myself. But you, no, you are too talented to meet that fate. I think you would be better served as one of my personal bodyguards, like Ogre here." He motioned to the hulking vampire next to him, and received nothing but a grunt from the beast in greeting. "You'll have to excuse him, he's spent the last few centuries guarding me while I sleep. Not having another living thing to converse with has detrimental effects on the brain."

"Yeah, well, good luck with that, bud." TnT started up his chainsaw with a *whirr* and *roarrr,* shooting a menacing grin at the enemy duo. Ogre chuffed like a horse and smacked one cement fist into his own hand, stepping forward with murder in his eyes. The midget met the gaze with his own maniacal eyes, lips curling up into a sneer.

Ogre's head suddenly exploded in a fantastic fan of explosive flesh, and his body staggered a few more steps before keeling over in front of the unused chainsaw.

"Sorry I'm late," Rose said from behind TnT, stepping through the dilapidated doorway.

"Ah, my Rose." Kyran stood, spreading his arms like Jesus on the cross. "So good of you to make it in time for our big moment together." The redhead scowled at him, and stepped firmly beside the midget, reaching out to squeeze his shoulder before assuming a battle ready stance.

"Looks like the lady has made her choice," TnT smirked at the vampire.

"Rose, why would you give up this opportunity?" The pale dead man with the slicked black hair cocked his head, looking absolutely mystified as to why she would refuse him.

"You mean, why would I give up the opportunity to have a demon spawn rip its way out of my uterus? Why wouldn't I want to spend the rest of my life in agony?" She raised an eyebrow. "Is it really that hard to figure out?"

"True, the birth would decimate you," Kyran nodded thoughtfully. "But if you wish, I could be there for you, right by your side to bring you back. Think of it, you'd have eternal life."

"As a mindless killing machine," Rose snapped. "And not sure if you've seen my partner in action or not, but I don't think eternity would last as long as you think it would."

"Goddamn right!" TnT cried, revving the chainsaw, and she glanced down at him with a stern expression in her hard eyes.

"What? Only if you were fanged." He shrugged, and she continued to stare at him. "Oh come on, you know you'd do the same to me if I were a vamp."

"I might do it to you anyway," she retorted.

"Save the foreplay for later babe, we got work to do." He winked at her and she rolled her eyes. Kyran cleared his throat in irritation.

"Very well then," he cut in loudly. "I gave you an opportunity to be immortal and you turned me down. Now I shall take what I want and leave you to rot as you wish. As for you little man, you will watch as I do this, and then stand at my feet for centuries to come."

TnT squared his shoulders and revved the chainsaw again. "Bring it, bitch!" he bellowed. Rose fired immediately, but Kyran *whooshed* out of the way at lightning speed. He was far quicker than anything they'd ever faced, and he wasn't holding back. He appeared behind TnT, grabbing him by the back of his shirt to whip him aside like a rag doll.

Rose fired again with a frustrated grunt as the Ancient vampire dodged once again.

"Get back!" the midget roared, and swung his bladed chain around like a skip-it of death, catching Kyran's leg. The vampire stumbled for a split second, and Rose took her shot, catching him in the shoulder.

The Holy Smoke erupted in his shoulder with a little mushroom cloud of blue haze. Pain sizzled inside of Kyran's collarbone and he screamed, the shock of feeling pain for the first time in at least a century smacking into him like a tidal wave. He grasped his knee and ripped his leg across the calf with a squelching *crunch*. Rose shot two more times as he leapt from the room, diving out the door and through the hole that TnT had sprung up from earlier.

The midget in question retracted his chain and tossed aside the mangled foot.

"How many you got?" He asked.

"Two shots," Rose replied as she slammed the last two shells into the chamber with a sharp *clack*.

"You go down the stairs, I'll take the fast route," TnT instructed, raising the chainsaw. "Hopefully he's slowed enough and we can flank him." She nodded in reply and they darted out the door, her barreling down the stairs as he skidded to the edge of the hole in the next room.

Kyran had discovered a severed hand from one of his fallen comrades, and shoved his exposed leg bone into the gaping wrist.

"That's new," TnT muttered at the brand new leg-hand, and then jumped. The chainsaw screamed as the midget bore down on top of Kyran, and the Ancient vampire reached up to protect himself. He caught TnT with his left hand and the blade with his right, the latter chewed up spectacularly by the spinning apparatus.

With a scream of frustration, Kyran whipped the midget across the room, kicking the saw in the other direction where it clattered to the floor, losing power. TnT groaned as he crumpled to the floor, forcing his sore body back to his feet just in time to see Kyran jam his shredded wrist into the neck hole of a nearby vamp head.

"What the actual fuck?" the midget exclaimed as the newly reanimated head snarled and tried to bite the air.

"Desperate times, my future servant."
Kyran sneered. "Desperate times." He
lunged forward, pushing off with his hand/
foot, and TnT reached up to catch the
vampire head hand with the gauntlet.
Strong teeth gnawed on steel blades, but
neither gave up as they pushed back and
forth in a gruesome arm wrestle.

A shotgun blast rang through the air,
and Kyran shrieked in pain again, back
arching from the blessed bullet that found
its mark in his spine. Rose fired again,
but the Ancient vampire managed to dodge
the headshot, taking the Holy Smoke in his
good leg, blowing it right off of his
body. Still he didn't give up, pulling
himself towards her with his actual hand
and his leg hand, and Rose raised the
empty shotgun to bring it down on his
head.

TnT lashed out with his bladed chain
and caught the vampire head hand with it,
pulling it back to hold it in place.

"You got your phone?" He asked, and
Rose raised an eyebrow.

"What?" she asked.

"Your phone? Take a picture of this
shit." He grinned. "I need a new Agency
profile pic." The redhead shook her head
in disgust, and slipped the UV syringe
from the back of her belt, stabbing Kyran
in the back of the neck. He screamed in

frustration and pain as the liquid
sunlight permeated his body, and then
finally went limp.

TnT dropped the head/hand with a
huff. "Man, you are just no fuckin' fun at
all."

"Well *excuse* me for wanting to finish
off the asshole that wanted to rape a
vampire spawn into me before posing for
pictures," Rose snapped.

"Wait, you mean you'll take my photo
now?" He grinned.

"Ugh." She sighed. "Fine, you get *one*
pose then we gotta get him back to base
before the UV wears off."

"That's my girl!" The midget punched
the air happily.

CHAPTER TWELVE

The duo dragged Kyran's limp body out
of the house in a garbage bag. Rose
reached the trunk first, and popped it
open to see George mumbling muffled
obscenities through his gag. She pulled
the fabric from his mouth in amusement and
he scowled at her.

"You goddamn motherfuckin'
cuntwagon!" he cried. "I'm gonna rip your
fuckin' throat out and shit down your
esophagus!" The agents blinked at him, and
then glanced at each other.

"Given he doesn't have an ass
anymore, I'm guessing that's an idle
threat," TnT spoke up, a lazy grin
crossing his features.

"What should we do with him?" Rose
asked.

"Do you really want to drive four
hundred miles with him banging his head
against the trunk?" The midget motioned to
their mangled prisoner of war with a
raised eyebrow.

"That's a good point," she
acquiesced, and grabbed George by the
hair.

"Whoa, wait, what are you doing?!" he
cried.

"Sorry bud, this is where we part
ways," Rose replied, and dragged him along

the hot tarmac to a nearby tree. The
blisters on his skin from his tanning
session protected him from the brief stint
in the sun, but he still wasn't impressed
as she planted the two by four into the
dirt.

"Oh, come the fuck on!" He wiggled on
his stick, looking the part of a grim
scarecrow.

"Well, I was going to just kill you
and be done with it," Rose said pertly,
hands on her hips, "but you called me a
cuntwagon. So I'm going to leave you here
to think about what you've done. I figure
you have about an hour or so until the sun
gets low enough to fry your foul mouthed
ass." She jabbed her thumb over her
shoulder towards the west.

"Oh please." George rolled his eyes.
"You are a beautiful flower that no man
would ever be good enough for."

"Why thank you, I'm very aware of
that." She smiled cruelly. "Now enjoy your
last hour on earth."

"Fuck you!" he screamed, spittle
flying from his dried and cracked mouth.
"I swear I'm going to survive this and
fuckin' get you! You and your little
fuckin' half-pint fuckin' cocksucker!"
Rose sashayed back over to the car,
swiping her hands across each other as if
you wash her hands of the situation. TnT

heaved the garbage bag into the newly
vacated trunk, and the redhead slammed the
door shut, hopping up onto it with
effortless grace.

The midget dialed his phone and
leaned casually on the car, as if there
wasn't an impaled vampire torso still
screaming obscenities just across the
street.

"Yo, Baptiste, it's TnT," he greeted.
"Hey man, we got the package in tow and
are about to hit the road."

"That is fantastic news," Baptiste
replied. "How is Miss Rose?"

"Feisty as ever," TnT admitted. "Just
planted half a vamp in the ground like a
fuckin' scarecrow."

"I…" the attache paused. "I don't
know what to do with that information."

"Don't worry kid," the midget said,
"you'll get the hang of things before you
know it." He waved a hand dismissively as
if they were within sight of each other.

"There's a reason I'm not in the
field, sir," came the reply.

"So, what's the plan with Kyran the
Ancient?" TnT changed the subject, knowing
that they were short on time. "You want us
to bring him back to base?"

"I am going to dispatch a transfer
team that will meet you halfway." Baptiste
regained his professional composure. "I'll

send you the coordinates. They'll take him off your hands, put him in a special containment facility where we can keep him paralyzed indefinitely."

"That's probably a good thing, since he wasn't able to blow his wad." The midget shook his head, pursing his lips in sympathy. "He ever gets mobile again and he's going to go on the rampage to end all rampages."

"Don't worry Sir, our new facility is top of the line and is capable of holding things much, much worse than him," the young man promised, and TnT's eyebrows shot to the sky.

"Oh great, so there are worse things than Ancient Immortal Rapist Vampires that can use dismembered heads as hands?" he asked sarcastically, and Rose scoffed.

"You've won the day sir," Baptiste said firmly, "worry about those things another time."

"That doesn't sound fuckin' ominous at *all*." TnT's voice continued to drip with sarcasm, and he rubbed his forehead.

"Travel safe, Sir," the attache concluded. "Please give my regards to Miss Rose."

"A pleasure as always, Baptiste." TnT ended the call and sighed heavily, turning to his red haired companion.

"Well, George is taken care of," she
said lightly as she slid from the car,
hopping over to the passengers side.

"Pretty sure you made the right call
with him," he replied as he got into the
driver's seat. The engine roared to life
and he grinned. He'd never get sick of
this puppy.

"Agreed." Rose nodded, and clicked
her seatbelt into place, rolling her head
to blink her big round eyes at him. "Well,
you ready to hit the road?"

TnT grinned, and threw the car into
gear. "Let's do it, babe."

END

CURSE OF THE BLUE DIABLO

© 2018

"Come on you bunch of pansies, you wanna make the show one day or don'tcha?!" Blackwell barked up the hill, shaking his head at the seven wrestlers huffing and puffing their way to the top. They were just beyond the Anarchist Championship Wrestling Promotion training camp, pushing their bodies to perform harder and faster.

Frankie and Brian were the first to hit the bottom of the hill again, collapsing next to each other in the dirt with fatigue. Brian flopped over onto his back, running his hands through his blonde hair. Frankie remained facedown, the neon green of his tight jogging pants making his ass a giant beacon for the others in the evening sun.

Sarah barreled down after them, skidding in the gravel on the bottom half of the hill and tripping over Frankie. She let herself fall, just to have the chance to rest, and left her legs propped up on the blonde's chest. She was happy she'd wound her long brown hair into a bun for this, as she felt like she'd sweated out twice her body weight that night.

Dave and Tommy leaned on each other, their dark hair looking the same shade in the dusky light. They supported each other as they panted for breath, clearly staggered from running up and down this hill so many times.

"Come on, line up!" Blackwell demanded hoarsely, and Dave and Tommy groaned in unison, facing the hill again. The last two to jog gracefully down the hill joined the line, and they couldn't be more different.

Tate, the tall All-American wrestler with the bulging pecs and flowing blonde hair grinned smugly as he joined the lineup, flexing to show that he wasn't fazed in the slightest by all this hard work. He gave his short masked companion a hard shove.

"You ready to get your ass kicked, boy?" He sneered. "I'm the star of this promotion and I'm gonna show you why."

The stocky wrestler in the black and blue mask didn't betray any emotion from his face being hidden. "Big words from a small man," he rasped with a throaty Spanish accent.

"Bitch please, I got at least six inches on you," Tate snarled.

"Not where it counts," the masked man replied, a hint of amusement in his voice, and the taller wrestler lunged for him. Tommy and Dave recovered their breath enough to hold their blonde firecracker of a coworker back.

"Jesus Christ, Tater Tot, keep it in your pants," Blackwell barked, his grizzled face deep in a frown.

"Sorry, Mister Blackwell," Tate muttered, shrugging his friends off violently. He turned to the hill, scowling at it as if it had done him a great disservice.

"Alright, one more trip to the top, ladies," the old wrestler grunted. "Whoever gets there and rings the bell first doesn't have to do the six mile fun run tomorrow morning. So is everybody who hasn't already shit themselves ready to go?"

"YES SIR!" The four left standing yelled.

"On my mark," Blackwell bellowed, "Three… two… one… GO!" Tommy and Dave made it about twenty feet before tripping over themselves in a heap, having spent the last shreds of their energy on holding their coworker back. Tate, the man in question, tore up the hill in perfect synchronicity with the man in the mask despite their height difference.

The shorter man managed to pull ahead right at the crest of the hill, and reached out for the bell, but Tate lunged forward and knocked him clean into the bell post. He stood there, smugly looking down at the man he'd knocked over, and

smirked at him as he rung the bell several
times.

"That's right, you second class piece
of shit, I'm the champion," he said, voice
laced with warning. He cackled as he
turned and strutted down the hill, chest
puffed out like a caveman. The masked man
picked himself up off of the ground,
brushing the dirt from his legs and
shoulders as he clomped down the hill to
the others.

Tate stopped abruptly halfway down,
leaning until he was nose to nose with his
masked opponent.

"Just remember, you're always gonna
be a loser when you're up against me," he
growled, and then his eyes lit up with
mischief. "Maybe if you took off that
mask…" His hand shot out to grab the
bottom of the mask and started to jerk it
up, but the short man immediately punched
him in the throat. As the blonde's eyes
bugged out of his head and he gasped for
air, the shorter man shoved him just
enough to send him tumbling down the hill.

"This mask is sacred and never leaves
my face in the presence of others," the
short man declared as he traveled the rest
of the way down. "You touch it again, and
you're gonna have a problem." Tommy helped
Tate back to his feet, the blonde's eyes
blazing with anger as he caught his

breath. Blackwell stepped between them, and stared at his prize pony.

"Serves you right, Tate," he began, "you may call yourself the American All-Star, but you're really just an American Asshole. You just can't stand that the new guy kicked your ass, can you? I saw what you did at the top of the hill. Because of that and you're little display here, you get to go check the morning fun run trail for downed branches. I suggest you get goin unless you want to be checking by moonlight."

Tate simply grunted in response, tugging Tommy along with him as he stared the shorter man down. He lowered his mouth to Tommy's ear. "Give me two hours, then bring him up to Fire Rock. Tell him whatever you need to, just get him there. It's time for his initiation."

"You got it," the dark haired wrestler replied with a nod.

"Now shove me like you're on his side," Tate instructed, and his coworker complied, pushing him hard towards the trail.

"Go on, get out of here Tate, serves you right!" He cried, and the blonde shot him a petulant middle finger.

"Fuck you, Tommy!"

"Tate," Blackwell growled sternly, "run, *now*." The blonde turned and took off down the trail, disappearing into the trees as Tommy approached the masked man.

"Hey, look man, sorry about Tate," he said apologetically. "He's just stressed out about some scouts from the biggest Texas promotion coming to our next show."

"It's okay," the masked man shook his head. "It's not your fault he's a prick."

"So, what's your story, man?" Tommy asked conversationally, shoving his hands into his pockets and bouncing on the balls of his feet. "You've been out here all day running with us and you haven't said barely anything until now."

"My character is silent," the shorter man shrugged. "I usually employ that when I'm around others. It's nothing personal, I just don't often break character."

"I understand that." Tommy nodded. "Being professional is a big part of the business. Well look man, I'm Tommy and that's my brother Brian. We're the Brain Bashers, the top tag team." He motioned to the blonde still flopped on the ground, who gave a lazy salute. "That's Dave, he has a heavy metal persona and goes by Shredder in the ring."

"What's up, man?" Dave strolled over and extended his hand. "Hey, if you ever want to team up and do a mariachi metal tag team, I think we can kick these guys asses!" He grinned and the masked man nodded, shaking his hand firmly.

"That bright green ass over there is Frankie," Tommy pointed to the neon clad man who was doing some yoga stretches to wind down after all the running. "He goes by Hollywood in the ring, total 80's motif. You know, like Frankie goes to Hollywood?" Tommy received a nod and then motioned to the brown haired woman who was just getting to her feet, daintily brushing dust from her irresistibly tight jogging pants. "And finally we have Sarah, who is our little debutante, Southern Dee-Lite. Only thing sweeter than her is the tea." Tommy concluded, and she smiled brightly at the newbie.

"Nice to meet you," she said, eyes alight with charm.

"Likewise," the masked man replied.

"So, what's your name?" Tommy asked, keeping the conversation rolling. "Obviously you're a Luchador, but what do you go by?"

"Coming up in Mexico I was known as Diablo Azul, which translates into the Blue Diablo," the short man said thoughtfully. "Blackwell has suggested if I want to get a following outside of the region I should go with the English translation. I haven't decided yet."

"So what should we call you?" Tommy shrugged. "Neither of those exactly roll off of the tongue in conversation.

"Just call me BD," The shorter man replied, and then his lips twisted into a small smile. "Or Mr. Diablo." There was an awkward silence and he glanced around the group. He chuckled awkwardly. "Got ya." There was a smattering of laughs throughout the wrestlers, and Sarah started the procession inside.

"So, BD, we have a bit of a tradition at this camp," Tommy said as they walked. "After we survive the first day, we all head down the trail a bit to a place called Fire Rock. We grab some beers and swap some of our more colorful wrestling stories. You want to join us this evening?"

"I'm not exactly the talkative type," Blue Diablo protested with a shake of his head.

"Oh, come on," Sarah drawled, eyes big and pleading as she slipped her arm into his. "It would be great to get to know you."

"Yeah, come on bud, a couple of beers ain't gonna kill you," Frankie piped up, and the short masked man figured it would be easier to give in than to argue. And this group seemed like they were a lot better company than that insufferable Tate.

"Okay," he agreed.

"Fantastic!" Tommy grinned. "Let's go get cleaned up and we'll take off."

That night, atop a large rock deep in the woods, Dave stoked a well built campfire surrounded by stone seats. Brian opened the cooler Tommy had hauled out there, and passed out beer to everyone. Sarah offered one to Blue Diablo with a hand on her hip and a smile on her lips, but he graciously refused.

"So yeah man, I was on the undercard of this show somewhere out in west Texas, and I swear to christ there were more scorpions in the building than people," Dave was saying as he added more logs to the fire. "It was one of these small towns where their normal source of entertainment during the week was seeing how far they could slingshot roadkill."

"Oh come on," Sarah wrinkled her nose as she popped the cap off of her beer. "The town couldn't have been that bad."

"Sarah, I swear, right hand to *god* if I had asked the audience for a soda and some meth, I would have had a wider variety of meth to pick from." Dave put a hand over his heart and the other in the air, gaze so serious she giggled. "This,

this was not a great town. So anyway, I was facing off against this local kid. He didn't know suplex from a supermarket, but for some reason he was popular in the town. Well, he decided to get bold and refused to sell a couple of my punches. Just stood there like he was a methed up Superman. The crowd started going wild, chanting his name, which kind of rubbed me the wrong way." He squared his shoulders. "So I laid him out for real."

"Bullshit, man!" Brian exclaimed.

"Swear to fucking god, Brian, swear to god!" Dave nodded emphatically. "This kid didn't fall to the mat though, I hit him so hard he went through the ropes and into the front row!"

"And how did that work out for you?" Sarah raised an eyebrow.

"Well, turned out he had a couple of brothers and a few cousins, all with a mean streak." Dave shuddered. "Next thing I know, I'm knocking out his extended family and trying to get the hell out of there before I end up in jail. Hardest forty bucks I ever made."

"Wait, the promoter still *paid* you?" Frankie blurted, eyes wide in disbelief.

"Hell yeah he did!" Dave laughed. "Said that was the biggest reaction he's ever seen at one of his events. He offered to double my pay if I came back to smack his momma around at the next show."

"Did you do it?" Sarah asked, excitement in her voice.

"Come on, Sarah." He rolled his eyes.

"Come on, Dave," she replied, mocking him complete with the eye roll. "We all know you're a whore and will do anything for money."

"This is true, but goddammit I'm a high priced whore." He straightened and pretended to preen himself. "Gotta at least hit triple digits before I'll smack somebody's mother."

"Yeah, well, that still doesn't hold a candle to what I have go to through," she replied with a grimace.

"Oh, why's that?" Dave teased. "Because you're a delicate little flower?"

"You're goddamn right I'm a delicate little flower," she agreed, striking a little pose and flipping her hair. "And yeah, you try looking like this and walking through a crowd of drunken rednecks whose wives won't let them go to the strip club. They have to settle for grabbing *my* ass on a Saturday night."

"To be fair, it is quite grabbable," Brian piped up with a lopsided grin on his face.

"Of course it is!" she agreed. "Do you have any idea how many squats I have to do in order to keep this up?" A chuckle rippled through the group around the glow of the fire.

"So, BD, you have any crazy wrestling stories?" Tommy prompted, motioning to the short masked man with his beer bottle.

"Eh, you know, nothing out of the ordinary," Blue Diablo replied with a shrug. "I mean I was pretty popular in some parts of Western Mexico. Got such a following that I would get booked for private events."

"Like what, kid's birthdays and shit?" Tommy asked.

"More like private shows for the cartels," the shorter man corrected, and a hush fell over the group. They glanced at each other, and then back at him, until Dave broke the silence.

"Like, drug cartels?"

"No Dave, like the Maple Syrup Cartels in Canada," Sarah retorted with another eye roll. "Of course the fucking drug cartels." She turned to Blue Diablo with softer eyes. "Please excuse Dave. He's a moron."

"It's quite alright," the masked man nodded in acceptance. "But yes, the drug cartels. Now, I don't know about the stress of having to perform in front of some methed out desert people, but I'm guessing that it's a little less stressful than performing with one of the cartel boss' family members."

"Holy hell dude, that's nuts," Frankie blurted, eyes wide.

"Yeah, not my best show by far," Blue Diablo agreed. "One of the bodyguards pulled me aside before the show and said if anything happened to the kid that my family would receive a map to all the places where my body was buried."

"Yeah, BD, I think you got me on the stress level with that one." Dave shook his head in disbelief. "Holy shit."

"How did you even perform that night?" Sarah inquired, leaning forward with anticipation.

"It was kind of a blur, to be honest," Blue Diablo replied, spreading his hands with his palms up. "Only thing I remember is being amazed that I figured out that there is a middle ground between a body slam and gently tucking a child into bed." Everyone burst into laughter, bellies clenching with the force of it.

"Well, looks like everyone is having a grand old time here!" Tate bellowed, stepping into the firelight, and the laughter stopped immediately. The silence was palpable, everyone tense and ready to spring, except for Blue Diablo, who simply smirked through his mask.

"You still upset, Tate?" he asked. "Or have you had a chance to work through your frustrations on your hike?" The blonde wasted no time lunging forward to shove the masked man from his seat. Brian and Tommy dove to help pick him up, but Blue Diablo got to his feet, squaring his broad shoulders.

"Just getting started blowing off steam." Tate crossed his arms, grinning wide as Brian and Tommy grasped the masked man's arms to hold him in place. The others flanked him and he glanced from side to side smugly, asserting his position as Alpha of the group.

"What are you doing?" Blue Diablo asked, though he didn't sound worried or afraid.

"I'll tell you what we're doing, you mask wearing freak," Tate snarled, narrowing his eyes. "We're giving you your walking papers. Now, I don't give a fuck what Blackwell wants for a promotion. *I'm* the star, *I'm* the one who puts asses in those seats. *I'm* the one who is destined for greatness."

"So, what's stopping you?" the masked man prompted, a hint of sarcasm in his tone.

"You and Blackwell. You come in here with your Luchador act and want to compete in the same ring as *me*?" Tate scoffed, putting a hand to his chest in disbelief. "I know he wants to make you champ so he can get those dollars from your beaner fan base. They would throw down the pesos by the fistful to watch their Mexican homeboy whoop up on the American All-Star. In the blink of an eye I go from Champion to a fucking joke! We all do. Playing second fiddle to *your* kind." He reeled back and spit on the rock that Blue Diablo had been sitting on, face twisted with disgust. "As soon as that happens, those scouts stop coming to the shows, and I end up stuck doing these House bits in high school gyms until I'm a broken fucking old man.

"The rest of these guys will never move up, and have to spend the rest of their days in this industry being mocked in fucking *Mexican*. I'm not gonna let that happen!" Tate finished shrilly, eyes wild and fists clenched.

"Wow, you are one racist piece of shit, you know that?" Blue Diablo was in awe, and shook his head. Tate punched him in the gut with all of his muscular glory, causing the masked man to slump forward.

"Now, here's what's gonna happen," the blonde put a hand on his opponent's shoulder, buffed up from being top dog. "You are gonna walk back to your car, hop in, and drive off before the sun comes up. You understand me, cocksucker?"

"Not gonna happen, Tate," Blue Diablo shook his head, and Tate growled, hooking his fingers into the collar of his shirt, fingering the bottom of the mask. Before his captive could protest, he drew the blue and black fabric up over his face, and the Mexican wrestler struggled as if his life depended on it.

"Motherfucker!" he screamed. "I'll kill you!" The blonde simply punched him again, fist hard and winding, causing Blue Diablo to fall to his knees. Tommy and Brian let go of him in shock, staring down at the veteran wrestler on his knees. Tate strutted over to the fire, examining the fabric by the dim light.

"This shit's made in Mexico, so it's gotta be flammable." He sneered and extended his hand as if to drop the mask into the flames. Blue Diablo roared a fierce battle cry, launching himself off of the ground at the tall American All-Star. Tate dove out of the way, shoving him in the process, expecting to have to turn and fight.

Instead, a sickening *crack* resonated through the still forest air, and six hearts skipped a beat in unison.

"What the fuck, Tate?" Sarah's shrill question cut the silence. "What did you do?"

"What can I say?" The blonde shrugged, trying to appear nonchalant through his fear. "He went crazy, fell and killed himself."

"Fucking *hell*, man!" the brunette cried, shoving him with all her might.

"What are we gonna do?" Brian piped up, clenching and unclenching his fists. They were so sweaty all of a sudden, and almost made little squelching sounds at the movement.

"Calm down," Tate rolled his eyes, putting his hands up.

"No seriously, this is bad, this is really bad," Frankie rambled, crossing his arms as his body temperature seemed to drop ten degrees.

"Calm *down*," Tate repeated.

"We…" Dave ran his hands through his hair, hands shaking, eyes darting around everywhere in the darkness. "We gotta call the police!"

"Everyone calm the *fuck* down!" Tate yelled, and the tense silence returned, heaving breaths the only sound. He looked down at the pool of blood rapidly forming beneath Blue Diablo's head, his eyes open in bugged out shock. "Brian, you run back to the camp and get some shovels."

Brian gaped at him. "What?"

"Just do it!" Tate barked, sounding so much like Blackwell that it made them

all want to line up in front of him. "Go,
right now!"

Brian clenched his jaw and darted off
down the trail.

"Dave, Tommy, Frankie, help me pick
him up," the blonde continued, motioning
to the body. "We have to go deep into the
woods to a spot that nobody will ever find
him."

"What about me?" Sarah's voice was
small, the Southern lilt making her sound
almost childlike in her fear.

"We're going due north, half a mile,
maybe even a mile," Tate replied, "when
Brian gets back with the shovels, lead him
to us, okay?" She swallowed hard but
didn't answer, nor acknowledge his
question. "Okay?!" He demanded harshly,
and she winced, biting her lip.

"Okay!" She snapped, hating the
quiver in her voice. "Goddammit, okay."

"Good, let's move like we have a
purpose, people," Tate instructed, and
hooked his arms under the dead wrestler's
torso.

CHAPTER ONE

One year later…

"Hey Boss, I'm at my first match."
Alex Nantz cradled a cell phone between
his shoulder and cheek as he adjusted his
blue wrestling boots. He straightened up
and stretched his arm high over his head,
and then switched the device to his other
hand so he could stretch the other.

"Good, good," the older man on the
other end said, "you been able to locate
the target?"

"If all goes to plan, I'm going to
make the offer this weekend," Alex
replied, and leaned against the row of
lockers with surprising grace despite his
six foot frame.

"Fantastic news," came the response.
"There's a shitstorm of epic proportions
on the horizon and we are going to need
all hands on deck." That was the
understatement of the century.

"I understand, Boss." The brunette
nodded, and started to bob back and forth
from his left to his right foot. "But I do
want to go on record as saying that this
is an incredibly risky recruit for the
Agency, sir. I mean, you know his
background after all."

"Duly noted, Nantz," his superior acknowledged. "I know you'll do the job and deliver the Agency a valuable new recruit."

"As always, sir." Alex saluted, regardless of the fact that the man on the other end couldn't see him.

"Contact me when it's done," the Boss instructed.

"You got it, Boss," Nantz said, and then ended the call, tossing his phone into the locker he'd been provided. A grizzled old wrestler strode into the locker room, eyes sweeping the room.

"Nantz!" he barked. "You're up!"

"Coming, Mr. Blackwell," the brunette said with a smile, and popped his neck as he approached the man in the doorway.

"Look kid, I know you were big time a while back," Blackwell said firmly, "but you've been out of the game for a while now and have to pay your dues again, you got it?"

"I'm just here to work, Sir," Alex assured him.

"Good." His new employer nodded his appreciation. "Now I don't want you going in there doing no-sells and getting this idea in your head that you're gonna beat the American All-Star tonight, okay?"

"Yes, sir." He nodded.

"You got any questions?" Blackwell raised an eyebrow.

"How long do you want the match?" Alex rolled his shoulders.

"This is your first time with us, so we can't have you do too good of a job against the champ," the older man mused, "anything more than ninety seconds will be too much."

The blue clad wrestler nodded. "Yes, sir."

"One more thing…" Blackwell prompted.

"Sir?" Alex raised an eyebrow.

"What's your ring name?" The older man rolled his fingers in the air as if searching for a word. "You know, Crusher, Magnum, shit like that?"

"Alex Nantz." The Agent shrugged.

"Going with your real name, that's a bold move that rarely pays off." Blackwell chuckled to himself. "But what the hell, there's only like seventy people here anyway. Have at it." The newest wrestler strode over to the staging area, and bounced on the balls of his feet again.

"... NEWCOMER, THE INVADER IN BLUE, ALLLLEX NAAAAANTZ!" the announcer cried, and the entire crowd hooted a chorus of *boos* as he walked to the ring, arms in the air.

Well, at least if they're booing that means they're paying attention, Alex thought, grinning at the snarling audience. They were spitting mad, and he admired their passion. If they only knew what was going on out in the world; but ignorance was bliss, as they say.

"AND IN THIS CORNER, DEFENDING REIGNING CHAMPION, THE PURE-BRED U S OF A... THE AMERRRRRICAN ALLLL STARRRR!" the announcer bellowed, and the crowd erupted into a rising crescendo of cheers. As Tate burst into the arena, everyone got to their feet, throwing fists in the air and screaming their heads off. The golden haired giant wore a full length black robe, and strutted along the front row of fans, high fiving them with a wild smirk on his face.

Remember Nantz, you are here to do a mission. Recruit the target at all costs. You are not here to kick this schmuck's ass and win the title. Alex repeated this in his head like a mantra, his annoyance at the idiot growing the more he tried to build up the crowd. He finally slipped out of his robe, hopping into the ring, and puffed his chest out, clenching his fists in anticipation.

Alex extended his hand to shake, and Tate sneered at him, grabbing his hand and using the momentum to sucker kick him right in the stomach. Alex grunted and narrowed his eyes, staggering backwards and then instantly launching himself forward. His fist connected with Tate's chest, but the blonde simply grinned and flexed for the insane crowd, flexing his muscles, unfazed. He chopped and Alex sold it like a pro, flying backwards into the ropes. He bounced back and they grappled momentarily, Tate gaining the upper hand and flipping the brunette around, throwing him at the edge of the ring.

As Alex rebounded back to him, the blonde leapt into a flying dropkick and connected with significant power, shattering his opponent's nose. The man in blue hit the floor, blood pouring from his face like a river, half dazed by the carnage. He didn't know if it was sloppiness or a complete disregard for his well being, but he wasn't impressed.

The crowd somehow got even louder as Tate planted his foot casually on Alex's chest for the three-count, and after his official win he dove out of the ring to do a victory lap. He punched the air, eyes wild, jumping up and down like a kitten on cocaine. Alex rolled over and ducked out of the ring, leaving a trail of crimson in his wake, and one of the attendants passed him a white towel.

Alex nodded in appreciation, not wanting to open his mouth for verbal

thanks lest he get a mouthful of the
Niagara Falls that was his face.

When the American All-Star finally
strolled into the locker room, he shot a
lopsided grin at the brunette inspecting
his broken nose in the mirror.

"Oh damn, new guy, looks like I did a
little damage to you," Tate said, though
he didn't sound very regretful nor
surprised. He chuckled. "Well, I guess
that's a significant enough welcome to the
promotion."

"You know, the scouts don't like it
when you botch moves like that," Alex
commented casually, gently pinching the
bridge of his nose to assess the break. It
was clean, at least.

"Ex*cuse* me?" The blonde's eyes were
menacing as he stepped forward,
unimpressed with the new wrestler's
insinuation.

"I assume you don't want to say at
this level forever, so I wanted to give
you some free advice," Alex straightened
up and turned to address Tate face to face
instead of through the reflection of the
mirror.

"Who the *fuck* do you think you are,
newbie?" The All-Star snarled, just as
Blackwell strode into the room.

"That's Alex Nantz, you dipshit," the
old man snapped.

"So?" Tate crossed his arms petulantly.

"Dude was a legend in North Texas for years." Blackwell motioned to his newest employee. "Big, athletic, one hell of a high flyer. Was on his way to The Show before a table throw didn't go as planned. I saw the video of that, holy shit that was hard to sit through. I mean the way your leg was bending… ugh." He grimaced, motioning to his own leg in sympathy. "What kinda damage did that cause?"

"Torn ACL, MCL, and a dislocated knee cap," Alex replied. With a flick of his wrist, he crunched his nose back into place. "Four surgeries and six months later, I was finally allowed to walk without crutches."

"So why are you back?" Tate narrowed his eyes.

"I'm a recruiter of sorts." Alex shrugged, and the blonde's eyes lit up like a kid in a candy store.

"A recruiter? Really? For who?" He blathered.

"After your performance in the ring tonight, you'd better hope he's taking the night off," Blackwell scoffed.

Tate put his hands up in a placating gesture. "Oh shit, damn dude, yeah, I'm so sorry about your nose." His voice was sickly sweet, and Alex resisted the urge to roll his eyes. "I mean, we just haven't had a chance to work together and our timing is off."

"That's why Nantz is going to the retreat this weekend," Blackwell put in firmly, crossing his arms across his chest.

"Oh, man, that's awesome," Tate grinned massively, though his eyes were pleading and desperate. "Hey look, to show that there's no hard feelings, the group and I are heading up after the show tonight. Blackwell isn't gonna be up there until tomorrow afternoon, but we go up to have some drinks and shoot the shit, you know? Why don't you come with us?" He was still grinning as Blackwell wandered off, and Alex nodded.

"I'd be honored," he said, and the blonde clapped him on the back. The Agent resisted the urge to break his nose for touching him.

"Oh *hell* yeah!" Tate exclaimed. "Well hey man, I gotta go press the flesh with some fans and go save Hollywood from getting his ass kicked by the Shredder. But after the show, we have a driver to take us up so we can drink on the way. Just meet by the ring."

"I look forward to it," Alex replied, and the blonde gave him two thumbs up, backing out the door and scurrying off.

The Agent finally got to roll his eyes, dabbing the last of the blood from his face before tossing the towel into the laundry. It was going to be a long night.

CHAPTER TWO

The group sat in a circle at Fire Rock, exchanging beer and hotdogs over a little inferno that Brian continued to stoke up. The mountain air was clean and enriching, all pine and earth. The fire crackled happily.

"So, what do you think, Nantz?" Dave asked, a twinkle in his eye. They'd only allowed him to drop his bags before shuffling him up the trail to their drinking spot, giving him only a glimpse at the outside of the buildings in the compound, but he'd gotten an idea of the size. "Not a bad place for training, huh?"

"Pretty impressive for a small end promotion." The newest wrestler nodded, cracking open a fresh beer. He took a deep gulp and relished in the cool bitterness sliding down his throat.

"Yeah, Blackwell used to run one of the higher up promotions back in the eighties," Brian piped up from the woodpile they'd built. "Like most of those they went by the wayside, but he ended up with his place as a nice consolation prize."

"Yeah, there's a full sized ring in the warehouse, and an old but totally sufficient gym," Sarah added. "The bunk house makes Motel 6 look like the Ritz Carlton, but at least there's heat."

"Simple works," Alex replied with a shrug. "So, what's the plan for this evening?"

Tate squared his shoulders. "Well, Mr. Nantz-"

"Just Nantz." The Agent put up a hand.

"Alright, Nantz," the blonde corrected himself. "You're looking at it. This is Fire Rock. Usually we come up here after the first day of training to unwind, but seeing as how Blackwell won't be here until tomorrow, figured we'd go ahead and do it tonight. Give you a chance to get to know everybody." He motioned around the circle.

"Sounds good." Alex nodded. He clinked his beer bottle against Tommy's, who launched into a story that had absolutely nothing to do with wrestling. The others made noises of awe or disapproval as Brian grinned lazily the whole time, poking at the fire with his stick. It was an easy routine, one he felt like they'd been doing for a long time.

"... and that's when Brian and me had to sneak out the back before her husband came home," Tommy finished, and they high fived.

"Why in god's name did you think it was okay to tell that story in mixed company?" Sarah groaned, brushing her long honey brown locks over her shoulder.

"Oh *please*." Dave rolled his eyes. "If we all whipped it out right now, there's a good chance you'd be bigger than most of the guys here."

"Fair enough," she conceded, and everybody laughed.

"So Nantz, what's your story man?" Frankie inquired, passing fresh beers out from the cooler. "Heard you were on the way to do The Show before a botch."

"Come on Frankie, he doesn't want to relive that," Tate hissed.

"It's all good." Alex waved him off and turned to Frankie. "Yeah, I was on my way to the top. My agent was hammering out a deal with The Show, and in a matter of weeks I was due to be on the main card. Out of a sense of loyalty I wanted to play out my character for my current promotion. They had been so good to me over the years, and I didn't want to leave them hanging.

"I was set to hand off the belt to this evil German character named The Baron. He was a great guy, hard working grinder, been with the promotion for years. With me leaving, everyone felt like he deserved a run at the top."

"So what happened?" Tommy asked, and everyone stared at Alex expectantly.

"We were having a hardcore match," he continued, "just beating the ever living fuck out of each other. Barbed wire bats, chairs, you name it. Blood was everywhere, the ring looked like the set of a chainsaw slasher flick.

"The finishing move that night was that he was going to throw me against the ropes, and when I came back he was going to flip me over the top rope and onto a flaming table. Everything was set perfectly, except when I got to him for the flip, his foot slipped on a pool of blood. So instead of gracefully flying through the air, I tumbled over the top rope, missed the table, and came crashing down onto the pavement. My leg was just destroyed."

There was a series of groans as everyone imagined what that must have felt like, and Alex nodded. "Ya'll ain't kidding. It killed me to get that close to achieving my dream and missing it. Took four surgeries and six months of waiting before I could really get back into rehab, but even then something was off. I tried everything I could think of to recover. New rehab exercises, every single supplement I could get my hands on.

"Hell, I even hired a witch to teach me some spells to remove the hexes from my injury and give me a black magic edge." He threw his hands up and chuckles rippled through his audience.

"How did that work out?" Sarah inquired with an amused tone.

"What, the witchcraft?" Alex shrugged, and she nodded. "I never made it back to the show, but got my recruiting job shortly after that. And I'm back in the ring, so I'll let you be the judge."

"Can you… can you do me?" she asked shyly, a blush creeping up her cheeks.

"What man hasn't?" Frankie snickered, and she flipped him the bird.

"Fuck off, Frankie," she growled, and then turned back to Alex. "I mean, can you do a spell on me? You know, to boost my chances?"

"Sarah, come on, give it a rest." Tate rolled his eyes.

"No, it's okay," Alex spoke up, and turned to the Southern belle. "So you want me to perform a little spell, huh? I think I can do that." His eyes lit up with mischievousness and she grinned triumphantly.

"Man, I think I'm gonna need another beer for this," Brian said loudly, and toed Frankie's leg. The spandex clad man reached behind him and pulled out a cold one, handing it to Brian.

"Toss one my way too, bud," Tommy prompted, and Frankie lobbed one over. Sarah stood up and sashayed over to Alex, lowering herself to sit in front of him, cross legged. She settled in, brushing her hair back over her shoulders and sitting up straight, looking as sweet as possible.

"What kind of spell do you want?" The Agent asked, crossing his own legs and cracking his knuckles.

"You know more than one?" Her eyes widened in excitement.

"After the first one I cast on myself, I got my recruiting job," he explained, "so I became a student of the black arts after that." Somebody snorted, he wasn't sure who, but Sarah kept her attention solely on him.

"Okay." She pursed her lips in thought, and then fluttered her eyelashes at him. "Give me one that cleanses my aura and puts me on the right path."

"Okay, you ready?" He held his arms out, hands hovering on either side of her.

"Oh, yes," she breathed, closing her eyes in anticipation.

"Furias Vocat Daemonem Hyacintho," Alex bellowed, and it was as if the entire forest had gone still. "Et Reposcere Quae Egrediuntur De Vita Tua!" He cried the last three words loudly, and the flames huffed up a bit at at the same time. It was as if the air had thickened to soup, and for a few seconds nobody could breathe. The core group of wrestlers all felt a sudden sinking in their bodies, dread gripping their hearts with icy fingers, and then just as soon as it had come, it was over, and the fire returned to normal.

"Dude!" Frankie recoiled from the flames. "How the hell did you do that? You an amateur magician as well?"

"Can't tell you my secrets," Alex said slyly, lowering his hands.

"So, was that it?" Sarah asked, and he nodded.

"Yes," he promised, "by the end of the night, you'll be cleansed."

"And with that epic display, I think it's about time we head back," Tate piped up, and stood with a groan and a belch. "Blackwell is going to run us ragged tomorrow, and a hangover isn't a great idea." He also figured being the responsible one might endear him to the recruiter, so it was a win/win situation.

"Yeah, yeah, okay," Dave grumbled. "Brian, Tommy, grab that cooler and let's head out."

Sarah put a hand on Alex's arm as they stood. "I… I really feel like

something changed. Like I have a clean
slate and my sins have been washed away."
Her big eyes glittered at him, amazed that
something like that could actually work
for her.

"It takes a little time, but I assure
you, by the time the sun rises, your life
will have changed drastically." Alex
smiled at her, and they headed back down
the trail.

A little ways to the north, a slight
mound of dirt impacted and cracked.

CHAPTER THREE

The group trundled back to the small cluster of buildings that made up the training camp. As they strode across the dirt driveway there was a haunting *ding, ding, ding.* It reverberated in the air like a ghost, hanging over their heads with that same sinking aura as Alex's spell earlier.

Frankie was the first to stop, brow furrowing, and Brian bumped into him, jerking Tommy with the cooler.

"Ow man, what the-" Brian started, but he was cut off by another *ding, ding, ding.* It was clearly the bell for the wrestling ring, as if somebody was trying to get a match going.

"Oh what the hell, man?" Frankie exclaimed, motioning to the warehouse. "Is Blackwell already here and wants us to get training going already? It's the middle of the night!"

"Come on, we'd better go check," Brian sighed and set his end of the cooler down. "If we ignore it, we're going to be running the hill until morning." Sarah yawned loudly in protest, wandering after the group as they changed direction. Tate pushed forward to take the lead, and shoved through the side door.

"I would have napped if I'd have known he was coming early…" Sarah sighed, stretching her arms above her head before slamming into Tate's back.

He'd stopped short, the others piling up behind him, blood running cold. His heart pounded in his ears so loudly that he didn't even hear the snarky protests of the others as they pushed inside.

There, in the middle of the wrestling ring, was Blue Diablo, in full costume, beneath an eerie teal-tinged spotlight.

Ding, ding, ding.

"What the fuck is he doing here?" Tate breathed the words, blinking rapidly, hoping that the image would just go away. He wanted to be hallucinating; it was the only explanation for what was happening.

"*How* the fuck is he here?" Dave blurted, and the blonde smacked him in the chest to shut him up. The rest of the group stared open mouthed at the wrestler that was apparently back from the dead, save for Alex. He glanced back and forth at his new coworkers, eyebrows raised.

"Dave, go see what he wants," Tate demanded in a low whisper.

"What? Fuck that, you go!" Dave hissed back.

"We got your back," the blonde insisted, "stop being a pussy and go check it out." Dave gulped hard, and glanced

back at the rest of the group. He received
a series of nods and thumbs up as
encouragement, and he turned back to Blue
Diablo, sweat springing to his skin.

"Fucking hell," he muttered, and
started to shuffle slowly towards the
ring.

Ding, ding, ding.

"Who is that?" Alex inquired, keeping
his voice low. "Doesn't look like
Blackwell."

"This wrestler called the Blue
Diablo," Tommy replied, crossing his arms.
"Some Luchador out of Mexico. He lasted a
whole day in this camp last year before he
went AWOL."

"Yeah, he wussed out and ran away the
first night," Brian added, shaking his
head in disgust.

"Well," Alex said with a shrug,
"looks like he's here to redeem himself."

Ding, ding, ding.

Dave ducked into the ring
reluctantly, examining the man he hadn't
seen in a year. He was wearing his
signature black and blue mask, and
matching couture. He looked like he'd had
a roll around in the dirt. *Or maybe*, Dave
supposed, *crawled out of a grave.* But he
didn't have a single scratch on him, no
blood, just bulging muscles and a thick
neck.

"Uh, hey there, hey BD," he stammered, and glanced around nervously, realizing that the bell had stopped. It was disconcerting and made his stomach sink down into his toes. "How… how you doing, man?"

The wrestler remained motionless, arms at his sides, eyes staring straight ahead like an eerie blue and black clad statue.

"So yeah, look, sorry about the last time we saw each other," Dave scratched the back of his head, swallowing hard, mouth dry as sandpaper. "I mean, everybody is really sorry." Still no movement, and his skin began to crawl. "Can I… can I get you anything? Some water or something?"

Blue Diablo cocked his head suddenly in a sharp movement, causing Dave to take an involuntary step back. He wasn't yet sure if the guy was real or an apparition, but he wasn't exactly keen to find out. Blue Diablo lifted his arm slowly, pointing a finger at the bell.

Dingdingding.

Dave furrowed his brow, and glanced back to the group with a shrug, unsure of what to do. When he turned back, he met the underside of Blue Diablo's chop, and crumpled to the floor. He rubbed his chest absently, looking up at the demon looming over him. Not an apparition, then.

"What the hell, man?" Dave grunted as he sat up. "I said I was sor-" The rest of his sentence turned to a gargle as Blue Diablo hooked his entire hand into the lower half of Dave's mouth.

"Holy shit, man!" Frankie ran forward, and Dave smacked the floor to tap out. The bell rang to signal the end of the match, and Frankie slid underneath the bottom rope, flipping his poofy hair out of his eyes. "You want a piece of me?!" he roared, and Blue Diablo pointed at the bell again.

Dingdingding.

As soon as the next match began, the Blue Diablo jerked his hand back, taking Dave's entire jaw bone with it in a sickening *snap*. The hole where Dave's lower mouth used to be gargled and glugged, and the entire group gaped in horror. Blue Diablo shoved the gooey bone directly into Dave's eyes, like a pair of gory sunglasses.

"Holy fuck!" Frankie shrieked. "I'm outta here!" He practically flew through the ropes, and backed away from the ring, not wanting to take his eyes off of the murdering wrestler that was back from the dead.

Blue Diablo looked squarely at him, and held up a fist. His thumb unfurled, then his pointer finger, then his middle, and so on, as if counting.

"Dude, get Dave out of there, man!" Tommy screamed and the rising of Blue Diablo's ring finger.

"Fuck you!" Frankie cried shrilly as the pinky finger made an appearance. "I ain't going back in there!"

"We're getting the fuck out of here, then," Tate backed up, arms scrabbling behind him for the door.

Alex narrowed his eyes as Blue Diablo raised his second fist, his thumb poking out for number six, and he took Frankie's arm before they could all run back outside.

"You have to get back in the ring, now!" He hissed.

"Fuck that!" Frankie shrieked, jerking his arm out of Alex's grasp. Pointer finger.

"Do it, now!" the newbie yelled. Middle finger.

Ring finger. "Or what?" Frankie shoved Alex in frustration as Blue Diablo raised his second pinky finger.

Dingdingding, the bell signaled the end of the match, and the blue and black clad wrestler vanished. The group collectively gasped, heads darting around like spooked chickens, and then Sarah squealed as Blue Diablo reappeared directly behind Frankie.

He punched right into his back, his hand coming through his chest , bloody hand gripping a still beating heart. Frankie coughed a mouthful of blood and looked down in shock, eyes widening in fear at the sight of his own heart before they rolled right back into his head and his body crumpled to the floor.

Tate screamed something unintelligible, flinging the door open behind him, and the rest of the group sprinted after him, adrenaline pumping. They fled across to the bunk house, Alex bringing up the rear, and Tommy locked the deadbolt, collapsing against the wall.

Sarah peeked out the window. "He… he's not following us," she panted, and crossed her arms over her stomach. She shivered, despite the fact that it wasn't cold.

"What in the everloving *fuck* was that?" Tommy blurted, voice strained. "He… I mean… he just ripped Dave's fucking jaw off and stabbed him in the eyes!"

"And Frankie…" Brian scrubbed his hands down his face, eyes wide with fear. "What the hell?"

Tate growled and shoved Alex against the wall, bringing himself nose to nose with their newest coworker.

"Tate!" Sarah stepped forward. "What are you doing?"

"This piece of shit knows something," the blonde snarled. "He told Frankie to get back in the ring and I want to know why." Alex pushed him back and stood up straight, running his hands through his hair.

"He challenged the Blue Diablo to a match, and the bell immediately rang," he explained. "Frankie jumped out of the ring, and then the Blue Diablo started counting to ten. He was counting him out."

"Like a disqualification?" Brian raised an eyebrow.

"Exactly." Alex nodded. "Frankie lost the match, so the Blue Diablo took took his victory trophy, which happened to be Frankie's heart."

"Man, how the fuck do you know that?" Tommy asked, exasperated.

"Because the Blue Diablo is an avenging spirit, and they have rules," Alex replied, and every one of his coworkers backed up a step, bodies tensing. Tate and Brian shared a pointed look, and Sarah's eyes darted back and forth with nervousness.

"Wha… what?" she stammered. "What is he avenging?"

"Generally speaking, avenging spirits come back after their life is cut short in a nefarious way," Alex replied casually, as if he were talking about the weather. "Their anger keeps them tethered to this realm, and when the opportunity presents itself, they strike back."

"But… but what if we didn't do anything?" she asked shrilly.

"The avenging spirit might not see it that way," came the calm reply.

"Man, how would *you* know?" Tate barked. "I thought you were a recruiter?"

"If you'll recall, I never said *who* I was a recruiter for," Alex said. "You just assumed I was here for wrestling."

"You have about two seconds to come clean before I whoop your fucking ass," Tate growled and took a step towards the now implicated newcomer.

"I work for the Agency." Alex took a seat on a nearby dresser, unaffected by Tommy and Brian pulling the blonde back from his threat.

"Which one?" Brian asked.

"It's just called the Agency," the newcomer explained. "We're a ragtag group that battles demons, spirits, and every other nightmarish thing you can imagine. I'm here at this compound because we've had someone on our radar for a while."

Tate froze, his shoulders drawing back as he shook off Brian and Tommy.

"Well, who is it?" He inquired, raising his chin.

"Sorry, but I can't divulge that information." Alex shook his head. "It would skew the results of the test."

"Test?" Sarah cried. "You… you mean you *knew* that this spirit would start killing us? Why the fuck didn't you warn us?!"

"Because my orders are to test and recruit the target," the Agent replied. "Everyone in this room is expendable. We're headed towards a massive war and we're pulling out all the stops to recruit the best of the best, regardless of the cost. If we don't, then it won't matter if you survive the night." He waved at them flippantly, and then turned his gaze on the southern belle. "Besides, if I came up to you in the locker room and said 'hey Sarah, you shouldn't go to the camp because there is an avenging spirit that will rip your head off,' would you have actually listened to me?"

She paused and then blushed slightly, shaking her head in the negative.

"So how do we kill this fucker?" Tate squared his shoulders, cracking his knuckles.

"Don't know if we can." Alex shrugged.

"So what do we do?" Brian moaned, wringing his hands.

"Well, we have no transportation." The Agent sighed. "We are twenty miles from the nearest main road, and would die of exposure or wildlife attack if we tried to make a run for it. And we have no cell reception. The only thing I can think of is to split up."

"Split up?!" Tommy exclaimed. "Are you crazy?"

"Yep, we split up." Alex nodded, ignoring the outburst. "This particular avenging spirit has picked wrestling as his form of vengeance. If he challenges you, you have to fight, and fight clean. As Frankie found out, you don't want to end up with a disqualification."

"To hell with that, man," Tommy cut in. "If you want to go off on your own you have at it, cowboy. I say we pair up, search this compound for a phone or something to ride and get the fuck out of here."

"Hell yeah!" Brian clapped his brother on the back. "If he shows up in front of us, he's gonna have to face the Brain Bashers! And we'll send his taco eating ass back to the netherworld!" They high fived and bumped chests.

"That's fine, if you want to go off in pairs," Alex conceded, but there was a note of warning in his voice. "Just something to contemplate when one of you gets challenged. You saw what he could do, both to Dave and Frankie. I can pretty much guarantee that you don't want to face off against him and his tag team partner."

The brothers shared a worried glance.

"Noted." Tommy nodded gravely. Tate stepped forward, waving for everyone's attention, clearly attempting to take charge.

"Alright, here is what we're going to do," the blonde said loudly, commanding the room. "Brian, you and Tommy look through the office. See if you can find a landline that works, or any keys. Sarah and I will check the storage shed to see if there are any ATVs or anything. Nantz—" He turned to the Agent perched on the dresser, who stared back at him incredulously. "Ahem." Tate swallowed. "Nantz, what do you think you should do?" he inquired politely.

"Well, if this is a rampaging avenging spirit, he's going to want to see me eventually." Alex shrugged. "So, I'm going to go to the place where I feel most comfortable. The ring. You guys do whatever you have to do, and if any of you survive head on back to the ring and we'll figure out what's next."

"Okay man, well, look. You just be safe," Tate said gently, his tone laced with condescension and desperation for acceptance. "I'm going to figure out a way to get us out of this. I mean, you said this was a test, right? Well, I'm gonna ace it. Then you can buy me a beer and tell me all about the Agency."

"I look forward to seeing what my future recruit can do," Alex replied with a nod, and the blonde grinned with excitement.

"Alright, come on everybody, let's do this!" Tate clenched a fist, and turned to the door. He unlocked the deadbolt and flung the door open, tugging Sarah along in the direction of the storage shed.

CHAPTER FOUR

Brian kicked open the door to the office, heart pounding with newfound adrenaline. The avenging spirit of the guy they'd killed—no, the guy that *Tate* killed—was back to kill them all, and they had to figure out a way to live through it. So that somebody could get recruited by a demon hunting agency? He shook his head. It had been a crazy day.

"Check those filing cabinets," he instructed his brother, "I'm going to check the desk."

"Got it," Tommy replied, and scurried over to the far corner. He jiggled the metal drawers, but they were locked. Brian picked up the phone, hope making his heart leap, but there was no dial tone.

"Dammit, line is dead." He slammed the handset down in frustration. "Guess Blackwell cheaped out on his bill. You got anything?"

"Man, this fucking thing is locked up tight," Tommy grunted, and then threw the filing cabinet over on its side.

Ding, ding, ding.

"Oh shit," the black haired brother moaned. "What was that?"

"I… I don't know man," Brian whispered, and then the room began to light up. It was as if someone was upping

the exposure on a photograph, the very air
illuminating until both brothers covered
their eyes to avoid blindness. After a
moment, Tommy peeked through his fingers
to see the light dimming, and his hand
dropped to his side in shock.

"Fuck me, man," he breathed, smacking
Brian's arm to get his attention. There
were neon glowing ropes lining the room,
making it into a makeshift wrestling ring.

The Blue Diablo materialized into
existence before their very eyes and they
both cried out, taking an involuntary step
back in surprise. Blue Diablo looked back
and forth between the two men,
accentuating the movement of his head.

"Well, come on!" Brian had enough and
threw his arms up. "Who do you want?!"

Blue Diablo stared at him for a
moment longer, and then turned to Tommy,
extending his pointer finger. He curled it
up in a 'come hither' motion.

"Goddammit," Tommy muttered, his
blood pounding in his ears.

"Go get him man, you got this!" Brian
cheered, simultaneously terrified for his
brother but also relieved that it wasn't
him going in.

"I don't know man, what if I just
don't get in the ring?" Tommy wondered,
and Blue Diablo tilted his head to the
side slightly. He raised his fist, and

then poked out his thumb, then his pointer finger.

"I think that's your answer." Brian inclined his head.

"Yeah, no shit man." Tommy let out a huge whoosh of breath.

"Come on, you gotta get in the ring," his brother urged.

"Brian, promise me," the darker haired Basher pleaded. "Whatever you do, don't interfere. I don't want my heart ripped out on a disqualification."

"Okay man, just go, go get him," Brian agreed, and clapped his brother on the back as Blue Diablo was halfway through his second hand of counting.

Tommy screamed in anticipation, and ran full tilt at the ring, hopping over the top rope. The demon put his hands down, effectively ending the count.

Dingdingding.

"Come on, you got this!" Brian cried, clapping his hands with encouragement. His blood pounded in his ears and his skin crawled, icy fingers clutching at his heart. He didn't think his brother had this at all.

Tommy managed to land the first blow, right across his opponent's masked face, and Blue Diablo reciprocated with a quick uppercut jab into the dark haired wrestler's chin. Tommy's teeth clanked together painfully and he grunted, throwing his shoulders into Blue Diablo's stomach. The blue clad wrestler flipped over his opponent gracefully, punching him in the lower back on the way down.

Tommy fell towards the ropes, running and bouncing back into the ring. He rolled his shoulders and bounced back and forth on the balls of his feet, glaring at his otherworldly opponent. Blue Diablo darted to the left, then quickly rolled to the right, leaping up and landing his knees on either side of Tommy's head. He twisted his body and flung the dark haired wrestler to the floor, flipping back and landing his ankle directly on Tommy's throat.

"Come on, man!" Brian screamed, voice strained as his brother rolled over, wheezing and coughing as he slowly got to his hands and knees. Blue Diablo cracked his knuckles as Tommy staggered to his feet, and then lunged forward with a dropkick, catching his opponent in the side of the head. Blue Diablo fell to the side, but tucked into a roll and bounced right back up. He came at Tommy with a powerful haymaker, sending the dark haired wrestler to one knee.

Blue Diablo climbed up to the top rope and leapt off, kicking his opponent

square in the face. Tommy hit the floor
hard, barely able to move.

"Get up, man!" Brian screamed, fists
clenched tight. "Come on, get up!" He
watched as Blue Diablo strutted around the
ring, chest puffed out, as if trying to
pump up a crowd. The masked demon turned
and stared right into his eyes.

"What?!" Brian yelled. "What are you
waiting for?! You have him beat, just pin
him and let him go!" His voice cracked at
the last word, and his heart skipped a
beat as Blue Diablo slowly shook his head
in the negative, drawing his finger across
his throat in the signature sign for
death. Brian clutched the top rope, ready
to leap in to save his brother, but Blue
Diablo executed a lightning fast jump
kick. His foot landed right in the middle
of Brian's chest, flinging the blonde back
into the far wall.

He grunted as he crumpled to the
floor, struggling to breathe from the
force of the stunning kick. "Tommy!" he
managed to croak, but all he could do was
watch with wide eyed horror as Blue Diablo
wedged his foot under his brother and
flipped him over. He took one of Tommy's
legs on either side of his hips and then
turned, flipping his dazed opponent back
over onto his face. He leaned back, using
the dark haired wrestler's ass as a seat,

bending him in a classic sharpshooter
move.

Tommy shrieked something incoherent
as his lower back bent back at a near
impossible angle, and tapped himself out
frantically.

Dingdingding.

Blue Diablo didn't let up, muscles
bulging as he continued to bend Tommy's
body back, until there was a sickening
crunch and his dark haired opponent went
limp against the floor. He stood and
twisted the last shreds of Tommy's
midsection apart and whipped the lower
half of his body over the ropes.

Brian recoiled in horror, blinking
almost dumbly at the severed half of his
brother's body strewn across the office
floor in front of him, blood pooling. The
blonde let out an anguished cry and leapt
to his feet, rushing the ring with fists
flying. Just as he reached the ropes, both
the ring and the Blue Diablo vanished,
leaving just the live brother and the dead
brother behind.

"What the hell?" Brian whipped around
in a circle, heart clenched in anger and
fear. "Oh god, Tommy!" He scrubbed his
hands down his face as he approached the
mangled top half of his brother, face
frozen forever in a grimace of intense
pain. Brian knelt, not caring that the

blood billowing from Tommy's torso flooded
his knees.

He screwed his fists into his eyes,
clenching his jaw, and then let out
another scream.

"I'm going to kill you!" He yelled at
the ceiling, hoping that the Blue Diablo
would hear him, from whatever plane of
existence he resided in. "You hear me?!
I'm going to rip your fucking heart out!"

CHAPTER FIVE

The warehouse that doubled as the compound's garage was dusty and full of old broken training gear. There were no vehicles to be found, and Sarah's heart sank as she ran her hands through her honey brown locks. She tried to control her shaking fingers as she did so, and jumped when Tate angrily kicked a pile of broken ring equipment.

"How the hell are there no vehicles here?" he barked. "Does Blackwell not enjoy fun?"

"You've known him for years, does he strike you as the type of man that enjoys fun?" She pursed her lips and clasped her quivering hands in front of her. "I mean, other than torturing us on those runs?"

"Point taken." Tate sighed, and yanked down a stack of blankets in hopes that there was an ATV or something hiding beneath. "Fuck, I've got nothing over here. You?"

"Nothing except training equipment," she replied, eyes darting around the garage jerkily.

"Come on, let's get back to Nantz," he waved her towards him, and she scurried to his side, happy to be leaving.

Ding… ding… ding…

"Oh god he's here!" Sarah shrieked, blood running ice cold in her veins.

"Run!" Tate grabbed her wrist and took off towards the warehouse doors, but skidded to a stop at the sight of the Blue Diablo standing there, arms crossed across his chest in an intimidating display. He took in each of them separately, shifting his head back and forth to size each of them up.

"Well?!" The tall all-American blonde dropped Sarah's wrist and slammed his fist against his own chest. "Come on motherfucker, let's do this!" Blue Diablo cocked his head and then pointed at Sarah. Her breath caught in her throat and her heart sped up double speed, and she looked to Tate with wide fearful eyes.

"Oh god, what do I do?" she asked, chest constricting.

"You fight, and be sure to make it clean," he replied, not taking his eyes off of Blue Diablo.

"How?! There's no ring!" she exclaimed, and turned to her opponent. "Where's the ring?!" The blue clad wrestler waved his arm in the air, motioning to the room around them.

"What?" Sarah's voice was shrill and panicked as she turned back to Tate. "What does that mean?"

"I think it's a backstage match," he replied with a shrug.

"What?!" she cried.

"Backstage match?" he asked, eyes on Blue Diablo, and the demon wrestler nodded slowly and menacingly.

"What does that mean?" Sarah panted, mind going blank on any rational explanation.

"It means you use anything and everything you can find to hit him with," Tate explained, "nothing is out of bounds."

"But…" She wrung her hands in front of her. "I…"

"Sarah, focus," he demanded, and grabbed her shoulders. He turned her to face him, eyes blazing as he forced her to look at him. "Find whatever you can and beat him down. You can do this." She nodded jerkily, and stepped back, hopping up and down a bit and taking a deep breath to try to psych herself up.

Tate looked at her opponent, who dismissively waved him away. He reluctantly backed up, jaw and fists clenched. Sarah tried to gain the upper hand right away by running full steam towards Blue Diablo and sailing through the air. Her elbow connected with his throat, and he stumbled back, but quickly regained his footing and charged at her.

He lowered his shoulder and caught her right in the stomach, sending her crashing into a stack of boxes. Glad for the cushioning, she rolled over and grabbed two five pound dumbbells, springing back to her feet.

Blue Diablo lunged forward, a flurry of fists, and she lifted the weights with expert speed to meet each punch, his knuckles cracking against the weights every time. He grunted into a backflip and grasped a large ring bell from a pile of old equipment, whipping it through the air as if it were light as a feather. Sarah ducked, the metal hitting the wall behind her with a loud resonating *clang* that made her wince.

Blue Diablo took advantage of the distraction to leap into a flying kick, catching her right in the chest. She flew backwards, losing her grip on the weights, back hitting the floor and knocking the wind right out of her lungs.

"Sarah!" Tate cried. "Get up! Come on!" He urged, voice wavering but trying to sound as demanding as possible. He took a step forward but Blue Diablo instantly raised his hand, wagging his finger in a clear motion that indicated *no*. Tate reluctantly stayed put, eyes hopeful as the brown haired bombshell managed to get to her feet.

She lunged for a short metal pipe
next to her, and swung it up like a golf
club at Blue Diablo's chin. He dodged, and
then dodged again, then dove forward and
caught the pipe in his armpit. She tried
to wrench it free but quickly gave up and
punched him in the face instead. He barely
moved from the impact, and took the pipe
in his free hand, swinging viciously at
her head.

Sarah didn't even have a chance to
cry out before the metal connected with
the side of her head, and her body flopped
to the concrete floor like a rag doll.

"You won, motherfucker, now let her
go!" Tate bellowed as Sarah struggled to
regain her bearings, trying to get to her
knees. Blue Diablo shook his head at his
spectator, malice in his eyes, and dropped
the metal pipe with a sharp clang. He
kicked at her chest and then whipped
around with inhuman speed, grabbing her
head over his shoulder and dropping to the
floor in a stunner, snapping her neck.

"Sarah!" Tate screamed as her body
flopped lifelessly on the floor, and his
desperate eyes found Blue Diablo, who
glared back at him before vanishing. The
blonde wrestler scrambled over to his
unmoving coworker, slipping a hand down
around her throat to confirm that she was

dead. He clenched his jaw and growled in
anger, shaking his head in disbelief.

326

CHAPTER SIX

Both Tate and Brian entered the training warehouse at the same time from opposite directions, wide eyed and terrified and full of purpose as they strode in.

"Tate, you okay, man?" Brian blurted, jogging to rush towards his coworker. "Where's Sarah?"

"That motherfucking Luchador got her," the taller wrestler shook his head in disdain, running his hands shakily through his hair.

"Yeah, he got Tommy too," the shorter man's voice cracked at the mention of his brother's death. "Ripped his fucking legs off with a sharpshooter."

"You boys okay?" Alex yelled over to the duo, and they both turned to see him casually hanging out on the edge of the ring. "Find anything?" He was the picture of perfect relaxation, arms resting on the bottom rope, legs dangling off the edge of the training ring. The only thing missing was a beer in his hand and maybe a cigar to complete the look.

"Fuck no, we aren't okay!" Brian cried, as they started towards the ring. "Sarah and Tommy are dead!"

"And we came up empty," Tate added as they walked. "No vehicles. There's no way out." The duo suddenly froze, faces going pale, and Alex furrowed his brow.

"Why did you stop, guys?" he asked, confused.

"Nantz! Get out of there!" Tate cried, and their newest team member slowly turned his head to see the Blue Diablo standing in the center of the ring. His shoulders pulsed with rippling muscle beneath his signature blue and black outfit, and a smile broke out on Alex's face.

He casually got to his feet and faced the demon, stepping forward so they were within arm's reach of each other. He raised his hand as if going in for an arm wrestle, and Blue Diablo stared at his hand, then back up to Alex's eyes. He slowly raised his own hand, and they clasped their fists together in a power handshake.

"Been far too long, brother," Alex said with a grin, and the Blue Diablo silently nodded in agreement. The duo on the floor were frozen in disbelief.

"What the fuck, man?!" Tate cried, breaking up the reunion.

"Well gents," the newest wrestler bellowed, turning to face the two remaining members of his team, "back when I first started my wrestling journey, nobody in my home state of Texas would

give me a shot. In fact, the only
promotion that would pick up my contract
was a small indie group down in Mexico.
That's where I met the Blue Diablo.

"He not only took me under his wing,
but we had great chemistry in the ring, so
we joined forces and created Tex-Mex, the
most feared tag team in the region. Spent
a year kicking ass from town to town.
Didn't take long after that for me to
catch on here in Texas, rise through the
ranks and actually have some pull with the
promoters.

"That's when I started to pull some
strings to get my old friend a spot here
in your little promotion. I knew Luchadors
can be a hard sell, but I didn't realize
he would face this kind of racist
backlash." He shook his head.

"You *betrayed* us, man!" Brian
blurted, pointing a shaking finger at the
ring.

"I betrayed you?" Alex narrowed his
eyes, all traces of humor gone from his
face. "I betrayed *you*?! Why? Because I
stood by and watched as the avenging
spirit of my friend that you assholes
murdered came back for revenge?" He
snarled the word *murdered*, and both the
remaining wrestlers swallowed hard, side
glancing each other nervously.

"What… uh…" Tate stammered, "what are you talking about?"

"I've known the Blue Diablo for years, and he is the most dedicated wrestler I've ever worked with," Alex said firmly. "So when I got word of his disappearance and the story from you dickheads was that he just wussed out and went AWOL, I knew something was up. Took my months of researching the area and walking these hills until I found where you buried him.

"And I'll be honest with you, it took every ounce of restraint to not just turn this over to the local authorities and let you rot in prison for the next twenty or thirty years. But I did my job and reported it back to my Boss, who came up with a plan." Alex grinned with malice. "See, I'm not here to recruit you, Tate. I'm here to recruit him." He pointed to Blue Diablo, who crossed his considerable arms across his chest.

"Well congrats, Nantz, you got what you wanted," Tate said, and put his hands up in surrender. "So, we'll just leave you to your reunion."

Ding… ding… ding…

Tate and Brian gulped, both taking a step back from the ring.

"Yeah, Tater Tot, remember when I said you wouldn't want to face off against the Blue Diablo's tag team partner?" Alex grinned. "You're about to find out why, you murdering racist piece of shit."

Tate growled, his ego having taken far too much of a beating that night to back down. "Alright Nantz," he hissed. "I kicked your ass last night in the ring, I can do it again!"

"No script this time, bub." Alex sneered, and Blue Diablo lifted his hand, beginning his signature count to ten. "Well, it seems as though my partner here is anxious to get started. You… you care to join us in the ring or do you just want to forfeit and save yourselves a savage beating before death?"

Tate squared his shoulders and planted his feet, ready for an extra deadly game of chicken. Brian looked from his partner to the duo in the ring and grabbed the taller man's arms, trying to pull him towards the ring.

"Come on man, get a move on!" he urged, though having no luck trying to move his last remaining coworker. "At least in there we have a chance!" he begged, but Tate still didn't want to move. Brian gave up trying to drag him, and ran full tilt at the ring just as finger number eight made an appearance. He slid under the rope just in time, making him the legal opponent and giving his partner time to get to the side of the ring.

Blue Diablo put his hands down, officially ending the count.

Dingdingding.

"Would you like to do the honors, or should I soften him up a bit first?" Alex asked, motioning to Brian, and his long time friend waved flippantly as if to say *go ahead*. The demon's partner grinned and lunged forward, landing a haymaker on Brian's face for first blood.

The blonde landed his own haymaker, and they viciously jabbed at each other. Brian grunted and growled, fighting for his life, as Alex seemed amused by the exchange, happy to be raining revenge on one of the men that killed his friend.

They fell into a fierce grapple, and Alex was able to get a grip on Brian's arm, hooking his thigh up over his head to bend him over. He wrenched the arm out straight, bending it back enough to incapacitate his opponent. Blue Diablo climbed up to the top rope and leapt off, knee first into Brian's elbow, the sickening crunch of it shattering echoing in the large space.

Tate winced at the sound, inching towards the ring, not sure what to do. He stubbornly didn't want to be a part of this fight, now being the last man standing with nothing to lose. He didn't have anyone to one up, and there was no recruitment in his favor. He didn't know if he was going to survive or not, and maybe all he could do was just stall until Blackwell arrived. If they could just stall, keep Alex and the Blue Diablo fighting until help arrived...

Brian collapsed into the floor, screaming in pain as he tried to get to his knees, slithering along the ground towards Tate. Alex tagged his undead friend, jogging to the side as Blue Diablo grabbed Brian by the hair. The blonde reached out and missed Tate's hand by a hair's breadth, unable to tag him, and then his world went white as Blue Diablo violently chopped him three times in the throat.

"Please..." Brian gasped and wheezed, his arm hanging limp and useless next to him. The pain was intense and all encompassing, and he felt nauseated at the sight of bone sticking out through flesh. "Please... no more..." His opponent took a step back and glanced at his partner, who shrugged.

Alex inclined his head to Blue Diablo with a mischievous grin on his face. "You heard the man," he said, and his partner picked up the moaning man with seemingly no effort whatsoever. He held him like a

bodysurfer, his face pointing at the
ceiling, and then brought him down hard
over his knee for a backbreaker.

The sharp *snap* rendered Brian
lifeless, his back literally breaking in
two, and Blue Diablo tossed the body onto
the mat like a crumpled up piece of
garbage. He brushed his hands together as
if to wash his hands of the fight, and
then turned to Tate.

The blonde's fists were clenched so
tight his knuckles were white, and he
clenched his jaw as Blue Diablo pointed at
him. He flipped his hand and bent his
finger in a *come hither* motion, and Tate
raised an eyebrow, shrugging as if
regretful.

"You know, I'd love to, but rules are
rules," he said, proud of the way he was
able to keep his voice from shaking. "If I
come into the ring for more than a few
moments, you can disqualify me since I
didn't tag."

Alex scoffed and lowered his face
into his hand, shaking his head in
disbelief. Blue Diablo stopped for a
moment as if thinking, and then turned to
Brian's lifeless body. He reached down and
grabbed the floppy shattered arm, twisting
it to snap it the rest of the way off at
the elbow. He flipped it in his hand like

a drumstick and held it out to his opponent.

"Are you kidding me?" Tate threw his arms up.

"As you said, rules are rules," Alex replied with a smirk. The All-American star, the last of his crew, gingerly brushed his fingers over Brian's cold dead digits and reluctantly stepped into the ring. He could only hope he'd stalled enough. How long could he survive now? Help would come… help had to come.

Blue Diablo stood in the center of the ring, arms outstretched like Jesus on the cross, offering his opponent a free shot. Tate let out a strained cry and leapt forward, jabbing his fist right into his mouth. Blue Diablo shook it off and patted his face, clearly smiling beneath his mask to show that the punch had been nothing more than swatting at flies.

Tate growled as he received the *come hither* motion again, and leapt forward with another jab. Blue Diablo shook his shoulders and wiggled his head a little, still unfazed and mocking him with his body language. Tate screamed in frustration, despite everything he couldn't *stand* the insinuation that he wasn't strong enough to at least make a dent in this guy, demon or no. He punched him again with a scream, and this time

Blue Diablo smacked his arm away like
nothing and then came in hard.

Before Tate could even register it,
he'd taken four punches to the face and
was falling towards the ground. He felt
weightless for a moment, as if time had
slowed down, and couldn't believe what was
happening. He barely felt the floor rise
up to meet him, stunned into unmoving
stupidity from his shock.

Blue Diablo climbed up to the top
rope and executed a graceful swan dive,
ending in a flying headbutt to Tate's
face. Cartilage crunched with the impact,
shattering the blonde's nose, and this
development struck Tate out of his reverie
and he began to moan in pain, rolling back
and forth on the ground, spreading his
blood about everywhere.

Blue Diablo strutted around the ring
once, chest puffed out in magnificence,
and he stopped next to Alex, tagging him
in.

"You want a setup?" Alex grinned, and
his old friend nodded. "Double drop kick,
or something a little more vicious?" he
inquired, and Blue Diablo simply cocked
his head in response. "Okay, okay, I hear
ya." Alex waved him off as Tate managed to
peel himself off of the floor. He wavered
on his feet, brain clearly not firing
properly in his daze.

"Come on," Tate slurred, raising weak arms. "What you got, Mr. Agent man?" He flung his arm limply forward and Alex easily dodged it, ducking under his arm and popping up behind him, curling one arm under his chin and the other over his head in a sleeper hold.

"You took my friend from me," Alex snarled in Tate's ear, squeezing his arms tight. "Before you're sacrificed to bring him back to me, I just gotta know. Why? Why did you kill him?"

"He…" Tate sputtered and choked, gasping for air, and Alex let up the tiniest bit to allow him to speak. "He was a threat… I wanted to move up…"

"A threat?" Alex snapped, and tightened his arms exponentially, causing Tate's arms to flail around, his lips turning purple. "You murdered my friend, my tag team partner because you were worried about your pathetic little career?" Alex resisted the urge to choke him right to death, and let him go.

Tate collapsed, dragging in huge gulpfuls of air painfully into his lungs, stars exploding behind his eyes with the sudden oxygen filling him. Alex ran at the edge of the ring and leapt, launching himself up off of the ropes back towards his gasping opponent. He landed squarely on the side of Tate's head, his ass driving the blonde's cheek into the mat. He jumped up, grabbing a fistful of his victim's hair in his hand to drag him across the ring.

He lifted Tate's neck to rest on the second rope, the American All-Star now limply accepting his fate, unable to fight back. His legs dangled off of the edge of the ring, his body in a relaxed position, reclining against the outside of the ring like he was chilling around the campfire.

Blue Diablo dashed forward and vaulted over the corner post, swinging his feet in a graceful arc straight at Tate's face. The force of the kick against the taut rope decapitated the blonde head and straight at Alex's form, who had to duck to avoid taking it in the nose.

"Holy hell man, good velocity on that one!" he exclaimed, grin breaking out on his face. Blue Diablo hopped over the rope, and met him in the middle of the ring. He extended his hand and they shook again, this time with reverence for one another.

"Now… what?" Blue Diablo asked, his voice thrumming deep like a bass guitar.

"My friend," Alex said with a smile, "you have two choices, and I am not going to pressure you to pick one over the other. The first option is that I can perform an incantation that will set your spirit free. You'll be able to move on to the afterlife and live in peace. From what I hear, it is quite nice on the other side. And after everything you've been through, you have more than earned that peace.

"Now, the second option is a bit more complicated. I work for a group called the Agency, and in a nutshell we go around fighting demons, creatures, and pretty much anything that wants to do the world harm. So if you entrust your spirit to me, you can help me fight against the forces of darkness.

"I won't lie to you, this isn't a pleasant option. In addition to facing down some of the most terrifying things known to man, when you entrust your spirit to me, you are essentially a passenger. You'll be trapped in my body and will only be able to experience what I experience, except for the times when I release you.

"I'll be honest, I've never had a spirit, avenging or otherwise, be a passenger before, so I don't know how long you'll be able to stay out at a time. We are kind of in uncharted territory here, but from the research I've done it would be in short bursts. A few hours at most before you'd need to recharge.

"Now, I know I said I wasn't going to pressure you, but there is one more bit of info. Things have been ramping up as of late. Bad things. We don't know what this means in the grand scheme of it all, but there's a storm brewing. And I could use your help." He opened his palms to surrender the decision to his friend.

Blue Diablo inclined his head. "You came for me," he said, dark gravelly voice reverberating in Alex's head. "I will help you."

"Thank you, my friend." The living wrestler grinned. "Are you ready?" Blue Diablo nodded, and they clasped hands again, arms bent at the elbows, wrists curled. There was a bright flash of light and the undead wrestler felt like he was falling, falling fast into an endless abyss, before snapping still, and looking out of a pair of eyes that had been opposite his own only moments before.

Alex looked down at the blue and black mask in his hand, and carefully folded it, tucking it into his pocket.

EPILOGUE

Alex grabbed his bag from his bunk, having not even had to unpack it after the night's events. He slid his phone from the side pocket and hit a single number, cradling it between his shoulder and ear. He carefully slipped the folded up mask into the duffel bag, and straightened up as the line went live with a *click*.

"Hey Boss, it's Nantz," he greeted. "The mission was a success."

"That is excellent news!" the Boss' voice bubbled with excitement on the other end. "Were there any casualties?"

"Everyone that came up here with me," Alex replied with a noncommittal shrug. "The Blue Diablo laid waste to them."

"Eh, good riddance," came the tart reply, "bunch of murdering assholes." Alex barked a laugh, agreeing wholeheartedly with the sentiment.

"I will need a cleanup crew to plant a body that can pass for me," he said. "We have enough things going on without explaining to the police why there are six dead bodies up here instead of seven. Oh, and have someone run interference on Blackwell. He's supposed to be up here in the morning. That should buy enough time."

"I'll have Baptiste get one dispatched immediately."

"So, what's my next assignment?" Alex took his bag in hand and headed outside into the crisp mountain air.

"I'm sending you the coordinates of a town that is about a six hour drive from your location," the Boss told him. "Real nasty situation going on there that could really use your help."

"Got details?" Alex raised an eyebrow.

"Baptiste can give you specifics on the way, but there is a nasty Pestilence Demon that is laying waste to the town. Took out two of our agents too."

"So why not just firebomb the place and call it a day?" The Agent asked, lips twisting in thought.

"Because there is a survivor who is immune," the Boss replied. "From what Baptiste has told me, he's well trained and has enough weaponry to invade a small nation."

"So… you want me to recruit him?" Alex confirmed.

"If you can," came the reply. "We can use all the help we can get."

"No doubt Boss, no doubt." Alex took a deep breath, staring off into the horizon. It looked like any other horizon, but he knew what lay over it for him was a lot different than people not tasked with saving the world.

"Check your phone for coordinates of
a drop car," the Boss said with finality.
"Happy hunting, Nantz."

"Thanks, Boss," he said, and ended
the call. He swung his duffel bag over his
shoulder, and strode up the training hill,
staring down at the blinking red dot on
his GPS app.

END

PESTILENCE A GO-GO

© 2018

CHAPTER ONE

"Yeah that's right, sit there and
bleed, ya pussy," Jimbo sneered, flexing
his muscles for effect. He stood over his
opponent in all his crew cut glory,
kissing his own bicep where his favorite
stripper was tattooed across the rippling
muscle. The young man groaned as he tried
to pick himself up, but Jimbo slammed his
fist down in a cheap shot to knock him
right back down to the ground. "Oh yeah!
Ain't nobody can beat me in this pissant
town!" Jimbo hooted and hollered, shooting
his fist triumphantly up into the air.

"I'll give it a go," a man said, and
Jimbo turned to stare down a well built
guy that looked to be in his early
forties.

"What?" He raised an eyebrow in
amusement. "You want to take me on, old
man? Hey guys, get a load of this!" Ted
and Frank, who of his fellow farm boys,
approached the ring from the bench press
on the far side of the room.

"Oh now, look out there Jimbo, that's
not your ordinary old fuck," Ted warned
when he laid eyes on the newcomer.

"Yeah Jimmy, this here used to be the
pride and joy of this shitberg," Frank
added, shaking his head. "Right after
those planes hit the towers he ran off and

joined the military. Went off to fight the good fight as a marine."

"Delta Force, actually." The man put up a hand.

"Oh, well, excuse *me*, Mr. Delta Force." Frank rolled his eyes.

"So, you some sort of fancy pants war hero?" Jimbo pursed his lips.

"More like a fuckin' disgrace," Ted scoffed. "Word is he abandoned his squad out in Afghanistan."

"What, you some sorta coward or something?" Jimbo cracked his knuckles and stared menacingly at the old man he was now looking forward to crushing.

"Little more complicated than that," came the mellow reply.

"I doubt that." The ripped farm boy in the ring squared his shoulders. "Regardless though, I'm gonna whoop your ass." The old man stepped into the ring and slid on his gloves, waving forward his opponent who was half his age.

"You gonna keep running your mouth or you gonna fight?" he asked, and Jimbo narrowed his eyes.

"Oh, it's on," he said, and rushed forward. He attempted to land several punches, but the old man bobbed and weaved out of the way, dodging each hit with ease. He didn't bother trying to hit back, just letting his opponent swat at the air.

"Come on, Jimbo!" Ted barked. "You got this fucker!" Frank added a hoot to pump up his friend, and the man in question was starting to get frustrated.

"You gonna fight or dance, you fucking coward?" he grunted, and the old man winked at him. He was taken aback by the gesture, such a sly little thing to happen in the middle of a fight, but he didn't want to show fear. He threw another punch and the old man blocked it this time with what felt like a steel tricep, and then immediately countered.

The flurry of blows into Jimbo's torso stunned him, the younger man unable to even keep track of each hit they were so fast. His opponent's fist connected with his jaw in a vicious uppercut and he flew backwards, hitting the mat with a hard *thud*.

"Next time you should respect your elders," the older man said casually as he started to remove his gloves. Before he could react, what felt like a brick house barreled into his back and he hit the floor. Ted and Frank began kicking him, and he tried to reach up to catch a leg but had to concede that it was too much, curling into the fetal position to defend himself. A third leg joined in and he peeked around his arm to see that Jimbo had joined his dishonorable friends.

"You ain't so tough, are ya soldier boy?!" Ted cried, thick drawl echoing across the gym. A few of the other gym patrons hopped into the ring and pulled the young firecrackers off of the older man.

"You shouldn't have come back to this town, you coward!" Frank spit as he struggled against the guy dragging him away. The bloodied man on the floor sat up, gingerly poking at his cheekbone as he righted himself.

"You okay, Rutger?" David asked, and leaned down to help him to his feet.

"Yeah, I've had worse," Rutger replied, patting the owner of the gym on the arm as he steadied himself on his feet. He accepted the offered towel from his friend and dabbed gently at his nose.

"Look, I knew your daddy, him and I were friends," David said slowly, running a shaky hand through his grey hair. "Frankly it's the only reason I agreed to let you into this gym after your, uh… military difficulties."

"David, it's okay, I understand," Rutger assured him.

"I'm sorry Rutger, I just can't have this sorta thing in my gym." The older man frowned, his wrinkled jowls deepening the expression almost comically. "It's hard enough keeping the doors open in the off season."

"David. It's cool," the younger man said, and offered a smile. "I'll manage. Promise." He turned and ducked under the ropes of the ring, wincing as he straightened up. At least one of his ribs were surely bruised.

"Rutger, wait," David said, and leaned on the top rope, lips pursed, and lowered his gravelly voice. "If you want, come by here tomorrow night around closing. I'll have you a key made so you can come work out after hours."

"Thanks, David," the younger man replied, his dark eyes softening at the sincere expression on his old friend's face. He reached out his clean hand and they shook firmly.

CHAPTER TWO

Mel's Diner was known for miles around as the place to go for country fried steak. It was one of the only shops still open in the off-season, and the heart and soul of the small downtown core. Rutger trudged in like his shoes were made of lead and took his regular seat in the booth against the back wall.

He gazed down the seating area, which was essentially a long tube of black and white checkered tile with booths on one side and a counter on the other. The giant fan mounted in the kitchen wall kept the cooks from overheating, and the squeak of each rapid undulation was almost comforting. He was pretty sure that same fan had been here when he was a kid; that same sharp old metal with that same *squeaksqueaksqueak*.

JoJo was the lone waitress that night, an early 50s southern lass that looked like she'd been around the block a few times. She checked on the two middle aged couples on her way to Rutger's table, and set a cup of coffee down in front of him.

"You look like you could use this, hon," she said with a note of concern in her voice.

"Thanks, JoJo," he said with a smile, and wrapped a hand around the warm mug. The coffee here was one step up from sludge, but it caffeine was caffeine.

"Rough night at the gym?" she inquired as she pulled the pencil from behind her ear.

"Yeah, you could say that." Rutger shrugged and took a sip of the black liquid.

One of the three farm workers scattered along the far booths hollered for her attention, and she waved at him to acknowledge she was coming. "You want your usual?" she asked Rutger.

"Yep," he said with a grin. "You know I can't get enough of your special gravy."

"Well, if you ever get around to taking me out maybe I can say the same thing about you." JoJo winked and sashayed off down the line of booths, leaving Rutger to grimace into his coffee cup. The mental image of the sloppy waitress enjoying his *gravy* made him die a little inside.

The bell over the door tinkled happily as a man in dirty jeans and a wool poncho walked in and stopped right inside the door.

"Just seat yourself anywhere you like hon, and I'll be right over," JoJo called as she stepped around the counter to put

in Rutger's order. He watched the man
curiously, just standing there motionless
in the doorway. He couldn't get a good
look at his face, as it was shrouded in
the woolen hood of the poncho. But there
was something in the air then, something
that made his stomach sink.

"Sir?" JoJo returned from around the
counter, wrinkling her nose at the dirt
caking the new patron's clothes. "Are… are
you okay?"

He lifted his arm ever so slowly, a
gloved hand peeking out from the tasseled
hem of the poncho. He rolled the woolen
fabric back, revealing crusty and decrepit
skin. It looked like someone had taken a
cheese grater to a roll of toilet paper,
and JoJo simply stared at it with wide
eyes. When his nasty forearm was parallel
to her face, he took a deep breath and
then blew hard, flakes of skin flying
right into the waitress' disgusted face.

She recoiled in horror, squeezing her
eyes shut for a split second, but then her
demeanor changed completely and she stood
at attention, back ramrod straight.
Rutger's blood ran cold at the sight, a
cold death in her eyes, as if they weren't
seeing anything anymore. The lower lids
began to pool with redness, and as crimson
spilled over the edge to waterfall down

her face, he realized it was blood. Her eyes were bleeding.

Her cheeks began to crack and bubble, sores pushing through her thick foundation to explode, pus oozing down her face like sludge.

"Hey, JoJo, more coffee over here," one of the ladies on the far side called, clearly having not paid attention to the altercation happening by the front door. The waitress turned on her heel and stalked over to the table, snatching up a steak knife from one of the farm workers on the way. She plunged it into the back of the woman's neck, her head hitting the table as JoJo continued to stab her over and over.

The man across the table shook himself free of his shock and lunged forward, catching the knife happy waitress around the waist and wrestling her arms behind her back. The knife clattered to the floor, and the remaining patrons took this as their cue to dart into the kitchen, as the entrance was blocked by the mysterious newcomer.

Rutger stayed in his seat, simply watching the events unfold, trying to stay subjective and suspend his disbelief at what was happening before his very eyes. The newcomer took a deep breath and blew more of his flaky skin towards JoJo and her captor, the latter taking a faceful and immediately letting go of the waitress. The two of them spun on their heels and stalked to the kitchen door, pounding on it with fists that were forming even more bulging pustules.

The cooks and patrons held the door, screaming as they took in the bleeding faces through the window. The poncho wearing catalyst turned his head towards the kitchen fan and turned his hand towards himself, taking his pinky finger and snapping it clean off. He tossed it into the wall fan and the rapidly spinning blades easily chopped the intensely dry digit into dust.

The screaming in the kitchen came to a halt as the powdered finger coated the kitchen, and the brick forming in Rutger's stomach gave him a kick. It was time for him to attack this situation head on. He strolled up behind the mystery man and grabbed his shoulder, spinning him right around. The force of it caused the hood of the poncho to fall back, revealing the face of a man who looked like he'd gone bobbing for apples in industrial waste.

His skin was melted with burns and boils, his left eye sagging in its socket so deep it looked like it was about to fall out.

"Holy shit," Rutger said, "you need to moisturize."

The scarred man raised his hand quickly and *poofed* a cloud of skin dust point blank into his new opponent's face. Rutger chuffed in annoyance, blowing off his face and brushing off the front of his jacket.

"Really, dude?" he groaned, and caught a quick flash of confusion in the melted man's face. He stumbled back in shock and snapped the fingers on his less mangled hand, causing one of the cooks to leap over the bar counter like an ape. He sprung through the air and tackled Rutger right into the front door, shattering the glass and sending them tumbling to the concrete outside.

The ex Delta Force reacted by reflex, smashing the cook's face with his elbow and leaping to his feet. He spun in a tight circle, his boot connecting with the cook's head. As his opponent slumped to the concrete, Rutger glanced up through the broken glass to meet the livid eyes of the melted man. The decrepit poncho wearing newcomer lowered his chin and the swarm of possessed diner workers and patrons surged towards the busted door.

"Fuck," Rutger grunted, and took off running towards his truck. He retrieved his keys from his pocket as he bolted, flung open the door and dove inside, slamming it behind him. The engine roared to life as four diner zombies reached the truck and he popped it into reverse, flooring the gas pedal with as much force as he could muster.

JoJo leapt up onto the front bumper just in time, pulling her now completely blistered body up onto the hood. Rutger snapped the handbrake and did a one-eighty turn, flinging her into one of the storefronts like a rag doll. He couldn't help but pause a second as her body crumpled to the ground, but at the *thud, thud* of his pursuers jumping into the bed of the truck, he floored the gas.

He sped down the highway, bobbing and weaving to try to dislodge the two diner zombies still attached to his vehicle. They started to crawl onto the roof, and upon seeing a gnarled hand snake down over the front windshield, he hit the brakes hard and they both went flying. He wasted no time in speeding off, glancing in the rearview mirror to see two shadowy figures peeling themselves off of the asphalt to stagger after him.

Rutger parked his car and hopped out, heart still rattling around in his chest like a jackhammer. He didn't know what the hell was going on, but he was going to find out. He slammed the truck door as he darted inside, throwing all of his deadbolts closed with expert ease. He moved swiftly into the front room while removing his still dusty jacket, tossing it on the hallway table.

He immediately picked up the phone and dialed nine one one, and slammed the receiver down at the sound of a busy signal. He ran his finger down the piece of paper next to the phone and dialed the number for the local police station directly.

Ring… ring… click.

"Hello? Can anybody hear me?" Rutger demanded, but the only answer was a clatter in the background, as if somebody had dropped the receiver. At the sound of screams and gunshots, he gripped the edge of the table.

"Oh god help me!" a voice pleaded from the other end. "Help me!" More gunshots. Rutger dropped the phone, letting it hang from the cord off of the edge of the table, wandering away as the screams faded. Cops becoming zombies, likely.

He reached his desk and opened the top drawer, revealing a 9mm and a clip. He slapped the clip in with a deadly sounding *click*, and cocked the gun.

"Okay, Rutger, now what?" he asked himself, turning and leaning on the desk. He chewed his lip for a moment and then darted back over to the phone, pushing down on the hangup button a few times before finding the dial tone once again. He dialed another number from the paper.

"Yeah?" a familiar gruff voice asked from the other end.

"Ronny, it's Rutger."

"What's up, brother?" The voice brightened. "You change your mind about joining up with us?"

"We can talk about that later," Rutger shook his head. "You boys need to seal up that compound and do it now."

"Man, look at you," Ronny replied with amusement. "Not even a member yet and you are already barking out orders."

"Listen to me," Rutger pleaded. "Some weird shit just went down at the diner. JoJo chopped a woman's head off and one of the cooks tackled me out of the front goddamn door."

"Wait, JoJo did *what*?" Ronny blurted in confusion. "That don't make any sense. Boy, you on the sauce again?"

"Ronny, I'm not fucking around!" Rutger barked harshly, begging for compliance with his no-nonsense tone. "There was this… guy, all kinds of fucked up. He blew something in their face and they just went insane. I called the police station and it sounds like they're overrun. You guys are only a couple miles away from downtown. Thought you'd want to know and take appropriate action."

There was a moment of silence, and if it weren't for the ragged breathing, he would have thought he'd been hung up on.

"Okay, Rutger," Ronny said finally. "You ain't usually one to get freaked out, so I'm gonna take your word this is serious."

"Thank you," Rutger let out a deep breath of relief.

"This is what I'm gonna do," Ronny continued. "The boys are gonna seal the front gate and stand guard. I'll make sure they know to expect you. How long do you think it'll take for you to get here?"

"Few hours, probably," Rutger said. "I don't really want to go through town, ya know?"

"Alright buddy, you be safe," came the reply. "We'll be on the lookout for you." The *click* almost sounded like a nail in a coffin, and Rutger stared at the receiver for a moment before gathering himself. He hung up and headed towards his bedroom, where he kept his go-bag for emergency situations.

He froze as he passed the front window, seeing the two diner zombies from the highway stalking towards the house.

"Motherfucker," he muttered, and cocked his gun. The sound of tires squealed in the distance and headlights screamed up the road, straight for the house. Rutger watched with fascination as a black car slammed into the two diner zombies, pinning them under the front wheels. The doors open in perfect synchronicity, and two men in suits stepped out, circled around, and put a bullet in each of their heads.

One of them pulled out a bag and the other started for the door. Rutger ducked before he could be seen, holding his gun at the ready.

Knock, knock.

"Sir, please open the door." The voice was controlled, but the urgency was there. If they were some kind of federal agency, and they were nervous, then shit was really bad. "We need to talk to you about the incident at the diner."

Rutger chewed his lip for a moment before answering. They obviously knew he was in there. "I was just defending myself, officer," he replied, raising the pitch of his voice a bit to sound less threatening. "If you can find anybody who isn't drugged out of their mind, they'll back me up."

"Sir, I'm not an officer, and we know you aren't at fault," the man assured him. "We are from the Agency and we are here to deal with whatever creature you encountered."

"Creature?" An image of a melted face with angry eyes flashed in Rutger's mind and he shuddered. "What are you talking about?"

"Sir, please open the door," the Agent reiterated, "we will explain everything."

He knew he had to. What did he have to lose at this point? He'd called the cops and they were a no go, so this was the next best thing, no? Rutger opened the door reluctantly, revealing the two suited twins.

"Sir, can we-"

"The name's Rutger," he insisted.

"Rutger, can we please come in?" the first Agent asked. "It's a little dangerous to be standing out here."

"Yeah sure, just no sudden moves until I know what's going on," Rutger replied, revealing his gun.

The Agent nodded. "Fair enough." They strode into the front room as he closed the door behind them. "I'm Agent Wiggins, this is Agent Johnson." The first man introduced them as Johnson set up a laptop on the desk.

"Alright, let's hear it," Rutger prompted with a nod. "What the fuck is going on?"

"Sir, you experienced a demon attack at the diner." Johnson spoke up.

Rutger stared at them blankly for a moment. "Oh. Okay." He scrubbed his hands down the sides of his face. "How could you tell? Did you have cameras in the diner or something?"

"No sir, we got a hit on our satellite imagery that showed an intense concentration of demon activity," Wiggins explained. "We were able to watch as you fled the scene and came here. Before we confront this particular demon, we need to know what we are up against. We're hoping that you can help us fill in the gaps." He crossed his arms across his chest and leaned back against the wall. "So, can you tell us what you saw?"

"Sure thing," Rutger sighed. "In a nutshell, this fucked up looking dude came into the diner, blew his skin flakes into people's faces, and they went batshit. A fifty year old waitress breathed it in and twenty seconds later she was using a steak knife to fillet a woman who wanted more coffee."

The Agents shared a quick look that Rutger wasn't sure he liked. "Sir, this is very important," Wiggins began, "did this demon breathe anything onto you?"

"Yep," came the reply, "head-butted the motherfucker after he did, too."

The Agents immediately drew their guns, training them at their informant's face.

"Whoa, whoa, what the hell, man?" Rutger exclaimed. "I'm answering your questions!"

"Put your gun on the ground!" Wiggins barked. "Hands up! Do it now!" He moved forward a step and the older man tossed the gun on the carpet, raising his hands above his head.

"Okay, calm down there buddy, I'm complying," he said calmly, and Wiggins took another step forward. One more step and Rutger lashed out, grabbing his arm and throwing it back, using the momentum to grab his head and slam it down onto the table. He held the Agent's head against his jacket on the table, bending his gun arm back at a painful angle. Wiggins cried out briefly before quieting.

"Okay, you made your point, let him go," Johnson warned, his gun still pointed.

"Put down the gun there, bucko," Rutger countered. "You don't and I'm gonna snap his arm, maybe worse."

The Agent sighed and set his gun on the desk. Rutger released his prisoner and backed away, eyes on Johnson as he moved towards his discarded gun. Wiggins turned around slowly, revealing bloody smears beneath his eyes and boils cropping up along his cheekbones.

"Johnson," Rutger gulped. "Pick your gun back up."

It was too late. Wiggins leapt onto his partner and they toppled over, smashing his head into the floor.

"Let him go!" Rutger cried. "Let him go right now, goddammit!" After the wet squelch of blunt force trauma, Rutger fired twice, catching the demonic Agent in the back. He exploded into a cloud of dust and the older man immediately bent down to check Johnson. No pulse.

"Baptiste here." A voice came out of the laptop. "Hello? Hello? Agent Johnson? Agent Wiggins?" Rutger slowly got to his feet, into view of the computer. A young man with kind confused eyes stared out at him. "Oh, hello Sir. Perhaps you can help me. I'm looking for two well dressed Agents who are nearby. Could you please let them know I'm on the line for them?"

"I'm… I'm sorry, but they are both dead." Rutger sighed.

"Did you kill them, Sir?" Baptiste raised an eyebrow.

"No. Well, maybe. Only one of them, possibly."

"Could you be a little more vague, Sir?"

"I'm sorry, been a hell of a day." Rutger sighed, not even irritated by the sarcasm from the polite man. "So these two showed up at my door, claiming to be from The Agency, whatever the hell that is. They wanted to know about the diner incident, and as I was laying it out for them one of them pulled a gun on me. I disarmed him, and a few seconds later he went crazy like the people at the diner and killed his partner. I kind of put him down after that, which caused him to explode in a puff of dust. So you can see my hesitation for taking the blame for killing them."

"I understand Sir," came the understanding reply, "and I do apologize for the position you currently find yourself in. My name is Baptiste. Who do I have the pleasure of speaking to?"

"Name's Rutger."

"Rutger, let me lay it out for you," Baptiste said. "There is a Pestilence Demon on the loose in your town, and you may be the only one who can stop it."

"Pestilence Demon?" Rutger scrubbed his hands down his face. "Are you shitting me?"

"No Sir, I am deadly serious."

"Okay." The ex Delta Force soldier nodded. What was even the point of resisting at this point? "I'm listening."

"Is this the demon from the diner?" Baptiste lifted a photo to the camera. The face was incredibly familiar, just a little less melted.

"Yeah I think…" Rutger bit his lip. "Only the guy I saw was a lot more fucked up."

"This is what we classify as a Pestilence Demon," Baptiste explained. "This particular one is named King Leper."

"King Leper? Really?" The older man didn't even know why he was surprised anymore.

"Yes, colorful I know." Baptiste nodded. "In a nutshell, Pestilence Demons are regular demons who have been unable to feed for many years, often decades. The lack of fresh souls causes the demon infestation to begin to eat itself. This

results in the demon looking like a
heavily infected leper.

"When they reach this status, they
can easily infect humans who breathe in
their shedding skin. Those humans become
deathly ill and completely under the
control of the Pestilence Demon that
infected them. To make matters worse, when
those infected are killed, they explode in
the poof of dust you witnessed, which is
also highly infectious.

"King Leper was dropped down a dried
up well back in the eighties that was
subsequently filled in. One of our
maintenance teams found that something had
dug itself out about a month ago, so we
were on the lookout. We had no idea he'd
be able to get this far."

"Holy hell." Rutger rubbed his
forehead. "That's a lot to take in."

"That's what yo momma said."

The older man blinked at his new
acquaintance. "Excuse me?"

"My apologies, Sir." Baptiste
coughed. "It's a reflex brought on by my
boss."

"Uh, it's cool, man." Rutger
shrugged.

"Now." The Agent recomposed himself.
"I have some questions for you. I need to
know your background. I need to find out
why you weren't infected."

"Kinda curious about that myself," Rutger replied. "Okay, well, I'm ex Delta Force, got dishonorably discharged back in two thousand and eight."

"May I ask why?"

"You want the company line?" Rutger rolled his eyes. "Or the real reason that nobody wants to believe?"

"Sir, I deal in a world where Pestilence Demons are a thing. Chances are I'll believe you."

"Fair enough," the ex soldier conceded with a nod. "My squad was at this Afghan outpost that was closer to the moon than anything resembling civilization. We got approached by some shady looking higher ups that were looking for a volunteer for a vaccine project.

"I guess the first red flag I should have picked up on was that they were doing this in the middle of a hot zone, but I was gung-ho about serving my country every way I could. So I volunteered.

"They took me to this compound built into the side of a mountain. Real complex science shit. There was this doctor, I think his name was Dr. Shultz, he injected me with this stuff, said it was to protect against bio-weaponry.

"I don't remember much over the next week as the stuff made me sicker than I've ever been. When I woke up, the facility was emptied out except for a few MP's and a four star. He thanked me for my service and said my sacrifice was invaluable and would save countless lives. He then informed me that my squad had been wiped out in an attack, and that I had two choices.

"They could take me back to the site and burn me with the rest of my squad, or they could claim I was a deserter, get a dishonorable discharge, and go into exile for several years. They needed a plausible cover story as to why I wasn't with them during the attack, so I chose the latter and spent several years honing my skills in the orient… but that's another story."

"It's all making sense," Baptiste replied. "Dr. Schultz is a highly regarded scientist that was using demon artifacts as a way to combat other conditions. Whatever bio-toxin he was using you to develop a vaccine for must have made you immune to the Pestilence Demon. In fact, it's possible his testing on you helped develop the vaccine we use for our own agents."

"If you have a vaccine, then why did this guy go batshit crazy?" Rutger asked.

"Unfortunately the vaccine has a short half-life, so each injection only gives a few days worth of protection," Baptiste explained. "Whatever concoction he gave you ended up being more permanent, apparently."

"Well, great, mystery solved." Rutger shrugged. "So I got a question for you."

Baptiste nodded. "Okay."

"What the fuck am I supposed to do now?" The ex-soldier's voice raised an octave in volume. "I have this King Leper asshole running around my town turning people into pestilence zombies."

"Well, normally we have a lengthy review process before bringing someone into The Agency, but given your military service and the fact you're all I have at the moment, allow me to be the first to officially welcome you to The Agency." Baptiste smiled brightly.

Rutger deadpanned. "Yay."

"Okay, now that we have that taken care of, the next question: do you have weapons?"

"I'm ex Delta Force and live in rural America, what do you think?" Rutger scoffed.

"Please disregard the previous question," Baptiste corrected. "Once you are armed you need to figure out a way to dissolve King Leper."

"Dissolve him? Can I just pop this motherfucker in the head and call it a day?"

"Well you can, but it won't stop him." The Agent shook his head. "Bullets have little effect on demons this powerful."

"So. Dissolving it is, then."

"Yes, dissolve." Baptiste nodded. "His flesh is the contagious part, so if you can destroy that we'll be good to go."

"Will dismemberment work?" Rutger inquired. "I saw him break off his pinky finger and use it to infect people."

"Unfortunately no, as Pestilence Demons can attach new flesh," Baptiste replied. "It isn't instantaneous, but after a few days the new limb will be ready to infect."

"What about fire?" Rutger mused.

"As a last resort, this could buy some time," Baptiste acquiesced. "Normal fire just isn't going to be hot enough to melt away the flesh. So unless you are able to make some thermite all it would do is immobilize him for a bit."

"Fantastic."

"So, what do you have in town?" Baptiste asked.

"There's a hardware store, and that's about it."

"If they have hydrofluoric acid that would work best."

"Dude, it's a small town." Rutger threw his hands up. "We're lucky if we have more than two beer brands to pick from."

"The next best option is lye. It's a slow burn, but if you can trap him somehow it will do the trick."

"Great, so the plan is to find some lye, put it in a barrel, and chop a Pestilence Demon into tiny bits and throw him in while avoiding his infected army of the damned who all want to kill me," Rutger summarized flatly.

"Good, you understand your mission." Baptiste nodded.

"So what do I do about the infected?"

"Whatever you deem necessary." The Agent said gravely. "They are infected and are going to die in a matter of days. If you are able to start the dissolving process on King Leper, they won't be mind controlled any longer, but they'll be gone by the weekend."

"So there's nothing that can be done for them?" Rutger asked, incredulous. "I mean I'm not a huge fan of the assholes in this town, but they don't deserve to go out like that."

"I'm sorry, but there is no known cure."

"Just make me a promise." Rutger held up a finger. "If I help you take this motherfucker down, you will do what you can for them."

"You have my word, sir," Baptiste promised.

"Good enough for me."

"Okay, before you go, look inside the Agent's bag," Baptiste instructed. "There should be an earpiece."

Rutger rummaged around in the discarded duffel bag and produced a small black earpiece that he held up to the laptop in question.

"This will allow me to keep in touch with you," Baptiste explained. "I'm going to be sending you some assistance. I have an Agent and a new recruit nearby and I think they can be useful."

"Just make sure they take their vaccines," Rutger warned. "I don't want to be cleaning up another dust pile."

"Will do." Baptiste nodded. "Contact me with status updates or any questions." The new Agent nodded and shut the laptop. He pushed the earpiece into his right ear and turned to enter the den. He grasped the edge of a specific bookcase and shoved it out of the way, revealing his weapons stash.

After strapping on his ninja sword, a handgun with fresh clips, and an assault rifle with a mid and long range swappable scope, he sighed.

"Some days I wonder if I shouldn't have taken the first option….

CHAPTER FOUR

The crickets were out in full force
that night, nature unperturbed by the
demon activity all around it. As Rutger
parked his truck in the bushes on the side
of the highway and hopped out, he vaguely
wondered if the Pestilence dust would have
any effect on animals or insects. He was
quite sure that he didn't want to find
out. Bleeding murderous swarms of crickets
were not on his bucket list that night;
though neither were bleeding murderous
swarms of townsfolk either.

He ducked down the ATV path that
would lead him back into town, under the
cover of brush and darkness. He moved at a
brisk pace, not quite a run but faster
than a jog, weapons slung around him and
fingers firmly on the handgun. He froze
at the sight of two silhouettes in the
moonlight down the path, and ducked and
rolled quickly into the bushes.

Rutger stood up behind a thick tree
and peeked around it, getting a closer
look at two boil covered faces. He raised
the gun, but then thought better of it.
The noise might attract unwanted
attention; he needed to be stealthy. He
holstered the nine millimeter and
unsheathed the long sword on his back. His
back pressed to the tree trunk, he waited

for the mindless drones to shuffle past
him.

As soon as they were level with his
hiding tree, Rutger burst out onto the
path. He put his first opponent into a
headlock and then plunged the sword right
through the head of the second. The
impaled zombie flopped over, taking the
sword with it so that it swayed back and
forth upright, as if somebody had driven
it into the ground like a signpost.

Rutger spun and and shoved the
headlocked figure into the tree, snatching
up his sword and lunging forward in a
flash to bury it into his opponent's gut.
The infected man growled at him, seemingly
unaffected by the stabbing, and the ex
soldier sliced upwards, gutting his enemy
from belly button to chin. Guts spilled
everywhere, wet organs slapping against
tree leaves, and the creature finally
fell.

Rutger stepped back out onto the path
and wiped the blade clean of blood on the
first dead guy's shirt. He sighed and
sheathed the sword, resuming his combat
walk with the handgun back towards town.

The hardware store wasn't too
difficult to get to through the back
alleys. He had to stop and duck a few
times to avoid being seen by passing
infected, but soon he reached the fire

escape in the back and climbed to the top of the two story building. He jogged to the front sign, staying low, and sank down on his haunches under cover.

He peeked through the hole in one of the A's, and was surprised at the flurry of activity down on the street. A few dozen of King Leper's mind slaves were moving bodies off of the road into a considerable pile on the street corner. Others were loading goods into several waiting cars.

He tapped his earpiece and produced a set of binoculars, squatting behind the A to get a better look.

"Baptiste, you there?" he whispered.

"Yes, what's the situation?" Baptiste replied immediately.

"It's a fucking war zone down here," Rutger said. "Bodies are everywhere, and those infected zombie things are looking incredibly busy."

"Might I inquire as to what they are doing?" So polite, even in times of crisis.

"They are packing up cars," Rutger explained, examining the cars with his binoculars. "There are half a dozen large sedans in the middle of the street. I can't be certain but it looks like they are putting gas cans in the trunk. What the hell are they trying to do? Make the world's wimpiest car bomb?"

"If only that were the case," Baptiste sounded apologetic. "No, I fear his plan is much more sinister."

"Well, out with it," Rutger prompted. "What am I up against?"

"Do you want the good news or the bad news first?"

"Wait." The ex-soldier blinked. "There's good news in all of this?"

"Of sorts," Baptiste replied. "If I'm correct in my thinking, twenty-five or thirty of the infected are going to be driving off in the near future. So the good news is you'll have less of them to deal with."

"Almost afraid to ask how that equates to bad news."

"Your hesitation is well founded, Sir." The Agent paused. "I fear as though his plan is to start a pandemic."

"How the hell is he going to do that with only a couple dozen goons?"

"There are two major cities within a few hours drive of your current location," Baptiste explained. "The infected will be able to get there before dawn and find their way to the ventilation system of high rise buildings."

"And let me guess, this King Leper asshole can command them to shoot themselves in the head." Rutger's head felt light.

"That is correct," Baptiste confirmed. "In a matter of moments, twenty-five infected become an army of twenty-five thousand. From there, untold thousands will die every hour until the King is dealt with."

"So, a ticking time bomb." Rutger let out a low humorless chuckle. "This day just keeps getting better and better."

"I have faith in you, Sir."

"Well, that makes one of us," Rutger retorted. The zombies finished packing up their cars, hopped inside, and peeled out down the road. "They're on the move, so the clock is officially ticking."

"Can you make it to the hardware store?" Baptiste inquired.

"I'm on the roof," Rutger replied, "I'm going to head down and see what I can find."

"Contact me as soon as you can," the attache said. "I will also update your backup, Nantz, on your current location."

"Got it. Rutger out." He tapped the earpiece to end the call and jogged back over to the ladder to climb down. As soon as his boots hit the asphalt he ducked behind a dumpster to avoid a few more passing zombies. He darted back into the alleyway once the coast was clear, and slithered along the side wall to the main road.

Upon jiggling the handle of the front door of the hardware store, Rutger found it locked—of course. He glanced over his shoulder to make sure there were no infected townspeople nearby and then slammed his elbow into the glass.

The old door shattered to pieces, and he flinched at the loud clatter that echoed across the streets. There was a scream around the corner.

"Shit." Rutger dove through the broken door, ducking behind a display of ninety-nine cent duct tape. He stared through one of the rolls as three zombies bustled inside, and then branched off, each taking an aisle.

He drew his gun and held his breath as one of them approached, a twenty something man with fists clenched, blood streaming down his face to stain his plaid shirt. Just as Rutger aimed his gun through one of the duct tape rolls, the shelving unit behind him groaned and fell towards him.

He dropped his hands and ducked low, abandoning his shot to keep his head from getting crushed. The shelving unit caught on a support beam above, raining various small boxes of screws and washers down on him. The plaid guy dove into the shelf tunnel, causing Rutger to kick backwards, scrambling as best he could on his ass to get out the other side. He dodged arms shooting down through the shelves at him from above, one of the infected enemies having climbed up on top to try to get at him.

As he got to the opening at the end of the shelf tunnel, a pair of arms grasped him around the chest. "Oh no you don't," Rutger warned, pointing his gun directly over his shoulder to blow the face off of his captor. Brains splattered all over the ceiling, smacking into the face of the overall-wearing woman leaping from atop the tunnel at him.

He aimed and caught her in the shoulder as plaid guy rushed him, tackling him to the ground. The gun clattered away and Rutger grunted, bringing his knee up into his attacker's stomach. He flipped him up over his head, following the momentum to land on top of him, curling one of his legs around the back of plaid guy's neck. He squeezed his calves together, applying as much pressure as he could to the wriggling infected towns boy.

"Come on. Come on…" Rutger grunted, pressing harder until there was a satisfying *snap* as plaid guy's neck snapped in two. The body went limp and the ex-Delta got to his feet with a groan, stepping over to retrieve his gun. As he holstered it, he turned and realized the woman in the overalls slowly regaining her footing.

"Really?" Rutger sighed. "You couldn't just stay down?" As she opened her mouth to shriek at him, he unsheathed his sword and brought it down in a fluid motion, taking off the top left half of her head. A wimpy moan left her mouth as she joined her comrades on the floor and Rutger sheathed his sword, shaking his head at the carnage.

"Alright, let's find that lye," he muttered to himself, and turned on his heel. He pulled his assault rifle, knees bent as he crept down the paint aisle to the back of the store. Against the back wall a bright yellow SALE sticker advertised an empty lye shelf. He groaned softly, but raised the rifle at the sound of shuffling behind the rubber strips separating the main room from the storeroom.

He nosed the tip of the rifle between two strips and gently eased it to the side, peeking in at the sound of spraying water. His blood turned to ice at the sight of two infected townspeople dumping what looked like the last jug of lye down into a floor drain and washing it down with a hose.

"No!" He screamed and pulled the trigger, riddling the two zombies with bullets in his desperation. They flew backwards, the hose slapping the concrete floor like a nail in the coffin as Rutger hurried forward to see if they'd gotten it all. He lifted every jug and they were all empty, his heart pounding harder with each light canister. He threw the last one against the wall in frustration, letting out a sharp yell.

"Sorry to disappoint you," a cracked voice rasped from the shadows. Rutger took a step back, raising the rifle as King Leper himself emerged into the flickering fluorescent light of the storeroom.

"Oh, so you can speak," he snapped, while taking stock of his options. The rubber curtain was just about as far behind him as the loading bay doors on the far side.

"Some," his demonic enemy slurred. "It's been a long time since I've had the need."

"Well, don't get too comfortable because you aren't going to need it very long," Rutger warned, preparing his stance to fire. King Leper simply chuckled, a lilting ghastly sound that gave the ex-Delta pause. He furrowed his brow and the nose of the rifle dropped a touch, as he

strained his ears to see what the demon
was laughing at.

It was an odd standoff, with a gunman
and an unarmed smirking pestilence demon,
the former very unsettled and ready to be
done with it. Nothing happened.

Rutger peppered a few shots into King
Leper's torso, and the bullets whipped
straight through in little *poofs* of dust.

"Shit," he pursed his lips, lowering
the gun in disdain. "Well, that didn't
work."

"No." The demon grinned, showing a
toothless decaying smile. "It didn't." He
took in a sharp ragged breath and let out
a piercing scream, a high pitched shriek
that was a hell of a lot stronger than the
harsh rasp of his speaking voice.

The loading bay doors flung open and
a huge pack of infected townspeople
bustled inside, as if on call. Rutger
backed up towards the rubber curtained
doorway, unloading more bullets wildly
across the throng of attackers. Bodies
dropped in puffs of dust, but many were
still in pursuit as he dove through the
curtain.

He ran full tilt for the front of the
store, slinging the rifle back over his
shoulder so he could pump his arms faster.
He leapt through the broken glass of the
front door, and skidded into the middle of

the street. A small infected army ran towards him, about fifty yards away, and he blinked dumbly in shock until the crunch of the hardware store's front door being ripped from its hinges startled him.

He turned on his heel and sprinted down the street in the opposite direction of the horde, blood pounding in his ears and almost drowning out the sound of a roaring car engine. He looked over his shoulder to see a dark blue sedan crash through the army and speed towards him, a zombie clinging to the roof. It skidded to a stop next to him, and he drew his handgun, popping the infected woman in the forehead.

The windows rolled down and a well built guy with brown hair leaned over, eyes wild. "What are you waiting for?" he cried. "Get in!"

"Right!" Rutger dove headfirst into the back passenger window as his savior hit the gas, leaving tire tracks on the asphalt as the townspeople screamed after them.

"You okay?" the driver asked, glancing into the rearview mirror at the shell shocked looking ex-soldier.

Rutger just blinked at him. "What?"

"Are you okay?" he asked again, raising his eyebrows with impatience.

"Oh yeah." The bewildered man threw his hands up. "Just peachy. Just been a long evening of gunning down my neighbors because they've turned into pestilence demon infected zombies. You know, the usual."

"Yeah, Baptiste filled me in on the details." The driver waved him off. "Were you able to get the lye?"

Rutger barked a laugh, motioning to the empty backseat. "Did you see me jump in with an armful of shopping bags?" He narrowly missed hitting the back of the passenger seat with his face as his rescuer slammed on the brakes, the car screeching to a halt.

"Where is the lye?" He turned right around in his seat, face stern.

"It's gone."

"What do you mean it's *gone*?"

"I mean that King Leper asshole knew that's what I would be going for," Rutger snapped, chin jutting out. "So he had his minions dump it down the drain." The driver scrubbed a hand down his face, jaw clenched. He saw the horde still giving chase in the distance, and straightened in his seat, punching the gas again.

"We're in trouble," he said sternly.

"Gee, you think?" Rutger asked in exasperation. The brunette dug his cell phone out of his pocket, hitting a button and then tossing it on the passenger seat.

"Agent Nantz, have you made contact with Rutger yet?" A voice came through loud and clear, and the ex-Delta recognized it as Baptiste.

"Yeah, he's in the car with me," Nantz replied.

"I'm here, Baptiste," Rutger put in, clutching the seat back and leaning forward.

"Were you successful in your mission?" the attache asked.

"King Leper destroyed the lye before I got there," came the reply and a disappointed shake of the head.

"That is unfortunate." Baptiste clucked his tongue.

"So is it time for a fire drill?" Nantz cut in as he turned left onto a dirt road.

"I spoke with the Boss to authorize it should the mission fail, and he agreed it was the only option," the voice on the other end sounded regretful. "Unfortunately, the payload won't reach the town until an hour after his infection squad reaches civilization."

"Wait, what's a fire drill?" Rutger asked, putting up a hand.

"What sort of casualty projections are there?" Nantz ignored him, brow knit together.

"Conservative estimates have it at forty-five thousand," Baptiste replied.

"Hey, what's a fire drill?" Rutger tried to cut in again, throat beginning to constrict in panic.

"You going to have sweep teams ready?" the driver asked.

"They are en route as we speak," Baptiste assured him.

"What is a god*damn* fire drill?!" Rutger roared, slamming his fist down onto the center console. Nantz didn't even flinch, the only recognition a flick of his eyes into the rearview to meet his passenger's wild gaze.

"In a nutshell, we are going to have our attack choppers firebomb the fuck out of your small town," he explained. "Which will hopefully stun King Leper long enough for our sweep teams to locate him and get him put in a vat of acid."

"So that's it?" Rutger swallowed hard, hands clenched in his lap. "You're going to just burn a town full of people to ash?"

"I'm sorry Rutger, I know I said I would do what I could for your townspeople," Baptiste said with sincerity in his voice, "but without that lye we don't have much of an option."

"No, Baptiste, you gave me your word," the ex-Delta replied through clenched teeth. "That's a big difference. These people don't deserve to go out like that." He wanted to smash the door right out of the car he was so angry.

Nantz watched the passion in his passenger's face, and couldn't help but take pity on him. This was his town, his people. "Baptiste, how much time do we have before the birds get here?" he asked.

"You have four hours," came the reply.

"Alright Rutger, you heard the man," Nantz said with a nod. "We have four hours to do something. You know this town, so think. What can we use?" The ex-soldier met the Agent's gaze and he took a deep ragged breath, unclenching his fists. His eyes thanked his rescuer for the second chance, for suggesting they at least try.

A lightbulb went off in his head. "The high school!"

"Gonna have to be a little more specific there." Nantz furrowed his brow.

"The high school on the edge of town got shut down in the early nineties," Rutger explained. "The budget was cut and it was literally boarded up over the weekend. I had to spend half my senior year driving an hour away to another school just to graduate. That science lab was loaded up with chemicals, not to mention the janitor's closet. There's got to be some lye in there."

"So how are you going to lure him to the high school?" Baptiste inquired.

"We're going to have to make a pit stop," Rutger continued, "but I think I can get my hands on something that will attract his attention."

"Okay Baptiste, we're improvising," Nantz said firmly with a nod of his head. "We'll make contact in three hours to give you an update."

"Good luck gentleman," Baptiste bid farewell, and there was a click as he hung up the phone on his end.

Nantz slowed down a bit to take directions. "Okay Rutger, this is your show," he said. "Where are we off to?"

Rutger squared his shoulders. "How do you feel about militias?"

Rutger and Nantz walked up the last stretch of dirt road towards the compound, not wanting to startle the militia members into bombing an approaching car. The night air was much fresher outside of town, without the looming stench of pestilence laden flesh and blood.

"So how do you know these guys?" the Agent inquired as they strolled along the tree line.

"They know I'm ex-military, just like a lot of them are," Rutger began. "About three months ago, a couple of them confronted me when they heard about my supposed desertion. Needless to say they weren't happy with me. Thankfully the leader, Ronny, gave me a chance to explain myself."

"What did you tell them?" Nantz wondered.

"I mostly told them the truth." He shrugged. "I volunteered for medical experimentation, then after my unit was wiped out, the military fucked me over and made me out to be a deserter. Luckily these guys aren't huge fans of the federal government, so they welcomed me into their group."

"Wait." Nantz stopped short, turning to face his new comrade. "You're a member of this militia?"

"Oh, hell no." Rutger waved his hands back and forth in front of him. "I don't want anything to do with these anti-government nutwagons. I just remain acquainted with them because, well, I don't really have a lot of people who are friendly towards me. You never know when that friendliness might come in handy."

"Like now, you mean?" Nantz raised an eyebrow and continued walking.

Rutger nodded. "Like now."

The dirt in front of them suddenly exploded with gunfire, puffs of dry road shooting into the air. They immediately split apart and dove to either side of the road, taking cover behind the trees.

"Whoa, whoa!" Rutger yelled from his hiding spot. "What the hell, man?!" The area lit up as spotlights raked the area.

"You motherfuckers better get up on out of here!" A loud voice barked from atop a guard tower behind the eight foot fall fence at the end of the road.

"I'm Rutger!" the ex-Delta cried back. "I talked to Ronny a couple of hours ago and he told me to come up here!"

"I don't give a good god*damn* if you were a big titted stripper with a winning lotto ticket, you gonna get shot unless you get outta here!" the guard screamed down at them.

"Goddammit," Rutger grunted, and then raised his voice again. "Just go tell Ronny that Rutger is here!"

"Kiss my ass!" the guard barked back.

"You got any bright ideas, Nantz?" Rutger turned to look at his companion across the thin road.

"Yeah, I got one," Nantz admitted. "Now, you aren't going to freak out when you see some weird shit, are you?"

"Not sure if this day can get any freakier," his companion replied with a bewildered shrug.

"Well… you say that." The Agent sighed and removed a blue and black mask from his coat pocket. He began a low chant, in what sounded to Rutger like latin, and the fabric began to glow. It pulsed a deep blue color, growing brighter and brighter with the words, and then Nantz threw it up in the air where it froze.

The blue glow flashed and became the shape of a person, and then there was a person attached to the mask. He was a stocky muscular man in full on wrestling garb, and his feet hit the ground purposefully.

Rutger blinked, despite everything he'd seen that day, he hadn't been expecting *that*.

"You…" he stammered. "You had a Luchador in your pocket this entire time?"

"Don't worry." Nantz smirked. "I was happy to see you, too."

"Heh," Rutger chuckled, the tension dissipating from his shoulders. He knew he had to keep his cool; they were on a time limit. "So uh, how is he going to get past the gun happy guard over there?"

"BD, can you gently take out our friend over there?" Nantz asked.

"How gently?" The apparition wrestler replied with a question, and Rutger was surprised at the clarity of his voice. He'd been expecting an old rasp, maybe due to his demon exposure with King Leper.

"Just bruised," Nantz confirmed. "He's going to have a long night after we're gone."

"I'll take care of it," BD replied.

"BD?" Rutger asked.

"Blue Diablo," Nantz whispered as the wrestler stepped out from the tree line. He approached the gate, strolling towards it like he owned the place.

"You better stop right there!" the guard screamed, firing off a few shots near the newcomer's feet. It doesn't even faze him, and he continues his slow walk.

"Next shot is going right through your heart, you Mexican motherfucker!" the guard warned, but Blue Diablo continued to move forward. "I warned you!"

The guard fired a single round directly into the wrestler's chest. He stopped walking then, looked down at the wound that wasn't leaking even a single drop of blood, and then raised his gaze back up to the guard.

"Oh, shit." The guard blurted as Blue Diablo broke into a run. He disappeared and reappeared almost instantly at the top of the gate, landing a chop onto the surprised guard's exposed shoulder.

Rutger stepped out of the tree line, watching as the apparition—or at least, what he'd *thought* was an apparition—slammed his wrist down three more times, stunning and disarming the guard. He leapt and scissor kicked the guard in the head, sending him flying off the side of the tower to the road below.

Rutger and Nantz strolled up to the fallen guard.

"That… that was impressive," Rutger admitted. "Teleporting masked Mexican wrestlers. Wow. Where did you find him at?"

"Mexico," Nantz replied, and the ex-soldier shot him a pointed glare. He rolled his eyes and bent over, grabbing

the gate key from the guard's belt. He
unlocked it as the Agent grabbed their
fallen enemy under the armpits and dragged
him inside.

"It's probably best we bring him with
us," Nantz grunted as he moved.

"Even after he shot you and your
friend there?" Rutger raised an eyebrow,
holding the gate open.

"If the infected get here, they could
turn him," came the reply as the Agent
crossed the threshold. "Would rather have
him firing his weapon at them, than
fighting against us."

Rutger nodded. "Fair enough."

Nantz dropped the guard and turned to
make sure his companion was relocking the
gate, when a loud horn bleated. They
looked at each other wide eyed and then
saw the guard had woken up, and triggered
the compound's alarm on the wall above
him.

"You stupid asshole!" Rutger yelled.
"Turn that off before you get us all
killed!" Blue Diablo hurtled down from the
guard tower, landing his elbow directly
onto the alarm trigger, silencing it. The
momentum carried him down into the guard's
face, silencing him once again as well.

"Thanks for the assist, big guy,"
Rutger nodded to the wrestler, who simply
nodded back at him.

"We've got to hurry," Nantz urged. "That alarm will attract some unwanted attention."

"They are going to be in the main building over there." The ex-soldier pointed to the biggest building in the compound, a cement block amongst the huts.

"BD, go greet them for us, will you?" Nantz asked, and his partner teleported away from them. The two human companions headed towards the building at a brisk pace.

"Man, they are not going to be happy to see a Mexican wrestler," Rutger said, shaking his head with amusement. As if on cue, gunshots erupted inside, screaming permeating the night air through the windows of the main building. They drew their handguns and kicked open the front door, sweeping in simultaneously.

Bodies were strewn along the floor, Blue Diablo standing in the middle with two guys in a headlock, four more circling him with guns aimed. There was a flurry of movement as the two newcomers approached, everyone frozen in aiming weapons at everyone else.

"Whoa, whoa," Rutger said firmly. "Everybody calm down here."

"Rutger?" Ronny blurted, hair disheveled and eyes blazing. "What the fuck man? I thought we were cool?"

"Ronny we're cool, and I'm sorry for the rude introduction to my friends here," the ex-soldier said, sincerity lacing his tone. "But there's some shit going down and we don't have time for all of this." Ronny's dark eyes hardened as he chewed his lip, and then he lowered his gun, motioning to his guys to do the same. Blue Diablo let his prisoners go and they scurried behind Ronny, fear in their gazes.

"Alright man," the leader squared his shoulders, running a hand through his shaggy locks. "I'll give you the benefit of the doubt here. If you thought it necessary to bring a masked Mexican into my compound there's obviously something going on. So talk."

"First off," Rutger said, putting up a finger. "You need to get some guards on that gate, and they need to shoot anyone who comes close to it."

"Jack, David, Bobby, get up there," Ronny snapped his fingers, and three of his guys stood at attention.

"You boys have any sort of gas mask?" Nantz asked.

"We're prepared for anything," Ronny replied, almost sounding offended at the insinuation that he wouldn't have gas masks.

"Good," Nantz nodded. "Use them, and stay away from any dust coming from them."

"Man, what the hell are you guys into?" Ronny cocked his head, raising an eyebrow at Rutger. The ex-soldier and his Agent companion shared a glance, and the former nodded his head in understanding.

It's the government, man," he said, holding up his hands with a shrug. "They dropped something on the town that's making the citizens go crazy. It's highly contagious, which is why you need to shoot on sight."

"I fucking knew it, man!" Ronny cried. "Alright boys, let's show 'em what we can do!" He threw his fist in the air, and his militia sprang to action, scurrying about to grab weapons and equipment. The leader waved the newcomers to a quieter corner out of the way.

"Ronny, again I apologize for bursting in on you like that," Rutger said. "This is my friend Nantz."

"And that's my friend the Blue Diablo," Nantz added, and the wrestler in question simply grunted in greeting.

"If any of us are going to survive this, we're going to need some serious supplies," Rutger continued. "Can you help us out?"

"Let me see what we can do," Ronny replied with a nod. "Follow me." He led

them over to a large metal door, and
punched a ten digit code into the keypad
to the left of it. The door slid open by
itself, and the militia leader proudly led
them into a room full of military grade
weaponry.

"Welcome to the shop, boys," Ronny
spun around to face them, arms spread for
effect.

"Jesus Christ," both men breathed in
unison, and their host barked a laugh.

"I take it you approve?" he asked.

"Oh, yes," Rutger said with a nod.

"So what do you boys need?" Ronny
inquired.

"My friend Nantz could use a better
gun," the ex-soldier said, "and we'll
definitely need explosives."

"Gonna have to be more specific than
that." Ronny grinned toothily. "You need
grenades? C-4? Fertilizer bomb to take out
a city block?"

"Uh." Rutger scratched the back of
his head. "Ronny."

"Relax boys, I'm just fuckin' with
you," their host said good-naturedly.
"That bomb will take out a lot more than a
city block."

Rutger sighed. "I think some C-4
oughta do us."

"Back corner over there," Ronny
directed. "Take as much as you need.

Remote detonators are on the shelf beside it." He leaned on the doorframe, eyeing Blue Diablo, as the other two busied themselves in the corner.

"So what are you thinking?" Nantz asked quietly as they loaded up a bag.

"I'm thinking I'm definitely on a government list after making nice with these guys…" Rutger replied.

The Agent sighed. "I mean with our current situation."

"Well, I figure we get to the school, set a lye trap for King Leper, and have your teleporting Luchador friend plant some C-4 on the roof so that if everything goes to shit we can at least collapse it and trap that son of a bitch until reinforcements show up." Rutger took a deep breath to replace what he'd lost in his long winded explanation, and his partner paused.

"Not my first choice." Nantz shrugged. "But it's as good a plan as we're going to get. Let's load up." They finished packing the bags with explosives, and strutted back over to the door. Ronny held out a modified assault rifle to Nantz, who took it with a small smile.

"Here you go," their host said. "Best one I got. Full auto, hollow points, mid-range scope, and got you five full clips in addition to the one in there."

"Thanks Ronny," Nantz said as he checked it over, eyeing the scope. "This will do nicely."

"Glad to help out some patriots in their fight against the tyrannical government," Ronny replied with a grin. "You boys need anything else?"

"Yeah, you got any thermite?" Rutger piped up.

"Didn't they teach you chemistry in school?" Ronny chuckled. "It's just aluminum powder, magnesium and some run of the mill iron oxide. Or rust, if you will."

"Guess I played hooky that day," Rutger admitted.

"We should have the ingredients back at the lab." Ronny waved for them to follow him, but as they emerged from the armory they heard gunshots outside.

"That's our cue," Nantz said.

"Ronny, you got a truck we can use?" Rutger asked, and their host tossed him a set of keys.

"It's the blue one parked right outside," Ronny said.

"Alright, tell your men to keep firing and to be ready to open that gate in a hurry," Rutger instructed. "We're going to roll through them and draw them away from here." Ronny took the ex-soldier's hand in an arm wrestling

position and they shook, clapping one
another on the back.

"You got it, Rutger," their host
said. "You guys stuck your neck out for
us, so you survive this and you and your
friend are welcome here anytime." At this,
Blue Diablo grunted, and Ronny rolled his
eyes. "Eh, fuck it, him too."

"How far away is the school?" Nantz asked as he got into the passenger seat, Rutger buckling his seatbelt behind the wheel. There was a *thunk* as Blue Diablo hopped up into the truck bed behind them.

"Two, maybe two and a half miles," Rutger replied.

"If these infected follow us, it's not going to have us much time to get set up," the Agent mused.

"I'm open to ideas on how to stall them," his companion said, raising an eyebrow. Nantz reached into the bag of explosives and revealed a small block of C-4. He unrolled the window and stuck his head and arm out, addressing his masked friend.

"Hey, BD, think you can attach this to one of the infected as we go by?" he asked.

"Does he have to survive the attachment?" Blue Diablo asked gruffly.

"If he does, he won't be alive for very long." Nantz shrugged.

"Leave this window open," the Luchador replied.

"Okay then, I guess we have a plan," Rutger nodded, and honked the horn. He unrolled his own window and waved at the militia leader. "Ronny, your guys ready?" he asked.

"You're good to go!" Ronny gave him a thumbs-up, and then raised his other hand, shooting a bright orange flare into the night sky. This signaled the gatekeepers, and Rutger floored the gas pedal.

The tires spun for a moment on the dirt before gaining traction and the truck leapt forward towards the gate. One gatekeeper pulled open the door just in time, the other laying covering fire. The open door revealed a hundred or so infected townspeople, pale skin and bleeding eyes, momentarily frozen from the flare exploding. Their attention turned back to the gate just in time for the front bumper of the big blue truck to make impact.

Bodies flew left and right as the truck plowed through, and Blue Diablo wasted no time leaning over, using the open window as a handhold to snatch a zombie. As his hand tightened around a throat, he used the momentum of the speeding truck to flip the infected up onto the roof of the truck, head hanging towards him.

The zombie wriggled in his grip, but was no match for the Luchador, who shoved the block of C-4 right down its throat. When the truck crested the throng, Rutger

put thirty yards of distance between them
before slowing down, and Blue Diablo
tossed the explosive infected into the
middle of the road.

Nantz watched, and as the mass of
zombies stepped over their fallen comrade,
he detonated it, sending bodies flying
everywhere.

"That should buy us some time," he
declared as Rutger floored the gas again,
speeding towards the school.

It didn't take long to get there, and
they parked around the side of the
building, not wanting their potential
getaway to be in the line of fire. As they
got out of the vehicle, Nantz tossed a
block of C-4 into the bed of the truck.

"Just in case," he said as they
started to walk.

"Well, on the off chance we survive
this," Rutger replied, "just remember to
take that out before we hit the road."

"One step at a time," Nantz said.

"So, how are we going to lure King
Leper here?" the ex-soldier asked.

"He knows we're a threat, which is
why he send that army of infected after us
at the compound," Nantz explained. "So
don't worry, he'll show up."

"And if he doesn't?" Rutger raised an
eyebrow.

"Fire drill," the Agent said somberly.

"How much time we got?" his companion asked.

"Just over an hour," Nantz informed him as they busted the lock on the front door. In the lobby, they turned to each other.

"I'm going to hit the science lab," Rutger said. "You should probably head to the gym and get the charges set. At least there if you have to blow the building, you'll have a few seconds before the debris crashes down on top of you."

"Why don't you give Baptiste a call, and BD and I will get the party favors set?" Nantz nodded.

"See you on the other side," Rutger replied, and then turned to run towards the science lab. It was weird being back in this school after all this time, but he still remembered where everything was. He pressed on his earpiece as he reached the lab door.

"Rutger, I do hope that you come bearing good news." Baptiste's voice filtered into his ear.

"Well, it's not entirely bad," Rutger said.

"I shall take what I can get," came the reply. "Report."

"I'm headed to the science lab at the high school, and Nantz and the masked Luchador are planting C-4 charges on the ceiling of the gym," Rutger explained. "Worst case we are going to make a last stand here and trap the King so your boys can dispose of him properly." He rummaged through the chemical storage room, looking for anything they could use.

"They will be there within the hour, but if you are unable to break his spell over the infected I fear the damage will be catastrophic," Baptiste said. "We've already had a report of a night security guard being attacked at a high rise office building and there is currently a standoff."

"Goddammit!" Rutger cursed. "Am I really asking for too much today?"

"I take it they don't have lye?" Baptiste asked.

"Or acid, or much of fucking anything," the ex-soldier grunted.

"Read off to me what you have at your disposal and let's see if we can't come up with a viable alternative," the voice in the earpiece suggested.

"Okay, I've got sodium, lithium, aluminum powder, magnesium…" Rutger trailed off, a niggling thought in the back of his brain.

"Rutger?" Baptiste prompted. "Are you okay?"

"I just need to find some rust and I can make that thermite," he remembered. "I just need to know how to combine and detonate it."

"I can walk you through it," Baptiste confirmed, and before he could reply, the sound of machine gun fire echoed through the building.

"Give me the nickel version," Rutger urged.

"Okay, you need to do a 27 to 80 ratio mixture of-"

"I said nickel!"

"Fine…" Baptiste sighed. "Do a three to one mixture of the aluminum powder and rust, and use a magnesium strip as a fuse. Light it and stand back."

"There you go!" Rutger appraised, and grabbed the ingredients he needed. He turned and kicked a rusted old shelf, smashing at it with his boot until it shattered. He dumped the aluminum powder into the pile, and then took off out of the lab as more gunfire sounded.

Nantz stood in the gymnasium doors, popping off rounds into infected townsfolk as they entered into the school lobby.

"How you doing, Blue?" he called over his shoulder.

"One more!" Blue Diablo replied, teleporting to the last rafter to set the final charge.

"Good, because I'm going to need help down here!" Nantz cried as he unloaded the final clip into a pack of zombies tearing into the school. He dropped the now-useless weapon and drew his handgun and a detonator.

Infected townsfolk poured into the building like a tsunami, and he hit the detonator on channel one, blowing up the truck outside. Body parts fly into the school lobby, but Nantz slammed the door shut before he could see any more, blocking out the group still rushing towards him. The far door of the gym burst open, revealing another slew of infected villagers, and they tore across the basketball court to get to him.

Blue Diablo dropped out of the rafters and landed in center court, laying haymakers all around like a tag team partner on a hot tag. Bodies fell but didn't burst into dust, and Nantz started to lose his footing against the door.

"I can't hold 'em!" he cried, and the Luchador swiveled to look him in the eye.

"Hide," he said firmly, and his partner let go of the door, sprinting beneath the bleachers. As he reached the tangled mass of metal bars, he fired back

over his shoulder once, catching one of
the townsfolk in the arm. He dove through
the bars, dodging and chopping around
beneath the bleachers to avoid getting
hit. His movement was limited, but so was
theirs. He hoped his new friend was faring
better.

Rutger skidded around the corner
towards the lobby, stopping short at the
sight of infected swarming down the
hallway towards the gym. He dropped into a
crouch and fired, unloading a clip at knee
height to try to penetrate deep into the
throng.

This disabled some, but drew the
attention of a lot more, and they started
to march towards him before stopping
short. Rutger stood up straight,
adrenaline pumping, as the front doors to
the school opened.

In strolled King Leper himself, and
the ex-soldier grinned wildly.

"Hey, King Douche," he said
triumphantly. "Come and get me."

The King snapped his fingers and half
a dozen infected barreled past him to give
chase, the high Leper himself strolling
casually behind. "Rip him apart," he said.

Rutger ducked back around the corner
towards the science lab, leaving the door
open behind him. As soon as the zombies

tumbled in, they were met with a volley of
bullets, exploding into dust. Three more
enter through the cloud, and the loud
click of Rutger's empty gun caused them to
scream in amusement.

He tossed the empty gun at the middle
attacker, causing just enough of a
distraction for him to draw his sword. He
slid by, slicing right through the
zombie's waist, the top half of it
flopping over as it went *poof*.

The one to the left leapt at him,
throwing a punch, but its fist met sword,
the arm like a sheath as Rutger slid it in
until the hilt hit knuckles. The other
tried to get at him from the back, but he
reeled his leg in a fierce roundhouse kick
to the face. He grasped the infected's
hair and brought its throat down on his
knee twice, and then caught it in a choke
hold when the first one swung with its
sword fist.

Rutger managed to dodge the blow,
grabbing the handle as he snapped the neck
of the infected in his arm. He spun around
in a slicing arc, taking off the zombie's
head. The dust settled, revealing King
Leper standing in the doorway.

"Well, it's about time your royal
highness showed up," Rutger said, leaning
on his sword casually. "Why are you

sending all these town folks out to do your dirty work?"

"They are beneath me," King Leper rasped in that chalky dead voice. "Just as you are beneath me."

"Royalty, modest, and man that complexion." Rutger grinned. "You must be a hit with the ladies."

The demon threw off his shawl, revealing a grotesque body of rotting flesh. Lesions and boils littered his skin, cracked and flaking with crusted pus. The scent of death and decay hit Rutger in the face like a freight train and he turned to heave, his stomach trying to expel what little was inside of it.

At that moment, King Leper lunged forward, catching him in the chest with his rotten fist. Rutger flew backwards, a desk crunching beneath him, sword skittering away across the floor. He got up slowly just in time to see the pestilence riddled fist coming at his face, and he dodged, catching the King at the wrist.

Rutger flung his body back with all his might, pulling his enemy to the ground with him and putting a knee in his back, wrenching the arm back. Normally this would break an arm or pop a shoulder, but the ex-soldier was surprised when the arm just came right off of the body.

King Leper used the shock to slither
out from beneath his foe, jumping up into
a fighting stance. Rutger raised the arm
like a baseball bat, and smashed him
across the face with it. It was a
sufficient weapon to beat the owner of the
arm with, and after a quick and brutal
beat down, he finally manages to smack the
King in the back of the head, knocking him
to the floor.

Rutger stepped on the other shoulder,
and broke off the other arm, swinging his
prizes around as he strolled over to his
sword. His enemy screamed in anger and
frustration, managing to stumble to his
feet and stagger to the door.

"Nuh, uh, where do you think you're
going?" Rutger asked, and flung one of the
limbs towards its master, catching the
King in the back of the knee. The demon
tumbled to the ground in a heap, and the
sound of shrieks echoed down the hallway.

Rutger stepped over the now armless
demon and peeked out the door, seeing
another pack of infected running towards
him.

"You just don't quit, do you?" He
sighed.

"I have legions of followers who will
never stop pursuing you," King Leper said
with a sneer. "There is nothing you can
do."

Rutger shut the door and clicked the deadbolt. "Well, you say that," he said, as the throng banged on the locked door. "While I'm sure they would eventually get in here, they aren't going to have the time." He brought his sword down on the King's ankles, severing his feet in one fell swoop. "You wait here, stumpy."

He crossed to the pile of rust and aluminum scooping up a hefty amount of it in an empty glass jar. He grabbed the magnesium strip and returned to the King, who was trying to get up on his stumps to reach the door. Rutger grabbed his shirt collar and pushed him down onto his back.

"You know, if you weren't such a scum sucking demon from hell, I might actually give you some props for your effort." He grinned. "But given how you wiped out my entire town with your plague dandruff, I'm not going to give you the satisfaction."

"Talk, talk, talk…" King Leper rasped, rolling his crusty eyes. "That's all you can do to me boy. You don't have anything that can kill me."

"Well, you say that," Rutger repeated, and held up the jar. The demon squinted at it, and his pox riddled brows furrowed in concern just as the ex-soldier plunged his sword into his chest.

He dragged the blade down, and then stabbed again, dragging it back across to make a deep X in King Leper's torso. He swirled the sword around in a circle as if he were churning butter inside the demon's chest cavity, and then admired the hole he'd created as he lifted the jar again.

"Now see, this here is what we call thermite," Rutger explained as he nestled the jar into the putrid smelling crater. "I didn't have the best education, oddly enough in this very classroom, so I'm not entirely sure what's going to happen when I set this thing off." He inserted the magnesium fuse and pulled a zippo lighter out of his back pocket. "All I know is that I'm going to be on the other side of the room when it happens."

The demon muttered unintelligible words that sounded like they could be curses in another language as Rutger lit the strip's end. He flicked the zippo closed, and at the *click*, King Leper started to squirm as violently as he could.

"You can call me The Doctor." Rutger raised his hands as he backed up into the far corner of the room. "Because I just cured this whole motherfuckin' town!"

Magnesium hit powder and the thermite ignited, casting a bright red glow across the room. Rutger watched, wide eyed, as the demon melted down into a puddle of bulbous goo, smoke curling off of him

417

instead of skin flakes. His rasping curses dissipated, only the fizzle of the metal melting concoction echoing as what was left of King Leper melted away.

Rutger touched his earpiece, waiting for the telltale click of someone on the other end.

"Yo Baptiste," he said jovially. "The King has been usurped. You can call off the fire drill."

"Was the thermite successful?" came the voice on the other end.

"He's currently a puddle of flaming goo on the floor," Rutger replied, waving his hand in front of his face to try to waft away the smell.

"And the infected?" Baptiste asked.

"Well, they stopped banging on the door, so I'm going to assume that's a good sign." Rutger shrugged.

"If they've stopped attacking, then his control has been broken," the attache acknowledged.

"You're going to keep your word now, right?" the ex-soldier asked, a note of warning in his tone.

"Yes Rutger, I'm dispatching transport trucks to your location now," Baptiste said.

"Thank you," Rutger replied, shoulders slumping with relief at the sincerity in the man's voice.

"It's my pleasure," Baptiste replied. "I was wondering if I could ask one more thing of you."

Rutger scoffed. "Haven't I done enough today?"

"You most certainly have, Sir," Baptiste said quickly, "and if you decline my request I will certainly understand."

"Okay," the ex-soldier sighed, "shoot."

"Would you please accompany Nantz back to our storage facility?" Baptiste asked. "I would like to speak to you in person."

"Oh shit, Nantz!" Rutger cried, heart skipping a beat.

"Rutger?"

"Yeah, oh fuck," he cursed, and readied his sword, striding to the lab door. "I just remembered that Nantz and that Blue Diablo guy were facing off against a couple hundred of those infected. I need to go check on them."

"And my request?" Baptiste asked hopefully.

"I'll see you in a few hours," Rutger promised.

"Very good," came the reply, and then *click*.

Rutger took a deep breath and unlocked the deadbolt, inching the door open to peek out. At the sight of confused and weak looking townsfolk strewn about, he rushed into the hallway.

"What… what is going on?" one man groaned, hissing at the pain of trying to stand up.

"It's hard to explain," Rutger replied gently, putting a placating hand up. "Just trust me, stay here and don't move. Everything is going to be okay." He strode past them, sheathing his sword so as not to startle anyone, and rounded the corner to head towards the gymnasium.

The hallway was lined with dozens of sick people, leaning on each other and moaning, some crying. A few were staggering about, calling for their loved ones, not knowing how they'd gotten there.

"Folks, I'm Rutger," the ex-soldier called loudly as he walked through the crowd. "Most of you know me, and well, most of you don't like me. Be that as it may, some serious shit went down in this town and you were all affected. Actually, infected. You are all very, very sick." He was halfway down the hallway, and the murmurs amongst the townspeople rose into more agitated concern. "Everybody please calm down, help is on the way. I just need everyone to remain calm and stay where they are."

"Why?" a woman shrieked from behind him.

"What's happening?" A man on the floor tried to grab at Rutger's leg on the way by.

"Why aren't you sick like us?" another man asked, voice wavering with fear and confusion.

"Everyone!" Rutger reached the gym doors and turned around, putting his hands up again to stop the rabble. "Please, I will explain everything shortly."

He ducked into the gym, eyes nearly popping out of his head at the mass of bodies squirming in pain. They'd clearly been littered about by the Luchador standing tall in the center of them mayhem.

"Holy hell Blue," Rutger said, bewildered. "This place looks like a bomb went off at the Royal Rumble."

"I'm good at what I do," Blue Diablo replied proudly, arms crossed over his considerable chest.

"Nantz!" Rutger called, head swiveling around. "You still with us?" The Agent climbed out from under the bleachers, raising his hand.

"Yeah, I'm here," he greeted. "Going to need some help over here, though. Got some injured people trapped beneath the bleachers."

They approached each other and Rutger nodded, not wanting to verbally admit how happy he was to see his new friend alive.

"So, I'm guessing you were able to get him dissolving in some lye?" Nantz inquired.

"Thermite, actually," Rutger replied. "He's a puddle of goo and won't be a threat to anyone anymore."

"Rutger, you've done a hell of a job here," the Agent scratched the back of his head. "I'd hate to think where we'd be without you. At the very least, Baptiste would have burned this city to the ground." His eyes widened. "Oh fuck, I gotta call that off!"

"Relax, I called him as the King was going up in flames," Rutger said.

Nantz smiled. "I'm sure he appreciated the news."

"I assume so," the ex-soldier said with a shrug. "He wants me to accompany you back to the storage facility, whatever the hell that is. Says he wants to talk to me in person."

"Alrighty then," Nantz replied, nodding. "As soon as the cleanup crew gets here, we'll see about hijacking a chopper and heading in."

"Sounds like a plan, especially since you blew up Ronny's truck." Rutger grinned.

"Think he'll be upset about that?"
Nantz raised an eyebrow.

"Nah." Rutger waved him off. "Knowing
those boys, they're probably already,
ahem, acquiring some new transportation
from some of the unguarded homes in the
area.

Nantz chuckled. "Yeah… you're totally
on a government list now."

EPILOGUE

The storage facility looked like somebody had turned a distribution warehouse into a military grade bunker. As the helicopter lowered onto the landing pad, Rutger noticed a dark skinned man in a pristine white lab coat approaching from one of the bay doors. He held a clipboard and a pen, looking ever the part of secret agency scientist.

As he and Nantz dismounted the helicopter, the blades slowed and they approached the young attache on the walkway.

"Nantz, Rutger," Baptiste greeted them, shaking each hand in turn. "Glad you survived this ordeal relatively unscathed."

"Yeah, me too," Nantz replied, running a hand through his hair. "Been a hell of a few days."

"I can imagine, Nantz," Baptiste agreed. "Why don't you go get some rest before writing up your report? I'd like to discuss some things with Rutger."

Nantz nodded, and turned to his new friend, extending his hand. "It's been a pleasure," he said, eyes tired but sincere. "Hope to work with you again."

"If it does come to that," Rutger replied and shook the Agent's hand, "hopefully it will be on a project that's a little less funky."

Nantz barked a laugh. "Probably not in this line of work." He shot Baptiste a little salute and strode into the building.

The attache opened his mouth, but Rutger put up his hand to stop him from speaking.

"Okay Baptiste," he said firmly, "before you give me your pitch or whatever you wanted to talk to me about, I want to know what's going to happen to the sick people in my town."

"Fair enough," came the reply. "Please follow me." He started down the walkway, leading the ex-Delta into the facility, where a golf cart waited for them. He got into the driver's seat, and shot Rutger an expectant look. His companion reluctantly got into the passenger seat, looking around the concrete hallway.

"This facility is six hundred thousand square feet with multiple levels of security," Baptiste began as he pushed the gas, propelling them into a massive room full of steel boxes. "There are resident quarters, training facilities, a vault for various demon artifacts, and one of the most advanced laboratories in the world. Deep in the heart of this facility is our storage unit, where we keep the most dangerous demons we come across but have no way of disposing of. For most of them we put them into a deep freeze, which not only keeps them contained but gives our scientists the ability to draw blood and tissue samples for testing."

"So you can figure out how to kill the unkillable?" Rutger inquired.

"Precisely." Baptiste nodded, turning a corner down another hallway. "And seeing as how this is a relatively new facility, we have plenty of storage space here. According to the latest information I have, two hundred and thirty seven people from your town survived the encounter with King Leper, however they only have about forty eight hours to live. We will put them on ice here, and use every resource at our disposal to attempt to find a cure."

"How confident are you that you can find a cure?" Rutger asked, and pursed his lips.

"I won't lie to you Rutger, our hopes aren't high." Baptiste shook his head as he parked the cart, stepping off to lead his guest to a white railing. "More than likely these people will either remain frozen forever, or will have a weekend to live out the rest of their lives. But I gave you my word I would do everything I

could for them, and I will." He inclined
his head and Rutger approached the
railing, looking down at the room below.
Men in white coats loaded up frozen glass
caskets, each with an infected townsperson
inside.

"That's all I ask," Rutger said, and
took a deep breath, letting it out with a
whoosh.

"Thank you for your understanding."
Baptiste bowed his head a little in
appreciation.

"Okay, now that we have that business
out of the way." Rutger turned and leaned
on the railing, crossing his arms. "Go
ahead and ask me what you want to ask me."

"Very well," the attache stood up
straighter, clasping his hands over the
clipboard in front of him. "As you have no
doubt seen, there are some evil things out
there that need dealing with. You have
shown yourself to be quite capable in a
fight, and are quick on your feet. While
you are older than our typical recruit,
you have shown the rare ability to
complete high risk missions. If you are
interested, I'd like to bring you on as a
special operations agent."

"Does it pay well?" Rutger asked.

"Hardly," Baptiste replied, shaking
his head. "But you get your own room here
at the facility, access to some

otherworldly weapons, and the cafeteria
isn't half bad."

Rutger pursed his lips in thought for
a beat, and then shrugged. "I'm in."

END

SMOOTHEN SILKY VS THE WERECOUGAR
© 2018

CHAPTER ONE

It was Thursday night, and Kerr was on the prowl. He casually walked along the upstairs balcony of the two story dance club, the very walls shaking from the generic beat of the overproduced techno music. The robust bass pounded through the railing and into his hand as he leaned on it, eyes raking over the packed dance floor below.

His phone vibrated in his pocket and he pulled it out to see Rose had texted him.

Silky says, and I quote, she'd written, *"What you got, Cracka?"*

He rolled his eyes and took a swig of the cheap beer that was rapidly warming in the sweaty air of the club. He set it down on a tall round table next to him, clinking against the dozen or so empties sitting there.

Tracking a pack of potentials. He typed back. *I'll be in touch.* He pocketed his phone, and narrowed his eyes as he honed in on a group of frat boys huddled in the corner of the dance floor. There were four of them, three having ganged up on the fourth in some kind of twisted pep talk ritual. They popped his collar and sprayed him down with so much cologne that

Kerr was sure he could smell it on the dank updraft.

Fucking frat boys. He *hated* fucking frat boys.

Kerr reached back for his beer but the table had been cleaned by what felt like a ghost waitress, and he swallowed his disappointment to turn back to the dance floor. The popped and loaded frat boy strutted across to the bar, where there was only one figure sitting alone that he could have possibly been targeting.

Her back was to him, her elbow resting on the bar, unlit cigarette raised in the air. Her nails were six inches long and the brightest pink he'd ever seen, practically glowing under the lights of the club. Her leopard print top had three quarter length sleeves and was more form fitting than it maybe needed to be given the shape of her. The back of her neck was obscured by shoulder length black hair in a puffy perm that didn't particularly look like it was from the current decade.

The likely stank-filled frat boy approached, clearly nervous, biting his lip and visibly shaking as he leaned on the bar next to her. It was clear he was trying to look cool, but failing miserably if his tomato red cheeks had anything to say about it. Leopard Print laid a

dangerous looking hand on his arm, claws
and all, and that seemed to calm him down.
She leaned closer to him, appearing to
whisper something in his ear, and he
totally relaxed, a giant grin erupting on
his douchebag face. She hopped down from
her barstool and took the kids hand, and
Kerr caught a glimpse of a giant hoop
earring before they were obscured by the
throng of dancers.

The Agent was instantly torn. He knew
that his mission was to take out as many
demons as he could at any given time, but
he didn't want to risk this poor woman
being ripped apart. He pulled out his
phone and opened the surveillance photo of
the demon marked 'Ezra' that had been
provided to him. He eyed the group of
remaining frat douches in the corner, but
none of them fit the picture. That was the
deciding factor for him, so he hurried
down the stairs, keeping an eye on the
woman's fluffy hair as it bounced through
the crowd.

He swiped away from the picture and
sent Rose a quick text: *Got a live one.*

Leopard Print led the frat dick like
a poodle at a dog show, all the way to the
fire door that had been propped open for
ventilation. Two hundred sweaty, gyrating
twenty-somethings generated a hell of a
lot of heat, especially in Austin where

the average temperature hovered around the boiling point, even at night.

Kerr paused as they exited, and then slid up to the door, putting his back to the wall right next to it. He reached into the deep pockets of his jeans and casually slipped his hands into a set of brass knuckles. He took a deep breath and then slipped out the door into a wall of humid night air. He nearly gagged; it was like breathing soup.

He cautiously moved down the dank alleyway towards a nearby dumpster, and raised his brass fists at the sound of whimpering. It was not the happy whimpering usually associated with a young couple getting it on in an alley, and the Agent took a fighting stance.

"Alright, you demon possessed prick," he warned loudly, "let go of that innocent young woman and get out here for an ass beating."

The whimpering ceased, and an eerie quiet fell. The only sound was the creaking of the old building that struggled to maintain structural integrity from the onslaught of shitty techno bass.

"Well, come on!" Kerr urged. "Let's do this!"

There was a metallic groan and suddenly the dumpster rocketed towards the Agent. He dove out of the way just in time, hugging the wall at the *whoosh* of the deadly weapon narrowly missing his face. It landed with a gargantuan *clang-thud* right in front of the fire door.

Kerr leapt back out into the middle of the alley to face the demon, and blinked in confusion at the sight before him. The frat boy lay flat on the asphalt, spread-eagled, blood pooling rapidly beneath him from the massive hole in his chest. Leopard Print stood above him, revealing herself to be in her mid-forties, not the early twenties that he'd originally assumed.

The most grisly part of the demonic tableau, however, was the fresh heart in her hand, oozing crimson all up her forearm.

"What. The. Fuck." Kerr breathed, jaw dropping in horror as the woman took a hearty bite out of the heart, blood running down her chin to stain the crushed velvet animal print barely covering her cleavage.

The Agent banged his brass knuckles together to get her attention, and her head immediately flicked to him like a bird's. She screeched and pitched the partially devoured organ at him.

Kerr ducked and barely registered the sickening squelch behind him as the heart hit the brick wall before the harpy was on him. He managed to roll out of the way of her razor sharp pink claws as she tried to get him with her considerable speed. He attempted to hit her, but she easily dodged his blows, reciprocating in kind with kicks laden with stiletto heels.

He ducked down into a squat before launching his body forward, fists held in front of him like a battering ram. She leapt into the air with impressive grace, flipping forward and lashing out to scratch the back of his neck with one long fierce claw.

Kerr hit the ground and tucked into a roll, springing back up to his feet and raising his fists once again. But she'd already turned and sprung onto the wall, and he watched with his jaw on the ground as she parkoured up the building like a coked up cat.

When she vanished over the top into the night, his body relaxed and he fell down onto his ass to take a breather. What the fuck had just happened? The frat dicks hadn't turned out to be demons after all, but Leopard Lady sure was. Where she'd come from and what her purpose was remained to be seen, further than eating frat hearts that was.

His pocket vibrated and he fished his phone out, glancing at an SOS text from Rose.

"Well," he groaned as he pocketed the device, "looks like it's time for Kerr to go save the day." He paused as he was about to get to his feet and put a hand to his forehead in bewilderment. "Crap, that talking in third person stuff is contagious."

CHAPTER TWO

Silky ran across the hardwood floor, dragging his 9-iron behind him like a samurai running head on into battle. His white fur jacket fluttered gracefully behind him, giving the effect of an avalanche thundering towards his victims.

The first one to reach him was a stocky demon with wild stupid eyes, shouting a battle cry fit for a bad action movie. Silky swung his club upwards in a tight arc, catching his opponent in the armpit. There was a pop and a sickening crack as the force of the blow severed the demon's arm. He staggered backward, staring open mouthed at his sudden wound that was spewing blood like an uncapped fire hydrant.

Silky spun and whipped his club around like a baseball bat, smacking into the falling appendage and sending it sailing across the room to embed into the drywall. The pimp strolled casually over to the arm jutting out of the wall, palm up. He removed his precious jacket and placed it in the demon hand, punching the forearm to get the fingers to clench around the white fur. He inspected his handiwork, making sure that the jacket was safe from touching the ground on it's new organic hook.

He pulled down the sleeves of his white long sleeve shirt and smoothed his pristine white slacks, inspecting his shiny white leather penny loafers.

"Silky would like to give his humble thanks to each and every one of you demonic cocksuckers for patiently waiting while Silky be tendin' to his jacket," he declared loudly. The dozen or so demons glanced at each other in confusion, some scratching their heads in bewilderment. "With all the moral outrage these days it's becoming harder and harder for a pimp to be findin' real fur, let alone fur as rare as this.

"Now. Silky ain't gonna be borin' you with the details of how he acquired this magnificent work of tailored art, or which endangered species gets to live on in perpetuity thanks to the care Silky be providin' this jacket," he continued as he slung the club over his shoulder, strolling up next to Rose, who had her head in her hand in exasperation. "All Silky be sayin' is this. If *any* of you motherfuckers come within ten feet of Silky's glorious jacket, Silky is gonna be bendin' you over and shovin' his 9-iron so far up you ass that you gonna feel like you on a date with Long Dong Silver!"

"Really?" Rose sighed, cocking her head so that her long red ponytail fell down over her left shoulder. "The jacket speech again?"

"What?" He puffed out his chest a bit and raised his chin. "Silky be proud of the work his tailor did. You have any idea what that magnificent bastard had to go through to be gettin' that fur?"

"Yeah, yeah, I know," she said, rolling her eyes. "Australian outback, wiped out an indigenous tribe who didn't take kindly to him killing their god, and lost a toe or some shit."

"That ole honky lost his *big* toe," Silky corrected with a wag of his finger. "Now the man doesn't have the proper weight distribution to be supportin' his gigantic set o' balls. Brings a tear to Silky's eye when he's seein' that seventy year old mammoth of a man wobblin' across the shop to collect Silky's wares."

Rose sighed again. "Are you done?"

"One day Silky's gonna be educatin' you on the finer things in life." He shook his head.

Rose slipped a knife from the back of her dress' bodice, and pointed her signature metal baton at the group of demons eyeing them.

"You assholes want to fight now, or keep hearing about the jacket?" she asked, and her opponents looked back and forth at each other, then took fighting stances, echoes of cracking knuckles and necks permeating the dim space. "See, they're ready to go," Rose said to her comrade. "Are you?"

"Baby, Silky *always* ready to go." He grinned at her, revealing the custom grill that read S I L K Y.

Screeches ran out amongst the demons as they darted forward, and the two Agents sprung to action.

Rose sprinted forward, leaping into the air and catching a demon in the chest with a flying knee. She drove him into the ground and dipped into a lithe shoulder roll, whipping her knife in the upswing to slam right into the chest of another enemy. She reeled back with her elbow as the first demon sat up, knocking him back down as she rained three vicious blows to his face, caving in his head with her fist.

The redhead leapt to her feet and a pair of arms encircled her from behind. The attacking demon opened it's mouth with a hungry snarl, ready to take a bite out of her neck. She jabbed her baton back and embedded it directly into her assailant's throat. The momentary shock and pain staggered the demon back far enough for her to retrieve her knife and plunge it into it's chest.

Silky released twin blades on his 9-iron and swung into a surprised foursome of demons, whose panicked heads detached from their bodies from the force of his mighty backhanded swing.

"Looks like it's all y'all's turn," he declared as two more demons flanked him. "So y'all wanna spitroast ole Silky, do ya? Sorry to be disappointin', but Silky ain't into threesomes, at least not with the likes of you's ugly ass mothafuckas. I tell you what, though, Silky'll at least give you's a fightin' chance." He hit a button on the club to retract the blades, put the head extended out with a flash to smack one of his opponents directly in the face.

The other charging demon leapt as the first one fell backwards, and Silky managed to land a series of blows, bones crunching with each hit.

"Whoo-ee, Silky's workin' them ribs, got them crack-a-lackin'," he said with a grin. The first demon dove back in and the pimp dodged the first blow, retaliating with a golf club to the goody bag. As the demon doubled over, Silky smashed the head into his face, holding him upright against the wall, head slamming back against the brick with a thud.

The demon with the cracked ribs cried out as he ran full tilt at the pimp's

back, and Silky dropped into a split that
would have made James Brown proud. His
opponent's flying sucker punch sailed over
his head and directly into the demon
against the wall, and Silky leapt back to
his feet and hit the blade release. He
used the momentum of his spring to stab
the blade into the back of his opponent's
head, securing both of them to the wall.

He let go of the 9-iron and it stayed
in place, both demon heads pinned through
the center against the wall.

"Rose, you see this shit?" he cried
excitedly.

She grunted, shoulder to shoulder
with two demons. "Little busy right now."

"And you be thinkin' *Silky* needed to
hit the gym?" He puffed his chest out.
"Shiiiiit girl, Silky don't need to be
doin' free weights or any of that new age
yoga and shit."

Rose landed a direct shot to one of
her opponent's faces with her baton,
sending him tumbling backwards. The other
turned in shock and concern for his
partner, which gave her the opening to
stab him in the heart.

"No!" the demon on the ground cried,
throwing his hands up just a second too
late to protect himself from her plunging
blade.

"Now, what do you want?" Rose asked, turning to Silky, who was standing by his gruesome display of power like a proud five-year-old with his drawing on the fridge.

She opened her mouth to respond, but another demon ran towards her, screeching like a banshee. She unleashed a volley of blows with her baton, a vicious dance that drove her enemy back. He hit the ground with a groan, and Silky bristled.

"Mothafucka," the pimp snapped, tearing the 9-iron out of the wall and retracting the blades. The two pinned bodies crumpled to the floor in a heap as he stalked over towards Rose's victim.

"What is it?" she asked, brow furrowed.

"He better hope, he better hope," Silky muttered as he tossed the 9-iron to the ground with a clatter. He knelt and took the fallen demon's hair in his fist, lifting his lolling head to point it at the jacket on the wall. "Ten feet," he said firmly. "Ten mothafuckin' feet. You not listenin' to Silky? Silky be layin' it all out there for yo ass. One rule. One. Simple. God. Damn. Rule. Do *not* get within ten mothafuckin' feet of Silky's jacket."

"That doesn't look like ten feet." Rose sighed. "And besides, we need this asshole to talk."

"Don't be worryin', Rosie," Silky assured her. "This asshole can still talk with Silky's club hitting from the rough."

"Jesus Christ," Rose muttered, closing her eyes momentarily and taking a deep breath. "Can we just call it ten and a half feet and move on to the interrogation?"

The pimp dropped the demon's head with a *clunk* against the cement floor and huffed as he crossed to his jacket. He pulled out a tape measure and knelt, hooking it to the baseboard before moving towards the demon.

"Silky's got standards," he said, "we ain't eyeballin' this shit."

Rose crossed her arms in defeat, cocking her head as he stopped at the demon's toe.

"Nine feet, eleven inches!" he cried in disgust, and threw down the tape measure. It skidded across the floor as he snatched up the golf club. "Silky be apologizin', cracka ass demon, but he didn't bring no lube!"

His opponent's eyes went wide as saucers with fear, and Rose *humphed*, stepping forward to hook her arms underneath the demon's shoulders. She dragged him a few inches and then dropped him again, both he and the pimp staring at her in confusion.

"What?" Silky finally asked. "You gonna help Silky pop this demon's cherry?"

"No, I'm preventing you from doing that," Rose snapped. "For starters, just, *ewww*. Secondly, we need information from him and I guaran-damn-tee he's going to be a lot more likely to co-operate if he isn't feeling Mandingo's wrath. Thirdly, and the most important point, we don't have a place to stay in town yet and I'll be goddamned if I'm riding around in a car with something that smells like demon ass."

"Fine," Silky conceded. "Do what you gonna do. Silky's gonna go make sure his coat's okay."

Rose sank to her knees and slid her hand around the back of the demon's head, tightly fisting the hair at the nape of his neck as she lifted it.

"Look, I've had a long day, so I'm going to make this short," she said firmly. "Answer my question quickly, and I end you quickly. Refuse, and I'm going to let my friend over there do whatever the fuck he wants to you because I'm going to find a nice hotel with an even nicer bar. You with me so far?"

The demon nodded jerkily, as far as the movement was allowed with the fingers clutching his head.

"Good." Rose nodded. "Have you seen this demon?" She produced her phone, a picture of the demon Ezra on the screen.

"He's in town," her captive said shakily. "I don't know where exactly." He winced as she tightened her hold on his scalp, hair tearing free. "I swear. He summoned me two nights ago. I didn't even want to come up to the surface, he just brought me here."

"Is he doing that a lot?" Rose asked.

"Look around," the demon said, "we call came up in a single night."

She nodded and then slid her knife from its sheath, planting it like butter into his heart. He melted away into the floor as Silky strode back over to his partner.

"He got anything useful?" he drawled.

"Just that our boy Ezra is summoning demons at an alarming rate," Rose replied as she wiped her knife and sheathed it again.

"Silky gonna be puttin' a stop to him," the pimp stood up straight, and then the duo whipped around as the door flung open. They took defensive positions until they realized it was Kerr, gun in hand, ready for battle, and screaming shrilly.

"God*damn* it, shut the fuck up you dumbass honky." Silky rolled his eyes. "Rose and Silky done finished the job."

The Agent dropped his hands in disappointment, pursing his lips. "Damn, Silky, I'm sorry," he said. "I ran into some strange action."

"So you tellin' Silky you late because you be havin' some action with a piece o' strange?" The pimp crossed his arms.

"What? No." Kerr waved his hands in front of his face. "I had some action and it was strange."

"Well, first times can be like that," Silky retorted with a grin, and his comrade scowled.

"I'm late because I got attacked by something I've never seen before," Kerr began again. "I was tracking the target as he hit on a woman at the bar. They went outside and when I stepped in to take him out, she had ripped his heart out."

"God*damn*, that's why Silky never be messin' with Texas women," the pimp put in.

"It gets weirder." Kerr raised his hand as Rose's phone bleated. She pulled it out and her brow furrowed at the familiar name on the screen.

"I gotta take this," the redhead said, hitting the talk button. "Thorn? Everything okay?"

"Rose," a rough edged female voice greeted her. "How quickly can you get to Austin?"

"We're actually in town now," Rose replied. "We caught a case."

"Can you come by?" Thorn asked. "If you're working a case here, then it confirms my suspicions. Something really bad is going on."

"Yeah, absolutely," the redhead confirmed. "Can you give me a couple of hours?"

"Take your time, I have to drop off the rest of the band," Thorn confirmed. "We had a late practice for the gig on Saturday. Why don't y'all come by about six?"

"Okay, I'll see you then."

"Thanks, Rose."

The redhead ended the call and turned back to Silky and Kerr, noticing the long scratch on the back of the younger Agent's neck.

"Yeah man, she just climbed up the walls like a methed up monkey," Kerr finished, as Rose re-entered their pow-wow circle.

"Goddamn, Silky's needin' to be hittin that bar," the pimp said with a chuckle. "Those drinks must be magic."

"Kerr, that looks like a pretty deep scratch there," Rose teased. "Good to see you're toughing it out in the field."

"Don't make fun, you would have had trouble with her too." Kerr pouted.

"Trust me Kerr, I'm a lot better with women than you are," the redhead promised.

"Important call?" Silky asked.

"You remember Thorn, don't you?" Rose replied.

"You's meanin' your old partner Thorn?" the pimp asked.

"Wait," Kerr cut in. "Rose and Thorn? Really?"

Silky smacked the back of the young Agent's head. "Shut yo mouth before Silky be shuttin' it for you."

"Ow, sorry," Kerr muttered.

"Yes, my old partner Thorn," Rose confirmed, getting back on track. "She's here in Austin and needs us to come by."

"Rose, we's workin', we ain't got time for you to be havin' a booty call," Silky chastised, and Kerr turned and blinked at the insinuation.

"Shut the fuck up," Rose pointed at Kerr, and then turned to Silky. "It's about our case. She noticed something out of the ordinary and since we're here, she's convinced."

"Alright, Silky be likin' the idea," the pimp agreed. "Be good to work with that badass chick again." He collected his jacket from the organic hook on the wall and shrugged into it as Rose led the way out of the building of dead demon carnage.

"So, was he just joking about the booty call?" Kerr trotted in front of her, and the only response was another swift smack in the back of the head, this time from his redheaded companion. "Nope. He was not." He gulped, eyes wide at the revelation.

The three Agents piled out of Silky's white Cadillac, and Kerr stretched his arms over his head, taking in the older house in front of him. It looked like it hadn't been updated since the fifties structurally, but the decor was newer with the punk band flags hanging in the windows. The faint sound of crunchy metal guitar permeated the early morning air, and he bobbed his head to the beat.

"Sounds like Dead Under Three Strippers," he commented.

"That's yo dream death, ain't it, cracka?" Silky sneered.

"Isn't it every man's?" Kerr shot back.

"With your income, you might want to reconsider given the quality of stripper you can afford," Rose teased, and the younger Agent begrudgingly nodded with her assessment.

The front door creaked open, revealing a tall statuesque dark skinned woman. Tattoos snaked all over her body, topped with a perfectly tight mid-sized afro.

"Agency still underpaying ya'll, huh?" she drawled, and Rose's eyes lit up.

"Thorn!" She darted forward and the women embraced tightly. A lopsided grin erupted on Kerr's face, and Silky smacked him on the back of his head.

"Sorry," the younger Agent muttered, but didn't avert his gaze as the two women pulled back just enough to look at each other.

"Damn, Rose, it's good to see you girl," Thorn said. "You still kicking ass?"

"Just as much as you remember," Rose replied with a smirk. "You?"

"I've been out of the game for a while now, focusing mostly on my metal band, Queen of the Demon Blade," the dark woman replied. "Although I do have to throw down in the pit from time to time."

"Queen of the Demon Blade?" Rose raised an eyebrow. "I thought you ceded that title to me when you left the Agency?"

"Girl, you wish," Thorn teased.

"Ladies, Silky be hatin' to break this up, but we's got work to do," the pimp interjected, stepping forward.

Thorn reeled back and punched Silky with a vicious right hook, and his head snapped to the side. Neither he nor Rose looked surprised by the violence, but Kerr's face lit up like he'd just seen the Pope paying for a private dance in the Champagne Room.

"Silky's gonna assume you's still holdin' a grudge for the rigorous training program Silky insisted upon?" the pimp asked, flexing his jaw as he straightened back up.

"Bitch, you sat on your ass while I took on a dozen demon motherfuckers," Thorn snapped.

"You's kicked they asses, didn't you?" Silky crossed his arms.

"No thank to your dumb ass," she shot back.

"Come on now, Silky be shoutin' encouragement." He rolled his eyes.

"Yeah, like a fluffer cheering on a Nebraska farm girl who thought L.A. sounded like fun but ended up in the middle of a demon gangbang." Thorn shifted her weight, left hip jutting up to accentuate her point.

"That's a vivid visual," Kerr piped up, eyes going a bit glassy.

"Bitch, ain't nooooobody talkin' to your cracker ass," Thorn snapped, pointing a finger at him. Kerr recoiled and took a step back as if slapped, realizing that maybe he should have been seen and not heard.

"Aight girl." Silky put his hands up. "In the spirit of collaboration and shit, Silky would like to offer his formal apology."

Thorn clenched her jaw, but Rose reached over and took her hand in an effort to calm her down.

"Not ready to forgive your ass yet," the ex-Agent said in a low threatening tone, "but there are things we need to address. Why don't y'all come inside?" She stepped aside and Silky strutted past her as if he owned the place. Kerr trotted forward and she jumped at him as if she were going to throw a punch. He flinched violently back, and Thorn threw her head back and barked a laugh.

"Rose, when the hell did the agency start investing in jumpy white boys?" she asked, wiping fake tears from her eyes.

"Eh, Kerr's not so bad." Rose shrugged. "Most of the time."

He smiled sheepishly and Thorn reached out again, tussling his hair a bit before shoving him after Silky.

"Alright, go on in," she said, and he scurried through the door. She grasped Rose's hand again as the redhead slunk by. "It really is good to see you," she said sincerely.

"You have no idea." Rose smiled.

The living room was exactly what one would expect of an indie metal band. Cinder blocks and plywood acted as a makeshift coffee table covered in beer cans, eighties band posters hanging where family portraits would normally reside. On the worn and faded couch lay an unconscious older bearded white man in a jean jacket with no sleeves.

"Silky's always amazed at how you honkies just pass the fuck out anywhere y'all like," the pimp said, he and Kerr standing over the couch to inspect the sleeping bear.

"That's Abe, don't mind him," Thorn instructed as she and Rose strolled in. "Just give him a good poke and he'll move."

"You's been whinin' how lonely you is, now's yo chance to get a poke." Silky winked at Kerr and the younger Agent scowled.

"I said a *good* poke," Thorn teased.

Silky smirked. "Sista's gotta point." He kicked the couch and Abe sat up, eyes bloodshot as he peeled them open.

"Abe, go crash in the back," Thorn instructed. "My friends and I have some shit to take care of."

The bear grunted and grabbed a beer can from the table, giving it a shake. It was empty, so he tried another and shot her a partially toothless grin at the sound of liquid swishing inside. He stood with a groan and then ambled out of the room.

"He seems classy," Rose commented.

"Yeah, ole Abe is a bit rough around the edges," Thorn agreed. "But he's a hell of a roadie and works for cheap beer."

The Agents took up residence on the stuffy couch, and the lady of the house pulled up a chair across from them.

"So girl, whatcha got fo us?" Silky asked, back on topic. "We's on a case and Rose said you could help."

"Well, my band has a regular Saturday gig at Concussion," Thorn began.

"Concussion?" Kerr piped up.

She sighed. "You got two left."

"Two what?" He furrowed his brow.

"Interruptions," she replied firmly, and he pursed his lips. "Now, Concussion is one of the local metal bars. We have about fifty regulars that come out for every show. Over the last few weeks, I've noticed some of my most dedicated fans have gone missing."

"Bitch don't be modest, you missin' yo groupies, ain't ya?" Silky's lips curled into a smile.

"These guys wanted some badass brown sugar," Thorn seethed through clenched teeth, trying to ignore him. "Like any good front woman, I provided them with the illusion they had a chance with me, and it kept them front and center every show. Then poof, they vanished."

"You drug us all the way over here because you lost some cock you didn't even want?" Silky scoffed, and stood up. "We's dealin' with some serious shit, we ain't got time fo this."

Thorn jumped to her feet and effectively blocked the pimp's path, raising a finger. "I will lay you the fuck out and have Abe cuddle your black ass until you wake up," she threatened, and he sat back down.

"Perhaps Silky acted rashly," he conceded. "Why don't you be finishin' your story?"

"As I was saying," she huffed as she sat back down. "I lost my three, ahem, groupies. Over the course of the next couple of shows, our crowd thinned out as well. Last week we only had twenty-two people at our show, which is unheard of for us. Abe noticed we did gain a new hardcore fan though, that showed up right as the disappearances began. Here, I got a picture." She pulled up a photo on her phone and handed it over to Rose.

The redhead's face paled. "Mother fucker." It was Ezra. She showed it to the others.

"You know this asshole?" Thorn asked.

"His name is Ezra, some shitheel demon that leveled up to being a summoner," Rose explained.

"Christ, that's all we need," the
lady of the house replied, taking her
phone as the redhead handed it back. "How
powerful is he?"

"We got word a couple weeks ago that
a newbie demon summoning was happening at
a higher than normal rate, which is when
we were dispatched."

"So nothing more powerful?" Thorn
pursed her lips. "No Gateway Demons?
Zombie Ogres?"

"If so, the Agency techs haven't
detected it." Rose shrugged.

"Well, let's keep it that way," the
ex-Agent replied with a roll of her eyes.
"Sixth street is chaotic enough on a
weekend."

"So, do you have any idea of where to
find him?" Kerr piped up.

"Abe's asked around to some of the
other bands and club owners and he
thinks…" Thorn trailed off and squinted at
him. "What the fuck is up with your ears?"

"What are you talking about?" His
brow furrowed.

"Gold looks good on you, Wonder
Bread," Silky said with a smirk.

The younger Agent touched his ears
and shrieked. "What the fuck?!" His hands
closed around the hoop earrings that were
suddenly in his ears and tore them from
his earlobes, throwing them on the table.

"Now that Vanilla Bean is done showin' off the fall collection, can we be gettin' back to the task at hand?" Silky asked. "How we's gonna find this demon summoning groupie hoarder?"

"Abe thinks he's found where Ezra is set up," Thorn replied. "An old buddy of his runs this little dive bar just outside of town, and it's been closed the last few weeks. A couple of bands told him that they saw the owner on the street and he was acting strangely. Put two and two together, and yeah, it's pretty fucking flimsy."

"Flimsy or not, it's better than anything we have," Rose added. "Kerr's spent the last week freelancing for leads, and Silky and I cleared out a hive last night and he wasn't there."

"Well unless Bo Derek here has any mo accessories to model for us, Silky thinks we should be gettin' this demon cock sucker."

"Austin traffic is a motherfucker at rush hour," Thorn glanced at the cracked clock up on the wall. "Why don't y'all catch some sleep here and head out in a few hours."

"If you's and Rose wanna put on some Barry White and get freaky deaky, all you's gotta be doin' is sayin' so," Silky teased with a grin. "Don't need to be throwin' out excuses."

Thorn clenched a fist. "Motherfu-"

"Thanks Thorn, we'll get some rest," Rose cut her off, and the lady of the house calmed down.

"You boys can have the living room." Thorn motioned to the couch. "Unless you wanna share a bed with Abe in the back."

"The couch will be just fine…" Kerr began, and Silky raised an eyebrow at him in incredulity. "...for Silky," the young Agent finished quickly. "That floor looks mighty comfortable for me, and too good to pass up."

"I'll toss you a pillow and a blanket so your bony ass don't break on the hardwood," Thorn said with amusement.

"Night guys," Rose said with a little wave, and headed into the master bedroom.

Kerr leaned over, trying to peek through the door, but was met with a flying pillow to the face.

"I have knives and deadly aim," Thorn called from the bedroom, "in case you feelin' pervy."

Kerr gulped. "Ya'll sleep tight!"

CHAPTER FOUR

"Good lord, what time is it?" Kerr moaned from the backseat of the Cadillac.

"You's ask that one mo time and Silky is gonna be plantin' yo ass in the ground so you can sundial that shit," Silky warned.

"It's damn near seven," Rose replied, eyes glued to the multiple video feeds on her phone. "And still nothing." She sighed.

Kerr leaned forward, putting his hand on the front seat to Rose's right, leaning over the left to peer down at her phone.

"You think this is a wild goose chase?" he asked.

"Um, Kerr," Rose said, shrinking away from the six inch long ruby red nails poking her shoulder from the young Agent's hand. "I know you're bored but what's with the fingernails?"

"What the fuck?!" He gasped, holding up his hand in front of his face. "Where did these come from?!"

"First earrings and now those lucious nails?" Silky teased. "You tryin' to tell Silky you wanna be shakin' it on the corner for him?"

"I swear, I have no idea what the hell is going on," Kerr replied, voice shaking as he continued to stare at his hands, face pale. "I'm not doing anything, this stuff is just appearing."

"You ain't gotta be self conscious, Silky don't judge," the pimp promised.

Kerr slumped back in his seat and tried to pull the nails off, but to no avail.

"Sit up and turn around," Rose instructed.

"Why?" Kerr asked petulantly.

"Just fucking do it," she snapped, and he did, shifting around so she could inspect the scratch on the back of his neck. "Ew," she muttered.

"What?" he asked, voice laced with fear.

"What did you get in a fight with last night?" Rose mused.

"I told y'all, I don't know," Kerr replied, throwing his hands up. "It was some older lady who must have been possessed or something with the way she moved."

"When we get back to Thorn's, we've got to call Baptiste," the redhead said.

"First things first," Silky interjected. "We's gotta get this Ezra mofo off the street before he be doin' any real damage."

"Sorry Kerr, we'll get to you," Rose promised.

"Don't you be worryin' about that dainty doily, he be aight." Silky waved his hand dismissively. "Stay focused on the task at hand."

After what felt like hours, a loud snap from the backseat broke the silence. Silky and Rose turned around to see Kerr sitting there with a long chunk of crimson nail in his hand.

"Looks like I broke a nail," he said with a grin, and the other two Agents sighed as they turned back to face the front of the car. He rolled down the window and chucked the busted piece out onto the sidewalk, but upon turning back to his hand the broken nail had magically repaired itself. "That could be useful," he muttered. "Hey Rose, you have a nail file?"

She rummaged in her purse and produced a nail file, passing it back to him. Kerr spent the next half hour filing his new claws down to sharp points. He admired his new weapons, wiggling them in front of his face, as Rose perked up from the passenger seat.

"We got him," she said.

"You sure it's him?" Kerr leaned forward, careful not to stab anything.

"If it's not, he has a doppelgänger," Rose replied.

"Bout goddamn time," Silky declared. "Aight, let's go wipe the floor with him so Silky can be hittin' the clubs."

The trio stepped out of the Cadillac and stretched their legs and arms, then headed up to the front door. Silky stood in front of the door in his form fitting blue suit, golf club resting on his shoulder, Rose and Kerr flanking him.

He kicked the door in and stepped through, taking a beat to pose, hand on his hip, before pointing his club at the pack of demons on the other side of the room. "Aight, which one of you motherfuckers wants to die first?" he asked loudly.

Rose stepped in to the left, extending her baton with a *shink*, demon blade in the opposite hand. Kerr moved in to the right, flexing his claw hand.

"Who wants to know?" A twenty-something male demon stepped forward out of the group. He looked like he would have been at home in the back of a gaming shop being Dungeon Master to a Dungeons and Dragons campaign. It was Ezra.

"Silky be takin' offense at yo stupidity," the pimp replied, raising an eyebrow.

"Ah, you must be the assholes that took out my hive last night," Ezra said, connecting the dots. "No matter, those demons are a dime a dozen. Just means that more innocent lives are going to be lost thanks to *your* actions. My summoning powers are growing by the day, and there's nothing you can do that will stop me."

"Well, you's be sayin' that." Silky smirked, and hit the button on his 9-iron to eject the blades. He whipped it like an axe, end over end, and it embedded in an unsuspecting demon's chest.

Ezra shrugged, seemingly unfazed. "Just one more I get to replace," he said, a huge smile erupting on his face as he began to chant in a foreign language. It was guttural and lilting, with an ominous tone that caused the hairs to stand up on the back of Kerr's neck.

"Rose, what's he trying to summon?" he asked.

"Don't know, but I'm not going to wait to find out," Rose replied, and leapt into battle. She drew two demons away from the group, both diving forward to attack her at the same time. She sidestepped and slammed her knife into a temple, eliciting a blood gurgling moan before her victim collapsed and slowly disintegrated.

The other demon lunged into a backhand, and Rose ducked, punching her opponent directly in the knee. She spun with the momentum as he knelt, catching him in the side of the head with her baton. She retrieved her knife from the puddle of demon goo next to her and buried it in the chest of her stunned enemy.

Meanwhile, Kerr brandished his ruby claws, wiggling his fingers with a smirk. His enemies simply laughed, one of them motioning to the ridiculous-looking hand.

"What are you gonna do, scratch us to death?" one demon taunted him, and stepped forward to make a grab for the Agent's wrist. Kerr jabbed forward, all five of his razor sharp nails stabbing his opponent right through the heart. Blood poured down over his hand and he wrenched it violently to the side, breaking all of the nails.

The demon fell to his knees, and Kerr spun into a roundhouse kick, boot landing directly on the jagged cluster of nails. The demon fell backwards, a shocked and confused look on his face as he ceased all movement.

A second demon stepped forward with a growl, and Kerr held up his claw hand again, ready to go with fresh nails.

"Come on big boy, get some," he purred, and his opponent lunged forward. The Agent slashed his face on his way by, and the building shook violently, causing them all to waver with the sudden movement.

Silky stepped up behind his own opponent, who had turned his back with the earthquake, and casually snapped his neck.

"Come on now, don't do Silky like that," the pimp commiserated as the claw-slashed demon scurried away in the confusion. "Expectin' a workout and not even be gettin' a warmup."

As if on cue, Ezra finished his chanting and slammed his fist into the floor. The wood cracked apart and giant fingers curled up from between, grabbing the wood to pull itself up. The smell wafting up from the hole was enough to make Kerr gag, and he staggered closer to Silky, eyes wide as a seven foot tall decaying ogre emerged from the hole.

"Well, if you wanted a workout, here you go," Ezra teased with a wave, and retreated into the back room.

"Fuck me," Rose breathed, stepping closer to Silky as he readied his 9-iron. "Ideas?" she asked as the muscular zombie grunted, casting more of it's putrid scent their way.

"Silky gonna be sweepin' the leg like he's Johnny Goddamn Lawrence," the pimp explained. "Once this big bitch is on the ground, Silky be hopin' that blade of yours works." He tightened his hand around the handle of the club, and nodded to his two companions. "Well come on now, Silky's got shit to be doin'."

The ogre opened it's moldy maw in a wet roar, and lumbered forward, swinging a heavy arm at the pimp. Silky dropped to his knees and slid along the floor, using every bit of force he could muster to swing at its knee. The club bounced off like it was made of plastic, and did little more than to agitate the grotesque demon.

The ogre send a fist down towards Silky, who rolled out of the way to narrowly avoid being tenderized. He dodged two more blows, but ran out of momentum against one of the walls. Kerr jumped up onto the beast's back, grabbing a fistful of its matted hair so he could repeatedly stab and break his claws. The ogre reached back to try to grab his new assailant, but Kerr didn't let up.

Silky used the distraction to pop the blade on the 9-iron and sliced with a precise strike at the base of his legs, severing both the demon's achilles. Kerr leapt to the floor as the ogre fell to its knees, its back resembling a porcupine with all of the bright red quills sticking out of its back.

Rose came down on the back of the ogre's head with all of the strength she could muster, and then straightened up as it stopped moving but didn't immediately dissolve.

"Shouldn't this asshole be melting right now?" Kerr inquired.

"I've never used it on a zombie ogre before," Rose mused. "Not sure what's supposed to happen." Boils began to rapidly form along the demon's skin, and then rapidly grew, bursting and sending streams of pus through the air. The Agents looked at each other for a beat and then dove for cover as more geysers of goo flew. The entire creature exploded in an impressive array of thick slime, covering the walls in demon gunk.

"Silky is very glad he opted to keep his jacket in the car for this one," Silky commented as he strolled back through the puddle towards the far door.

"Let's go get this asshole before he summons something else," Rose said, and the trio moved towards the back room.

Ezra's scream permeated the thick air, and they burst into the back to see his legs sticking out from beneath the form of a woman in a leopard print onesie.

"Holy shit," Kerr blurted at the sight of a head of puffy black hair, "I think that's the woman who attacked me."

"Takes a brave ass cracka to be admittin' to getting his ass beat by a woman," Silky said with a grin, and then rolled his eyes at Rose's noise of disapproval. "Baby, Silky knows yo balls be bigger than any man. Silky notwithstanding o' course."

"Damn right," the redhead confirmed.

"What the fuck did you do to me, you bitch?!" Kerr cried shrilly, and the woman whipped around with lightning fast speed. She held Ezra's heart in one hand and his head in the other, fingers in his eye sockets and mouth like a bowling ball. Her eyes glowed yellow as she fixated on Kerr, and her red painted mouth grew into a massive grin.

"Ah, my protoge returns," she purred. "You ready to come home with mama so she can teach you a thing or two?"

"Fucking hell, it's a WereCougar," Rose breathed.

"What the hell is a WereCougar?" Kerr exclaimed.

"It's what she is," the redhead replied, motioning to their new opponent.

"Well, how do we kill her?" Kerr asked impatiently.

Rose shrugged. "Not a fucking clue."

"Silky be havin' an idea," Silky piped up, and before anyone could react, he whipped his 9-iron, blade out, at neck level. It flew like a spinning lawnmower blade, and sliced right through the WereCougar's neck.

She dropped what she was holding with a sly grin, the expression an eerie contrast as her head flopped backwards off of her body. The rest of her crumpled to the ground and Silky spread his arms, spinning around to take a bow.

"Whoo!" He punched the air in triumph. "Silky done fucked that bitch up worse than menopause did."

"Uh, Silky," Kerr said, tone laced with warning as the WereCougar's decapitated body began to rise to it's stiletto-booted feet.

"Not now, Vanilla Thunda, can't you see Silky be struttin'?" The pimp put his hands behind his head and rolled his hips suggestively.

"Silky," Rose put in, pointing behind him, but he ignored her, all the while the demon cougar was lifting her head back onto her body.

"Silky ready to hit the cub tonight, be showin' off his jacket and attractin' them fine young ladies," the pimp continued, raising his hand into a disco dance move and pulling off a spin.

"That's probably for the best, since you don't have the skills to satisfy someone with a little more experience," the WereCougar said as she finished reattaching her head. "Maybe those young girls won't mind that you underperform."

"Nah, baby, you got it *all* wrong," he
wagged his finger as he glared at her.
"Silky was worried you was gonna hurt
yoself, so he went easy."

"Uh huh," the WereCougar replied,
sarcasm dripping from her overly made up
face.

"You be thinkin' you can handle round
two?" Silky asked and cracked his neck.

"Ohhh, now you're talking, big boy."
She leered at him as he sprinted towards
her, throwing haymakers. He drew air, and
she lashed out with her claws to try to
scratch him in retaliation, but he dodged.
She grunted with the force of a horizontal
strike, but he leaned back, landing a kick
to her stomach.

She staggered back, and the other two
Agents stepped forward, flanking Silky.
The WereCougar screamed and snatched up
the fallen golf club, whipping it back
towards them. Silky and Kerr hit the deck
and Rose tried to dodge, but the blade
tore into her bicep. Their opponent used
the distraction to parkour up to the top
of the room and burst out a window into
the night.

"Son of a whore!" Rose seethed, blood
pouring from her arm and rapidly soaking
her clothes.

"Oh, quit yo whinin'," Silky chastised as he inspected her wound. "Silky's seen you take worse hits."

"I don't care about the cut," Rose snapped. "I just really liked this outfit."

"I bet your girlfriend Thorn has something you can borrow," Kerr piped up as he strolled over, and she immediately jabbed at him, causing a wicked charley horse. He doubled over in pain, groaning at his seizing muscles.

"Yeah, the arm's fine," Rose confirmed as she flexed her bloody arm. "Come on, we gotta call Baptiste and figure out how to deal with a WereCougar."

CHAPTER FIVE

The trio strolled into Thorn's living
room, Rose holding a bandage to her
bloodied arm. Kerr had grown a crushed
velvet leopard print shirt to go along
with fresh hoop earrings and thick makeup
caked on his face.

The lady of the house rushed forward.
"Oh my god, what happened?" she asked.

"I got infected by a WereCougar,"
Kerr raised his claw hand in defeat.

"That sounds like white boy problems
to me," Thorn retorted, and shoved him out
of the way. "Baby, what happened? You
okay?"

"Yeah, I'll live," Rose replied with
a nod. "This WereCougar bitch got the jump
on us and I got nicked by Silky's 9-iron."

"Girl, you need to come with me so I
can get you fixed up," Thorn instructed,
her voice laced with concern.

"It'll have to wait, we need to get
the Agency on the line." The redhead
argued.

"Which is something your
transgendered cracka can handle," her
companion shot back. "Or do you need to
spend some time staring in the mirror?"
She turned her hard gaze on Kerr, who
visibly shrunk away from her.

"You's go on and be gettin' patched up," Silky assured Rose. "Silky'll supervise while Nilla Wafer here be takin' care o business."

"Yeah, sure, not like *I'm* having any issues today or anything," Kerr muttered with a roll of his eyes, and started setting up the laptop as the women retreated to the master bedroom. He struggled to open it with his giant claws, and when he finally got it sitting upright he couldn't help but scoff at his treatment.

"Oh, what you be bitchin' about?" Silky asked in amusement. "Silky be known' lots o' ladies that would scratch your eyes out for lookin' as good as you is."

Kerr sighed. "I really need to find a new line of work."

"I would ask for a mission update, but I'm almost afraid to ask," Baptiste said, his concerned expression popping up on the computer screen.

"As well's you should be, brotha," Silky replied, sliding on to the couch next to Kerr.

"Have you eliminated Ezra?" the attache inquired.

"Yeah, he be gone," Silky confirmed. "But this cracka here be presentin' us with a complication."

"Rose can probably describe things better than I can," Kerr replied, defeated, and stood. "Let me see if Thorn's finished patching her up."

Silky put his feet up and leaned on his elbow, ever the picture of relaxation. "So, brotha, how you likin' things heading up the storage facility?"

"Absolutely loving it, Silky," Baptiste replied with a big smile. "I don't have to engage in fisticuffs, I get to explore demonology, and with the constant stream of new recruits I get to toss out the occasional yo momma joke. Life is good. The artifact archive here is magnificent, too."

"Doesn't really sound like Silky's bag, other than the insults o course." The pimp shrugged. "But if it be gettin' ya there, more power to ya, my man."

Kerr stood at the master bedroom door, waiting for a moment to be able to interrupt the ladies sitting on the bed.

"Baby, you gotta be more careful," Thorn said firmly. "This is a deep cut."

"Well, maybe you need to come back to the Agency so you can start watching my back," Rose teased, raising a perfectly sculpted brow.

"I'm not sure I could work with Silky and resist the urge to murder that motherfucker in his sleep." The dark skinned woman rolled her eyes as she tied off the last stitch.

"Let me talk to the Boss," Rose insisted. "I had my first solo mission recently, so maybe I can convince him to team us up."

"Or," Thorn replied, "you can quit the Agency and come be with me." She slid her hand gently around the back of the redhead's neck and stared into her eyes, sincerity in her big brown orbs. "Lot less dangerous, even with the mosh pits."

"You know I'd love a life with you," Rose said quietly, taking the woman's other hand in her own and caressing it with her thumb. "But I'm doing a lot of good with the agency. I've saved a lot of lives."

"And you've done your part," Thorn argued gently. "It's time to let others do theirs."

"You might be right." The redhead sighed heavily with a small nod. "But I think Kerr is in trouble and I owe it to him to do what I can to help. Once he's not in danger anymore I kind of like the idea of being the bouncer at your shows." She smirked as Thorn leaned in, crushing their lips together.

"Guess every Rose has its Thorn," Kerr declared from the doorway, and then blinked, stunned, as a knife embedded itself in the doorframe barely an inch from his head. "I'm going to go now… when you're done, Baptiste is on the line." He backed out of the room slowly.

"Thought you had deadly aim?" Rose chuckled. "Don't tell me you're slipping?"

"You just said I get you as soon as that cracka is out of trouble," Thorn confirmed with a grin. "Didn't want to waste time on an emergency room visit." They shared a laugh and a sweet embrace.

"We'd better get in there." Rose sighed, and they reluctantly headed back into the living room. Silky and Kerr sat on the couch, and the pimp shoved the infected Agent over to make room for Rose. Thorn knelt down next to her on the floor, her hand discreetly resting behind the redhead's ample ass on the cushion.

"Ms. Rose, it is good to see you," Baptiste greeted her. "Hope you have been well."

"I have, Baptiste, thank you for asking," she replied politely.

"And who is your friend there?" he inquired.

"This is Thorn," Rose replied. "She was with the Agency before you came aboard. She's helping us out with this case."

"Nice to meet you, Thorn," Baptiste said, inclining his head in the hostess' direction. "The Agency would like to thank you for your assistance in taking down Ezra."

"My pleasure," she replied with a little salute.

"So now that the pleasantries have been exchanged, let us get down to business." The man on the screen faced front. "Rose, what do you have for me?"

"Late last night as Kerr was pursuing leads, he was infected by what I believe to be a WereCougar," she explained.

"Are you certain?" Baptiste blinked.

"Well, we just had an encounter with one," Rose informed him. "Silky was able to lop the bitch's head off and it didn't do a whole lot to slow her down. She just picked it up and reattached it like she was putting on a hat. And over the past twenty-four hours, Kerr has been exhibiting symptoms."

"Such as?"

"Gaudy earrings appearing," she listed off, "six inch fingernails, and as you can see, crushed velvet leopard print attire appearing out of nowhere." As she motioned to her companion, they all realized that a very large set of breasts were threatening to bust out of the fabric across his chest.

"Goddamn, them's a fine set o' titties there," Silky complimented, and a dejected Kerr shook his head in defeat.

"I need a fucking drink." He scrubbed his hands down his face with a groan, and stood up to amble away to the kitchen.

Thorn leaned forward. "Baptiste, how often have you seen-" There was a clatter and an 'oof' as Kerr fell onto his face, legs tangling up in the carpet from his newfound stiletto heels. "That's two!" Thorn growled, holding up two fingers at him as he sat up in a daze.

"I didn't even say anything!" he argued petulantly.

"Don't matter, you interrupted me," she replied. "That's two." She turned back to the computer as Kerr struggled to get to his feet, knees shaking.

After a few failed attempts, he gave up and crawled on his hands and knees to the kitchen, muttering obscenities as he went.

"As I was saying," Thorn continued, "how often have you seen a WereCougar infection?"

"They are exceedingly rare," Baptiste replied, hammering away at his keyboard and looking at his screen to the left. "In fact, there are only two known cases of a WereCougar encounter in the Agency database. The first one was in the early eighties and the last one was in the mid-nineties."

"So what do you know about them?" Rose inquired.

"Well, they stalk their prey over a three day period on the first and fifteenth of every month," he replied, brow furrowing as he read his screen.

"So every two weeks, then?" she asked.

"No, always beginning on the first and fifteenth," Baptiste corrected with a shake of his head. "We initially thought it was every two weeks, but the nineties attack happened over a four month period that started in January. Our team was caught off guard when March first rolled around and one of them was infected on the first night of the hunt. As you've witnessed with Kerr, the transformation into a WereCougar was a gradual one."

"How much time we got before we's needin' to get him a carton of Virginia Slims?" Silky piped up.

"By the end of the third night, he'll be fully transformed and under her control," Baptiste replied.

"Great, so we'll have two of them running around?" Rose sighed.

"For a few hours at most," he continued with a nod.

"What the fuck do you mean, for a few hours at most?" Kerr staggered back into the living room, barefoot and holding a beer. "What happens after I turn?"

"For lack of a better term," Baptiste explained slowly, "you will progress rapidly from a cougar to a turkey vulture."

"What in god's name is a turkey vulture?!" Kerr exclaimed.

"Let ole Silky break it down for ya," the pimp said with a wave of his hand. "See, cougars be vicious unrelenting huntin' machines that be pickin' a target and rippin' it to shreds in pursuit of its own selfish goals. Which, for most cougars, means havin' a much younger man be servicin' them until the point of exhaustion. A cougar's prime typically bein' a short one, given that old bitches ain't that durable. Once they be losin' a step and breakin' a hip attempin' a double deluxe with a couple of cubbies, they reach turkey vulture status."

There was a long moment of silence, before Kerr threw his free hand up. "What the *fuck* does that even mean?"

"It means that this time tomorrow, you's gonna be lucky to pick up a middle aged man wearin' a fanny pack," Silky replied.

"I'm afraid it's worse than that,"
Baptiste put in. "If the curse isn't
broken by the end of the hunt tomorrow,
then Kerr is going to rapidly turn into a
turkey vulture, aging years in a matter of
minutes. The aging process will continue
at that pace until he is incapable of
movement."

"So if we don't kill this bitch
tomorrow, then I'm going to die?" Kerr
rubbed his forehead, eyes big as saucers.

"You'll only wish you were dead,
unfortunately," Baptiste corrected. "For
six days each month you'll morph into the
WereTurkeyVulture, and have an
overwhelming desire to gum someone to
death. The rest of the time you'll be in a
near vegetative state due to your extreme
age."

"Alright, so how do we find and kill
this bitch?" Kerr demanded.

"The first part is easy, as she'll
find you," Baptiste informed him. "Since
you were cursed by her, she'll be drawn to
you." At this, Thorn leapt to her feet,
fists clenched.

"I'll secure the door," she said
quickly.

"That won't be necessary, Thorn," the
attache put up a hand. "If she was as
injured as Rose said, she'll spend the
rest of the evening hunting and feeding so

that she can regain her strength. And she only hunts during the evening, so you'll be safe until tomorrow."

"Okay," Rose spoke up, and took a deep breath. "So, how do we kill her?"

Baptiste sighed. "I wish I had an answer for you, Rose."

Another silence fell over the room, until Kerr barked a hysterical laugh. "That's a good one, Baptiste!" He pointed his beer at the laptop, sloshing a little bit of the liquid over his hand. "But seriously, how do we kill her?"

"I'm sorry Kerr, but it's a mystery," the man on the screen replied, shaking his head solemnly. "The WereCougar from the eighties just vanished from our radar, and the one from the nineties is locked up in storage. All the typical things that kill a WereCreature, and demons in general, are ineffective. Silver, beheadings, demon blade. But in the spirit of full disclosure, our research team hasn't done much work on the issue since one hasn't been seen in over twenty-five years."

"Well, this might be a good goddamn time to get them on it, don't you think?!" Kerr cried.

"Yes Kerr, I will put a rush on it," Baptiste assured him.

"In the meantime, we'll brainstorm here and come up with a plan of attack," Rose said, and received a nod in return.

"Sounds good," the man on the screen agreed. "We'll be in touch." The screen went dark, and Thorn heaved a sigh.

She squeezed Rose's shoulder gently before turning for the kitchen. "I'll put some coffee on."

CHAPTER SIX

Rose took a sip of her hot comforting
brew and leaned forward on the couch, brow
furrowed.

"Okay, so we have a day to figure out
how to kill a creature that the Agency
hasn't been able to kill in thirty years,
so let's get to it," she began. "We know
what doesn't work, so let's start thinking
outside the box. What do we know about
cougars?"

"Well," Kerr stretched out, leaning
casually on one arm and inspecting the
massive fingernails on his other hand. "In
my many, many hours of internet research
I've noticed a common theme. There is one
thing that always seems to satisfy them,
so maybe that can be her weakness?"

There was an anticipatory silence as
everyone waited for him to continue, but
he simply took a sip of his coffee and
smiled.

"Well?" Thorn prompted. "What is it?"

Kerr blinked at his companions, as if
it were obvious. "A BBC."

"A *what*?" Rose raised an eyebrow.

He cleared his throat, suddenly
remembering that he was in mixed company,
and a light pink blush crept up his
cheeks. "A big black cock."

There was another beat of silence, and then all three turned their gazes on the pimp in the chair opposite them. He flashed his signature silken grin, grill and all, and leaned forward from his previously lounging position.

"As y'alls well knows," he began, "Silky is all about takin' one for the team, 'specially when it be involvin' gettin' a piece o' trim. That bein' said, Silky has learned a very valuable lesson during his time with the ladies, which is…" He put up his hands and lowered his head, as if about to preach a sermon. "You nevah, *evah* be stickin' yo dick in crazy. And based on what we's witnessed thus far, this bitch be crazier than a methed up daytime stripper. So while Silky be appreciatin' the request to deep dick this whore to death, Silky is gonna be humbly declinin'."

Rose nodded in understanding, and turned to the hostess.

"Thorn, you know anybody else who may be up to the task?" the redhead asked.

"Nobody I want to try to explain this shit to," Thorn declined, crossing her arms.

"Maybe we could just use a giant black dildo?" Kerr asked.

"While there be no substitute for the real thang, beatin' this demonic harlot to death with a big black dildo might be an option," Silky agreed.

"Alright, I'll add it to the list," Rose said, tapping away at her phone. "Thorn, you have any idea where we can get a massive black dildo?"

"Yeah, pretty sure Abe has one in his room," came the reply, and it was met with wide eyed stares. "What?" She shrugged. "He never learned Silky's life lesson about not sticking your dick in crazy. Hell, based on the noises that come out of that room I'm leaning towards he likes the challenge."

"Finally, a cracka Silky can be respectin'," the pimp piped up, tipping his hat.

"Alright," Rose said, bringing the conversation back around, "death by dildo is on the list. What else can we possibly use against her?"

"Don't older white women love white wine?" Thorn tried.

"Yeah." The redhead nodded. "White zin or chardonnay."

"So, whatcha thinkin?" Silky mused. "Forcin' her to be bingo drinkin'?"

"I was thinking we drown her in it," Thorn finished with a shrug.

"Silky can get behind that."

"So which one do we get?" Rose asked.

"Well, if she is a true cougar then she'll have a few racks of the stuff," Kerr theorized.

"And if we can't find her house?" Thorn held out her palms. "Then what?"

"I guess before we can answer that we need to figure out where we want to bait her into coming," the animal print clad Agent replied, pursing his lips.

"I have my show tomorrow night," Thorn suggested. "If the guys in the pit think I'm being threatened they'll throw down."

"Given how powerful she is, I think we could use all the help we can get," Rose added.

"I'm going to go out on a limb and guess the club y'all play at isn't known for their wine selection?" Kerr asked.

Thorn chuckled. "Does Boone's Farm count?"

"Maybe if we were trying to drown a sorority girl," Rose replied.

"I'll make a wine run in the morning," Kerr confirmed.

"Given your current appearance, I'll have Abe go get some stuff for you," Thorn cut in. "He owes me some beer anyway."

"I appreciate it," the half-cougar replied sincerely.

"Oh, oh, I got one." Rose leaned forward. "What if we stab her with designer heels? Maybe in the heart?"

"Good one, girl!" Thorn commended. "Given Cindy Crawford here and her magically appearing cougar gear, we'll just borrow a pair when we get to the club."

"Well what about-" Kerr's voice suddenly became muffled around the lit cigarette that appeared between his lips. "Goddammit." He took it out, looked at it with disgust, and then tossed it in his almost finished mug of coffee. "As I was saying, why don't we-" Another cigarette cut him off, a tendril of smoke curling up directly into his eye. He hissed and threw his hand against his burning eyeball, trying not to inhale at the same time.

"Maybe we be settin' the hussy on fire with a Virginia Slim?" Silky asked.

Rose nodded. "Couldn't hurt to try."

"Oh!" Thorn snapped her fingers. "We could use a martini as an accelerant! Cougars like martinis, don't they?"

The pimp put up his hands as if to say *whoa, nelly.* "Silky does *not* condone the wastin' of good alcohol."

"It's a dive bar." Thorn rolled her eyes. "The only good stuff that will ever be drunk in that place is brought in by a customer underneath their jacket."

"Silky withdraws his objection," the pimp conceded.

"I like it, but I was thinking I could gouge her eyes out with my nails," Kerr said quickly as he snuffed out the second cigarette in his coffee.

"Not sure eye gouging is going to be enough," Rose countered.

"Yeah but it'd make me feel better." Kerr scoffed, happy to note that another cigarette didn't immediately grow in his mouth.

"Well if you be feelin' it, live it up, homie," Silky said.

Rose looked around to her comrades. "Anybody got any other ideas?" There was a thick silence, and then she turned to her infected coworker. "Okay. Kerr, it's your life on the line. If there's anything we can do, just name it."

"Well, I could use some help learning to walk in heels," he replied sheepishly.

"Goddamit honky, how difficult is it?" Silky retorted. "Heel toe, heel toe!"

"You ever tried doing it with double fucking d's?" Kerr snapped.

The pimp sighed in defeat. "Silky withdraws his taunt."

"I got you, Kerr," Rose patted his crushed velvet shoulder.

"Alright y'all, it's late as hell," Thorn said, and got to her feet. "We need

to get some rest. Tomorrow is gonna be a
beast of a day."

CHAPTER SEVEN

Bong… bong… the bass twanged across the dingy one room club as the band did their sound check. Thorn nodded over some sheet music with the drummer as Abe leaned on one of the speakers, drinking a cheap beer and perusing a dirty magazine.

"So, you be thinkin' that any of that shit we came up with last night gonna work?" Silky asked as he leaned on the bar, chest puffing out at the fact that he was clearly the best dressed present.

"I honestly don't know," Rose replied with a shrug. "But we're going to try every single of one them. We owe Kerr that much."

"You know, Silky be givin' that cracka a lot o' shit, but damned if he don't take it and keep on truckin'," the pimp said with a respectful shake of his head. "White bread be deservin' a better end than being a zombified turkey vulture."

"You know," the redhead said, avoiding his gaze and taking a long sip of the swill the bartender had assured her was a Long Island Iced Tea. "This has got me thinking about the life… and I don't know if I'm cut out for it anymore."

"Aw come on girl." Silky waved her off. "Don't be talkin' like that."

"I'm serious," she replied, eyes bright but firm as she raised her gaze to his. "Just in the last few months I've nearly been sacrificed to a legendary demon, nearly involuntarily impregnated by an ancient vampire, and now I'm more than likely going to watch someone I've fought beside be condemned to a fate worse than death. I mean, there has to be more to life than this, doesn't there?"

"You's wanna shack up with Thorn, don't ya?" Silky raised a knowing eyebrow, and she lowered her gaze again.

"That is playing a part in this," she admitted. "But that's not the only reason."

"Silky be understandin' where you comin' from," he said, and reached out to give her shoulder a reassuring squeeze. "And afta we be gettin' through this situation, Silky'll be lendin' his ear and hear yo concerns. We's got a deal?"

Rose smiled. "Deal."

"Aight, so where is our cougarlicious mothafucka at?" Silky asked, rubbing his hands together.

"He'll be in shortly," Rose informed him, back straightening as she fell back into work mode. "Last I saw he was getting his nerve up in the car."

The front door of the club swung open as if on cue, revealing a completely cougarified Kerr. He stood proudly on black stiletto heels, clad from ankles to shoulders in leopard printed crushed velvet. His massive tits looked like they were struggling to escape a push-up bra to punch him in the chin. His dirty blonde hair was a teased mop on top of his head, accentuating the thick makeup caked onto his face. To complete the look he had an oversized animal print purse slung over his elbow, and a lit cigarette glued to his bottom lip.

"God help the poor sucka that be hittin' on that tonight," Silky muttered, shaking his head.

Kerr strutted in with surprising grace, heels stomping as he crossed the dance floor to the bar. He hopped up on the bar stool like he owned the place, a few seats down from his coworkers.

"That was impressive," Rose said as she watched him.

"Even ole' Silky will be givin' that cat some props," the pimp declared. "If we's ever have to be infiltratin' a band of demon drag queens, that fierce bitch be takin' point."

"You just don't want to wear a dress," Rose teased.

Silky nodded. "You ain't wrong, Rosie-girl."

Kerr smacked the bar to get the attention of the bartender, who finally turned around and lazily leaned towards him.

"Yeah, what'll it be?" the bartender asked, tone bored.

"Martini, two olives," Kerr replied.

"It's happy hour, so it'll be five bucks," the bartender replied. The cougarified Agent reached into his purse, but before he could even find his wallet in the depths of cigarette packs and lipstick tubes somebody smacked a ten dollar bill onto the counter.

'Don't you worry baby, I got this for you." It was a frat boy, couldn't have been two or three years into college, all blonde hair and blue eyes. He wore a light pink polo shirt with a popped collar and his giant douchey smile was all for Kerr. "I'll take one too, barkeep," he said.

"Coming right up," the bartender replied.

"So baby," the frat boy cooed, "I'm Jordan, what's your na-"

"Let me stop you right there." Kerr put up a ruby nailed hand. "Thank you for the drink, but I'm not interested."

"Baby, baby, you got me all wrong!" Jordan put his hands up in defense. "I'm not looking to hit it and quit it, I'm looking for something *real*." He put a hand over his heart.

"Then you are in the wrong fucking place," Kerr snapped.

"Oh, you got a bit of a dirty streak, don't you?" Jordan licked his lips and winked. "I like that."

"Oh, you like it dirty, huh?" Kerr grinned. "Okay." The hand still in his purse closed around a twenty-four inch black dildo and produced it, slamming the silicone down onto the bar. "This is my friend the Violator. Over the years he's seen some shit, both literally and figuratiely. If you don't back the fuck up in the next three goddamn seconds I'm going to bend you over the bar and use your asshole as a storage facility. Is that dirty enough for you?"

Jordan visibly gulped, and took a step back from the bar. "Barkeep, give both drinks to her," he said loudly, and then turned on his heel, crossed the dance floor, and exited the club completely.

"Goddamn, you is some sorta super cougar, ain't ya?" Silky raised an eyebrow.

"Well, if I'm going out tonight, I'm taking some assholes with me." Kerr shot back his first martini in one gulp. "Even if it's just their self esteem."

"You might want to take it easy there, Kerr," Rose warned as he lifted the second glass into the air.

"I downed one of the bottles of white zin we got before I came in here," he replied with a shake of his head and downed the second drink. "Didn't phase me in the least. Apparently in addition to everything else, I have the alcohol tolerance of a cougar as well."

"Well, don't be worryin' too much there vanilla bean," Silky piped up. "Just be thankful that there be one thing that bitch can't be takin' from ya." He physically recoiled at the burning horror in Kerr's eyes as their gazes met, and the pimp swallowed.

"Um." Silky nodded in realization, and stood up. "Silky is gonna go see if Abe be havin' another magazine."

"Good call," Kerr seethed.

"Don't worry, we'll get you out of this," Rose assured her coworker.

"Glad at least one of us is optimistic," he muttered.

"I am, Kerr," she said, and hopped a stool closer to him. "And I also have something for you."

"I don't think a good luck charm is gonna help." He sighed and tried to lean his head on his hand, but then thought

better of it so that he didn't stab
himself.

"It's a tracker," Rose slid a small
rectangular device along the bar to him.
"If you really are turning into a
WereCougar then you might be the only one
that can keep up with her if she bolts."

"Sorry Rose," Kerr replied with a
nod, picking up the device. "Just a bit on
edge."

"It's okay, Kerr," she said, and
patted the soft fabric on his back gentle.
"It's okay."

CHAPTER EIGHT

Silky flicked through a few pages of
articles until he got to a curvy olive
skinned goddess in a golden bikini.
"Goddamn, Silky wouldn't care if *she* be
crazy," he murmured, and Abe grunted from
behind his own magazine.

Rose stood by the front door, keeping
an eye on Kerr at the bar as Thorn grabbed
her mic.

"What's up, Austin?!" She roared,
throwing a fist into the air. "We are
Queen of the Demon Blade and we are gonna
blow the roof off of this *motherfucker*!"
As she screamed the last word, the drums
exploded into a fast lead in, and the band
kicked into high gear. The thrash coming
out of the amplifiers rattled the glass in
the skylight, and the twenty or so patrons
on the dance floor started to throw
themselves around in excitement.

Rose straightened as the front door
opened and a familiar looking demon
entered the club with a set of deep
scratches across his face. She waited
until he was just past her before raising
her fingers in a signal to Thorn that
there was trouble.

The singer nodded and continued to
screech into the mic, taking a fighting
stance that simply looked like a metal

move. Two of the demons spotted Silky and made a beeline for him, while scarface and two lackeys start for the stage.

"Hey boys!" Thorn cried across the crowd, over a thick crunchy guitar lick. "Looks like we have some newbies in the pit! Make 'em feel welcome!"

The random moshing became a well oiled machine of a circle, Thorn's fans creating a human barricade that entrapped the trio of demons. They shoved them back and forth like rag dolls, and the dark skinned front woman grinned.

"That's it fellas, you keep em there til I give the word!" she egged them on, and Rose crept up behind the last stray demon that had trailed in behind scarface. He braced himself to take a run at the crowd, but she planted her knife in his back for a silent kill.

Silky glanced up from his magazine to see the two incoming demons heading for him. "Yo Abe, you wanna take them out? Silky don't wanna be imposin', given how this be yo terrority and all."

The bearded man sighed and set down his magazine, stomping over towards the two newcomers.

One of them raised a finger. "You better back up old man-" *SMASH-BONGGGGG...* Abe smashed a bass guitar into the side of the demon's head, teeth flying everywhere

in a fantastic spray of crimson. Before
the second demon could recover from his
stunned shock, Abe swung the instrument
down onto the top of his head, crumpling
the demon body to the ground.

There were a few more wet squelches
complete with deep vibrato as he finished
them off into quivering messes on the
floor. He dropped the guitar casually and
slunk back over to Silky, who handed him a
fresh cold beer.

"This ain't yo first rodeo, is it
white beard?" Silky asked.

Abe shook his head. "Nope." The pimp
simply smiled at him and turned his
attention back to his magazine.

The trio of demons were still trapped
in the fan circle on the dance floor.
Scarface's agitation reached its peak and
he dropped his human form, letting out a
mighty roar as the first song ended. The
metal crowd wasn't even fazed by the noise
or the hellish skin of the exposed demon,
still raring to mosh.

Kerr leapt over the human wall,
extending his hand to slice right through
a demon's neck as he gracefully landed on
his heels inside the circle. The head
slicked off and hit the dance floor, and
the cougar Agent Pelé'd around the
wavering decapitated body and booted the

head straight at the other underling,
catching him square in the face.

Scar growled, pointing at his face.
"I owe you for this!" He lunged forward
but Kerr punched through his chest,
grabbing his heart and shoving it through
the other side. The fan circle stepped
back as the cougar raised his arm, posing
with his trophy and a wild grin on his
face. Rather than simply pull his arm back
out, he dug his second arm into the wound
and tore the demon in two, showering the
crowd in a blood and bone.

The underling that had been smashed
in the face with his buddy's head managed
to get to his feet, and clenched his
fists. He attempted to look menacing, but
the fear in his eyes betrayed him.

"Really?" Kerr sneered. "I just
ripped your boss in half and you want to
face off with me?"

The demon looked conflicted, but
before he could make a decision, there was
a *crunch* and *shink* as the skylight
shattered above. In a flash of red and
gold, the WereCougar flew down and landed
on top of the demon, driving him into the
ground with claw and stiletto.

"Well, well," she purred as she
kicked the carcass aside. "Looks like my
cubbie is all grown up. And momma didn't
even have a chance to play with him first.

What a tragedy." She clucked her tongue and the fan circle broke apart. The concert goers backed up, giving the two cougars space to face off.

"Somebody get me my purse," Kerr demanded, eyes narrowing beneath thick mascara encrusted lashes. A random metalhead jogged up to him, holding the massive animal bag, and Kerr reached in, curling his hand around the giant cock for the second time that night.

When he raised the Violator over his head in triumph, the metalhead stood next to him, frozen in confusion.

"You can go now," Kerr prompted. "Just put that behind the bar, will you?" The metalhead nodded jerkily and scurried away, purse in hand.

"Oh, that's a *big* one," the WereCougar said, putting a hand to her chest. "You wanna use that on lil' ole *me*?"

Kerr whipped the dildo around like a set of nunchucks, a certified S&M Bruce Lee. "You can't handle what I'm about to dish out," he warned.

"Ohhhh, I love it when they get cocky." She licked her ruby painted lips and then rapidly dove forward.

Kerr countered by whipping the giant phallus at her face, the tip bonking off the bridge of her nose. She staggered back

in surprise, a massive grin forming on her
foundation-caked face.

"Playing rough I see," she cooed.
"Don't worry baby, I like a little pain."
She readied her claws and then grunted at
the sharp shocks licking up her back.

"You'll *love* me then," Thorn
declared, and brandished more of her
knives before expertly flinging them at
the WereCougar. The old demon managed to
dodge the last few, but in the distraction
of it all landed Silky's 9-iron in her
gut. The impact forced her to double over,
and Silky took a golf position, ready to
tee off.

"Hope you don't mind if Silky be
finishin' on yo face," he said with a
smirk, and swung.

The WereCougar lashed out and grabbed
the shaft, holding the club down. "What's
the matter, hon?" She cocked her head.
"Having trouble getting it up?"

Silky struggled against her, trying
to wrench the club from her hands. "Bitch,
Silky's gonna-" Kerr interrupted the scene
by flying in, landing a blow to the
WereCougar's face with a dildo uppercut.

She let go of the 9-iron and
staggered back in a daze, taking a few
more big black blows to the face as Kerr
moved forward on the offensive. She
managed to steady herself and launched

forward with her claws outstretched. He
countered by leaping heels over head,
landing directly behind her and using the
Violator as a noose.

He pulled back as hard as he could,
planting his stilettos in the top of her
back for leverage. She struggled and
thrashed wildly, gasping for air and
clawing at the dildo with all her might.

"We need the wine, now!" Rose cried,
and the bartender pushed a giant tub out
from behind the bar. As he slid it across
the floor, Kerr steered her in the right
direction like a cowboy on a bucking
bronco. Silky swung and connected with her
knee, forcing her to tip over into the
tub.

Kerr kept the pressure on her
windpipe and her back, keeping the
thrashing old bitch in her wine filled
coffin. Finally the struggles subsided,
until he felt he could release the
Violator and step back, though his guard
was still very much up.

"Did we get her?" he asked, but he
could still very much feel that he wasn't
cured.

"Well, you's still a chick, so Silky
wouldn't be celebratin' just yet," the
pimp seemed to read his mind.

Rose crossed to the bar, pulling a
cigarette out of Kerr's purse and lighting

it up. She took a deep drag as she lifted
an abandoned martini and dunked the cig in
it, lighting it on fire. She strode over
with the flaming chalice.

"Maybe this will help," she said as
she tossed the flaming liquid onto the
WereCougar's lifeless body. Thorn hopped
down from the stage as her band and most
of her fans seemed to realize something
incredibly terrible was going on that they
didn't want to be witnesses to.

"Looks like you did it, babe," Thorn
said as the patrons cleared out.

"If she did, then why am I still like
this?" Kerr whined.

"Silky, give her a good poke," Rose
instructed.

"Did Silk not expressly fuckin's ay
he weren't stickin' his dick in no crazy?"
the pimp snapped.

"I meant with the golf club." The
redhead sighed.

"Silky gettin' a lot more info on
y'all's sex life than he be wantin'," he
muttered, and extended the club to test
for any sign of life. Just before the head
ghosted over the flaming WereCougar she
leapt up with a shriek, sending her
opponents startling backwards.

She grabbed the sides of the wine tub
and lifted it over her head. The white zin
soaked her, extinguishing the flames and

leaving her clothes clinging to her middle aged form, lopsided nipples pointing in opposite directions.

"So rude," she scoffed as she flung her wet black locks over her forehead. "Not only wasting good alcohol, but messing up my hair in the process."

"Why the fuck won't you die?!" Kerr roared.

"Now baby," she licked her lips, enjoying the taste of the wine on top of her cherry lipstick, "you know I'm just playing hard to get." She winked and leapt up onto a set of floor speakers, grabbing onto the rafters and swinging up through the busted skylight.

"Oh no you don't!" Kerr screeched, following her parkour path a little clumsier due to the newness of his powers. As he hurled himself up through the roof, Rose waved her comrades forward.

"Come on!" she cried. "I've got a tracker on him!"

"Abe, clean this shit up, will ya?" Thorn motioned to the clusters of demon guts everywhere and he nodded with a grunt, licking his finger to turn another page of his magazine as the trio ran outside to the van.

CHAPTER NINE

The wine-slicked sin of the WereCougar glinted under the light of the full moon as she raced across the Austin skyline, rooftops crunching beneath her shoes. Kerr bounded after her, eyes on the prize, noting that she didn't seem to be pushing herself. She flipped back and forth across obstacles, adding little flairs to her movements such as hair flips and fluttering fingers.

Kerr growled at her showing off; she was toying with him.

"My poor cubbie." She cackled as she backflipped up onto a flat roof, staring down at him with her hands on her hips. "Struggling to keep up with momma. It's a shame you tire out so easily."

"Bitch, I'm just getting started," he warned, and sprung up suddenly, catching her off guard. His flying knee landed into her chest and knocked her right back off of the edge of the roof. He landed on the ledge on the balls of his feet, wobbling slightly as he watched her crashing into a table of the rooftop patio just below them.

Patrons and their drinks flew everywhere, bits of wood crunching beneath them as they caused a chain reaction of mayhem.

"How'd you like that?" Kerr puffed out his tits and held out this claws menacingly. The WereCougar simply grinned and popped back to her feet, diving from the patio to a nearby condo balcony. She beckoned him with a single long nailed finger and disappeared through the sliding doors.

Kerr leapt down to the patio bar, dodging a few confused patrons before jumping down to the balcony, taking a deep breath. "Rose, I hope you aren't far behind…" he murmured as he stepped over the threshold into a giant loft apartment.

It was minimalist, with a few plush couches against the walls and a black and white deco rug perfectly symmetrical between them. He let out a low whistle at the expensive looking four-poster bed in the far corner, and then turned at the sharp *clang* of something hitting sink in the kitchen area.

The WereCougar strolled out from behind the stainless steel island, glass of white wine in hand. She had dried off a bit from her run, but still looked a bit disheveled and sticky from her zinfandel bath and shower.

"Well, well," she purred, putting a hand on her hip as she sipped at her glass. "Looks like I finally have you in my posh condo. Unfortunately given your current state it's likely the only thing of mine you're going to be able to get in to."

"I may not have a lot of time left, but I guarantee that you are going to wish I had a lot less when I'm done with you," Kerr warned, fighting the urge to clench his fists to avoid stabbing his palms with his own nails.

"Honey *please*." She rolled her eyes. "You already drowned me, beat me, and set me on fire. What else do you possibly think you are going to be able to do to me before becoming my slave?"

"Slave?" Kerr's furrowed his brow in confusion. "I thought I was going to wither up and wish I was dead?"

"Well, that last part is true, but a good momma knows how to take care of her cubbies," the WereCougar explained, motioning to him. "Why do you think I went to the trouble of getting you here alone?"

"Frankly, I don't wanna know what you had planned for me," he retorted, and reached between the pillows of his cleavage to produce the tracking device. "But you should be aware that I'm not alone."

The front door imploded, Silky standing behind it with his signature grin and leg extended. The trio burst in as the WereCougar watched, jaw hanging open, wine glass slipping from her hand. Kerr took advantage of the distraction to leap into a flying dropkick, driving the tip of his stiletto directly into her heart.

She screeched as he jerked his foot to the right, kicking off of her with his free leg to snap the heel off inside of her.

"Batter up, bitch." The words dripped from Silky's mouth smoothly, and he swung his golf club as hard as he could, driving the busted heel deep into her old Were heart. She screeched again, seemingly unaffected as she dug her sharp nails into the wound and tore the foreign object free, tossing it aside to clatter across the hardwood.

She came at the pimp in a flurry of fists, and he knocked them aside with his 9-iron, focusing all his energy on keeping up with her quick moves. She changed her strategy in frustration, going for overhand claws, and Silky slid back a few times to avoid getting scratched. He dove into a roll, gracefully attempting a leg sweep, but she anticipated it and leapt over him, landing a kick to his face.

Rose swung in front of him, baton connecting with the WereCougar's face square on, but the bitch didn't even bat an eye. She grabbed the redhead by the throat and threw her across the room, smashing against an inn table, papers flying everywhere.

Thorn growled, stalking into the foray like a feral beast. "Alright cuntwagon," she snarled, "you can beat on the boys all you want but you just messed with the wrong-" A sharp pain in her side cut her off and she grasped her rib in shock, turning with her knife raised to see Kerr, eyes glazed completely over.

"You were saying, honey?" The WereCougar teased, wiggling her fingers. Her eyes twinkled with triumph as Kerr's fingers mirrored her own, following her mental commands.

Thorn completely ignored her, drawing a second knife and glaring at the WereCub. "That's three, motherfucker!" she cried, and threw both knives.

They hit their marks in Kerr's shoulders, and in the second of shock from the pain, he left her an opening for the dark warrior to rush him. She landed a rapid succession of bodyblows and headshots, smacking him around like a flyweight boxer. He slumped to the ground, blood pooling on the monochromatic rug.

"Alright, you fossilized cock cobbler," Thorn wiped her hands on her pants with a sneer. "Where were we?" She snatched up one of her knives from Kerr's shoulder and whipped it with deadly aim, but the WereCougar slid underneath it and leapt back up to land a punch to her opponent's chest.

Thorn went on the defensive, body slightly sluggish from the wicked hit to her solar plexus. She attempted a few hits, but they were easily dodged, and the WereCougar caught her fist, twisting her wrist upwards. She wrenched it to force the ex-Agent to her knees, cackling all the while.

Rose blinked a few times to try to get out of her daze, the sounds of Thorn's hissing keeping her grounded. The redhead attempted to get up but slipped on the papers that had billowed around her. One stuck to the sweat on her fist and her eyes widened. It was a personal check for eight thousand dollars, and in the memo line it read *Alimony Payment*.

"Motherfucker," Rose breathed in realization, "the first and the fifteenth." She quickly pulled out her zippo, flicking open the lighter with a *shink* that caught the WereCougar's attention. The demon's eyes widened double size as her nails dug into Thorn's tricep with rage. She let go and sprinted across the room just as Rose touched flame to paper.

"Your sugar daddy's gone, bitch." The redhead grinned as the fire engulfed the check. As it happened, the WereCougar erupted into flames as well, screams echoing as she continued to try to walk towards Rose.

Soon she was reduced to nothing but ashes, and Rose scampered to her feet, rushing over to Thorn.

"Are you okay?" she demanded, inspecting the divots in her lover's skin.

"Yeah, I'm fine, girl," Thorn replied with a nod, showing off her arm as not having even broken skin. "What the fuck did you do to her?"

"I burned her alimony check," Rose declared.

"God*damn* girl," Silky groaned as he got to his feet, stretching his arms above his head. "That's *cold*."

"Eh, fuck her." Rose shrugged. "She can burn."

"Is it over?" Kerr moaned weakly from the rug, flopping over onto his back. He grasped the edge of one of the couches and dragged himself over, propping his shoulders up so he could see everyone.

"Well, you ain't got bitch tits anymo, so Silky's gonna say yeah," the pimp motioned to him, and the younger Agent started to paw his body. He reached down to his crotch.

"Oh please, oh please…" He cupped his junk and sighed with relief. "Thank fucking *Christ!* The boys are back in town!" His grin was short lived at the sharp pain from the stab wounds in his shoulders. He eyed Thorn with incredulity. "And *you*, you fucking stabbed me."

"Don't go blaming me for your inability to follow simple instructions." She put up a hand in defense. "You were warned there would be consequences if you interrupted me three times."

"But you fucking stabbed me!" Kerr cried. "How is that an appropriate response to an interruption?!"

"If you think that's bad," she replied with a smirk, "just imagine what's gonna happen next time."

He gulped. "I'll be good."

Rose's phone trilled a happy ring, and her brow furrowed at the caller ID.

"Who is it?" Thorn inquired.

The redhead looked to Silky. "It's the Boss."

"Aw hell," Silky said, "this can't be good."

A mysterious man stood at the edge of the storage facility grounds. He was thin and wiry but a surprising amount of muscle tone beneath his lean frame. His chocolate hair topped pasty white skin, and he lifted a pair of binoculars to his cobalt eyes.

The phone in the pocket of his black suit vibrated, and he didn't break his view, reaching up to gently press on the bud in his ear.

"Go for The Phaser," he murmured.

"Your contact, Ezra, has been killed," a deep voice came through over the speaker, and the Phaser sighed.

"Then who the hell is gonna pay me for this heist?" he snapped irritably.

"He put five thousand in an escrow account to get this job moving," the voice replied. "It's yours, minus my fee of course."

"Are you fucking kidding me?" The Phaser threw a hand up, finally lowering the binoculars to hiss the words. "Five k? That's it? Do you have any idea how much research I had to do for this job? There's a reason I asked for fifty to pull it off."

"That is none of my concern," the voice replied in a bored monotone. "You

knew what the deal was when you signed
up."

"Well I'm on site already." The
Phaser sighed. "Surely there has to be
some useful stuff in that storage room."

A short pause. "Perhaps."

"If I can get my hands on some stuff,
can you move it for me?" He asked, shoving
a leather gloved hand in his slacks
pocket.

A longer pause. "I can't guarantee
you I can move it, or what prices I can
get," the voice finally conceded. "But I
will make calls on your behalf."

"And reduce your fee for my
troubles?" The Phaser prompted.

An even longer pause. "Fifteen
percent on final sale price," the voice
replied firmly. "Twenty if you wish for my
people to handle delivery."

"Consider it a deal," he confirmed.
"I'll be in touch after." He clicked off
the earbud and ducked low, jogging through
the shadows to the outer wall of the
facility.

He leaned down, stretching out his
back and touching his toes. Then he curled
his hand back to grasp his right ankle,
stretching his thigh. He repeated for the
other thigh, and then did a few jumping
backs to limber himself up.

Once prepped, he closed his eyes and touched his right thumb to the pad of his right index finger in an *a-okay* sign. His body engulfed itself in digital translucent static, and then he casually stepped through the solid wall, phasing through it as if it weren't there at all.

He poked his head out of the other side, looking back and forth down the hallway, and then stepped out when the coast was clear. He unphased and touched his left temple, activating a heads up map display in his left eye. The map quickly plotted him a course through the infield of the storage facility, around a fleet of trucks and storage containers.

He dove behind a large red container, and at the heel clicks of an approaching guard, quickly phased and slipped inside the container. He crossed to the far side, sticking his head out just enough so that he could hear the footfalls echoing away before exiting the solid metal like a ghost.

He unphased and continued on his way, reaching the inner wall of the storage facility. It was a several foot thick barrier of reinforced steel and concrete, but it was no match for him. He backed up a few steps with a smirk, to get a running start.

He tore full tilt at the wall, hitting the trigger just before connecting with the concrete. He hit the floor on the other side and slid across the hallway, then dipped into a shoulder roll right through a vault wall.

The security guard raised his eyebrow, a chill creeping up his spine, but didn't see anything.

The thief stood up and unphased in the center of the vault, eyes wide with the variety of demon artifacts within. He walked up and down the aisles, putting small random items in his backpack to try to maximize the return on his money. There weren't any labels on anything, so he figured it was better to have a lot of items to sell as opposed to fewer large ones that might not be worth as much.

He paused at the sight of a pedestal in the far corner. It contained an egg shaped item, roughly the size of a football.

"Well, well, what do we have here?" he asked, rubbing his hands together. "What are you doing all by yourself?" He looked closely, not seeing any obvious signs of alarms or traps. He shrugged and reached out to grab the item, and a small metal arm immediately shot out of the wall and clamped around his hand.

An alarm bleated loudly above his head. "Dammit," he cursed. He grasped the egg tightly before phasing, removing his arm from the claw. He unphased and dropped the egg into his bag before turning to leave.

A half dozen armed guards greeted him, led by a cinnamon skinned man in a white lab coat.

"I don't know who you are, but you are in a whole lotta trouble," Baptiste said, crossing his arms across his chest.

"With most people I'm sure you're right," The Phaser said with a grin, "but I'm not most people." He winked just before the signal to fire was given. The first bullet reached him just as he phased, and it passed though him harmlessly as he sprinted through the firing line.

"Code red! Code red!" Baptiste screamed into his walkie talkie, whipping around to see the body shaped static disappear into the wall. "The intruder is escaping via the grounds!" The entire facility went into overdrive but the thief ran straight through the storage units and trucks, not unphasing until he was twenty yards away from the facility.

His heads up display blinked *LOW POWER* instead of the map, and he sighed.

"Man, that was close," he muttered to himself as he casually walked off into the darkness. "Maybe next place I steal from will have some stronger batteries."

The Boss strode into the vault, quickly coming up on Baptiste, who stood with a clipboard and pencil in hand.

"How bad it is, Baptiste?" the Boss asked, worry laced in his tone.

"It's bad," the attache replied regretfully. "They got some lesser artifacts, but they also got the Egg of Orion."

"Motherfucker," the Boss breathed, scrubbing his hands through his white beard. "How the hell did he get in here?"

"He had some advanced technology that allowed him to phase in and out of reality," Baptiste replied with a hint of curiosity and awe in his voice. "He literally ran right through us and the walls."

"We're going to need all hands on deck for this one," the Boss said firmly. "Who's close?"

"Rutger is on site," Baptiste listed off. "Not sure where Nantz and TNT are. Silky, Rose and Kerr are in Austin with some former Agency asset named Thorn."

"First bit of luck we've had today," the older man said, eyes lit up. "Give me your phone." He took the cell after Baptiste speed-dialed Rose, and at the connection he didn't even wait for her greeting.

"Rose, it's the Boss," he said brusquely.

"Boss, don't worry," she replied quickly, "we have everything under control with the WereCougar."

"That's good to hear, but not why I'm calling," he said. "The storage facility vault was just hit."

"Oh my god," Rose breathed. "How bad?"

He winced. "We don't know the full extent yet, but we do know they got the Egg of Orion."

She paused. "Holy fuck."

"Understatement of the year, my dear," the Boss agreed. "It's an all hands on deck situation. I need all of you to get to the storage facility as quickly as you can."

"Of course," Rose replied.

"And Baptiste tells me that you have Thorn with you," the Boss continued, "please explain the significance of the situation and persuade her to help."

"You got it, Boss," she agreed. "See you soon."

He ended the call and tossed the phone back to Baptiste.

"Put the word out to every contact
you have ever made," he said firmly.
"Finding whoever took the Egg of Orion is
the Agency's top priority."

        END

www.ingramcontent.com/pod-product-compliance
Lightning Source LLC
Chambersburg PA
CBHW070645310726
48982CB00001B/427